Trilogy in Blue

From the Ashes

A Novel by T.A. Perry

PublishAmerica
Baltimore

© 2009 by T.A. Perry.
All rights reserved. No part of this book may be reproduced, stored in a retrieval system or transmitted in any form or by any means without the prior written permission of the publishers, except by a reviewer who may quote brief passages in a review to be printed in a newspaper, magazine or journal.

First printing

This is a work of fiction. Names, characters, places, and incidents either are the product of the author's imagination or are used fictitiously. Any resemblance to actual persons, living or dead, events, or locales is entirely coincidental.

PublishAmerica has allowed this work to remain exactly as the author intended, verbatim, without editorial input.

ISBN: 978-1-61546-140-0
PUBLISHED BY PUBLISHAMERICA, LLLP
www.publishamerica.com
Baltimore

Printed in the United States of America

For Sherry the patient and organized love of my life

My thanks to my friends who took the time to read and give me an honest evaluation:
Milt Morris
Bill Haverstick
Mike Stringer
Marti Duncan

A special thanks for her critical editing:
Alison Lockhart

Prologue

He heard grey eyes walk up to where he was laying in the in the filth of the alley. "Well lad, it's time for you to take a little sea voyage. The salt air will do you good."

My God, I'm being shanghaied. As the man leaned over to grab him, Thad kicked out as hard as he could. His foot struck home in the man's groin. "Umph, oh shit," gray eyes doubled over in pain.

"You son-of-a-bitch!" The pain was evident in his voice and so was his anger.

Thad tried to scuttle away on the ground and get to his feet, but when he tried his legs wouldn't hold him. His head still spinning, he went to his knees. Instantly he felt the first kick to his kidney. The pain was excruciating, causing the air to rush out of his lungs, followed closely by the remaining contents of his stomach. His bladder emptied as the second kick hit its target. He was jerked to his feet and punches slammed into his face, rib cage and stomach. He felt himself being smashed into the rough brick wall of the alley. As he drifted into blackness, he could no longer remember how many times he had been punched and kicked. He just knew that he was about to die. He wanted to scream, 'stop, enough, stop,' but the sounds would not come out of his mouth. He could hear them, loud, aggressive, forceful, echoing in the alley, in the darkness that surrounded him, "Stop, stop or I'll shoot." The explosion thundered in his ears as Thad slipped into a black abyss...

The year was 1899 and it would turn out to be a historic time in the Pacific Northwest and a pivotal time for Seattle to become the dominant city in the Puget Sound basin. Gold had been discovered in Alaska and hundreds of thousands of people were streaming into the Northwest on their way to the gold fields. The city was still recovering from the devastating fire of 1889 that had charred the major portion of the downtown core. Everything had been constructed from the abundant forests surrounding the struggling seaport and most of it including the interiors of those few buildings made of stone had been destroyed. Even those stood stark in the smoldering ashes, gutted of any material that was combustible. In this time of recovery, much like the Phoenix of legend, a new city emerged from the ashes. Stone and steel replaced plank and timber, men and women with little or nothing but initiative became financial and political leaders in this time of renewal.

News of the Klondike gold strike had been trickling into the Northwest but it was solidified by the arrival of the steamer Portland carrying in excess of one ton of gold. The die was cast; the only thing that had been missing was a reason for the city to continue to grow. Timber and fish could only last so long but gold and what it brought would be validation for Seattle's existence. Storefront retail shops sprang up from nowhere, huge mercantile stores, carrying everything that a well-stocked miner would need, and some that he wouldn't, opened to receive the dollars that were streaming into the city. Anywhere men with money gather, there will be those more than ready to relieve them of it. Granted the honest and slightly dishonest business faction of the city would get their share, the dishonest and immoral would also get theirs.

The largest city on the Sound never lacked for entertainment for those who had money to spend. From the early traveling sin shop, a ship named the "The Gin Place Polly" that plied its trade up and down the Sound, to the "sawdust flats" where small houses were on stilts in the shallows of the bay at high tide and dry at low. Here a man could find a drink, a game of chance, or in most cases of little chance, and the touch and services of a woman. The box houses of the later "Tenderloin" district would uphold the tradition of immorality "below the line." A great deal of the money coming into the city was spent on activities that were less than honorable in their pursuit.

This fledgling of a city had a well-defined duel personality. On the one hand there were those devout church going citizens that made up the bulk of the movers and shakers. Business was good, the economy was stable, for the present, and for those with the money, life could be good. This was the faction that abided north of the "Red Line," the invisible boundary at Yesler Street that separated the elite and the devout from the "undesirables. They consisted of women of the evening, gamblers, con artists and saloonkeepers who had taken up residence south of the "Red Line." The Tenderloin was rough, tough, and delightfully sinful. It was a place, where on any given night a man could get drunk, laid, robbed, murdered or shanghaied on a ship bound for some foreign port of call. Although the line was invisible, socially the distinction was clear. Those in the north did not associate with those from the south. Of course, there would be times when a few from the north would discreetly slip into the Tenderloin to enjoy some of the delights. Into this turmoil of sin, greed, growth and opportunity would come many men and women of vision looking for that opportunity to establish their name in the annals of the history of this place in the woods. Chadwick Mitchell was one of those men who knew he was destined to become such a person. Bringing his wife Becky and his son Thad out from Vermont to the Pacific Northwest he would embark on building a financial empire. The strife between father and son would cause them to move off in different directions and the impact on their lives would be strikingly different as they too would rise from the ashes of disaster.

Chapter 1

The Nor-Easter had been blowing for two days and was finally settling down. The surf against the rocks in front of the bungalow was still beating but it was less ferocious than earlier in the day. The dark clouds scudded across the ocean's expanse, low and ominous but the rain had let up almost stopping at times only to start again beating against the windowpanes and drumming on the roof. The lights had been out for two days, but with the heavy drapes pulled tightly closed, the great stone fireplace kept the cozy home warm. Becky laid her head back in the overstuffed chair and let her mind drift. *It seems like a hundred years ago that Chadwick and I started our lives. How in the world did it ever get to this place?* The loneliness gnawed at her like salt on an open sore. *Will it ever end? Will I ever feel whole again?* She closed her eyes drifting back to Vermont.

Chadwick, to his family, friends and business associates, was a product of his strict up-bringing. He was brought up in a devoutly religious home where the work ethic was taught sometimes with the use of a switch or well placed slap by the large callused hand of his father, Jacob. His place and the place of his brothers and sister in the family were to share the load. The family farm in Vermont, north of Montpelier, was not a fun place to live. Except for Sundays, which were mostly taken up with church, prayer and supper, the rest of the week was devoted to his chores and there were always chores to do. The horse stalls seemed to always need cleaning, tack needed repair, animals needed feed and milking was a never-ending job. If the chores did not get done or were not done satisfactorily, Chadwick suffered the wrath of his stern father. Growing up had not been a fun time for Chadwick. He was up before light and worked till dark with a break for lunch. At 15, after a particularly bad time with his father, he left. Alone and broke he headed to Montpelier where quite by chance he would cross paths with Amos Benton the local blacksmith.

The two clicked immediately and Chadwick was offered a job as the smithy's apprentice. Amos was everything Chadwick's father was not. A large man fully six foot four and over 200 pounds with flaming red hair and beard. He looked ferocious. The man, however, was quite the opposite. Amos was good natured, kind and gentle. Mistakes by his new apprentice were corrected with a gentle word instead of physical pain. It was not long until each had taken a genuine liking to each other. Amos looked at Chadwick as the son he did not have; Chadwick looked to Amos as his father figure. Few people in his life would ever call him Chad. One was Amos and the other was Amos's daughter, Becky.

Becky with her blue, blue eyes, silky red hair and at fifteen a fully developed young woman. From the first time he laid eyes on her, Chadwick was like a man possessed. He thought of her in his dreams, when he woke and most of the time when his workday was done. Becky's mother had died in the summer of her 10th year and Becky had stepped in to run the house for her father. Amos moved Chad into the house with them after a few months and it was almost more than Chad could stand. Being near her, the smell of her, the touch of her hand, Chad could hardly wait for the workday to end so that he could get back to Becky who gave him cold sweats, chills and an ache in his gut that would not go away. Watching her in the afternoon removing clothes from the drying line, her body silhouetted through her light cotton dress by the sun behind her, made for flights of fantasy in Chad's mind. He would relive incidents of closeness with Becky, like the time she noticed that he had lost a button on the work shirt that he was wearing. She had undone the first two top buttons to get to the missing space. Sliding her hand into his shirt, she sewed on a new button her fingers brushing his chest. When done, she had looked up into his eyes and started to say something. He was struggling in an attempt to control his breathing and reaction to her touch. His very being wanted to take her in his arms and kiss her. She must have seen it. Whatever she was about to say caught in her throat. She suddenly fussed about something that had to be done in the kitchen and hurried away.

My God I've frightened her, thoughts swirled through Chad's head. *She must think I am some kind of animal when all I wanted to do was be close to her and tell her how I feel. Will she reject me, laugh at me, am I even worthy of such a woman?*

Becky too had been thinking about Chad, this strong, good looking young man that her father had brought home for dinner and moved in several months later. He was beautiful. Tall, muscled with soft gentle eyes that seemed to look deep into her soul. She remembered the first time she had seen him shirtless out back, washing for dinner after work. She savored the sight of the water running down in rivulets over his chest and arms; she knew that she would have just died had he caught her watching him. She remembered discovering a missing button on his shirt and insisting on sewing on a new one just to be close to him. Unbuttoning his shirt caused ripples of excitement to run through her body and actually touching him while she sewed on the button had caused her knees to go weak. But when she looked into his eyes when done, the thoughts shocked her. The desire to slide her hands fully inside of his shirt, wrap her arms around his body and pull herself close, to kiss his chest, his neck, his mouth, what must he think of her, she had to stop. She remembered fussing about something but did not remember what she had said or even if it had made sense. She found herself in the kitchen trying desperately to catch her breath.

Had he seen my face flush, did he know what I was thinking, would he think less of me, would he laugh at me?

Becky would watch Chad as he went about his chores, worked in the shop or when they just sat on the porch with Amos in the evening. When he wasn't watching, Becky would look intently at him and fantasize how it would feel to have his body pressed against her. Three weeks after her 16th birthday she would find out. It was innocent enough. Chad was in the barn pitching hay from the loft to the feed bins for the horses. Amos had gone to an auction and would not be back until after dark. It was summer and the day was hot, but the work needed to be done even though business was slow. Becky, knowing that Chad had been at it for several hours, knew that he would be thirsty and she brought lemonade to the barn for him. When she called, Chad came down from the loft, with no shirt his muscled body glistening with sweat and bits of chaff clung to his skin. There seemed to be a pounding in her chest and a catch in her breath as Chad descended the ladder. Their eyes locked for a moment, she quickly handed him the container of lemonade, which he gratefully began to consume. As he did, she began to brush the chaff from his chest and realized that he had stopped drinking. Her hand still on his chest she looked up at him to find his warm brown eyes looking deeply into hers. There was no awkwardness. It was natural as their lips touched once, twice and then more fiercely as their mouths opened and they probed each others mouth passionately, she felt on fire. She did not remember him undoing the buttons on her dress or when they moved to the back stall and settled into the soft sweet hay. There in the hay, exploring, learning, experiencing what it meant to become one, they shared each other completely and lovingly. After, buried in the hay, they clung together savoring the experience they had just shared. In all of his seventeen years, even as a small child, Chadwick Mitchell had never cried. His father had never allowed it; "men don't cry" he would growl.

In their nakedness, with their arms wrapped around each other holding tightly, they cried. They cried tears of release, of wonderment, of fulfillment; of joy. They were one, they were complete; they were in love. On Becky's 17th birthday Chadwick asked Amos for Becky's hand in marriage and four months later they were wed.

Chad's status in the business changed on that day, Amos now considered him a partner and Chad began to take a greater role in the running of the smithy shop. Chad approached Amos about selling tack to the horse owners and later they added feed and general hardware items to the inventory. Chad had turned into a prudent businessman and business was good. The time that Chad spent in the business became an obsession for him. Those lessons beat into him by his father began to foster money and power. Businessmen and politicians curried his favor. He loaned money, expanded the business, purchased property as an investment for the future; he had a son.

In the second year of their marriage Becky presented him with a son. He was a strapping baby boy who weighed in at nine pounds ten ounces and healthy. Chad's first impulse was to continue his presence into the future and wanted to name him Chadwick Mitchell Jr. Becky, however, had other ideas. She wanted the boy named after her father and her will was as strong as Chad's. The compromise would be Thaddeus Amos Mitchell, they would call him Thad. As Chadwick held his son he knew that this child would ultimately be the beneficiary of the wealth and power that he was going to build. By the time Thad was 15 he had been well incorporated into his fathers business. He started young with chores around the store and shop. He must have the drive, Chadwick would sometimes lay awake nights fretting that the boy did not have the drive to succeed. He knew that he must succeed or all that Chadwick was trying to build for him would go for naught. The child must have a solid work ethic, he must not shirk his responsibilities, and he must share the power.

Chadwick Mitchell, for all he hated about his childhood, had turned into his father. He pushed Thad hard and demanded only perfection from him. Although he knew better than to use physical force against his son, Becky would never have allowed that, he found psychological ways to punish Thad for what he felt was imperfection.

Thad's saving grace was Amos. His grandfather had been slowly backing out of the business and had more time to spend with him when he wasn't working. Amos and his mother Becky would be Thad's island of retreat from the wrath of his father. From them he would learn love and understanding. When Amos died Thad lost much more than a grandfather, he lost a protector and his life too started to become unbearable. The situation was reaching a head. Becky did not know or understand the man she had clung to in the barn that long ago summer. Chadwick had changed and not for the better. The gentle soul that had cried with her there in the hay had grown cold, distant and driven. His constant tirades against Thad had bothered her for some time and she could see the boy withdrawing from his father and it had to stop. As the situation was reaching a head their lives were turned upside down. Word spread across the country, there was gold in Alaska.

Alaska, that unknown place that seemed to be on the other side of the world was sending out a siren call for men eager to become rich. For Becky there was no attraction, she was quite happy where they were. *Why in Gods name would one leave this civilized world of comfort for the wilds and incivility of the Pacific Northwest and Alaska?*

For Chad however, the draw was strong. He had seen what wealth could do for a man. It brought comfort; it brought prestige; most of all it brought power. He had businesses, money and an abundance of property. Sacks of gold would solidify the power he needed so badly.

Chadwick could remember his father's words still burning in his ears, "your lazy, you'll never amount to anything, you're going to be a drag on others, you'll burn in hell for your laziness and if you leave, you are not welcome back into this house."

He remembered the burning in his gut, the tears that welled in his eyes and the pain in his throat when he choked the sobs back. He would not let this bastard see him be less of a man than he was. He would not let this monster of a father revel in the pain he was causing, he would show him, and he would show the world. The gold, ah, the gold, with it he could go back to his fathers farm posses it, throw him off and obliterate all memory of him ever existing.

Over the next month, Chad sold the business. Although Becky protested, he foreclosed on the loans he had made to friends and business associates. The property he kept for insurance. He provided for his wife and child and informed Becky that he would be back in two years or less. Becky protested vehemently but he was after all her husband and she did have a duty to him. With great trepidation Becky relented. Chadwick packed his bags and on July 17th 1897, the day that the steamship Portland would dock at Seattle with a ton of gold, Chadwick Mitchell left for Alaska in his quest to put his stamp on history. Seattle had to be the first stop on his journey

***

This place in the wilderness of the Northwest was alive with activity. Men were streaming in from all over the world ready to throw everything they owned into the prospect of becoming rich beyond imagination in Alaska. Chadwick had the financial base to build a successful foundation for an assault on the Alaska gold fields. What Chadwick didn't have was the experience to know what he needed to make a successful assault. That would change with a chance encounter of an officer from the Seattle First Bank where he had deposited his money.

Chadwick strolled into the Kansas Steak House on Second Avenue. The place was packed and it startled him when he heard someone call his name.

"Mr. Mitchell."

Chadwick turned abruptly to find the bank officer who had assisted him when he had deposited his bankroll.

"Well hello, its Hodge isn't it?"

"Oh please" the man extended his hand, "it's James but please call me Jim."

"And Chadwick will do nicely for me" Chadwick pumped his hand eagerly thankful that at least he knew someone here.

"Come sit at our table, you'll have to wait for at least an hour before one opens up." Hodges led the way to a table against the wall.

Chadwick noted that there was another man already seated at the table. He appeared to be about Chadwick's age, not as tall but he appeared stocky and strong. This was a man who had worked hard for a living.

"Chadwick let me introduce to an old friend of mine from California." The man stood and extended his hand, "Chadwick Mitchell I'd like you to meet

Andrew Windom." Chadwick took his hand and in a firm handshake, *this man has the power of a bull*, "pleased to meet you Andrew."

"I think that Andy will do just fine Chadwick, where're you from?"

"New England, are you up here on business Andy or looking forward to the gold fields?"

"Oh, the gold fields are my main objective, but I have to find a stake first. Jim and I grew up in California and I just stopped to see him on the way up. I have a couple of prospects for a stake, but they want more than sixty percent of everything that I get."

"Over sixty percent and you do all the work and all they risk is the money?" Chadwick could not believe what he was hearing. "Just out of curiosity, what makes them think you'll be successful?"

"I have the experience Chad...is it okay if I call you Chad?"

"That's fine...what experience?"

"Well, I learned the gold mine business from my Dad. He was a forty-niner when they found gold in California. I worked a mine for most of twenty five years before I lost it all making bad investments. I grew up digging and panning for gold."

Chadwick sat back in his chair. He had forgotten all about being hungry, this could be the answer to his lack of experience. "Andy, what do you think about partnering with me?"

Andy looked him in the eye almost suspiciously. "Don't know Chad, what experience you got?"

"None, but I have the money and the difference is that I would be working along with you and we would split everything fifty-fifty"

"Why would you do that?"

"Simple, my money, your know-how and a lot of hard work by both of us, we just might be successful."

Jim Hodge had been sitting quietly listening to all that was taking place. "Are you gentlemen sure a..."

Andy held up his hand cutting him off. "There's no guarantee Chad, were getting a late jump on the rush, we could go bust in a year. On the other hand, I know more about mining gold than probably ninety percent of these fools buying junk they don't need or can't use before they head out. Most of them aren't even sure where to go or what to look for. They've been buying books on gold huntin'. I looked at em' and their full of misinformation and bullshit."

Chadwick grimaced, remembering the two books he had purchased that afternoon.

Andy leaned forward in his chair and stared at Chadwick. "Okay Mitchell you got a deal, fifty-fifty." He stuck out his hand and they shook on it.

Hodges cleared his throat, "uh…Andy what about the meeting with the two investors tonight?"

"Jim old friend, tell em I got a better deal, I found me a partner."

***

The next few days were filled with buying the equipment they would need. The Canadian authorities were requiring a years worth of supplies to enter into the Yukon. They would take only the essentials that were necessary. Food stuffs were of vital importance as they would not be able to find retail establishments once in the wilds. Equipment for mining the gold and building shelter were also essential. Oil lamps, axes, clothes and cooking gear were among the basics that the two men gathered prior to boarding the ship that would take them to gold fields.

When the Portland was ready to load for Alaska, Andy and Chadwick had all their equipment dockside to be loaded. What they were taking was barely half of what the other prospectors were stacking up on the dock. Andy smiled as he watched one man load almost three times what they were taking.

"Ya know Chad, they have to get that stuff inland and will wind up throwing most of it away. If we watch closely and hire the right people we'll be able to use some of the things they discard."

"How many men are we going to need? I heard that there are some men up there that are stealing from the miners they're hired to help."

"I wired some men I know that are already up there. They're old friends and can be trusted. Oh yes, I also got us some equalizers yesterday while you were at the bank. I'll show you when we get to our cabin." Andy marched up the gang plank with Chadwick close behind. Once in their stateroom, Andy hauled out a bag and produced three revolvers and ammunition.

"In our gear…I also have a 30 caliber carbine in case we need to hunt game for food. The pistols are for our protection in case anyone tries to jump us once we become prosperous. Ever shoot one of these Chad?"

Chad picked up one of the revolvers and hefted it in his hand. "Can't say that I have, its kinda' heavy"

"I like em' heavy, that way they don't jump as much when you fire em'.

TRILOGY IN BLUE

When we get to Alaska I'll show you how they work. You never can tell we may need em' at some point. I want to be sure you can hit what you are aiming at. We'll have to hide these in our gear. The Mounties at the boarder are restricting firearms from going into Canada.

It was early spring and the trip up the inside passage was uneventful. Andy and Chadwick sat on the aft deck of the steamship watching the thick wooded shoreline seemingly float past them.

"Ya know Chad you never talk about your family. If it's none of my business you can just tell me so and I'll never mention it again"

"No that's okay Andy it just never came up we've been so busy putting things together. I have a wife, Becky and a fine son named Thad." Chadwick's thoughts turned to Vermont. *I wonder how they are doing now. This will take longer than two years, I wonder if I'll still have a family when I get back?* "How about you Andy?"

"Had a wife, no kids, she died of the fever bout three years ago. Threw me for a loop when she died, spent what little money I had left on booze and woke up one day in San Francisco. I was dead broke and realized that I had to move on. Still miss her but it isn't as bad as it was in the beginning. I guess I'll never totally get over it, but she would want me to go on, she was quite a woman." Andy stared out at the forested shoreline his eyes tearing up. He took a deep breath, "you're a lucky man Chad. You've got a loving wife and son to go home to when we're done here."

Chadwick recalled his last blowout with Thad, *Becky's right, I've become my father and I've pushed too hard. They should be the center of my life not the money or the power. Alaska has to be a turning point in my life and things will change.*

After docking in Skagway things went just as Andy had predicted. Their crew was waiting and ready to make the trek inland over the Chilkoot pass. Because of the additional manpower they were able to pack all of their gear over in one load. Once past the Mounties station at Bennett Lake they boarded boats for the trip to Dawson on the Yukon River and the gold fields. There they would start the search. Andy had selected a location three days pack up a no name creek that few had ventured into. His knowledge told him that there was gold here and they just had to find it. He didn't want the tailings in the rivers and streams. That's where most of the prospectors ended up. Andy wanted the source where the tailings came from, he wanted the vein.

"This is it Chad we start our search here. Pay off the crew and we can set it up."

The crew paid they set off back to civilization, some shaking their heads at where the two had decided to set up.

"They don't think we made a wise choice Andy." Chad sounded a bit worried.

Andy just smiled, "we didn't. Our destination is about two miles further up the stream and up that ridge there." Chad looked where Andy was pointing at an out cropping on a small ridge above the creek. "It'll take us a couple of days to move this stuff. I trust em, but I'd rather they didn't know exactly where we are. What say we get started, we can get some of this stuff up there before dark."

After only a day and a half and much effort they had moved to the final campsite and set things up.

The next morning Andy was up early and started the coffee. Even though it was now mid-spring there was still a sharp cold bite to the air. Chad fixed breakfast and started to clean up.

"Where do we start Andy?"

"We already have. You stay here and guard the camp. We don't want anyone to stumble onto it and steal everything. I'm going to take a hike up toward those crags." Andy stared at the side of the ridge. "I can almost smell it Chad. Hang tight I'll be back." With that Andy picked up the pack he had loaded and started off through the woods. "Keep a pistol handy, you never can tell."

Night fell and Andy had not returned. Chadwick began to worry and when Andy had not returned the second day Chadwick had made up his mind that in the morning he would go in search of his partner. He cleaned up the campsite put everything away and closed the flap on the lean-to that he and Andy had built. It was close to midnight when the flap was torn back. Chadwick bolted wide awake, rolled to his right and brought the revolver to bear on the intruder who stood in the entrance to the lean-to.

"Shit, don't shoot Chad it's me, don't shoot."

"Jesus Andy you scared the hell out of me, where have you been I was worried."

TRILOGY IN BLUE

"I found. I found the damned thing right up there big as life."

"What did you find?"

"The quartz I found all kinds of quartz veins."

"Does that mean gold?"

"You got it partner, where there's quartz there's gold. What we don't know is how much and how deep. I brought back a sack full of material for us to look at in the morning. If it looks good we pan some of it to see if we have gold. Right now I need about two days sleep, I'm beat." Andy threw the pack full of samples into a corner of the lean-to, crawled into his bedroll and was asleep almost immediately. Chadwick was wide awake and staring at the bag. *What if it is gold? What if it's a lot of gold? We could be rich beyond our dreams. How can he just lay there and sleep?* Chadwick settled back down but he would not sleep this night.

They skipped breakfast settling instead for a cup of strong hot coffee. Andy started busting clods of dirt and breaking up rocks as soon as he had finished his coffee. "Look here Chad, see this white streak? That's quarts, milk quarts. It's usually found along side of gold, well, not always right beside it but near." He had busted open several specimens when a smile broke out on his bearded face. He turned to Chad, tears in his eyes.

"Here partner, right here, see these specks here and here?" He pointed with the sharp end of his hammer. He started smashing the clod in his hand. "Hand me the pan Chad, I'll show you how to find gold."

They hurried down to the stream, the clod now broken into small fine pieces. Andy quickly scooped up some water into the pan and began to swish the water across the dirt in the bottom of the large round pan with slopped sides. He tilted the pan allowing some of the water to spill out into the stream taking the dirt with it only to scoop up more water and continue the process.

"Watch this Chad. You see this dirt spilling back into the creek? That's the light stuff, the gold, being heavier settles to the bottom and if you do it right the gold will be the only thing left in the pan. Grab some of that stuff I busted up and a pan. Try it for yourself."

Chad poured some of the dirt into the pan and squatted down next to the stream and started the process. It took him about 10 minutes to wash off the lighter materials in the pan. The fourth time he scooped up water and swished it across the material in the pan he stopped. His heart was beating wildly in his chest and he saw the glitter in the bottom of his pan.

"My God Andy we have gold." He looked up to see Andy sitting in the icy cold stream grinning from ear to ear.

Over the next two days, Camp was moved a mile closer to the search site. The area was marked and staked over the next week and while Andy started the primary search for a vein of gold, Chadwick made the arduous trip back to Dawson and filed a claim on the area. By the time Chadwick had returned to the camp he was amazed to see that Andy had carried a large quantity of material from the ridge and was in the process of building a sluice box next to the river.

"How'd it go at the government office Chad?"

"Got the claim filed. The agent thought I was nuts."

"Nuts, what'd he say to you?"

"The first comment he made was if I was sure I wanted to file for this area. He then asked what we expected to find way up here. I told him that was our business and I filed the papers."

"I'm glad they think we're nuts. That way no one will be up here bothering us any time soon. Take a look Chad, over there in the container."

Chadwick picked up a small container with a lid on it. It felt heavy and he opened the top and looked inside, his breath caught, the container was over half full of gold in a variety of sizes. Some were quite small and the largest piece was the sized of the end of his thumb. He stared dumbfounded into the container and did not notice Andy walk up beside him.

"I found a vein yesterday, its three inches wide and a foot high. It runs straight back into the ridge. Chad, I got this in one afternoon, if it goes back five feet we're millionaires. It may not be the only vein either. I found another deposit of milk quartz not twenty feet away. Chad, close your mouth, we have a bunch of work to do. We have to build a cabin and finish this sluice so we can separate the dirt from the gold. It's faster than using a pan."

"What do we do first Andy?"

"The cabin so we can get out of the elements when the weather changes, then the sluice so we can process the materials and then we start digging the gold out, so let's get started."

Over the next three weeks the cabin was completed as was the sluice box. They were now ready to start making their fortune. They tapped out the first vein in about six months and Andy found two more that would take them at least another year to work. The more gold they obtained the more nervous they got.

TRILOGY IN BLUE

If anyone found out what they had here in the hills the word would spread. It would be then that they would be vulnerable to attack by those who would try to kill them and take their gold. Andy had seen it happen time and time again in California. They had no idea how much that temptation would effect them in the future.

Chapter 2

Chadwick was thankful for the calmer waters of the inner Puget Sound. The crossing from the Inside Passage across the Rosario straight had been particularly rough. His stomach was just now calming down and he was again enjoying the magnificent cedar forests that hugged the shoreline as they passed down the sound toward Seattle. His thoughts turned to Becky and Thad wondered if they were on their way from Vermont. He had not heard from them since he wrote telling them to go to Seattle where he would meet them. If everything worked out he would have the gold deposited by this afternoon and start looking for a house for his family.

Chadwick leaned on the rail and watched as the shoreline of Whidbey Island slid by. The giant cedars came all the way down to the shore and the pungent smell of them and the salt water of Puget Sound were exhilarating.

"Mr. Mitchell" the purser had approached quietly and startled Chad.

"Y...Yes" Chadwick's voice shook ever so slightly.

After seeing his partner killed in the Yukon over their gold, Chadwick was always edgy about being robbed or killed for the cache of gold that he now possessed. That traumatic event had come back to haunt him almost every night.

***

The sounds outside the cabin as they prepared dinner, were not loud, just noise that didn't sound like the usual animals. As it turned out, it was a far more deadly animal than they had ever run across before, these would be human. It was still vivid in his mind.

"Chadwick, get your gun I don't like the sound of this. There've been killings in some of the other camps lately." Andy loaded his rifle and blew out the lamp. "Cover me Chad, I'll take a look."

As Andy reached for it the door exploded inward knocking him backwards. The shadows came through the door guns blazing. Andy screamed as the bullets slammed into his body lifting him off of the floor. Chadwick, half in shock emptied the first pistol into the shadows not knowing if he was hitting them or not. With the second pistol he took better aim. The flash from the next round provided enough light for him to see that three of them were on the floor and two were now directing their attention toward him. They fired wild. Chadwick heard one of the bullets snap past his left ear. He delivered three shots and they too went down. Chadwick checked the bodies to be sure they were all dead, reloaded the pistols and checked his partner.

Andy was alive but barely.

"Chad…my will's in the bottom of my pack."

Blood seemed to be coming from everywhere on his body. Andy had been hit five or six times and a trickle of blood ran out the corner of his mouth.

"Don't worry about a will Andy. You're going to get through this." There was a deep rattle from Andy's lungs; he was drowning on his own blood. Chadwick knew that his partner was about to die.

"I don't have no family Chad, I left it all to you." Andy lasted just a few hours before he died. It took 5 days to get the RCMP to the cabin to investigate. They released Chadwick who would live with his partner's death the rest of his life. He would feel a lot better when the gold was safely deposited.

"Mr. Mitchell, are you all right?"

Chadwick was jolted back to reality, "yes, I'm sorry I was just thinking. Thank you for asking."

The purser handed him a slip of paper, "when the pilot came onboard at Port Townsend he gave me this message for you."

"Th…thank you" still a little shaken, Chadwick wondered who would be sending him a message. He opened the message fearing bad news but was delighted to find that it was from the acquaintance that he had made on his trip through Seattle. James Hodge Jr. had been a clerk at the Seattle First Bank when Chad had set up an account. Chadwick read the note again carefully;

"Chadwick: Am in receipt of your letter from Seward. I am so sorry about the death of our friend. I do want to wish you congratulations on your tremendous good fortune. Be assured that our bank is at your disposal. Seattle now has an Assay Office to process your assets after which the proceeds will be transferred to your account here at the bank. I have arranged for your ship to be met by bank security people with a

wagon. They will assist you in transporting your assets to the Government office. I look forward to dining with you at your convenience.

Sincerely,

James Hodge Jr., President

Seattle First Bank

Chadwick smiled as he folded the message and placed it in his jacket pocket.

What a stroke of luck, my first inroad in Seattle was now president of a bank. He will be invaluable for making contacts, and investments. This was it, the start of the march to the top and the power that was there for the taking. With the fortune that he had made and additional fortune he had inherited upon the death of his partner the possibilities were unlimited.

As they entered Elliot Bay he was amazed at how much the city had grown since he left. He had seen the devastation of the "Great Fire" when he was first here, but what he was looking at was a far cry from a city in ruin that he had seen before. The ram shackled clapboard buildings that had been so prevalent when he was here last were gone. In their place were buildings of stone, brick and mortar, some several stories high. This was a city reborn. The steamer headed for the waterfront piers, he could see people beginning to gather on shore. These were the curious wanting to see who would come off the boat with a ton of gold. He was amazed at the activity both in the harbor and on the shore. Wagons were pulling up onto the pier, they were headed for tradesmen. With dock workers, freight haulers and the curious they all made an odd looking mixture of people. It was the sheer numbers of people that impressed him most. This was a thriving waterfront and commercial center and it would be lucrative for him in his future monetary endeavors.

Chadwick carefully watched as his cases of gold were loaded aboard the wagon with the four-armed security guards. A bank officer made Chadwick feel secure that his fortune was well protected.

"Mr. Mitchell," it was James Hodge hurrying across the street to the pier. "Sorry I'm a little late, tied up on bank business."

Chadwick took the extended hand and pumped it eagerly, "Please, there's no need to apologize, everything has been taken care of, congratulations on your promotion at the bank."

"Thank you," Hodge caught his breath, "why don't we ride in the wagon over to the assay office and when we finish our business there we can get some lunch and talk."

Chadwick looked at his watch and realized that indeed it was past noon and he had missed breakfast due to the rough water in the straight.

"That sounds great, lead the way." It was good to have a friend in a position to help with his financial future.

As they rode the three blocks to the Government Assay Office, Chadwick marveled at the changes that had taken place since he had headed north to Alaska. "The changes are striking Jim, fill me in."

Jim Hodge's eyes fairly glowed with excitement.

"Aside from all of that talk about recession and some panic about the millennium change we have entered the 20th century with new opportunities and a great deal of enthusiasm. You can see the new buildings that have sprung up here in downtown. The streets have all been redone and there are capital building projects for both the city and the county that will give an entrepreneur, such as yourself, ample opportunity to make sound and lucrative investments for years to come. We have a new transit system with cable cars up Yesler Street that go over to an amusement area on Lake Washington."

Chadwick let the possibilities soak in as Hodge burbled along about this thriving city of Seattle. "We have become the premiere city on the Sound with the terminus of the Great Northern Railway being right here. The Union Pacific had to shift their terminus from Tacoma to Seattle in order to stay profitable. Of course, the word is that the Seattle money helped to grease the skids, so to speak. Oh…and I found a house for you up on second and Virginia, but we'll talk about that over lunch."

The wagon bumped to a stop in front of the Assay Office and the guards jumped down and began to unload the boxes of gold. Once inside and inventoried it did not take long to check the quality and determine that Chadwick was possessor of 2.5 million dollars of gold.

"Jim, how long until the money can be transferred to my account at the bank," Chadwick was eager to get the process started.

"Be there in about 4 to 5 weeks." The clerk behind the counter had almost anticipated the question.

Hodge also jumped in, "Don't worry Chadwick; your credit is as good as the gold with the bank. You can start investing, spending and making your mark as soon as you want. The bank will cover it."

Chadwick put his hand on his new friend's shoulder, "Jim, what I need right now is a good steak. The food on the boat was less than adequate."

Hodge eagerly led the way out the door, "I know just the place right up the street. After, we'll go see your new house."

The house on the corner of second and Virginia was everything that Chadwick would have hoped for, an elegant two story that incorporated and reflected the architecture of the time. Scrolled fascia board trimmed the edges of the eaves and large spindle columns supported the over hang that covered a wide porch that ran across the entire front. The rail around the porch was secured by small spindled supports. The woodwork inside was of cherry and oak projected the image of elegance that befitted the mansion that would be owned by a man of wealth, power and importance. He knew Becky would be overwhelmed by the opulence. The view was more than Chadwick could have hoped for, a 180 degree view to the west. It included the Alki Point, West Seattle, Elliot Bay, the Sound islands, the Olympic Mountains behind them and then the bluff at Magnolia. It was breathtaking.

Chadwick stood on the large covered veranda and scanned the view, "I think that this will do quite nicely. Tell me more about it."

"Well the story is interesting. Captain John Abercrombie built it for his wife three years ago. He was the skipper of a four master named the Stalwart. He got a loan from the bank to build and furnish the place first class all the way including the chandeliers and the woodwork inside. He even had a basement put in. Anyway, last year in a spring storm he put the Stalwart onto the rocks off of the mouth to the Straight of Juan de Fuca. The good captain went down with his ship. His wife could not make the payments and moved back east where she had family. The bank took over the house and I would like to offer it to you for what's owing on it."

Chadwick was startled, "why on earth would you do that Jim, this house is worth three times the remaining mortgage?"

Hodge smiled, "I liked your style when I first met you two years ago. My intuition was verified when you returned. I think that we'll become good friends and on the banker side, I want you to stay with Seattle First for the future. I think that those are good reasons."

Chadwick was touched. He had known one other man, other than Amos, that he genuinely liked and trusted. That man had been killed in that Alaska Cabin almost a year ago.

"Thank you Jim, I'm sure that this will be an enjoyable and profitable friendship for the both of us. You've got a deal." The two men shook hands, turned and looked to the west as the sun was beginning to set behind the Olympic Mountains.

"Tomorrow evening Chadwick," Hodge turned slightly towards Chadwick, "I think it would be a good time for you to meet some of the power elite in this city."

Chadwick smiled and nodded, *tomorrow would be a good time to get started.*

The opportunity was at the Rainier Club which was hosting the monthly gathering of the power elite in Seattle. The place was impressive. The brick three story building covered the whole east side of the block between Columbia and Seneca streets on Fourth Avenue. Inside it was even more impressive. Meeting rooms, living quarters, bar and first class restaurant. The heavy floor to ceiling drapes, mahogany and teak woodwork as well as the huge stone fireplaces gave the inside the look of opulence. This is where the power elite would gather. This is where the contacts would be. This is where Chadwick needed to be. The contacts that he would make in this place would give him alliances and direction for expanding his fortune.

Chadwick was checking in at the front lobby when Hodge sauntered up from behind.

"Chadwick, I'm glad you could make it. There's a group in the lounge that you must meet." Chadwick glanced over the guest list. Names like Denny, Boren, and Yesler, names of the founding fathers and their descendants. Names that one saw on street signs as you traveled around the city. Other notable names representing the money elite on the list included, Burke, Lander, Chenoweth, Weyerhaeuser, Frye, Schwabacher and Furth, who owned the other bank in town. They were all there, the rich and powerful and Chadwick was about to join in.

As he entered the room the smell of cigars and cognac was in the air. Lively conversations were taking place mostly about the union problems and the railroads. There was much debate regarding the shooting of Police Chief Meredith by Bob Considine and his brother Tom down at the drugstore on the boarder of the "tenderloin" south of Yesler Street. Hodge and Chadwick made the rounds of the room Hodge introducing Chadwick to everyone.

"What do you think of the union problem Mr. Mitchell?"

Chadwick, being still new to town knew little of the problem but enough to answer as a business man. "I don't think it's a good idea for the workers to be in a position to dictate how we run our businesses."

Heads nodded all around, someone handed him a cigar and Chadwick became part of the good old boys club in Seattle. One person that he was introduced to was John Harrington, businessman and entrepreneur. Harrington did not care about the unions and he did not care about the dead police chief and whether the Considine brothers would be charged with the crime. He cared about business and making money and that was the subject that Chadwick was looking for.

"Chadwick," John Harrington was a big man, six four or better and two hundred pounds. He had an iron grip as he pumped Chadwick's hand. "Jim here has told me about you. Welcome aboard, we've got a money train here and it's on the fast track."

Hodge jumped in as Harrington took a breath. "Chadwick has purchased the Abercrombie property."

"That's a fine piece of property and a great house. Would have bought it myself but I already have a home up on the south side of Queen Anne Hill. That's really the upscale property right now."

Chadwick thought that Harrington was a little full of himself, but if he could make money he could live with it. Harrington steered Chadwick to a corner table near a fireplace big enough to walk into.

"Family Chadwick, do you have family out here?"

Chadwick had not thought of Becky and Thad, things had been happening too fast.

"Yes I do, my wife and 17 year old son are leaving from Vermont. They should be here in the next couple months. They'll be coming on the Great Northern."

"Ah," Harrington raised his glass. "Let us drink to the GN. If they could not have been bought off, we would still be slogging through mud filled streets. Best piece of negotiating we ever did. That made this town the center of everything."

Hodge raised his glass,

"And let's drink to jerking the rug out from under Tacoma, those backwoods interlopers didn't know what hit em."

Both men laughed rather loudly and Chadwick glanced around the room to see if anyone else had noticed. His eye caught Tom Weyerhaeuser looking disapprovingly at them.

Harrington's big hand clamped down on Chadwick's shoulder, "Look Chadwick, after your family gets here we'll get together at my house for dinner. I have two sons Patrick and Pauley. They're 18 and 19…that way your Thad will have some friends his age. Then you and I can talk about some business opportunities. In the meantime, Jim here will help you find office space downtown." Harrington suddenly jumped up.

"I've got to run some legal stuff by Burke. Jim, you take good care of Chadwick here."

Harrington hurried across the room toward a short rather stocky man with graying hair.

Hodge leaned closer to Chadwick. "Burke is a former prosecutor and judge. He knows where all of the skeletons are buried and uses that power wisely. He is a good man to have in your corner."

Chadwick looked at his new friend,

"Jim, tell me about Harrington, he seems a bit…overwhelming."

"He's good Chadwick; I've known him for about 4 years now. He had pull with Joshua Green the founder of Seattle First, and was instrumental in getting me the promotion to President. He blusters a lot but he's a shrewd businessman and good to know."

Chadwick had seen enough and it was getting late as the crowed started thinning after Lunch. This was going to be a lucrative place to be in the future and Chadwick had his foot in the door. *Now all I have to do is convince Becky that this is where we should spend the next few years. I'll even promise to take her back to Vermont when our fortune has been made.* There had been no response to his telegram telling her to sell everything and head for Seattle.

Did she do as I directed or is she still in Vermont and not coming? I'll check with the telegraph office tomorrow and see if there was a response. What would he do if she decided not to come? Did she still love him, or had she simply written him off after two and a half years and only two letters. His thoughts returned to the barn and the wonderment of the love they discovered there. Time had not erased those feelings but as Andy had told him, it seemed like Chadwick had a strange way of demonstrating his love for both his wife and his son. Life would be different now and Chadwick was determined to rekindle the love he shared with Becky and the love he felt for his son, Thad. *If only I knew for sure if Becky and Thad were on their way. Tomorrow, there would be a message at the telegraph office; I just know that it will be there.*

Chadwick decided to walk to the house and stopped along the way for dinner. There seemed to be restaurants everywhere and a wide variety of types of cuisine. Juneau had boasted to having some of the finest restaurants in the world. What with all the gold floating around busy entrepreneurs had worked on those endeavors that would quickly separate miners from their pokes the fastest. Those seemed to be whorehouses, saloons and restaurants. Though Juneau's restaurants were impressive there weren't any that met the quality of these in Seattle. Becky will like this place, it is most civilized.

Entering the house he saw that his things had been delivered and carefully placed in the foyer. He wandered through the house getting comfortable with the layout. The den just off of the foyer doubled as a library. The furnishings that had been left in the house by Mrs. Abercrombie were of high quality and would do quite nicely until Becky arrived. She might wish to change some of it. There was a large parlor, formal dinning room, breakfast nook and Kitchen. At the end of the hall was a moderate bedroom that could be accessed from the hall or through a pantry that led to the kitchen. Chadwick surmised that this had been servant's quarters when the Abercrombies lived here. *I don't think that Becky will have any part in that sort of thing, but we'll see.*

The grand staircase led up to a sitting area. The master bedroom was off to the left and there were three more bedrooms down the hall from the sitting area. Everything was heavy dark woods, cherry and mahogany and the railings looked like they might be teak. The house would have seemed dark and dreary except for the abundance of lighting and the floor to ceiling windows that were in all the rooms and at the end of the hallway. These allowed a great deal of natural light to flow through the house brightening it considerably.

Chadwick went back down the stairs and found the door that led to the basement. There he found a large coal bin and one of the new coal burning furnaces. *Ah that accounts for the fireplaces looking like that had not been used much.* There were after all fireplaces in all the rooms, but the furnace made them more decorative than a necessity. There was a large room at one end with shelves that must have been used for food storage. It was cool there with a large heavy door to keep the warmth out. At the other end of the basement there was a smaller room that had been used as storage. *This room will do nicely.* Chadwick pried off a panel from the wall and found that there was enough room to store what he wanted behind the panel. He hurried back up stairs to where his belongings had been placed and struggled with two heavy boxes as he took one at a time down to the storage room. There, he built a shelf between the outer and inner wall and placed the boxes on it. Replacing the wood panel he secured it. *There, I'm ready to get on with it, everything is secure. I think I'll unpack and get some sleep. Tomorrow I'll start the climb to the top.*

Chapter 3

Becky and Thad boarded the train in New York. They would transfer to the Great Northern in Chicago for the trip to Seattle. It was going to be long ride in more ways than one. Becky was not at all sure this was the right thing to do. When she had received the telegram from Chad, it had shaken her. "Sell everything. I am arranging for passage by train for both you and Thad. I will expect you next month. Yours, Chadwick."

Tears welled up in her eyes as she remembered sitting at the kitchen table reading and re-reading the telegram in between sobs. *My life and my roots are being ripped apart.* She had read the papers and heard the talk, murderous heathen Indians, killings, gun fights in the streets; he was dragging her and Thad away from civilization and into the frontier. It was abominable. The thought of divorce had crept into her head. She loved Chad but was not happy with him. She had other prospects after all, that nice Mr. Schoener who ran the newspaper; she had seen how he had looked at her. Mr. Schoener had offered to come by and help her if she needed anything fixed around the house. Life had not been easy for her and Thad after Chad left for the gold fields. She remembered the people who had trusted her husband. They had been hurt both mentally and financially when he suddenly tore their lives apart by foreclosing on loans that he had made to them. In some cases he had sold the property and homes right out from under some of the families they had considered friends. She had trouble looking those folks in the eyes when they met on the street. She had sensed the open hostility toward both her and Thad long after Chad was gone. A full year would go by before most of the townspeople would talk to her again. When they realized that she too had been abandoned by Chad she had become one of them and once again became socially acceptable in the community. She had been without a husband now for over two years and longed for the touch of a man. Thad in the meantime had blossomed into a strong willed handsome young man who loved and protected his mother. At seventeen Thad developed a cadre of close friends and he was particularly close to Eunice Mae Woodright, the sheriffs daughter. She remembered how she and Chad had felt about each other at that age. Now she was telling Thad that he must leave everything that he knew and loved and move to the frontier to be with his father. Oh yes, divorce had entered her mind more than once but it wasn't in her heart to break her marriage vows.

She sent the telegram telling Chad that they would join him and began to sell the remaining pieces of land they owned. It almost broke her heart to sell the livery stable and mercantile. She remembered how hard her father had worked to make a go of it. Now the last vestiges of her father were no more than a memory. A piece of property that she had been given by her father stood on the north side of town. Another two acres were located in Maine on the Atlantic shore. She could not bear to part with them and instead slipped the deeds into her financial papers just in case she might need them some day. They boarded the train out of duty; she still loved the young man in the hay. It seemed like a hundred years ago but the obligation was still there. Thad would go, out of an obligation to his mother. He had not been getting on well with his father before Chadwick had left for Alaska. He simply could not let her make this trip alone. Who would take care of her when she arrived in that God forsaken uncivilized corner of world? He had to go with her, but he knew he could also bring her back. His father could not bully him any longer; he was a full-grown man and was quite capable of making his own decisions and having his own way. Above all, no one would hurt his mother.

***

Expecting the worst, they approached the train in Chicago. The trip from New York had not been a pleasant journey. The seats were hard, straight backed planks. They had placed blankets on the seat to soften the ride but it was still rough and bouncy. When the train would stop in a small town to take on coal, water or mail, Thad ran to the nearest store and buy something for them to eat and then race back to the train as it was pulling out. Having experienced the short portion of the trip, they were not looking forward to the weeks it would take them to get across the country to Seattle.

Becky handed their tickets to the platform conductor not being sure where they were supposed to go. She was sure that Chad had purchased first class tickets for them but was not prepared for what happened next.

"Oh yes Mrs. Mitchell," the conductor became very proper, "your car was just attached to the back of the train, and I'll have a porter load your luggage. Come I'll show you the way." Thad touched his Mothers arm,

"Mother, look those people boarding, they're carrying boxes and bags of food and water." Thad stepped up along side the conductor, "Will we need to bring food or will the train stop often enough for us to purchase it?"

The conductor looked surprised, "Oh, young man that won't be necessary, the next car forward of yours is the dining car and you can either eat there with the other first class passengers or have your meals delivered, it's all been taken care of. Here we are."

They had stopped beside the last car on the train. It looked brand new and had windows that were larger than the other cars. It looked as though there were curtains on the windows and there was a covered open platform on the rear of the car. The conductor assisted Becky in stepping up on the step and then onto the train, Thad bounded up behind her. The connecting platform between their car and the dining car was open but covered. The door to their car had a sign posted on it with large white letters PRIVATE.

As they followed the conductor into the car, it was obvious that Chad had taken care of them. It was like walking into a parlor, tables, chairs, couches, and three small chandeliers. There were sconce lamps attached to the walls between the mirrors and not just curtains on the windows but fine burgundy velvet drapes that could be pulled across for greater privacy.

The conductor led the way through the car as if proudly touring a mansion.

"Toward the rear of the car through the door you'll find a restroom and sleeping quarters, at the rear of the car is a door that will take you out onto the observation platform. I would suggest that as we get in the mountains you dress warmly when going out." Having finished making his tour the conductor turned abruptly on his heel, "I'm sure that you will have a wonderful trip. If you need for anything, contact the porter in the dining car. He will also explain the eating arrangements and times." The conductor quickly exited the car leaving Becky and Thad to explore the lavishness of their surroundings.

Thad plopped down on the soft velvet covered couch, "maybe this trip won't be so bad after all mother."

Becky gave him a reassuring smile, but her thoughts were of the rough frontier and the savages. She had seen the stories in the papers and in the dime novels that had been written to tell the stories of the Wild West. She remembered seeing pictures of men and their families standing in front of sod houses with grass roofs, one-room shelters that should be called hovels rather than houses. The people were dirt poor and existed on shear grit and determination. She did not know if she would have that same determination to survive in such harshness. *It isn't fair of Chadwick to bring us to such a place. What kind of life and opportunities will there be for our son?* What frightened her the most however, were the Indians. The pictures in the news articles and books spoke for themselves, settlers that had been attacked and murdered, their scalps cut away from their heads, the women carried off to be raped, tortured and turned into slaves. She shuddered at the thought of the pictures that she had seen. What terrible fate would await them when they reached the North West? What in the world was she doing on this train traveling to what may be a terrible life in a God forsaken part of the world?

The days slipped by quickly traveling across the northern tier of the mid-West. The rolling hills and flat grasslands seemed endless. Herds of antelope, deer and elk broke the monotony; the grand herds of buffalo were, of course, not to be seen. Thad thought that he saw several in the distance, but was not absolutely sure. The army and the government had made sure the staple that the Indians needed to survive had been exterminated. This was a sure way to control the savages. Starve them and make them rely on hand outs from the government. Becky was still not sure that they had controlled the Indians further to the West.

Almost two weeks out of Chicago, there had been several stops in the middle of nowhere for track repairs, the landscape began to change. First the grasslands began to give way to scrub trees and brush. The lines of the hills became sharper and more in contrast to the flat lands around them. The scrub trees gave way to aspen and small pine, then larger sugar pine. The train slowed considerably as it began to climb. There was a definite chill in the air as they entered the lower reaches of the Rocky Mountains. Thad looked out the window and marveled at what he saw ahead of them. Tall craggy peaks that seemed to gouge into the sky, snow crested at the tops, casting long deep shadows as the sun was setting behind them. The clear blue sky and the thin wispy layers of clouds that looked like they were painted there turned red and orange. They made the sky look like it was on fire. An old sailors' saying came to his mind, *red at night sailor's delight, red in the morning sailors take warning.* It would be a wonderful day tomorrow, but he would remember to take a coat with him out onto the observation platform. He imagined what wondrous sights he would see. The mountains back home seemed like humps on the flats. These were mountains, the kind he had read about in school, wondrous, frightening, savage places of adventure and excitement.

The knock at the door jolted him back to the railroad car. "Dinner," the voice called. He suddenly realized how hungry he was. Becky ushered in the Porter with the trays containing their evening meal. They had eaten only a few meals in the dinning car. Thad did not mind, but his mother was uncomfortable with the stares and whispers from the other first class passengers. There were always curious looks as they wondered who these two people from the parlor car were. They were the subjects of discussion and conjecture over breakfast, dinner, desert and coffee. Becky was raised by a simple man during a simple time and it made her uncomfortable to be the center of attention. After several times of feeling scrutinized, Becky and Thad took their meals in their car.

Morning found them deep into the Rocky Mountains edging around deep canyons, raging rivers and mountains that towered around them. Thad was in awe of what he was witnessing, but Becky still felt a shiver of trepidation about where they were going. This wilderness they were passing through was only the start of wilds that lay ahead. If it was this desolate here, what would it be like further on? She could only imagine how terrible it would be for them when they arrived at the very edge of civilization. Her dreams were haunted by visions of teepees, rough hewn log shacks and mud huts. Lack of proper medical care frightened her the most. What would happen to them if they were injured or became ill? To Becky, at the turn of the century, the only real civilization was east of the Mississippi. Then there were the Indians, those savages that raped and murdered white settlers. Her mind raced, *my God what am I doing here*?

Their stop in Kalispell, Montana did little to allay her fears. The town was coarse, as were the people who lived there. This place gave her the first opportunity to actually see Indians. Fifteen or twenty had ridden into town to buy goods that would be delivered by the train. She shuddered at the sight of them. Many of them wore no shirts and only tight fitting pants and soft-shoes made of deer hide. All carried rifles and knives, their hair braided or flowing in the wind as they rode by. The fierceness in their eyes made her blood run cold. *These men could kill in a moment with little thought for their victims.*

I would kill myself before submitting to one of them. Even though it was not cold, Becky pulled her wrap more tightly around herself.

The streets of the town were dirt. The vast majority of the buildings in this little frontier town were of logs. Only a few were of processed lumber and they were unpainted clapboard. The sight was depressing for her to see as she knew that where she was going would be even more rustic. She retreated to the railroad car and wept for nearly an hour. Thad, on the other hand, was enthralled with what he saw. He was still a product of his father and had obviously inherited his father's risky adventurous side. He could hardly wait to get off the train and explore his new surroundings.

He walked the main street of the town and soaked up the sounds and smells. The cowboys, with their horses, lariats, boots, colorful shirts and weather-beaten wide-brimmed hats absolutely captivated him. Everyone either had a pistol on their belt or carried a rifle. Some had them in a leather sheath on the side of their saddles. He had studied the Indian wars in school. He knew how blood thirsty and violent they were. Look what they had done to General Custer at the Little Bighorn River. The armies were suppressing these wild men and most were now on reservations. However the Indians he saw here did not look tamed. They looked free, proud and fearsome. His heart beat faster when he saw them riding into town and he wished that he had a gun of his own. What if they attacked the town and the train? How would he protect his mother? Fear, excitement, apprehension, *my God this is a wonderful place.* As he watched from a respectable distance, he saw that the men of the town paid no heed to the Indians. They were not apprehensive about them being there and there was no fear or reaction to them. The Indians had started to unload furs piled high onto their packhorses. Merchants set up shop right beside the train station, as the goods were unloaded. The townspeople and Indians lined up side by side to both buy and trade for the goods received by the merchants. The sound of a gunshot at the far end of town caused the town Marshal to leave the crowd and head in that direction. He did not look happy as he waved at two deputies to follow him toward the shot, Thad, his heart pumping, fell in behind the three lawmen and started down the street a short distance behind them. The sound of the train whistle blasting brought him back to his senses. The train was leaving. He had to run for the train as it started to pull out. His mind was racing; *yes this was going to be okay! The west was exciting. Things were new and unusual. Living out west was going to be fun.*

As they continued west the mountains suddenly became less rugged. They were not as lofty but the cragginess was giving way to smoother formations. The tall pines gave way to fir and deciduous trees interspersed with velvety mountain meadows of colorful flowers. As they entered Washington, the mountains gave way to rolling hills and grasslands. The grassland once again gave way to forests of pine jutting mountains that would herald the Cascade Range. The crossing of the Cascades would be an impressive trip, but not the awesome experience of the Rockies. At times, it seemed the train was hanging on the walls of the canyons as they traveled along raging riverbeds.

By the time they crossed the Cascade Mountains, the weather had mellowed into a typical summer. The mountains were still severe. The trees had evolved from pine to deciduous, fir and gigantic cedars with their penetrating, yet pleasant smell. Becky noticed that the small towns they passed had processed homes in a variety of colors. As they approached Bellingham, they saw tarred roadways. Although wagons were plentiful, they saw a few delivery trucks. Even a couple of passenger vehicles were chugging slowly, bouncing along the narrow, rough roadways. Turning south along the Puget Sound, the six-hour ride relaxed Becky. The train ran down the shoreline almost all of the way. She marveled at the calm blue waters lapping at rocky beaches. Huge forests met the water where the blue summer skies silhouetted soaring eagles. The Indians that she spotted in small encampments along the waters edge were not the fierce eyed people that she had previously seen or imagined. These were short, stout, dark skinned people with deep lined faces and almost passive eyes. These were not fierce warriors of the plains, but rather a sheltered passive group. Fortunately at this time, she did not know about the fierce Nez Pierce who had, only a few years past, massacred the Whitmans near Walla Walla, or about the raids and murders committed by these passive people during the early days of Seattle. What she was looking at were a beaten people trying to eke out a living in a society they did not understand or fit into. She soon realized that she had nothing to fear from the Indians.

As the train approached the outskirts of Seattle, she also realized that this was not a collection of log cabins on a backwater in nowhere. This was a modern, civilized city with paved streets motorized vehicles and commerce. It was alive and growing, just the type of place that Chad would choose to bring his family. Thad, standing on the train's observation platform, inhaled the salty smell of the Sound mixed with the unique smell of the cedar trees. He leaned on the railing and soaked up the smells and sounds that bombarded from all sides. His mind slipped back to Vermont and Eunice, the smell of her, her beauty, and her touch. It was the most difficult thing he ever had to do when he told her he was leaving for the Northwest. She had cried, they cried, and he promised that as soon as he was settled he would come for her and they would be married. He leaned back against the wall of the car and remembered their last embrace.

"I'll come back for you," his lips brushed her ear and continued to the nap of her neck, her breath caught in her throat,

Her voice was almost a hushed whisper. "I love you Thad." Her hands caressed his back as she pulled his shirt up until she could press her hands against his bare skin. "I want to Thad...love me."

His thoughts were warm, passionate; *I will go back for her.*

Chadwick stood impatiently on the platform at the Union Station hearing, but not yet seeing the train. The activity had increased steadily for the last 30 minutes. The delivery trucks and wagons had begun lining up to load freight from the train and people moved in to greet friends and loved ones who would be arriving. Since it came only twice a month, it was always an event when the train came. Had it not been for the Great Northern, Seattle would have remained just another small settlement on the Puget Sound. With the Great Northern making their terminus Seattle, it had forced the Southern Pacific to abandon their terminus in Tacoma and lay mainline track to Seattle leaving Tacoma just a stop on the way.

He remembered the relief that he had felt when he found the response waiting for him at the telegraph office. She was preparing to leave and close things out. That would take some time and they would be there in four to six weeks. That would give him some time to get things set up for her. He had hired a housekeeper and gardener to keep the place up. They were about to become part of the power elite in this city and having the right amenities was part of the process. Becky would resist their new status, but he was sure that she would relent and accept their station in the community. Things were moving fast now and Hodge, being true to his word, had funded the projects that Harrington had lined up for them. The electric rail cars that serviced the south and north ends of Seattle were now owned by a conglomerate consisting of

John Harrington, Joshua Green, Jim Hodge and himself. They were already turning a profit and there was talk that the city was going to make them an offer to purchase the line. If that came to pass it would net them a tidy profit. With the two capital building projects for the county and city in the hopper, things were moving faster than even he expected.

The sound of the distant train whistle brought him back to the station. *They're almost here;* his heart began to beat faster. *How will she look? Will I recognize my son,* his apprehension was rising and he hoped for the best. Becky felt the train slowing as they entered the outskirts of the city. She looked in the mirror one more time to be sure her hair and make-up looked just right.

Thad was out on the observation deck,

"Mother, you have to see this," his voice was rising with excitement. "Just look at this place. It's bigger than Montpelier and I bet there are more automobiles!"

The train rumbled along below the edge of a high bluff on the left with water to the right. Becky looked out onto a beautiful bay. It was surrounded by forests and seemingly filled with the masts of ships at anchor waiting either to be loaded or unloaded at the active waterfront that was coming into view along the bays edge. The train suddenly entered a tunnel that ran under the city. It was dark as night on the train and Becky felt fearful. That was not helped by Thad's whooping and yelling to hear his voice echo off the rock wall of the tunnel. A mile or so later the train rounded a curve and exited the tunnel on the south side of the downtown area. As the train neared the station, Becky scanned the crowd on the platform looking for Chadwick. *Will I recognize him, has he changed, will I still feel that old love that I've buried for over two years now?* Suddenly, there he was. He stood out from the rest. He was taller, more handsome, more elegant and professionally dressed in what appeared to be a very expensive three piece suit. He was scanning the train as it pulled in and it was electric when their eyes met, those wonderful warm eyes that looked into her soul. She felt as though her heart would burst. Her breath caught and tears welled up in her eyes. She still felt love.

Standing on the platform, Chadwick watched as the train came around the corner agonizingly slow. He scanned the train even though he knew it was too far to see anyone clearly. *Will I recognize her*? It had been over two years after all. Had she remained true to him? She was a handsome woman when he left for Alaska. He was sure that some of the men in the town would at least make an attempt to woo her. He thought about his own infidelity and had a twinge of guilt. There had been at least two women that he had been involved with, both from south of the Red Line.

It had happened two months ago but it seemed like years.

"I'm sure there is something that I can do for you gentlemen." She could not have been more than 16 or 17 years old.

Harrington gave Chadwick a wink,

"the young ones are the best." He had slid his arm around the back of an attractive blond.

Chadwick felt out of place and awkward being in the box house. There, of course, had been prostitutes in Alaska. Whenever they had gotten to a settlement, Andy would disappear for a day and "rent himself a woman," as he put it. He would always come back looking worse than when he left from all the partying and sex, but always with a smile on his face. Andy had tried to get Chadwick to go with him telling him that he would feel better if he released a little tension. He knew Chadwick did not approve and had simply stopped asking.

"I'm Patty," the young girl had placed Chadwick's hand around her waist and pressed herself against him. Her hand rested low on his stomach as she looked up at him with her innocent blue eyes. Chadwick felt himself stir, it had been a long time since he had been with a woman and her scent and sexuality seemed to make his awkwardness fade away. He was after all a captain of industry and this would be just another service for him to use for his own needs. Upstairs, naked, her mouth exploring his body, hands touching, stroking made him understand how much power he had. He was in charge, he had control, and she was his to use however he wanted. His passion raged inside like a caged animal and he let it consume him as he listened to her moan in feigned ecstasy. It was not about love, not even about sex; it was shear power and control and as Andy would have said the releasing of the tension.

With Maggie it would be different. With Maggie, there would be an emotional attachment. Of course she was a prostitute, but she was his prostitute and her gentle loving way would cause an emotional bond that Chadwick did not expect. Chadwick had slipped south of the "Red Line" for a quick drink. He had been with Patty the night before and felt no need to vent his aggressions on a woman. He wandered into the Silver Slipper box house and encountered Maggie inside. Maggie was older, more his age, and comfortable to talk to. She had brought him a drink and sat down without the usual come on that the other women had. What had begun as a causal conversation over a drink culminated with a trip to an upstairs room. With Maggie sex was different. There was no aggression, no need to dominate and no need to abuse. This was about sex, about emotion and it was comfortable. Sex had been slow and gentle with touching and fondling. There was no rush, she did not urge or guide him to get on, get in and get it over with. After, they were comfortable just lying together, naked, spent, talking. There was no pay me so I can go get another customer. They had clicked and it was like talking to an old friend. There would be more trips to the Silver Slipper to be with Maggie. He had discovered that she was actually the owner of the place and did not normally sleep with men for money. It would not be long before they had a relationship that did not involve money at all. The problem was that she was from south of the "Red Line" and would not fit on the arm of a businessman, and then there was Becky. Maggie cried the night he told her that he would not be coming back. He had tried to explain how he felt about her but the words caught in his throat. He felt the tears welling up in his eyes and he had muttered something about being sorry and hurried out. He did not go back.

    The train whistle snapped him back to the railroad platform and he started scanning the cars. Suddenly there she was as beautiful as ever. Her smile seemingly brightened the whole station. She was still the most stunning woman he had ever seen. She would impress all of them when the power elite met her. Life was good and everything seemed to be in place.

    "Becky, over here," Chadwick waved his arm to be sure that she saw him.

    She stepped onto the platform a little unsteady from being on the moving train, but looking for all the world in total control.

    "Chad, Oh Chad," she rushed to him, throwing her arms around him.

    Chadwick was overwhelmed with joy to see her, she still loved him. As she looked up to his face, he kissed her full on the mouth and held her close. The familiar sweet smell of her encompassed him. As he held her, he looked passed and saw the young man coming toward them. My God this must be Thad, how much he had changed in just a couple of years. He no longer looked like the obstinate youth he had left in Vermont. This was a full grown, handsome, muscular man.

    Chadwick released his grip on Becky and stepped toward Thad.

"Thad, you've grown, you look great."

Thad met his father's gaze, "and you look well Father," both men stopped short of each other feeling unsure of themselves and not knowing for sure what to do. Chadwick finally put out his hand. Thad hesitated, then took it with a firm shake. Both men stood facing each other, old wounds churning around inside of each.

Becky broke the trance, "come on you two, we have luggage to get."

Chadwick turned away from Thad, his mind racing, *there is work to be done here, and I don't know this person anymore.* He looked to the side of the platform toward the men he had hired who were waiting by the delivery van. With a motion of his hand the men moved toward the train where they began to collect Becky and Thad's luggage.

Becky began to fuss,

"How will they know what to collect, Thad, go help and be sure they get it all."

Thad turned abruptly and moved toward the men and took charge of the process giving orders calmly and assisting when necessary. It was not long before the men and Thad were smiling, laughing and chatting casually. Chadwick made note of the attributes of his son.

"Chad, you look wonderful," Becky slid her arm around Chadwick and leaned against him.

"He's a wonderful young man, Chad," she too was watching Thad and the men load the luggage into the van.

"He's kind, gentle and very responsible. You should be proud of him."

Chadwick kissed her on the forehead,

"so it would seem. I know that we were not getting on that well when I left for Alaska. I hope that he has mellowed."

The crowd was beginning to thin out as they began to walk toward the edge of the platform. "It will take time Chad. You two need to get to know each other again."

Chadwick steered Becky toward the new sedan parked just forward of the van. "I can't wait to show you the house. I hope you will love it as much as I do. It's a grand place Becky, but we can afford it. It may seem a little much but…," Chadwick was rambling obviously concerned that Becky may not like the house.

"I'm sure it's wonderful, Chad," Becky's calm voice reassured him. She smiled to herself, *he really hasn't changed that much and I can still see pieces of the boy in the barn.*

They walked hand in hand toward the car. Thad had finished with the loading of the van and started to climb in for the trip to the house when his father pulled him up short.

"Thad, the car is over here, come get in."

Thad bristled,

"I would rather ride in the van with the men."

Chadwick was firm,

"your place is here in the car, Thad," his voice picked up an edge,

"Come, get in!"

Thad hesitated, looking at the men clamoring into the vehicle, he had never ridden in an automobile and the car would be okay, but not because has father had ordered it, "yes father, I'm coming."

Thad's heart skipped a beat as Chadwick turned the crank on the front of the Ford and the engine popped to life. He marveled as his father hurried into the drivers' seat and adjusted the levers on the steering column until the engine ran smooth. He felt a shiver run through him and a tingling in his scalp as Chadwick put the automobile in gear and they pulled away from the curb. Several horses hooked to wagons became skittish and had to be calmed by their drivers. Becky tried to look poised as they began to move through traffic up the street, although her heart was beating twice as fast as normal and she had a death grip on a passenger handle. Automobiles were becoming more common place but they were still a curiosity. It was thrilling.

They drove north from the King Street Station up Second Avenue followed closely by the delivery van. Chadwick honked the raucous sounding horn to get people and wagons out of the way.

"Must you make that terrible noise Chad?" Becky was not sure if he was doing it to get people to move as much as to draw attention to them.

"People dawdle, Becky and now and again they have to be woken up. Add to that, if I hit someone and did not use the horn to warn them, I could be held responsible. Just settle back and enjoy the ride."

On the other hand, Thad was enjoying the ride immensely. He marveled at the tall buildings that lined the street on both sides. There were people everywhere, men with straw and derby hats, suit coats and canes. Women with button shoes, long dresses and skirts, narrow at the waist, full at the hips, great hats and parasols. This was a wonderful place to be, it was new, it was exciting and there was so much to learn. He decided that he was going to like it here.

"Well here it is," Chadwick pulled up in front of the grand two-story house with the covered porch that ran all the way across the front.

Becky looked at it in awe, "Chad it's so large how will I ever take care of it?"

"Not a problem Becky, you have a housekeeper to help with the chores and cooking."

"Does she live here with us?" Becky was not so sure that this was a good idea.

"No, she lives south of town and will commute by trolley each day. She will work from 8 to 5 with Sundays off. She is a lovely woman Becky and has excellent references, I checked them all. We'll discuss her duties later. It will give you more time to spend participating in social obligations and enjoying the comforts that we have here."

Becky felt swamped,

"This is going to take some getting used to Chad, please be patient with me."

"You'll be just fine. Come let me show you our new home." Chad opened the door and stepped out, starting toward the house. Becky was startled, *why didn't he get the door for me? In Vermont he would have.* Becky reached for the door handle but Thad was already there, pulling the door open and helping her out of the car.

"Come on you two," Chadwick was already, excitedly, halfway up the walk to the house.

Chadwick stood at the entrance holding the door for her to go in.

"The interior is all cherry and mahogany and oh, look behind you at the view."

Becky turned and was speechless. It was late afternoon now and the sun reflected off of the bay and the Olympic Mountains still covered with snow. There was not a cloud in the sky and it was truly a magnificent view.

"Come let me show you the rest," Chadwick had taken her gently by the arm and ushered her into the house. The large entry opened into a foyer flanked by a large living room on her right and a smaller sitting room and library on the left. Both had large fireplaces and Becky was already placing furniture and hanging curtains and drapes in her mind. Thad was already prowling from room to room admiring the lavishness of the place. No place in Vermont that he had seen was ever as grand as this house.

"Where does this door go father" Thad's voice was the friendliest it had been since they met at the station.

"To the basement Thad, go take a look, we'll be upstairs."

Thad opened the door, turned on the light and bounded down the stairs. Becky and Chadwick climbed a grand staircase to the landing on the second floor. Chadwick steered her toward the left and through double doors into a large airy room with French doors onto a balcony and large windows that faced the spectacular view of the Olympic Mountains.

"This is the master bedroom. It has a balcony out those glass doors. They even put in a huge closet and it has its own bathroom and water closet. It has all the amenities one could hope for; it's quite modern; the previous owner spared no expense. I'm sure we will be quite comfortable in here." Chadwick stepped up behind Becky and put his arms around her. He kissed the nape of her neck,

"Becky you're going to love it here."

Becky felt a thrill run through her body as his lips brushed her neck. She had not felt this way for what had seemed like an eternity.

Becky turned and wrapped her arms around him.

"It's wonderful Chad, I do love the house and I love you." She hugged him and laid her head on his chest.

"I know what you're thinking, but now is not the time." She looked up at him, "Tonight Chad, tonight."

Chadwick reluctantly released his hold on her.

"You can still read my mind. You're right and I should tend to the luggage." He turned and started to the door as Thad bounded in.

"Which room is mine?" He had a couple of suitcases, "The men have unloaded the luggage and it's in the entry."

Chadwick looked back at Becky silhouetted against the glass doors with the mountains behind, her face flushed,

"I'll see to the luggage."

Thad looked at her,

"are you alright Mother?" Yes I'm fine dear; your room is down the hall, the last one on the right." She hoped that would be far enough away that he would not hear what would be going on tonight.

The bath felt wonderful. Becky slid down in the tub until just her face was just above the water. Her tired muscles from the train trip relaxed in the soothing hot water filled with her floral fragranced oils. Dinner had been very good; the little Italian restaurant was just two blocks from the house. Chad had talked about the movers and shakers that he was involved with and the business deals that were ongoing. They talked a little about the trip, but Chad and Thad had exchanged only a few words. That bothered her and she hoped that he and his father would be able to come to terms with each other. She sank deeper into the tub allowing the hot water and the oils to ease the tension she felt. The door to the bathroom opened startling her. Chad walked in, his shirt was off, his suspenders were hanging down and he was staring intently at her. She felt uncomfortable in her nakedness and tried to cover up as best she could.

"You startled me Chad. I'm not quite used to having a man walk into my bath."

"Well I should hope not," Chad smiled and knelt down beside the tub. He took her hands and moved them away running his eyes up and down her body, "my God you are beautiful Becky." He gently helped her out of the tub and dry off. Picking her up, Chad carried her to their bed. Snuggling under the down comforter they lost themselves in an embrace.

In the last room on the right at the other end of the hall Thad lay on his bed. He could not help but hear the noises coming from his parent's room. He heard the creak of the bed, the sounds of their voices. It was after all a natural thing for them to do. He thought of Eunice and their last embrace.

Chapter 4

"I know that we just got settled Becky but this is important." Chadwick was trying to explain why they must go to dinner at Harrington's.

"He's one of the business leaders in the city and we've partnered on several ventures. He has two sons about Thad's age, that's right, you will be going too Thad."

Thad just rolled his eyes and accepted the fact that his father would not be put off. Meeting some people his own age might not be so bad either.

"Tell me about Mrs. Harrington," Becky had obviously relented also.

"She died two years after the youngest was born, small pox I believe. That was 10 years before John moved himself and the boys out to Seattle."

Becky had now resigned herself to the dinner especially if it would help Chad in a business way.

The mansion on Queen Anne hill was as spectacular as the hill itself. Early settlers had seen the advantages of building their homes on the hill they had named Queen Anne. Any house built on the south side had a commanding view of the fledgling city and the sound. It was the place where the movers and shakers would build their finest mansions. These ornate three story dwellings on large lots, carriage houses and servants quarters dominated the south face of Queen Anne. The home of John Harrington was one of the finest of the finest. The cathedral ceilings, crystal chandeliers, hardwood floors and grand staircases leading to the upper floors of the three story house were impressive. The large fireplaces and a magnificent library humbled even the most affluent visitor. Becky and Thad were in awe of the grandeur of the home. The Harrington boys did not appear spoiled. They were both polite and seemed well behaved. They were courteous and comfortable, joining into the conversation freely and intelligently. It was obvious that they had paid attention to their father regarding business matters. They were able to converse on matters of business quite easily. Pauley, the oldest, had a bit of insincerity in his voice and Becky though that he might be saying what he thought others might want to hear. Patrick, the younger of the two had a sweetness about him and obviously adored his older brother. There was no doubt in her mind that Pauley was the leader. At eighteen, Thad fit right in the middle. The two Harrington brothers bracketed him on either side. Becky's mind had drifted away from the business discussion taking place between Chad and Harrington. *This could be a good relationship for Thad to have. The boys might just influence Thad's interest in business, which would please his father to no end.* Becky however, did not like John Harrington from the moment they were introduced. He was a big man fully three inches taller than Chad and 30 pounds heavier. He was not overweight, just big and strong. It was obvious to her that he had not always worked with his brain. He knew hard labor somewhere in the past. It was not his size, however, that bothered Becky, it was his attitude. First of all, he was full of himself and talked almost of nothing else. He was loud, obnoxious and used swear words that were left better not said in mixed company. Lastly was his crudeness and obvious disrespect for women. When Chad introduced her she noticed that he had looked her up and down with a particularly pleased look on his face. She had held out her hand to him and he had brushed past it to sweep her up in an embrace.

"I've heard so much about you that I feel that I already know you. Hand shakes are for strangers; hugs are for friends."

However, he had pulled her too close, pressing his body against her and moving ever so slightly from side to side, his hands rubbing her back and her bottom. She was held there for longer than need be, her arms pinned, unable to move or break the grasp. At the point when it would appeared too long, he suddenly released her and caressed her check with his hand,

"Chadwick, your Becky is even more beautiful than you told me. You are truly a lucky man." John Harrington looked at her in a way that made her feel dirty and she vowed never to be alone with this man.

After dinner the three of them John, Chad and Becky had wine and the men talked about the opportunities that were for the taking in Seattle.

Harrington finished lighting a cigar, "Big things coming up Chadwick. The county and city are both looking at redoing the sewage and water systems. That'll mean investment opportunities for those of us with the money to get involved."

Chad took a sip of his wine, "How do you see getting involved with the process John?"

"Two ways basically," John paused and took another pull on his cigar, he liked being in the roll of teacher and showing off some for Becky.

"We can loan the county part of the money at an inflated interest or we can bid the Job ourselves and inflate the costs. Either way we make big money."

Chad looked a little concerned, "I don't know John, from all I have seen the bank and your company are spread a little thin right now."

John sipped his wine, leering over his glass at Becky, "Nonsense Chadwick, we pool our money in a conglomerate and we have more than enough to be major players. Why in two years we can quadruple our investment at the counties expense."

Becky stayed as close as she could to Chad. Several times during the evening John Harrington had touched her in ways that would appear to be unintentional or inadvertent. It had just been too many times for it to be either. His hand had brushed her breast more than once and her bottom several more times. Chad seemed to utterly oblivious to what Harrington was doing and she was sure that if she had said anything that Chad would have told her that it was her imagination. Chad seemed different in the presence of John Harrington. He was no longer the take charge, in control man that she knew and loved. It was like he felt second best in Harrington's presence. He seemed to curry favor as she had seen others do with him back in Vermont, agreeing to everything Harrington said and laughing a little too loud or long at his jokes or anecdotes. The rest of the evening she managed to avoid contact or close quarters with Harrington and could hardly wait to go home and wash.

The boys had gone up to the billiard room and enjoined in a game. Thad felt a little out of place not being used to this opulence.

"So what do you like Thad," it was Pauley that started the conversation as he lined up a shot, "you fancy a drink or cigar?"

"I'm up for almost anything but I haven't had much experience with alcohol and I don't smoke." Thad didn't want to sound inexperienced but he was sure that he came off that way.

"If you don't drink or smoke, what else is there to be up for," Pauley made his shot and started to line up the next one.

"How about sex, you ever fucked a woman Thad? You ain't one of them sissy guys are you?"

Thad felt his face flush, "I've been with women and I like it just fine." *It's none of his business and where the hell is this going.* Thad was uncomfortable trying to justify who he was by his sexual conquests.

"Good, cause my brother and I don't associate with them sissy boys," Pauley completed another shot and Patrick congratulated him.

"How many Thad," Pauley was enjoying himself in his interrogation of Thad.

Thad was beginning to get irritated and wanted to say it's none of your damned business, but instead answered, "Enough to know what I'm doing Pauley."

Pauley stopped mid-stroke and looked up at Thad. He had obviously picked up on the sarcasm.

"Well good Thad. My brother and I can show you a good time where you can take good clean sex fun to new heights. We know where there are women who can suck an eight ball through a water pipe if you know what I mean."

Patrick, laughing chiming in, "Yeah, if ya know what he means and…"

"Shut up Patrick," Pauley cut him off mid-sentence, "he understands. At least one of these nights, if your mama lets you out, you can tag along and party with us. Who knows you may find it fun." Pauley finished with a crooked grin on his face that made Thad uncomfortable.

"Thad" his father called up the stairs, "we're getting ready to leave."

Pauley put his hand on Thad's shoulder, "We'll get in touch with you in a few weeks and set up a party night."

Thad muttered something in the way of agreement with macho overtones and went down the stairs hoping that day would not come. At the door Chad had put Becky's coat over her shoulders. She had managed to avoid another hug from Harrington by ducking behind Chadwick to retrieve Thad's coat and hand it to him. She avoided the second attempt by slipping out the door being held by Thad as Chadwick and John shook hands.

"It was very nice to meet you John, we will have to have you and the boys over to our house for dinner," although she didn't savor the idea. She saw the disappointment on his face at missing another chance to fondle her.

Chadwick started the car and they started down off of Queen Anne Hill toward home. The steep grade down to the bottom of the hill was always a test for the brakes on anyone's automobile.

"Thad I hope that you noticed how well versed the Harrington boys were about their father's business."

Thad saw it coming and there was no way to avoid it here in the confines of the car. It was going to be the old direction in your life lecture.

"You're 18 years old boy and it's time you got some direction in your life. You can't just sit around the house and do nothing son." Thad's mind repeated the words he had heard over two years ago, *why when I was your age.*

Chad continued, "why when I was your age, I had my life mapped out. I had married your mom and I had direction. I was doing things that assured our future and it's time you did the same."

Thad had finally had enough, "I know that I have to make some decisions about my life father but I'm not up to it tonight, I'm tired and I just want to go to bed."

"Well you're damn lucky that you have a bed to get into son. This conversation is not over by any means and we will visit it again." Thad slumped down in the back seat; *things had not changed at all.*

They entered the house and Thad immediately headed for the stairs. Half way up Chadwick stopped him.

"Where do you think you are going boy, I'm not done, come back down here. We have more to talk about."

Thad hesitated then turned up the stairs, "You may not be done, but I am, there'll be no more talk tonight, I'm going to bed. You want to talk tomorrow then we will, but not tonight." Thad's knees were shaking and his heart was beating triple time, he had never challenged his father before, this was a first.

Chadwick started up the stairs after him, "What the hell?"

"Chad," Becky's hand on his arm stopped him. "Let him be. Tomorrow will be better, you'll see." Becky was praying she would be right, how could she choose between the two.

In bed this night it was clear that Chad was back in charge. This was not making love, this had nothing to do with love, this was possession, and this was control. She had barely gotten into their bed when Chad was upon her, roughly stripping her, pinning her down. When done he rolled off and lay the quiet.

Becky layback on her pillows fighting back the tears. *Thad challenged his father and it obviously caused Chad a problem, or could it have been Harrington? Something set him off, this was not like him.* She lay back quietly when suddenly she felt his hands on her and he possessed her again. This time he fell asleep after and Becky quietly cried herself to sleep.

In the morning she awoke to find Chad sitting on the edge of the bed staring at her, tears running down his face.

"Becky I am so very sorry about last night. I don't know what came over me. It's not like me to be rough with you. Please forgive me, I will make it up to you, I promise."

Becky reached up and wiped the tears away and then kissed him on the cheek.

"I understand Chad, I really do and I do forgive you. I love you very much but you hurt me last night, don't ever do that to me again!"

Chad was taken aback, but he understood his wife's mandate, "I won't Becky, I swear to God I never will again."

Chad leaned over and kissed her, "I'll be home early this afternoon; there are things that I need to get done at the office." With that Chad left, leaving Becky to wonder what would happen when Chad and Thad locked horns again.

***

For the next two weeks the situation seemed to cool off. Chad was busy at his downtown office with meetings and paperwork for aligning the monetary resources that would be needed to get them involved with public works projects. John Harrington had decided that Chadwick should take the lead in this project. It would give him valuable experience and it would show the other movers and shakers that Chad had what it takes to be part of the "good old boy network." This would be Chad's opportunity to put his money up front instead of investing behind the scenes as a silent partner. It was his deal to make or break.

It had been weeks after the dinner with John Harrington and Becky had broached the subject of money. They were sitting in the drawing room, Chad reading the paper, Becky knitting, and Thad out for a walk. He seemed to be doing a great deal of that lately.

"Chad, what you said at Harringtons the other night, was that true about them being spread thin?"

Chadwick looked up over the paper a little startled. It was unusual for Becky to ask questions about money or business. She had left that up to him to be the businessperson of the family.

"I do have some concern about it, but John assures me that between Hodge, the bank and himself that there is more than enough capital to swing the projects."

"What about you, will you be solvent?"

Chad laid down the paper and there was a scowl on his face.

"Why all the questions Becky, are you loosing faith in me?"

"Of course not, I know what a good businessman you are, I guess I just got a little nervous. You're talking about a great deal of money."

"Thank you, dear, for your vote of confidence. Yes, we are talking a great deal of cash outlay, but we are also talking a great deal of profit when the projects are over. Please don't worry yourself. I know what I'm doing and my partners are rock solid."

Becky didn't know about Hodge, but she knew she did not trust John Harrington.

Thad walked down along the waterfront. What an exciting place it was. Ships with two and four masts lay anchored in the harbor and many more were tied up at the piers. Horse drawn carts and motor vans charged up and down the street along the docks delivering and picking up freight. Great warehouses bustled with the daily commerce that fed this thriving city. He wandered as far south as Yesler Street stopping there. He looked up the hill to the east toward First Hill. *How steep it is,* he watched as the cable car clanked its way up and over to Lake Washington. *How that must have looked when they used to skid the logs down from the top of the hill to the Yesler Mill here at the bottom. There's a public park and natatorium at the east end of the line. I'll have to go there to see it and maybe rent a boat to row out on the lake.* His thoughts turned to Eunice. *How wonderful it would be to row out with her, somehow I feel empty like something is missing in my life, quite possibly it's 'direction', what ever the hell that means.* He sighed and continued walking.

Before he realized it, Thad had turned up Yesler and then south on First Avenue. He had just crossed the line. The Tenderloin did not look as sinister as everyone had told him. Maybe that was because it was daylight. There were a few women lounging around inside of some of the bars. Thad could not help but look in; *they must be the prostitutes that people speak of.*

"Hey buddy," the man was dressed like a sailor off of one of the merchant ships and Thad didn't know where he came from, he just suddenly appeared beside him.

"How'd ya' like ta buy your girlie a genuine gold necklace?" The man opened his hand and the sun danced off of the gold chain that lay in his palm, "Guarantee that this'll get you over, if you know what I mean!"

"No thanks," Thad stepped away.

"Wait a minute boy, you ain't even heerd the price. How much money you got, we can work a deal."

"I said no!" Thad moved away not wanting to be rude.

"Wait," the man's voice was now menacing. "I asked you a question, how much you got, you tryin' to bug me off?"

The man now had Thad by the arm, stuffing away the necklace into his pants pocket he then used his free hand to grab the lapel of Thad's coat.

"Finely dressed gentleman like you surely must have some money on 'im."

The man had pulled Thad sideways and his freehand was now inside the jacket and grabbing at Thad's wallet.

Thad was startled and frightened, *this guy has four inches and at least forty pounds on me, I'm being robbed. This is what the Tenderloin was all about, what a dumb move I've made.*

There was a loud crack. The man's eyes bulged and his face screwed up with pain and he fairly screamed.

"Aaah, me fuckin' arm, ya broke me fuckin' arm!"

A large hand attached to a blue uniform jacket sleeve shot passed Thad and grabbed the man by the back of his jacket and snatched him sideways. The robber was then slammed into the brick wall face first. "Ugh" was the only sound the man made as he slid slowly to the ground at the base of the wall. Thad, frozen in place, slowly turned his head in the direction of the wall, almost afraid of what he might see. The police officer was handcuffing the man as he lay on the ground. A quick check of the man's throat with his fingers told him that he was alive, just unconscious.

"Told you I'd catch you wrong, Jake." The officer grabbed the back of the man's collar and started to drag him away while looking at Thad still frozen in position.

"Boy, you stay right where you are, understood?"

There was no doubt that the officer meant exactly what he said. *I would stand right here if he didn't come back for two days.* Thad's knees were weak and he was trying in vain to keep from shaking.

The officer drug the unconscious man some twenty feet to where there was a blue box on one of the light poles. There was a light on top of the box and the officer opened the door with a large brass key. From where he was, Thad could not see what the officer did in the box. Shortly after he closed it, a black open front van came around the corner. On the side, in large white letters, it said POLICE. The now conscious man, complaining about his arm, was loaded in and the van chugged away, Thad assumed, to the county or city jail. The officer now turned his attention to Thad.

"Where you from son," the officers voice was now softer and gentler than before. It was like he must understand how frightened Thad was. "Come over here and sit down on the stairs before you fall down."

Thad complied and did feel better once he was off of his feet.

"Where're you from?" The officer had produced a note pad and pencil and was starting to write things down.

Thad cleared his throat hoping that his voice would not crack, "Vermont, sir."

The officer got a slight grin on his face.

"No son, where're you from here. Do you have an address here in Seattle?"

Thad felt stupid. *It wasn't the officer's fault, I'm not thinking to clear.* Thad gave the officer his address, but could not for the life of him remember his phone number.

"What are you doing down here. You got business here?" The officer was looking very serious.

"I...I don't know I was just out for a walk. I haven't lived here long and I just wanted to get familiar with downtown."

The officer put out his hand and Thad took it and the officer pulled him to his feet.

"Look son, you're obviously an uptown person. You really don't need to be down here below the line. To these people, you're fresh meat. They can see you coming for two blocks and they start circling like sharks to bait fish. You take my advice and get yourself back uptown where you belong. I'll file this report and you may have to go to court and testify as to what Jake tried to do to you. He may plead guilty, in which case there's no trial. Now you think that you can negotiate the one block to Yesler without getting into trouble?"

Thad had stopped shaking and his breathing was back to normal.

"I can make that, I don't know where you came from sir, but I'm sure glad you were here. There's no telling what that guy may have done to me if it wasn't for you. Thank you."

Thad stuck out his hand; Officer Blackwell smiled and took it in a very firm handshake.

"No problem, it's what I do."

Thad turned and started up the block toward Yesler and safety of being north of the Red Line. Officer Blackwell, a smile on his face, watched him go. *Nice kid, not too many around these days.*

***

Becky was concerned that he was all right and that the man had not hurt him. His father on the other hand was angry after hearing the story of the robbery.

"What on earth possessed you to go to that part of town? There are dangerous people there. You could have been killed! For God's sake Thad, use you head, that's what it's for."

"That's not fair father," Thad was starting to get angry. "It was broad daylight. There were carts and automobiles on the street and there were people on the sidewalk."

Chadwick spun around glaring at his son,

"Don't you get it Thad? You're a wet nosed kid from Vermont and you haven't got a clue about the dangers of a big city. It's written all over you. You're fresh meat boy."

There's that phrase again, that's what the police officer said. Frustrated, Thad lashed out.

"Maybe I'd know this stuff if you hadn't walked out on us! You dropped us clean. You didn't give a damn what happened to us as long as you could do what you wanted. There was no one there to show or teach me the dangers and now all you can do is criticize. Well the hell with you!"

Chadwick's face tightened and he grimaced in anger. He started toward Thad drawing his fist back. Thad felt fear but he raised his fists to defend himself and stood his ground, rage in his heart. The two men were on a collision course.

"STOP!" It was not a request it was an order, both men seemed to freeze in place and looked toward Becky, who was standing at the table, tears streaming down her face.

"Who are you people?"

She was almost screaming at them.

"You're not my husband; you're my husband's father. And who are you," she was not yet done.

"You're not the son I gave birth to. You're not the son that for the last three years I have raised to be gentle, kind and polite. Who do you think you are to criticize your father and use that language to him? I don't know either of you and I will not have this behavior in my house. Get out!"

Chadwick was too startled to speak. *My God she's right, I'm acting like my father*. He backed away from Thad.

Thad's arms dropped to his sides. *Mother, I've hurt my mother, it's my fault, it's all my fault,* Thad turned and ran out through the front door fighting back his tears.

Thad sat and watched the sun setting behind the Olympic Mountains. It was like the sky was on fire. He remembered that same color from the train trip as they had entered the Rocky Mountains. *They're right, of course, I am young and inexperienced. The policeman could see it. The thief who accosted me could see it and my father had just rammed it down my throat. How am I supposed to get that experience? How am I supposed to learn about life except to live it? I can play it safe and go into my father's business, but that doesn't interest me. I could go back to school. I got good grades in the preparatory school in Vermont. Seattle does have a University, but what would I study? What else could I do? More importantly, would I be allowed back in the house after the mess I just caused?*

Thad walked away from the bluff overlooking the bay in the general direction of his home. At least he should try to make amends with his parents and try to find some resolution to this dilemma.

Auuugah, the blast from the automobile horn startled him and he jumped aside. He heard laughing and turned to see Patrick and Pauley Harrington sitting in a new Oldsmobile. Thad grimaced; *daddy must have money coming out his ears.*

"Hey, Thad where you been? We stopped by your house and your mommy appeared worried, said she hadn't seen you for three hours. Your father asked us to let him know if we found you. It's time my friend," Pauley had that crooked grin on his face.

Thad did not feel like a party tonight. *I should probably just go home and see if I can patch things up.*

"I don't think so Pauley I…"

"Oh sure," Pauley cut him off. "You're up for anything until anything comes along and then you chicken out. Come on Thad show us what you got. You got anything in your shorts or are you just a mommy's boy." There was that damn grin again, there was no doubt this was a challenge.

"I'm up for it Pauley, what did you have in mind." *Is Pauley serious or just throwin chaff in the wind? Besides, what better way to learn about life than to live it?*

"Things will be hoppin below the line tonight and we're going to take part in it. We'll stop for a little dinner and head down. I'll guarantee that you'll have a night to remember."

Patrick chimed in, "Yeah for a long time…"

"Shut up Patrick, he understands."

Thad got into the Olds and they headed south towards the Red Line.

Maggie watched the young men come through the door. *Boys,* she thought to herself and that uncomfortable feeling started to creep up her spine. It wasn't caused by the fact that three young men had just come through the door of her 'box house,' it was who they were. Two of them she recognized immediately. The Harrington boys had been here before as well as other houses south of the line. They were trouble. The third she had seen somewhere before but she could not recall where. His red hair and blue eyes gave him a look of innocence. He seemed unsure of himself, yet he looked somehow familiar. The Harringtons, however, were their usual selves, loud, profane and a little drunk. She remembered the stories from Honey's Place when the boys had taken a couple of the girls upstairs for a "party" and things got out of hand. One of the girls wound up in the hospital and the other was so sexually abused that she simply left town. Word had filtered back from Portland that she had died in the county mental hospital. Of course their father, with all of his money, had greased the right palms and the matter became ancient history.

Maggie knew that she would need to have her most experienced girls work with these guys. When Officer O'Shay came through on his rounds, she would let him know. She would definitely keep Cynthia out of sight of the Harringtons especially Pauley who, of the two, had the worst mean streak.

"Maggie" the buxom blond had walked quietly up from behind. "Did you see who just came in?"

"Yes I saw em." Maggie turned and spoke quietly. "You and Mary handle their table and no one goes upstairs without telling me first, is that clear?"

The blond nodded her head, glanced nervously at the table and left to find Mary.

Maggie turned

"Sandy, have you seen the new bouncer yet?"

"Yeah he came in about five minutes ago. Maggie I don't like him, there is something bad there, and he's just not right. He's already spotted Cynthia and I swear I saw his neck swell. You better get him straightened out and soon." Sandy continued off to find Mary.

The boys had settled into a table in a back corner. Maggie waited until she saw the two girls head for them before she set off to find the new bouncer and take care of some business.

"Come on Thad, loosen up" Patrick Harrington punched Thad's shoulder.

"Ya Thad, we're here for a good time" Pauley's speech was a little slurred but his eyes looked clear and sharp.

"Hi gentlemen, what can we get for you tonight?" Mary, put her hand on Patrick's shoulder. Pauley turned and eyed Sandy's ample cleavage. He slid his hand under her short skirt and patted her rear, "A little later I just might have to take a closer look at this" he squeezed her left buttock, "But for right now, we'll have three water backs and don't give us the cheap stuff." He gave her another little squeeze for good measure and removed his hand. The girls left to get the drinks.

"Jeez Pauley, was that necessary?" Thad could feel the red creeping up his face. Watching Pauley fondle the blond had embarrassed him.

"Come on Thad, these women are whores, they do it for a living" Patrick reached down to his groin and grabbed himself, "Give them enough money and they'll do anything you ever wanted or could have imagined." Go ahead and grab a handful when they come back, they won't stop you."

Thad was appalled. *What am I doing here, this is a mistake.*
"That's okay guys; I'm just not comfortable with it."

The brothers laughed, and Patrick punched his shoulder again.

"That's okay Thad, have a couple of drinks to loosen up and you'll be taking their clothes off."

Pauley gave a drunken bellow, "Hey wenches, where's the booze?" Thad felt like crawling under the table. *This is not a good idea at all. I'll have a couple of drinks and leave.* What he didn't know was that the Harrington boys had other ideas and leaving would not be as easy as Thad thought.

Maggie hurried to the back area and found the new bouncer sitting at a small table having a drink.

"Drago, we need to talk before you go to work."

Drago looked up, but did not offer to stand. He was a beefy guy, not tall but wide and solid. His greasy hair curled onto his forehead partially covering a small scar. Several of the girls had said that he was attractive in a rugged sort of way. Others had added the word sinister or tough to describe him. He had a square jaw, broken nose, obviously an old break that had been straightened by hand and a four inch scar that ran diagonally down his left cheek. These features, however, were not the sinister part. It was his eyes, his cold gray eyes that seemed to look right through you, never showing warmth or life. Bob Considine had told her he was a good bouncer who would work cheap.

"Look Drago, I have some rules that will be followed if you want to work for me."

That got his attention and Drago leaned forward in his chair.

"Like what Ma'am" his response sounded surly and Maggie didn't like it.

"Like you don't come to work drunk and while you are working you don't drink. I can't have you making bad decisions when dealing with my customers."

Drago's attention was diverted by one of the girls walking by and Maggie bristled.

"That's the other rule Drago," her voice was firm and got his attention. "The girls, they're off limits and that's absolute. If you want to get laid, go to one of the other houses in the area. There's no freebies here, mess with my girls and I'll fire you so fast it'll make your head swim. Are we clear on this?"

Drago's cold gray eyes stared at her for a moment.

"You got it boss" a wicked smile crossed his face. "When do I start?"

"Right now," Maggie was relieved that it had gone well. "Work the front door area and no rough stuff unless you have to; otherwise check with me."

"You got it," Drago sauntered out into the bar area looking the place over as he went. Half way across the large room, that was rapidly filling up, he looked at the table in the back corner of the room where three young men sat downing their third drink. Pauley looked directly at him and there was a brief and almost imperceptible nod between the two. *This is going to be a good night.*

Thad's head was swimming, he was not a drinker and in fact had only drunk hard liquor on one other occasion and then he had gotten sick. Beer seemed to suit him more. The whiskeys and water chasers had affected him far greater and faster than he thought they would. Patrick had been right. He did feel more relaxed and when he talked it sometimes came out slurred and everyone including him thought is was funny and would laugh. The woman named Sandy had let him put his hand on her leg. Sitting there beside him she had put her hand on the inside of his leg. He felt himself stir and begin to get hard as she stroked his leg. He put his arm around her, rubbing her side near her breast as another round of drinks arrived. *How many drinks have I had?*

Sandy cooed in his ear, "Ooh that feels good baby, I like that" her hand slid a little farther up the inside of his leg almost to his crotch and his growing hardness. Pauley was laughing at something Patrick had said, but Thad didn't know what it was and he felt confused. It seemed that he was in a barrel and everyone was talking down into it and the sound echoed around.

Pauley had shoved another whiskey in front of him

"I bet you can't pour the whole shot down without stopping."

It came as an echo, but Thad understood he was being challenged and he grabbed the shot glass and poured it down just as Sandy's hand grasped his erection.

The world suddenly went crazy his head was spinning; Sandy had fallen to the floor as he lurched out of his chair. His legs were wobbly and he felt as though he was going to fall but some how managed to remain upright. Nausea swept over him as he lurched toward the nearest door. *This is wrong, it's all wrong, I shouldn't have come, I shouldn't be here, what would mother think of me and my God what would father say, I have to get away.* He vaguely noticed Pauley holding his right arm moving him toward a door. He did not know the man on his left, holding him upright heading toward the door. The man's eyes made him afraid, those eyes, cold, gray, lifeless. Bursting out the back door Thad emptied his stomach in a stream as he hit the wall on the other side of the alley. He slumped to the ground retching, wishing he could die, afraid he wouldn't. Through his misery, drifting in and out of consciousness, he heard laughing. *They're laughing at me.* He wallowed around on the ground. *Conversation, they're talking, Patrick, Pauley and the man with the dead eyes.* What he managed to hear made his guts churn. *My God they sold me.*

"Where's the money?" Pauley was loud but his speech was no longer slurred. "You promised the money on delivery and this is it."

"Shut-up punk." The man with the dead eyes had a voice like the edge of a knife, "I got your fuckin money right here. Your buddy here thinks he's sick now wait till wakes up on the schooner Northstar on the Pacific Ocean."

"Hey," it was Patrick sounding angry. "There's only three hundred here, we were promised eight. You cheated us. Bullshit, the deals off."

The fist struck Patrick's face sounding like someone thumping a gourd. Patrick made a low moaning sound as his knees buckled as he slumped to the ground.

"You bastard." It was Pauley coming to the aid of his fallen brother, but the attack was short-lived "aaargh," Pauley choked as the gray eyed man grabbed his throat and squeezed.

"Would you like to die punk?" The sharp edged voice was soft now, cold, menacing.

Pauley managed to speak in squeaking sounds, "No, please don't hurt me." There was real fear in Pauley's voice.

"Pick up your fuckin' brother and get the hell out of here before I take the three hundred back."

Thad heard the brothers shuffling out of the alley. Thad was alone with the dead eyed man and was about to be shanghaied to a ship in the bay.

I have to get it together; I have to defend myself, what would Amos do? An image of the flaming red beard and large gentle hands flashed into his mind. His grandfather Amos, big, strong capable, but Thad was not fierce and he had never fought anyone.

He heard the man walk up to where he was laying on the ground.

"Well lad it's time for you to take a little sea voyage. The salt air will do you good."

As the man leaned over to grab him, Thad kicked out as hard as he could. His foot struck home in the man's groin.

"Umph, oh shit," Drago doubled over in pain. "You son-of-a-bitch!" The pain was evident in his voice and so was his anger.

Thad tried to scuttle away on the ground and get to his feet, but when he tried his legs wouldn't hold him. His head still spinning, he went to his knees, instantly he felt the first kick to his kidney. The pain was excruciating, causing the air to rush out of his lungs, followed closely by the remaining contents of his stomach and the contents of his bladder as the second kick hit its target. He was jerked to his feet and punches slammed into his face, rib cage and stomach. He felt himself being smashed into the rough brick wall of the alley. As he drifted into blackness, he could no longer remember how many times he had been punched and kicked. He just knew that he was about to die. He wanted to scream 'stop, enough, stop,' but the sounds would not come out of his mouth. He could hear them, loud, aggressive, forceful, echoing in the alley, in the darkness that surrounded him, "Stop, stop or I'll shoot." The explosion thundered in his ears as Thad slipped into a black abyss.

Chapter 5

Thad could hear faint noises. Sounds of people moving, foot falls, whispers, a faint, far away shrill but muffled female laugh, a honky-tonk piano, but it all seemed to be coming from outside. It seemed at though he was in the bottom of a well. It was dark, and it was painful.

"Are you all right O'Shay?" Maggie had come running out into the alley at the sounds of yelling and shooting. Big Bob O'Shay was walking back down the alley to where she stood at the back door.

"I'm fine Maggie; I think I may have gotten a piece of him."

Maggie straightened a bit, *ah* she thought, *but doesn't Officer O'Shay look simply grand in his dark blue tunic, brass buttons and shinny Seattle Police badge.* She always felt safer at night when O'Shay, the beat officer, came through on his nightly rounds of the Tenderloin. O'Shay was six foot four, dark hair, graying just a bit at the temples. He had a square jaw, rugged face and deep brown eyes that could warm your soul. Adding to his appeal was that he was as honest as the day is long. Maggie felt her face flush as she watched him come down the alley; *oh I could do a lot worse than take Robert O'Shay up to my parlor.* She was glad it was dark in the alley.

"Did you get hurt?"

O'Shay moved to her right, "No, but I'm a bit concerned about the lad over here in the garbage."

Maggie looked to her right and saw Thad face down in the alley blood pooling around his head. "Oh my God, It's the young man who was with the Harrington boys. They took him to the alley with my new bouncer when he got sick."

"Yeah, well the guy I shot at was trying to stomp him to death. I didn't see the Harringtons but they're always bad news." O'Shay checked Thad's pulse. "He's still alive, Maggie can we take him inside?"

"Aunt Maggie?" Cynthia had stepped out of the back door, "what's happening?"

Maggie turned, "Nothing that concerns you child, go back inside and get one of the bartenders."

"No, I can help." She moved up beside O'Shay and helped him pick up Thad, bringing him to his sagging feet. "Grab his legs aunt Maggie, we can get him inside. He needs help."

O'Shay frowned at Cindy, "Let's just get him out of the alley, I'll call an ambulance and we can get him some medical help."

"Bob, I know this boy from somewhere. I don't know where but I know him. Hold off on the ambulance. Let's take him upstairs and I'll call doc Brainard, he'll come down."

"Are you sure Maggie? We don't know who he is. He was with the Harringtons so he could be a wild one. I don't know if this is a good idea Maggie."

"I know, but I have this feeling. Let's just take him up the back stairs, Mario…"

The cook popped out of the kitchen, "Yes boss."

"Give us a hand getting this young man up stairs."

"Yes Ma'am."

They struggled up the back stairs and down the hall.

"Mario, get a mop and clean up the blood in the hall. We don't want the customers seeing it, bad for business."

Mario scurried off to get a mop.

Cynthia had taken control, "Put him in the room next to mine. Marco," the dishwasher had hurried up to help. "Go to the kitchen get me a basin of hot water and chip off some ice from the block into another and get towels."

Marco and Mario returned quickly with the requested items.

"The hot water, towels and ice Miss Cynthia," Marco set them on the night stand. "Will there be anything else?" Marco looked at Thad and grimaced, "Oh he's a mess miss Cynthia, he needs a doctor."

"It's okay Marco, Maggie's calling for one. You and Mario better get back down stairs, I know it's busy."

She turned back to the young man with the flaming red hair and began to wipe the blood and filth from the alley off of his face. She moved the cover down to his waist as washed his arms and chest. The bruises starting to form made a knot in her stomach and she wondered who he was and why anyone would want to hurt him. Her hand resting on his shoulder felt a quick movement that startled her. His breathing came in short gasps and his head rolled from side to side.

Thad tried to take a deep breath, but the pain in his chest was too much. He gasped and tried to open his eyes, but they seemed to be swollen and he could not see. He sensed the sweet odor of perfume and the softness of a feather bed. *Where am I, the gray eyed man,* Thad started to panic and his mind raced, *I'm being shanghaied, I've got to get away, the gray eyed man kicking me, the terrible pain, the perfume.* Thad drifted back into unconsciousness.

"Is he still alive?" Maggie burst into the room startling her. "The doctors here so let him have a look. Sandy will finish cleaning him up. I think you've done and seen as much as you need to."

For the first time Maggie looked closely at the man's face, now cleaned up but badly swollen. *Oh good lord, he looks like Chad, he could be Chad, but twenty years younger, he has to be Chad's son.* Maggie's hands started to shake and those buried feelings came rushing back.

"H...He'll be fine, let's go outside and let the doctor and Sandy take care of him for awhile."

Cynthia looked back as they began to work on the young man and could not understand the feelings she was having. *Why does it bother me that Sandy was cleaning and caring for him?* Maggie gently guided her out of the room and shut the door.

"Aunt Maggie, I want to take care of him." The words just seemed to slip out suddenly.

Maggie turned with a concerned look on her face.

"Why child, we have no idea who he is and Sandy has experience."

"I...I don't know why Aunt Maggie, I just need to."

Cynthia took a new tack, "I am a medical major at the University Aunt Maggie. This will give me valuable experience." Cynthia was resolute and Maggie was perplexed. Then the thoughts of Chadwick came rushing back.

"Okay, it's against my better judgment, but you can play nurse when the doctor and Sandy are done."

Cynthia felt a thrill run through her body followed by a sense of anticipation and excitement. She had not experienced this feeling since she and Billy Marshall had discovered and briefly explored the differences between boys and girls. That was in the barn out back of her house in Kansas, it seemed so long ago. Of course, it had only been four years yet so much had happened and changed in that time.

Cynthia's mind drifted back to that painful time. *Mom and Dad are gone.* Cynthia stood by the grave, heartbroken that life had dealt her close loving family such a disastrous blow. At 15 she was not prepared to handle all of this. It had happened so quickly. Her mother had gotten ill with what the doctor called "the fever" and her temperature was running far too high. She and her father had kept ice around her for two days until her father came down with it. Cynthia tried her best, the neighbors came to help but her mother died within two days and her father followed a week later. Mr. Baker, her father's attorney, was very helpful.

"I've sent a telegram to your mother's sister in Seattle and informed her of the situation. She's coming out to get you and you'll go to live with her in Seattle. It's going to be all right Cynthia; it's going to work out. Please accept my deepest sympathy."

Cynthia had only met her aunt Maggie once and she seemed like a wonderful person, happy and down to earth. Her mother and father had not spoken much of her in the past and she had only come out that one time. Cynthia had gotten the feeling that her parents did not approve of her.

Mr. Baker put his arm around Cynthia's shoulder, "I have followed your father's directives in his Will. You are the sole heir and I'm liquidating his business and holdings. That money will be placed in a trust from which you will receive a monthly payment and money for schooling."

Cynthia was numb; she heard what the attorney was telling her, but was unable to react.

What will I do? What will happen to me?

"Mr. Baker, what about our house, can't I live there?"

"I'm afraid not. The bank will call in the loan on it. I'll arrange to sell the house and property. The money left will be added to your trust."

Cynthia felt desperate. "Where will I live, when will my aunt be here?"

Someone took her hand; she turned to see Billy Marshall standing next to her looking very serious.

"It'll be okay Cindy. My mom said that you could stay with us until your aunt gets here."

Her best friend Billy being there to comfort her allowed her to unload. She had buried her face in his chest and the tears came. He wrapped his arms around her and rocked her gently as she wept uncontrollably. All that anguish that she had been holding in during this tribulation. All the tears that she had held back, trying to be strong for her dying parents, came flooding out. Her friend Billy was there to hold and comfort her. For now, at least, she was safe.

***

"Thank you Mrs. Marshall!" Billy and his dad had brought Cynthia's things to the room where she and Billy's mother were making the bed. "I really appreciate your letting me stay. It will only be two weeks until my aunt can get here from Seattle. I will be going back with her."

Mrs. Marshall finished smoothing the bedspread.

"Oh, it's our pleasure, and you know that you're welcome to stay as long as you want. I know your parents would do the same for us." Cynthia started to tear up at the mention of her parents.

"I'm sorry honey. I know how hard it must be. It's going to be alright."

"Is it Mrs. Marshall? Is it really going to be alright? When will it be alright?"

"It'll take time. Time will heal the wounds, and please call me Ann."

Cynthia felt a little better and at 15 she had a lot of time to heal. "Thank you Mrs…Ann," both laughed and finished making the bed.

The days seemed to pass quickly. The first day, Cynthia spent with Mr. Marshall and Mr. Baker at Baker's office and at the bank setting up the financial papers for the estate. The second was spent with Ann shopping and helping around the house. Billy seemed to hover just on the fringe of what ever was happening. It was like he was preoccupied with something and Cynthia figured he would get around to telling her what it was. Cynthia had begun to look forward to seeing her aunt again and Seattle sounded like an interesting and exciting place. She was able to keep busy during the days but the nights were bad. Laying in bed, her parents were in her thoughts and in her dreams. They were painful feelings and some nights she would cry herself to sleep. With each passing day, it was a little less painful and sleep would come a little easier. A week into her stay Billy could hold back no longer. It was after midnight when she heard the bedroom door open and then close. She turned over to find Billy beside the bed.

"Billy?"

"Sssh," Billy put his finger to his lips and sat down on the edge of the bed. "I need to talk to you," Billy leaned over and kissed her on the cheek then on the mouth.

This was not the first time they had kissed, so it didn't startle her. Last year in the barn was the first time she had ever seen a boy without clothes and for that matter had ever shown her self to a boy. Nothing had happened really. They had touched, looked and she remembered her amazement when he got an erection. She was almost afraid to touch it, they both laughed when she did. There had been other secret kisses but nothing more.

Billy brushed a curl off of her forehead and kissed her again, this time with more feeling. She was comfortable with Billy. She had a need for affection but not here and not like this.

"No Billy, stop, we can't do this here. If your parents should find out or come in we would be in trouble. I can't do this to them after what they've done for me. Go back to your room; we'll talk in the morning."

"Cindy, please," Billy slid his hand under her nightie and started to run his hand up her leg. "Please Cindy it'll be alright."

Cindy was starting to panic, *what if his parents come in, they'll throw me out, I know they will.*

"Billy, stop now." She grabbed his hand before he got to the top of her leg. "Billy if you don't stop right now I'll tell for your mom."

Billy snatched his hand back.

"Geez Cindy, it ain't like we never did this before."

"Billy Marshall you had more on your mind than touching and kissing."

Billy smiled, "Well maybe, but dang Cindy you know how I feel. We need to talk about it, I really want to."

"Tomorrow Billy, not now, go back to your room before we both get into trouble."

Billy got off the bed, "Okay Cindy, tomorrow." He slipped out of the room quietly shutting the door behind him.

"Cindy honey," Mrs. Marshall had just finished with the breakfast dishes and Cindy was putting away the last plate. "Would you mind taking care of the chickens and collecting the eggs this morning?"

"Of course not, I'd love to. Is everything okay?"

"Oh yes, Mr. Mitchell and I are going down the Johnson's for a few hours. They need help loading some of the cows and Agnes and I are going to can some beans."

"Well don't worry about the chickens; I'll take good care of them. Is there anything else I can do for you?"

"Well, you might give Billy a hand with some of his chores. He's always moaning that he has too much to do."

Cindy watched as they drove off, grabbed the egg basket and headed for the barn. Dust kicked up around her feet and the hem of her dress and there was a hum as grasshoppers rose up from the weeds in front of her scattering off in different directions. She opened the gate to the chicken yard stepping in quickly and shutting it as chickens seemed to come from everywhere in a chorus of clucks and squawks sensing it was time to be fed. She scattered the feed and then went inside and gathered the eggs. Most of the nests were unguarded and the eggs were easily retrieved. There were, however, a few hens who were brooding and gave up their nests only after Cindy physically pushed them out while they loudly squawked their complaint at having there eggs taken. She could hear Billy at the far end of the barn at the milking stalls.

"How're you doing with the milking Billy?"

"Oh, hi, I'm down to the last cow." Billy stood up and looked over the top of the cow at Cindy walking down the center aisle.

"You ever milk a cow before?"

Cindy set down the egg basket, "No, father always milked the cows. We only had two."

"Well come here, I'll show you how to do it. It's not hard."

Cindy went down to the milking stall and patted the cow whose head was firmly held in place by the stanchions.

"Will she kick Billy?"

Billy Laughed, "No Cindy she's not going to kick you. The worst that can happen is that you might get hit by her tail if she starts swishing flies. Here sit down on the stool."

Cindy squatted down on the low stool and Billy knelt on the straw behind her.

"Now, put your forehead against her side."

Cindy pressed her forehead against the cow; it was soft, warm and almost soothing. She stared at the udder and the teats protruding out of it.

"How do you get the milk out?"

"Take a hold of the two closest teats and hold them firmly."

Cindy grimaced and wrapped her fingers around the teats.

"This feels strange, doesn't she mind this?"

"No, she's used to it. Now start to squeeze the teat starting with the highest fingers and down to the bottom pulling the teat down slightly. Go ahead try it."

Billy leaned against her back and put his arms around her grasping her hands and showing her how to squeeze and pull. His cheek was pressed against hers as she labored to get milk from the cow. Her first and second attempts failed, but on the third try a small amount of milk squirted into the pail.

"Oh look, I got some."

"Keep going, you'll get more as you get better."

Cindy concentrated on squeezing down and pulling and shortly she was successful with every pull.

"I'm doing it Billy, I'm really doing it."

"You're a natural Cindy," Billy's hand left hers; went to the inside of her leg sliding up under her dress. She felt him kiss her neck. When she turned to say something he kissed her on the mouth. She stopped pulling the teats.

"Billy Marshal, this is not about milking a cow."

Billy stood up helping Cindy up off the stool and holding her hand, walked toward the hay stacked in a stall.

"Remember the first time we were in a barn and kissed and stuff? We were afraid your folks would find us, but we did it anyway, let's do it again. This time we don't have to worry about our folks, it's just you and me and this silly cow and she ain't gonna tell no one."

Billy pulled her close and kissed her, fumbling clumsily with the buttons on her dress.

"Wait Billy, I don't mind kissing and stuff but we can't have sex."

Billy was breathing hard as he started pulling her dress up.

"No Billy," the words hisst in his ear, "we can't do this, please Billy stop."

Billy let her dress fall back into place,

"Cindy, I love you, don't do this to me, I know you want it too."

"Thank you Billy, thank you for stopping when I asked. I think I love you too but doing it now will only cause us problems. I don't want to get pregnant and if we do it I just know that will happen. We'd be making a big mistake. The last thing either of us needs is for me to get pregnant."

"But I want to Cindy, I really want us to do it now, I know you want it too, I can tell the way you act." Billy was almost frantic as he started undoing her buttons again. "Come on Cindy we love each other, we can do it just this once, it'll be alright."

"No Billy I can't let this happen and if I lay down with you I won't be able to stop it." Cindy pulled away from his grasp and backed away. She buttoned the buttons Billy had managed to get undone and she ran from the barn. Cindy stood in the kitchen trying to catch her breath. *What should I do? I can't get pregnant; I just can't allow that to happen.*

Billy walked through the door carrying the egg basket.

"You forgot this," he set it on the counter and stood in front of her.

"Don't do this, we're not having sex and that's that."

"Cindy we need to talk about us."

"Not now Billy, I'm just not thinking clear what with Mom and Dad, how we feel about each other and Aunt Maggie coming down. Please let me think about it, please Bil…"

Billy stepped up and kissed her on the cheek.

"It's alright Cindy, but we only have a couple of days before your aunt gets here. I've got chores to finish before my folks get back."

Billy turned and hurried out the kitchen door. Tears of frustration and uncertainty ran down Cindy's cheeks as she watched him stride across the yard toward the barn.

Billy mentioned nothing about their discussion, neither that day nor the next. Cindy had lain in bed at night trying to understand her feelings and what she should do about them, about Billy; about Aunt Maggie.

"Good morning Cindy," Mrs. Marshall was getting breakfast ready and Cindy began to set the table. "are you alright, are you having trouble sleeping? You really look tired."

"I'm alright Ann. I guess it's just the excitement of Aunt Maggie arriving tomorrow."

"You'll be starting a whole new adventure. I guess that would keep me awake too."

Cindy got the jug of milk out of the ice box and thought of the incident in the barn. *Should I ask her about getting married or will that bother her?*

"Ann, what do…"

"Morning everyone," Billy came striding into the kitchen, upbeat and cheerful. "Gonna be a great day. How are you this morning Cindy?"

Cindy looked at Billy, *Why is he so cheerful, I'll be leaving tomorrow? Oh no, he's going to ask me to marry him, I know he is. Oh God, don't do it here in front of your Mom Billy.*

"I'm fine Billy. You're off to a good start."

"Yep, it's gonna be a good day." Billy slipped into a chair as the table as Mrs. Mitchell served breakfast.

Billy finished and got up. Cindy kept her eyes on her plate and would not look at him. *Don't do it now Billy, please don't do it now.* "I'm goin' down to the barn and help Dad. I want to get my chores done early so I can go fishin' this afternoon." Billy paused and looked at Cindy. "Want to come along Cindy? Should be a good afternoon for it"

"Oh I don't know Billy. I've got a lot to…"

Mrs. Marshall cut her off, "Oh go on down to the pond Cindy, it'll take your mind off things."

Ann, you have no idea what's going on here.

"Oh…alright Billy, let me know when you're ready to go."

Billy was beaming from ear to ear as he marched out the door. *Oh Billy what am I going to tell you if you do ask me.*

When they were out of sight of the house Billy took Cindy's hand as they walked down the trail to the pond. When they got there he leaned the poles up against a tree and took her other hand, standing squarely in front of her.

"Cindy, marry me."

"Oh Billy, I was afraid you were going to ask me that. You've had that look on your face for the last two days."

Billy moved a little closer, "Your aunt gets here the day after tomorrow and is that a yes or no."

I could love him, he would take care of me, I could take care of him, a house, babies…

"Billy, you're only sixteen and I'm just fifteen, we're too young."

Billy saw himself loosing, "John and Francine got married last year. They were only sixteen."

Cynthia let go of his hand and caressed his cheek with her fingertips, "Yes they did but that was because he got her pregnant. They're really struggling now."

Billy was looking dejected.

"We could rent the old Handy place. The land is good and the house and barn are still in pretty good shape. Given some time we may even be able to buy it, if we watch our money. I love you Cindy"

"Billy I love you too, I've never felt like this about anyone. Cynthia's thoughts raced. *What would mom and dad say? They even set money aside for me to go to school. It's too soon, I'm not ready, oh mom I need you.*

"I want to love you, I want to have sex with you, I want to have your babies, but I also want to see what's on the other side of the mountains. I want to see other places and experience new things. Billy there may not be anything for me there and I'll be back here with you, but I have to go see for myself."

Billy was now reaching, "Then as least let me make love to you just once" *Maybe it wouldn't harm if I did, maybe I wouldn't get pregnant,* "No Billy, we can't. Getting married because I'm pregnant is not the answer for us. Please understand." She reached out to touch him, but Billy stepped away, she could see the pain in his eyes. "Billy…"

He turned took the poles from the tree and headed back up the trail to the house.

***

Billy had left the house before breakfast and when he was there he was distant. He didn't try to talk to her that night and Cynthia lay awake, feeling guilty about not letting him make love to her. *Why does life have to be so complicated, why can't he understand that I need to get away, even if it's for a short time to let the healing happen. Oh Billy, I think I love you but how do I know. Will I ever really know?*

Cynthia had her things packed and ready to go when Aunt Maggie arrived. She was just as Cynthia had remembered her, colorful, happy and easy to talk to. The Marshall's insisted on Maggie staying for lunch before catching the next westbound train back to the coast. Billy was absent and no one seemed to know where he was.

"I think that Billy might be a little sweet on you Cindy." It was Ann Marshall who finally addressed his absence, "he may be having a problem with your leaving."

Cynthia looked around the table, *if they only knew what had been going on they might really understand,*

"I am very fond of Billy, he's been my best friend. He was there when I needed him. I do wish he would see me off."

They boarded the train and still Billy had not appeared. As the train pulled out of the station Cynthia caught a movement at the side of the last building on the platform. As they came abreast of it, she saw Billy standing there, tears streaming down his face. As their eyes met he gave a small almost imperceptible wave, as Cynthia's hand came up to wave he turned and ran towards the woods. Cynthia wiped her tears away as Maggie's arm came around her shoulders and pulled her close.

"That, I take it was Billy."

Cynthia simply nodded. She was not ready to talk. Maggie pulled her closer; "let me tell you a story about what I do for a living." By the time she finished three hours had passed and they were both crying with laughter. Aunt Maggie was wonderful and Cynthia already had begun to love her.

***

Cynthia straightened the cover over her charge and wiped the perspiration from his face. Her heart went out to this badly beaten young man with the red hair. *Why do I feel this affinity for him? I don't even know who he is?* She reached over and touched him lightly on the forehead. She pulled her hand back startled as his eyes fluttered open.

Thad started awake. *The man with the gray eyes, the punching, the kicking, the explosion, music, laughing, it all runs together, I'm going to die*, his eyes blinked open. His vision was blurred, but he could tell someone was there. He tried to focus but the bright light from behind made it difficult. *Where am I, who is this, I can't see clearly, I've got to stay awake but I can't*, He concentrated on focusing. Suddenly she was there. *She's beautiful, she's the most beautiful woman I've ever seen; she glows.*

Thad had to concentrate to speak.

"Are you an angel? Did I die? Please help me."

He felt her hand on his face her large brown eyes reassuring him. Her lips moved but he couldn't hear. She made him feel at peace. His vision blurred and he slipped once more into the blackness, but this time the face of the angel replaced the terror of the dream.

Maggie was faced with a dilemma. The boy had no identification and no one knew who he was. O'Shay had been asking around trying to find out who knew the boy, but no one had an answer. No one that is, except Maggie. *Should I tell O'Shay who he was? Would the question come as to how I knew? Should I make contact with Chadwick? He must be worried sick, but he had made it clear that there would be no contact between us. I have to do something, someone has to know. What does the boy want? I need to find out and soon.*

Maggie opened the door and poked her head in. Cynthia had stayed at his bedside all night and had fallen asleep in a chair. She woke up when Maggie came into the room.

"How's the patient? You look terrible!"

Cynthia got up from the chair with a groan from her stiffness.

"This chair is not the most comfortable place to fall asleep. He woke up once about three and muttered something but I couldn't understand it."

She dampened a cloth and tenderly wiped his face, "Aunt Maggie, he has been out for two days now. Will he be alright?"

Maggie put her hand on the side of his face, "Well he isn't hot any more and the swelling is going down. He took some nasty blows to the head. The doctor says it would be normal for him to be out for awhile. How are you doing? You look like you could use some rest."

"Oh, I'm okay," Cynthia stretched and yawned, "I manage to catch cat naps for an hour or two from time to time. I want to be here when he wakes up."

Maggie took her hand.

"Why Cynthia, what's going on here?"

"I don't know Aunt Maggie; I saw him earlier that evening and wondered why he was here. It was obvious that he was uncomfortable, not like the other boys he was with. They were rowdies!"

Maggie took her other hand and looked into Cynthia's eyes. "And..."

"I don't even know who he is Aunt Maggie, but something tells me I need to know. Does that make sense?"

Cynthia looked down at Thad.

"He may not be anything at all like I think he is," she looked back at Maggie. "On the other hand he may be exactly how I think. I just know that he's shy, vulnerable and hurt. I need to know more about him Aunt Maggie."

Maggie pulled her close.

"It's alright and it does make sense child. I once met a man very much like him. He broke my heart, but maybe this time it will be different. You go freshen up and get something to eat. I'll stay here till you get back and I'll call you if he comes around."

Cynthia hurried out of the room. She didn't want to be away for too long. Maggie walked over to the bed, took the cloth and wiped the perspiration from his face and chest.

"Well young Mr. Mitchell, will you break a heart too?"

She sat down in the chair touched his face and thought of Chad. Tears welled in her eyes. The decision was clear, Chadwick had to know. She wrote a brief note and tucked it into an envelope went down to the kitchen.

"Marco, take this envelope to a Mr. Mitchell in the Pioneer building. Give it only to him; no one else is that clear?"

"Yes boss" Marco took the envelope and hurried out.

Maggie went back to the room. *Chad has to know he must be sick with worry.*

When Thad did not return home that first night Becky had made Chadwick go out and look for him. Since his return late that night, Chadwick had suffered Becky's wrath and her guilt. She felt it was both of their faults, Chad's for fighting with Thad and hers for demanding that he get out. Chadwick had endured and tried to assure her.

"Becky, he'll be alright, he's just angry, hurt and confused. He'll be back by morning, you'll see."

Becky turned toward him, tears welling in her eyes.

"Are you sure, what if he's injured or does something stupid?"

"Stupid, like what Becky?" That possibility had not occurred to him.

"I don't know, get on a train, or sign-on to one of those awful ships in the bay. I've seen the men who work on them, they're dreadful!"

"I don't think that he'll do that honey, he'll be home when he works this through."

Becky began to cry again. Chadwick took her in his arms.

"I'm sorry, it'll work out. This happens between fathers and sons. Thad will clear his head and be home by this afternoon I'm sure of it."

Chadwick had stayed home from the office, but Thad did not return. By the second day Becky was insisting that Chadwick contact the police.

"No Becky, we don't need to involve the police. The whole world doesn't have to know about our personal problems. I've contacted John Harrington and he's checking with his boys. Remember that they were looking for him on the day he left. He may have hooked up with them."

The morning of the third day found Becky was absolutely beside herself.

"Chad you must find him or contact the police, something awful has happened to him, I just know it."

Chadwick held her hands and looked hard into her eyes.

"I fear for him too Becky. I'm going to the office and I'll get all of my resources working on it. We will find him and I'll contact you as soon as I know where he is."

When Chad arrived at his office his secretary pointed out the swarthy man seated in the waiting area.

"Mr. Mitchell, he says that he has something for you, but would not leave it with me. He said that it must go only to you and that was his orders. He sounds like he's Portuguese or something, he's hard to understand."

Chadwick approached the man, "You have something for me?"

"Only if you are Chadwick Mitchell, senor. My boss says it goes only to Mr. Mitchell."

Chadwick was starting to get impatient, "Who do you work for?"

"She own' the Silver Slipper."

"Maggie?" Chadwick blurted it out before he could think.

"Si, senor, I work for Miss Maggie, you must be Mr. Mitchell."

Marco dug into his jacket and produced the envelope. Chadwick's hands were trembling as he took the envelope and headed for his office.

"Please wait here, there may be a response." Marco sat back down. Chadwick fumbled with the envelope finally extracting the note inside.

'My Dearest Chadwick: I have struggled with the writing of this note. I know that you were clear that we would have no further contact and I have lived with that. This is a situation that you must know about. I have a young man here at my place that was beaten severely two nights ago. He has no identification on him and except for the red hair he is the mirror image of you. He must be your son. He will live and we are looking after him. A doctor, who assures me that he will make a full recovery, has seen him. If this is not your son you will not hear from me again.

My Love Maggie."

My God, Thad's hurt, thank you lord for letting Maggie find him. Chadwick opened the door to his office and looked at Marco, "there is no need for you to wait. Tell your boss that I will be there shortly."

"Si Senor," Marco popped up and hurried out the door.

Chadwick turned to his secretary, "Janet cancel all of my appointments and call my wife. Tell her I had to go out, I think I know where our son is and that I'll contact her as soon as I know for sure."

Janet looked a little perplexed.

"Yes sir...I'll get right on it."

Cynthia had taken her place next to his bedside when Thad's eyes blinked open. He was fully conscious this time and could feel the soreness in his body. He was staring at the ceiling and his eyes started to roam the room. *It's not heaven, I survived the beating.* He felt the hand on his arm and turned towards Cynthia. His face broke into a somewhat painful lopsided grin, "The angel, you're real, I didn't just dream you. Angels don't cry do they?"

Tears had flooded Cynthia's eyes and cascaded down her face when he spoke.

"I've been so worried; I thought you were going to die." She reached down and took his hand.

Who is this beautiful woman holding my hand?

"Who are you and where am I?"

Cynthia wiped her tears away, "I'm Cynthia, my friends call me Cindy and you're upstairs in the Silver Slipper."

Thad looked startled, "That's the box house I was in, are you a..."

Cynthia giggled, and put her fingertips over her lips. Her laughter sounded like bells from heaven to Thad.

"No, my Aunt Maggie owns the place. I just live here while I'm going to the University. I help out around here when I can. Right now you're my fulltime project."

Thad was totally captivated by her smile, it lit up the room. *Am I still dreaming, is she real, please don't let her be a dream.* Thad reached out and took her hand, "thank you for helping me, how can I ever repay you."

Cynthia felt a shiver of excitement; *don't ever turn loose of my hand*, "I'm glad we found you in time. If it hadn't been for Officer O'Shay, that man might have killed you in the alley."

Thad let it sink in for a second, *that's twice the police saved my tail.* Things started coming back in bits and pieces. *The Harringtons, those bastards, can't do anything about that now, but time will tell.*

"How long have I been here?"

"This is day three."

Thad sat straight up in bed, his eyes wide, "Good lord my parents, they must be in a state of panic. I've got to let them know I'm alright, help me get up." Thad suddenly realized that beside the excruciating pain, he was naked under the sheet and abruptly stopped moving.

Cynthia had a silly smile on her face after seeing his startled look.

"You had to be cleaned up a couple of times," She giggled nervously.

Thad gave her a wide-eyed look, Cynthia smiled, "No, I didn't, Aunt Maggie wouldn't let me. She had some of her girls do it. They're used to seeing men…you know…without clothes. She smiled to herself, *his cheeks are pink, he is shy, I just knew it.*

"You know me, who in the world are you?"

"I'm sorry, my name is…"

"Thad Mitchell," the answer came from the man standing in the doorway, cutting him off.

"Father!"

Chadwick came in through the back door, "I'm sorry sir, but you can't come in this way," a very large black man, most likely a bouncer, blocked his way.

"Where's Maggie, I'm a friend.

"Wait here" the man was emphatic and Chadwick did not follow.

"Chadwick," there was no mistaking the voice.

Maggie looked good and old feelings came rushing back.

"Maggie, I got your note. My son is missing, where's the young man that you have."

Maggie put her arms around him and hugged. She felt his hesitancy and then he melted and she felt the strength of his embrace. It was like he had never left but deep down inside she knew it was not meant to be.

"He's okay Chadwick. He's upstairs, but let me talk to you first." Chadwick looked past her to the stairs, "I want to see him now."

Maggie's boss voiced stopped him short, "Chadwick, sit down, we must talk."

Chadwick sat.

"I don't want it to be a shock to you, he was pretty badly beaten and I don't know how excited he should get. The doctor said that there could be some internal damage, he was kicked a number of times. My niece, Cynthia, has been with him ever since the doctor left two days ago." Chadwick looked nervously up the stairs.

"No Chad, she is not one of my girls, she's my niece. Her parents died and she lives here with me while she attends the University."

Maggie took on a small air of pride.

"She watches him like a hawk, takes care of him and he is coming along fine. He was out for over two days but woke up a little over an hour ago."

Chadwick was getting fidgety, "Chadwick, it wasn't his fault; we feel that he got set up."

"We, who exactly is we Maggie?" She now had Chadwick's full attention.

"Officer O'Shay and I."

Chadwick looked concerned, "Officer, the police know?"

Maggie put her hand over his and squeezed softly, "O'Shay saved his life Chadwick. The man in the alley would have killed him if O'Shay had not intervened. He saved your boy's life."

"How do you know he's my son, Maggie?"

Her eyes locked with his, "Because when I saw him this morning, with some of the swelling gone, I was looking at you…except for the red hair. He's you, Chadwick."

Chadwick slumped in the chair.

"We had a terrible fight Maggie. I was being a fool and he was being eighteen. He left the house hurt and angry. I've been looking for him for two days now. If it's anyone's fault it's mine. My stupidity could have gotten him killed."

***

"I'm so sorry for everything, father."

Thad felt ashamed and a little fearful, Cynthia released his hand and stepped toward Maggie and Chadwick in the doorway almost protective. Maggie looked her away and Cynthia stepped aside. *What was his father about to do, how would he react*? Words rushed out of Thad, "I know that you only want the best for me and you…"

Chadwick's raised hand stopped him from rambling.

"It's alright son, your safe and that's all that's important. Nothing else matters except that you're in one piece and by the look of you the pieces have been moved around a little."

Both men smiled, Thad breathed a sigh of relief. Chadwick moved to the side of the bed and sat down and took Thad's hand,

"Thad, sometimes we get so wrapped up in ourselves that we forget about others and their wants and needs."

Thad could not remember when his father had acted like this and it surprised him.

"Son, we say and do things that we don't mean and sometimes hurt the ones we love most. I'm proud of you Thad. You've grown into a fine young man." Tears were forming in Chadwick's eyes as they hugged one another.

"I love you father."

Both Maggie and Cynthia were wiping tears as they slipped out of the room.

"Thad, Maggie said that the doctor would rather you stay in bed and not be moved for at least another two days. That way he can be sure that you don't have any serious internal injuries. To move you too soon might cause problems, if you are indeed injured. So it looks like you stay here at least until the day after tomorrow." Chadwick smiled at his battered son. "How's your nursing care?"

Thad looked a little perplexed.

"Father she's not one of the girls here, she's…"

"I know son, she's Maggie's niece. She seems like a nice young lady."

Thad's eyes lit up, "Isn't she something? She's beautiful, she's gentle and kind, and she's just wonderful to be with. She's my angel father. I saw her in a dream and asked her to help me and when I woke up there she was. It's the strangest thing. She makes me feel so good inside and I don't even know her."

Chadwick put his hand on Thad's shoulder, *I know son I've had those same feelings before.* Becky was the person to pop into his mind not Maggie. But he owed Maggie a great deal.

"I'll explain to your mother what has happened. She is not going to like leaving you here until Friday but we'll sort it out. I better let her know that she still has a son and I'll see you Friday to take you home.

"Father" Thad's serious tone stopped him at the door, "I know I need direction in my life, but I want to check some things out before we discuss it."

"When you're ready son, when you're ready," *it's interesting what a good woman will do for your peace of mind. This should be interesting.*

Chadwick opened the door to find both Maggie and Cynthia standing outside with concerned looks on their faces.

"Well ladies it appears that your patient and my son are going to survive. Cynthia," he looked into her large dark eyes full of anticipation,

"You've done a wonderful job with him. Thank you very much, he's all yours." Cynthia's face broke into a smile as she slipped past Chadwick into the room.

"Maggie, I owe you more than I can ever repay. You have given my son back to me and I know the hurt that I caused you in the past. I'm so sorry about that, I would be lying if I said there was nothing there, but I do love my wife."

Maggie put her fingertips to his lips, "Shoosh Chadwick Mitchell, you get on home to your wife and let her know that her son is still alive. She has to be worried sick." They hugged and Chadwick slipped out the back door. She watched him stride up the alley, *you are something Chadwick Mitchell,* she felt the wound in her heart healing. It most likely would never totally heal, *well...maybe I can get on with it now.*

Cynthia was holding Thad's hand and they were talking softly. It was so comfortable for both to be in each other's company. There was no shyness. It was as though they had known each other for ever. It was different with Thad than it had been with Billy. The feelings were deeper, stronger, and more intense. She felt things that she had not when she was with Billy. Thad was telling her about the trip from Vermont as her thoughts swirled. *I told Billy that I had to see the other side of the mountains to see if there was anything there for me. There may be, it could be Thad, I could never have left him.*

"Okay, break it up in here." Bob O'Shay walked into the room with Maggie tagging along behind.

"Looks like they got all the pieces back in the right places son, I had my doubts when I first saw you laying in the garbage in the alley. You want to press charges against the guy who beat you?"

Thad was a little overwhelmed by the huge police officer.

"I...I don't know sir, can I?"

"Well you can," O'Shay walked over to the bedside, "Just a couple of things you might want to consider before you do. Now I'm not trying to talk you out of anything and if you want, I'll write it up and send it over to the prosecutor's office, but consider this." Thad and Cynthia listened intently, "He may be hard to find. I think I got a piece of him when I shot at him in the alley."

Thad perked up, "That's the explosion that I remember."

"Just how much do you remember about that night?" O'Shay took a hard look at him.

Thad thought for a minute, and then recounted the incident in the bar and what he could about the alley. He peeked over at Cynthia who just smiled at him. He felt embarrassed about his actions and he purposely left out Patty on his lap. *Man she must think I'm some kind of rounder or something.* If she did, she gave no hint of it.

O'Shay rubbed his chin.

"Ah the Harrington boys…now there's a bad pair. You'd be wise to steer clear of those two. There's also another problem. John Harrington is pretty well connected in Seattle. His money has gotten the boys out of a lot more serious stuff than this incident. You also have to consider that your dad is well on the way to being a political power here. You being caught up in a mess south of the line could affect that."

Thad looked a little shocked.

"Yeah son, I know who you are, but don't worry about it. I'm not going to broadcast it around. Besides if I did, my guess is that Maggie here would skin me alive."

He looked at Maggie and gave her a look and a wink that actually caused her to blush. She felt her face heat up. *Now what's this all about? You'd think I was Cynthia's age with no experience with men. This could get interesting.*

O'Shay had turned back to Thad.

"Last, but not least, I checked the hospital. Our gray-eyed friend, whose name by the way is Drago Banya, has a record as long as your arm. He hasn't turned up to get repairs done. I must have just nicked him or he left town. He could get medical aid in Tacoma. In any case, he may be hard to find. Well son, what do you think you might want to do?"

Thad was thoughtful,

"Officer O'Shay can I let you know in a couple of days? This may be something I need to discuss with my father, as it concerns him also."

"You can call me Bob and I'd say that's the smart move Thad," O'Shay started toward the door, "Glad to see your feelin' better son."

"Bob?" The tone of Thad's voice stopped the policeman.

"What is it?"

Thad was very serious.

"Do you like being a policeman?"

O'Shay looked intently at the young man sitting in the bed, "I love it. I wouldn't want to do anything else. I've been an officer for fifteen years and have seen a lot of changes in this city. It's a good job. The pays not great, but the benefits are okay." O'Shay thought for a moment. "There's a lot of personal satisfaction that goes along with the job. Granted there are some times of frustration too. Overall I'd say it's the fact that you're your own boss out on the street. No one is telling you what to do and when to do it. You call your own shots on every call. Each call is different and you get a real taste of what life is all about, both the good and the bad."

Thad had hung on every word.

"What does it take to be one and how old do you have to be?"

O'Shay walked back over to the bed.

"You serious about this Thad?"

"Yes…well I think so."

"Well it takes honesty, integrity and liking to work with people, those are some of the key ingredients. How old are you Thad?"

"I'll be nineteen in three months." The room was dead quiet for what seemed like an eternity.

"I'll tell you what Thad, when you turn nineteen, come see me. I'll show you around. If you still feel like you want to give it a try, I'll help you make application."

O'Shay turned and walked out the door.

Alone again Thad looked into Cynthia's eyes.

"Cynthia, you must think I'm a terrible person after hearing what I told Officer O'Shay."

"It's okay. You don't have to account to me. It's not important." The look on Thad's face made her heart melt, "It's important to me Cindy."

Cynthia's heart first seemed to skip a beat and then doubled its rate.

In the hallway Maggie had taken O'Shay by the hand, "I know you get off at three o'clock Bob. I'll be closing up, why don't you drop by and keep me company. I'd buy you some coffee."

Officer O'Shay was trying to be very casual but he felt like he had butterflies in his stomach.

"I'd like that very much Maggie. Thank you." His smile made her heart quicken but his smile had always done that to her. O'Shay went up the alley whistling softly.

Chapter 6

"Chadwick you can't just leave him in a house of prostitution!" Becky did not call him by his full first name unless she was very upset.

Chadwick stood his ground, "Yes we can Becky. The only other choice we have is to move him and risk serious internal complications. The doctor will know better by tomorrow and then we'll be able to bring him home."

Becky's face told him that he had won this round.

"How does he look Chad…is he in pain?"

"He looks awful Becky. He has bruises on his face, but most of the swelling has gone down. His lip is cut and there are some nasty bruises on his ribs, back and chest from the kicks. I didn't actually see them, but his nurse said that he suffered some kicks to his kidneys causing the bruising. He's a lucky young man that Officer O'Shay arrived as the assault was taking place and the man ran away. He was also lucky that Maggie Wilson, she's the owner of the Silver Slipper, found him in the alley and took him in and called a doctor. Her niece, she's a lovely young lady who attends the University, is caring for Thad and doing a wonderful job. If you wish, you can come with me on Friday and meet them."

Becky sniffed, "I don't believe I really have a need to meet anyone in that place."

"Now or later Becky, I have a feeling that you'll meet Cynthia at some point no matter how you feel."

Becky looked surprised.

"Who is this woman Chad? How old is she? Where does she come from? Why do you say that? I really don't like that look on your face." Becky turned suddenly and walked away. "No, don't tell me, I don't want to know. I'll be going Friday." With a toss of her curls she left the room.

Chadwick just smiled, *poor Cynthia.*

Thad had devoured his dinner. He had not felt much like eating before but tonight he was hungry. Cynthia had taken her dinner in the room with Thad and cleared the dishes. She had given him a robe and gotten him up for a walk around the room as the doctor had ordered. Marco had prepared a bath for him and Thad soaked in the hot water feeling the pain ebb from his body. He felt like a new man when finished. Cynthia was waiting when he came out into the room. Thad felt more than a bit uncomfortable being naked under the robe.

"You're to get back into bed Thad. Too much activity could be bad for you. Aunt Maggie talked to the doctor and he said it doesn't appear you suffered any internal injuries, but you should take it easy for awhile. He said that it will be okay for you to go home Friday. The extra days rest is just a precaution."

Cynthia was rambling as she turned down the freshly made bed. Thad started to remove the robe before he realized that Cynthia was now standing there staring at him.

He stopped.

"I still don't have any clothes, Cindy."

Cynthia's face suddenly turned red and she quickly turned around.

"I'm sorry, I forgot we dumped all of your clothes. They were such a mess. Your father will be bringing clothes with him Friday."

Thad gingerly slid under the sheet. It was too hot to use the cover.

"Okay I'm covered."

Cynthia turned around, a solemn look on her face.

"Cindy, what's the matter?" Thad was alarmed. "Did I do or say something that hurt you."

"No," Cynthia cleared her throat and sat down on the edge of the bed.

"It just hit me that you'll be gone the day after tomorrow. I may never see you again and it made me sad. Thad, do you think that you might want to see..."

Thad smiled and cut her off, "Just try and keep me away, I want to see you if it's okay with you. We might need to talk to Maggie about it." Cynthia smiled back and arranged his extra blanket at the foot of his bed. *She smells so good, she's so gentle, Am I falling in love? I wish I could stay right here just like this forever. I want to get to know her better.*

"We've been with each other such a short time and yet I feel like I have known you my whole life Cindy. There must be a million things that I want to ask you and a million things more that I want to tell you. I think I could talk to you about anything and it would be alright."

Cindy sat down in the chair next to the bed.

"What would you like to talk about?"

"I want to know everything about you, I don't even know your last name or how old you are."

She scooted up to the edge of the chair.

"Those are easy, I just turned eighteen, I came here from Kansas to live with my Aunt Maggie and my last name is Miller."

"What about your parents?"

Cindy had not thought about them for awhile. Their mention brought feelings flooding back. She suddenly had a lump in her throat and tears welled up in her eyes.

"I...don't have...they died three years ago, that's why I...it's hard for me to talk about."

"I'm sorry; I got too personal; you don't have to ans…"

"No, it's alright Thad. It helps to talk about it, it helps me sort it out and deal with the fact that they're gone." Cindy took a deep breath. "They died of the fever and we lost the farm. Well lost it, actually it was sold. The money went into an education fund for me. That's how I'm able to attend the University."

"What are you studying?"

"I want to be a doctor, but it's really hard. Not that the classes are hard, it's the pressure. They don't like women in Medical School. They put all kinds of pressure on us women in the program to not go on to Medical School. It's not really fair, but that's how it works."

Thad tried to not look embarrassed when he asked, "How about boy friends, do you have one now? There must be all kinds of guys asking you out."

"Oh there are a few who have approached me, but I've been to busy with my studies and helping out Maggie. I did have one in Kansas who actually asked me to marry him. Obviously I said no. I'm afraid I hurt his feelings when I did. I promised that I would come back and even thought about it until...I don't think that I will be going back. How about you Thad? How many young ladies are following you around?"

Thad smiled then grimaced as it hurt his split lip.

"None that I know of, I did have a relationship when I was back in Vermont. I never asked her to marry me. Now that I think about it I don't know that I loved her. How do you ever really know? What does it feel like?"

"Aunt Maggie says it'll happen all of a sudden and there won't be any doubt."

"I think your Aunt Maggie is right. Did you ever feel that?"

"I think so."

"Was it love?"

"I don't know yet." Cindy smiled and got up from the chair. "I should go see if Aunt Maggie needs any help."

"Cindy, the boy in Kansas, Billy, did you two ever…you know?" *My God what a dumb question.*

"Would it make a difference Thad?"

"No, it wouldn't, how about you?"

"No, it wouldn't make a difference." Cindy swept out of the room, "I'll be back to tuck you in." She shut the door.

Thad was tucked in, Cynthia had of course seen to that. Maggie also looked in and found him asleep. *I wonder what will happen after Thad leaves us. Will that invisible line at Yesler Street be a chasm between them that neither will be able to cross? Will my darling Cynthia get her heart broken like I did? The thought of it is so painful! Oh well, can't worry about it now. It's not yet a problem.* Maggie had checked on Cynthia to be sure that she was all right. *She was almost ecstatically happy. Thad's made quite an impression on my…Cynthia. What about the young man at the railroad station with the tears?* Almost all of the customers had left. There were still a couple at the bar, it was almost three and Marco had taken over the bar duties so that the regular bartender could go home. The last of the girls had left an hour ago and Marco was almost done cleaning up.

"Okay gentlemen, drain 'em. It's time we all went home." Both of the men finished their drinks and stumbled out the door.

"Marco, why don't you go, I'll finish up here." She looked at the clock. It was just coming up on three. If he was going to show, it would be soon.

"Thanks boss," Marco headed out the back door.

She started to shut and lock it when she heard the footsteps in the alley. Peeking out, she saw the very large shadow of one Robert O'Shay. Opening the door a little wider she saw him striding down the alley with a fistful of flowers. *Where the hell did he manage to get flowers at three o'clock in the morning?* Maggie felt her eyes filling with tears and choked them back…swallowing hard.

"Bob, they're beautiful! Where on earth did you get them?"

O'Shay looked at the floor and shuffled his feet, "I had a vendor up at the market stash them for me, so I could pick them up later. I thought you might like em."

Maggie kissed him on the cheek, "been along time since anyone brought me flowers Bob, they're wonderful, thank you." She put some water in a beer pitcher for the flowers.

"Drink, beer or coffee Bob?"

"Oh I'm not much of a drinker Maggie. Coffee will be fine."

She poured two and they sat in the bar and just talked for almost an hour. It was comfortable for both. Maggie watched O'Shay's hands as he chattered away. *He really is a gentle soul, big, strong and gentle, like a big toy bear.*

"Bob where would you be if you weren't here with me?"

"Oh, I'd most likely be at my apartment in Columbia City. Now that the trolley runs out there I understand that Seattle is going to annex it along with Hillman City. It's really expanding toward Renton. I heard that they even may take in Renton. Lots of coal coming through there," Maggie refilled his coffee,.

"That's my third cup Maggie. I need to make a little trip." O'Shay got up and headed for the men's room. When he came back Maggie had cleaned the table and washed the cups. O'Shay walked up behind her, "It's getting kinda late Maggie I…"

She turned, reached up, put her arms around his neck and kissed him. O'Shay literally picked her up off of the floor and returned her invitation. Maggie put her face in his neck trying to catch her breath and slow her racing heart, "You can put me down now Bob," he set her gently back on the floor, but held on to her. He kissed her again, passionately sliding his hand up to the side of her breast.

"Bob!"

He stopped, *Jeez, I went too far.*

"You missed the last trolley to Columbia City," she removed his hand and kissed it. "Why don't you just spend the night here?" She turned out the lights. Still holding his hand, she led him toward the stairs, "Come on, let's go upstairs."

Cynthia had lain awake in the bed, unable to sleep. Every time she tried, her thoughts would turn to Thad and her heart would beat faster and the gnawing in her gut would start. *I want so to be with him. Could he be the one? How will I know for sure? I have got to get some sleep.*

Thad kept tossing and turning thinking of Cynthia. *Am I going crazy? We've only known each other of a few days. There is no way we could be in love, but I feel closer to her than anyone I have ever known. What if she doesn't feel the same? I would feel so stupid if I talked to her about it, especially if she didn't feel the same. I am driving myself crazy, I have to get to sleep. If this is love why is it so confusing?*

Thad was sitting up in bed with his robe on when Cindy came in Marco was right behind her with their breakfast.

"My, but you certainly look better this morning. If it wasn't for the lumps and bruises you would look normal. Marco, please put the food on the table over there."

Cindy gently touched Thad's face in several spots.

"Well it looks like the ice has brought down the swelling but the bruising will take more time I'm afraid…hungry?"

"Starved, the food smells so good."

After breakfast Marco picked up the dishes.

"I only have you to myself for one more day so what shall we talk about today?" Cindy settled into the chair by the bed.

"I know let's talk about the girl in Vermont. What was her name?"

"Eunice…Cindy I hope that I didn't embarrass you with any of my dumb questions yesterday."

"No you didn't Thad. You said that you felt like you could talk about anything with me and I feel the same. Did you ever…you know…with Eunice?"

"We thought we were in love, I know now that we weren't, but when I knew I was going to come here, the night before I left we…you know. That was my only experience, your turn."

"Ah, Billy Marshal, we grew up together…anyway we learned the difference between boys and girls in my dad's barn. We too, thought we were in love. When my parents died I lived at his house until Aunt Maggie could get there and bring me here. We fooled around but we never went all the way."

"Did he see you without clothes?"

Cynthia's cheeks pinked, "yes."

Thad smiled and looked up at the ceiling, "I envy you Billy Marshall!"

Cynthia laughed that wonderful laugh of hers, got up and started for the door, "I should check with Aunt Maggie to see if she needs help."

Thad laid his head back on the pillow, "It will happen all of a sudden and you'll just know it." *I think its happening, how will it know it, when will I know it. She's wonderful, she's smart, she could be my best friend, is that what it's all about? Am I falling in love with her? I guess time will tell.*

Bob O'Shay could not remember the last time he felt this good, this early in the morning. He had worked the night shift for most of his career and mornings were not his best time of day. After the great sex with Maggie last night, he felt like a new man. It had been a long time. Six years since Janet had left him. She just could not handle his job. She lasted two years before telling him that it was his job or her. He was still a cop and she was in San Francisco, married to an attorney. *Well good for him, now he can try and cope with the crazy lady, she certainly left me with a ton of bills outstanding. The last straw had to be the trumped up allegations she laid on me in an effort to get me fired. She really was a piece of work.* O'Shay put his arm around Maggie, who was snuggled up against him. *How lucky can a guy get? Spending the night with an attractive woman I have admired since the first time I met her. Not only is she pretty with a great figure, but she's loving, gentle, attracted to me and is the best lay that I've ever had. Hopefully this could go somewhere.* O'Shay drifted off to sleep again feeling good about himself, Maggie and this whole situation.

Maggie slipped out of bed without waking O'Shay. As she got herself ready for the day, she looked in on him a couple of times just to reassure herself, it had been wonderful. *I should have made this move along time ago, but he was too shy and I had some serious doubts.* She finished dressing and sat down on the side of the bed leaned over and kissed him on the forehead. His eyes popped open and a grin spread across his face.

"Good morning love," Bob stretched and yawned.

"It's more like good afternoon sweet," Maggie kissed his cheek.

"It's almost one o'clock. We overslept a bit. I rounded up some stuff you may need in the bathroom and there should be plenty of hot water. Get yourself dressed and I'll have the cook fix you something to eat."

Maggie patted him on his butt and headed for the door. As she started out she stopped, "Robert you were very good this morning…I mean very good." Maggie gave him a lurid grin and left.

For the rest of the day Thad and Cindy talked about everything imaginable. They shared their deepest secrets and what they expected in the future. They took two walks down the hall to try and build up Thad's stamina. By the time they had finished there was nothing that they didn't know about each other and a bond was beginning to form.

"Cindy, I have never been able to talk to anyone like I have with you for the last two days. I'll be going home tomorrow and I will miss our talks terribly."

"Me too, I hate to see you go. Will I see you again?"

"I will be here as often as I can. I want to be near you all the time and we'll see where it takes us. I'm sure that you'll be welcome at our house when ever you want to come by. Would you want to?"

"Thad I'm scared to death about meeting your mom tomorrow. What if she doesn't like me, that would be horrible."

"Cindy, she's going to love you I know she will."

Cindy fluffed his pillow and tucked him in and kissed him on the cheek, "See you in the Morning Thad." Cindy quietly left the room without looking back. *If I look back at him I won't leave.*

The Mitchell's arrived the next afternoon precisely at one o'clock. Chadwick had parked the car in the alley, as it would be the shortest distance for Thad to walk. Maggie, feeling very uncomfortable, met them at the door. She had no idea what Chadwick had told his wife and how he had explained their relationship. She decided that being formal would be the best tack to take.

"Mr. Mitchell it is good to see you again and this must be Mrs. Mitchell. I'm Margaret Wilson, my friends call me Maggie. I must tell you what a nice young man your son is."

Chadwick held out a small suitcase, "Here are some clothes for Thad, and please don't be so formal. After all you saved our son's life. Please call me Chadwick and my wife is Becky." Maggie took the suitcase, noticing that Becky was looking her and the place over.

"Chadwick, Becky, please have a seat and I'll get these up to Thad."

O'Shay walked into the parlor, "I'll get that Maggie."

Maggie handed him the suitcase, "Thank you, Chadwick, Becky may I introduce you to Officer Robert O'Shay he is actually the one who saved your son's life. Chadwick and O'Shay shook hands and he accepted Chadwick and Becky's thanks for what he had done. Becky was impressed by the size of the man. *He must be impressive in uniform.*

Becky was still trying to assess the surroundings. It did not look like she had expected. It was not rundown and seedy. It did not reek of alcohol and cheap perfume; there were no half dressed painted women running around. It looked like a respectable hotel lobby with a dining area off to the left. She assumed that the bar and prostitutes were in the back or upstairs.

"Becky would you like some tea or lunch perhaps?" Maggie knew that there would be a wait while Thad dressed.

"Yes, thank you," Becky surprised herself.

"Good! Lets step into the parlor and I'll have someone bring us some…and you Chadwick?"

"Coffee will be fine, thank you."

Maggie shot a look toward the dining area where Marco had been waiting, he nodded and hurried away. Please have a seat, Maggie made sure that they were comfortable, "Maggie, I know that you must have incurred some expenses caring for our son." Chadwick was trying to be as tactful as possible, "I would like to reimburse you for those expenses."

"Please Chadwick that is not at all necessary. I'm just glad to have been able to help under these dreadful circumstances. Indeed it was my pleasure. I just don't understand what your fine young man was doing with those dreadful Harrington boys."

Becky looked at her sharply and started to say something when Marco appeared carrying a heavy silver service and set it on the table.

"Marco will you pour please, tea for Mrs. Mitchell and I, coffee for Mr. Mitchell and one for Officer O'Shay. Marco looked, for just a second, surprised.

"Yes Ma'am."

Maggie handed the sugar to Becky.

"I'm sorry Becky, you started to say something."

"Yes, did I hear you correctly that Thad was in here with Pauley and Patrick Harrington?"

"Why yes, he was. The poor boy looked like a fish out of water, I felt sorry for him."

"What were they doing exactly?"

Becky was concerned about her son's activities and the influence on him by the Harrington boys.

Maggie turned, "Oh, here he comes."

Thad was coming down the stairs slowly. His legs were a little weak and he was unsteady on his feet. Cynthia had helped him dress and was holding his arm to steady him. Becky could not help but notice how beautiful Cynthia was and noted the concern on her face as she guided Thad on the stairs. She especially noticed the way that Thad looked at her and how they radiated when they made eye contact. At the bottom of the stairs Thad gave a sigh of relief and his face lit up in a grin, "I wasn't too sure about the stairs; I'm still a little weak."

Becky felt sick at the sight of her son. The bruises were still vivid as they had not yet healed. There was still swelling in his face and abrasions were obvious from the kicks to the head. Tears welled up in her eyes as she thought of what his body looked like.

"Oh Thad," Becky jumped up and hurried up to him. Cynthia saw her coming and wisely stepped aside. "Oh my darling you look dreadful. Thank God you're alive!" Becky kissed his cheek ever so gently and was almost afraid to touch him. Thad smiled and kissed her on the cheek.

"I'd hug you mother, but I hurt all over. Mother I'd like you to meet my nurse, and Maggie's niece, Cynthia." Thad turned and took Cynthia's hand.

"I don't know what I would have done without her."

"Mrs. Mitchell," Cynthia extended her hand and Becky took it, "I'm so very glad to meet you. Thad has told me so much about you. I don't know your secret but you have raised a wonderful son."

Becky was taken aback, "Why thank you, Cynthia."

"Please Mrs. Mitchell, call me Cindy and hello again Mr. Mitchell. Here he is, just like I promised, all in one piece."

Becky was impressed with the girl and it seemed obvious that Thad was too. Becky and Cynthia helped Thad to the table and sat him down. Cynthia had sat at the table between Thad and his mother. Becky couldn't help but look at her battered son, "Thad, I must admit you look much better than I expected."

"Well mother, Three days ago I probably looked worse than what you expected. I can't begin to tell you what excellent care I received." Thad patted Cynthia's hand laying on his arm and smiled at her. Becky could not make up her mind about the girl, *who is she, is she a prostitute who sees dollar signs when she looks at Thad. He would be quite a catch for a girl in her position if she were.*

Cynthia had been sipping a cup of tea and abruptly set it down.

"If you would excuse me," she started to rise, Chadwick and O'Shay both stood Thad was unable to, and Maggie looked up, "Are you all right Cynthia?"

Becky made note that standing would not be Chad's response to a prostitute, "I'm fine Aunt Maggie, I'll be back in a moment."

Becky seized the moment, "Cynthia, could you show me to the restroom?"

"Certainly Mrs...er Becky...please call me Cindy."

Chadwick watched his wife move away from the table with Cynthia, *ah the tests begin, good luck Cindy.*

"Tell me a little about yourself dear." Cynthia began chattering away, where she lived, her parents dying, coming to live with her aunt and enrolling at the University in pre-med.

"My first year was been a real test. There is only one other female enrolled in the program. It seems the men are resentful and the professors put more stress on us women. I am determined to succeed though."

Becky was impressed, "Tell me Cindy, what is it like living in a..."

Cynthia smiled, "house of prostitution? During the day it's very much like what you see now, but let me tell you what happens at night!" Cynthia's eye grew larger and Becky was hanging on every word.

Maggie, Chadwick, Bob and Thad sat rather quietly drinking their coffee and tea. There was no doubt in anyone's mind what was taking place in the bathroom of the Silver Slipper. O'Shay finally broke the silence.

"Have you spoken with your father yet Thad?"

Thad choked on his coffee; *oh shit he's going to mention my wanting to be a police officer. I've got to break that to dad more gently than blurting it out in a box house.* He looked up at Officer O'Shay who had just a twinge of a grin at the corner of his mouth. Thad's mind raced but words weren't coming. O'Shay was reading Thad's mind, "You know about prosecuting your attacker."

Thad hoped that his relief was not visible.

"Oh, no I haven't, but now may be a good time."

All three of the men hashed over the consequences of prosecution or non-prosecution. Maggie sat quietly, stewing about what was taking place in the restroom. *They've been in there along time. Is my baby alright? What is that woman saying or doing to her? Oh lord, please don't let her be hurt.* The men were well on the way to resolving the problem when Maggie got up. The men tried to get up but Maggie waved them off.

"That's okay, don't spoil me."

O'Shay knew exactly what was going on in Maggie's mind, "Maggie."

She looked at him and O'Shay shook his head. Maggie frowned and looked toward the restroom. Suddenly the hallway was filled with laughter, not giggles or snickers but out and out belly laughs as Becky and Cynthia came out of the restroom. By the time they reached the parlor Cynthia was saying, "...And he ran right into the wall."

At which point both women broke into gales of laughter, tears streaming down their faces. Everyone at the table was bewildered. Chadwick looked at his son and gave him a wink, and Thad just smiled.

They were ready to load Thad into the car not 15 feet from where he had been beaten almost to death. Thad had bad feelings about even being in the alley, but controlled his emotions. Cynthia was holding his arm and Becky held the door open. Thad got one foot in and then changed his mind. He stopped and turned toward Cynthia.

"Cindy, I want you to know that I like you very much but..."

Maggie's stomach turned over, *oh God don't let this happen, not again.* Thad cleared his throat.

"I won't be able to come and see you right away. At least not until I heal up and can get around on my own. I'll call you every day, and I'm sure my parents won't mind if you come by if you have the time and really want to."

Thad turned and looked at Maggie, who now had tears in her eyes.

"Maggie, if you don't mind I would like to see Cindy and I want you to know that my intentions are honorable." *Oh Lord, I probably sound like and idiot.*

Maggie took a deep breath.

"Of course I don't mind, Thad."

Becky put her hand on Cynthia's arm,

"You're welcome at our home anytime."

Cynthia, tears brimming in her eyes, wrapped her arms around Thad's neck and kissed him gently on the cheek. Chadwick cleared his throat and went to the front of the Ford, cranking it to life. In 30 minutes they were home and Thad was safely tucked away in the library. It would be several weeks before he was able to negotiate the stairs well enough to move back to his room. Cindy was a regular visitor at the Mitchell home and took delight in helping Becky with dinner. It was also a great place to study for her classes, although Thad was a big distraction. By four weeks Thad was almost completely healed up and would pick Cindy up from school and drive her home at night. They would sit by the fire place for hours just talking and growing closer all the time.

"Father, we need to talk." Holding Cindy's hand they had walked into the sitting room where Chadwick was reading the evening paper. "I think I know where I'm going now. I've done some investigation and talked it over with Bob O'Shay and Cindy. I'm going to try to be a police officer."

Chadwick looked over his paper and studied his son for a minute.

"How do you feel about that Cindy?"

Thad plopped down on the sofa, Cynthia perched herself on the arm next to him.

"I was concerned about him getting hurt, but O'Shay says that it's really not that dangerous. I want what ever is right for Thad." Thad looked up and smiled at her.

"Thad, how do you know you'll like it? Do you really know what police officers do?"

"I turn 19 in a two weeks, father and Bob says that I can go out with him and see what the job is all about. I'll have a better feel for it then. Right now though it sounds like a really great job."

Chadwick put down his paper, "Have you told your mother yet?"

Thad dropped his gaze and then looked at his father.

"Yes, but she doesn't totally understand and is worried about the risks involved. I think at some point she's going to talk to Bob about it."

Cynthia rubbed his arm.

"I know that I want to talk to Bob some more. I have heard him say before that it is not really that dangerous, but I still want to talk to him. I'll go along with anything that Thad feels is right for him."

Chadwick smiled, "As will I Cindy. Whatever Thad does, he has to be happy doing it or it's not worth doing."

Becky walked into the room, "Dinner is on and will get cold if you don't get a move on." After dinner, Thad and Cindy cleared the table and helped with the dishes.

Thad picked up the keys to the new Ford that his father bought. "Father, I'm going to run Cindy home and will be back soon."

Chadwick was working on a ledger in the den.

"Take your time son. It was nice to see you again Cindy. When you see

O'Shay, would you tell him that we would all like to talk to him? I'm sure he'll be just delighted about it." Chadwick had a sly grin on his face.

Hand in hand Thad and Cindy headed for the new self cranking 1910 Ford four-door.

***

They had parked the Ford at the end of the road overlooking the Elliot Bay. The sun was just setting and the sky looked like it was on fire. Thad and Cynthia were oblivious of the sky or the Bay. They were locked in an embrace. Cynthia's shirt was open and Thad was ran his hands over her bare back and slid around to her breasts. Cynthia unbuttoned Thad's shirt and pulled it open to press her breasts against his bare skin. She tilted her head back as Thad's tongue flicked over her neck. She straddled his legs pushing herself against him.

Thad kissed her breasts, "take off your panties Cindy."

"No intercourse Thad, we promised remember? We have to both agree because I can't say no to you; I can't stop it from happening by myself."

"I can't promise Cindy, so you better leave 'em on."

Cindy stayed on his lap, pushing against him, while Thad pulled her dress up around her waist and ran his hands over her bare torso and legs.

Thad was so engrossed in what they were doing; he almost missed the sound of the automobile coming up the road. Cindy, her face buried in Thad's neck, never heard it, but Thad heard the vehicle come to a stop behind them. Thad turned and looked out the back and immediately recognized the Oldsmobile belonging to the Harringtons. Pauley was getting out from behind the driver's seat and Patrick was already out of the car walking toward the Ford. Anger consumed Thad when he saw them. Thad moved Cindy onto the seat and jumped out of the car. Cindy was scrambling trying to get her dress down and her top covered. She almost made it before she saw Patrick looking at her through the passenger window, a big grin on his face. Pauley was smiling at Thad's disheveled appearance.

"Well, Thad my friend, we playing a little hid the dip-stick in the front seat of the car are we? She got room for a couple more? You might as well share the wealth."

Patrick looked over the top of the car.

"Hey Pauley, you should see the tits on this one!" Cynthia got her shirt closed and locked the door just as Patrick tried to open it. *Oh no, we are in trouble, what are they going to do to us?* Patrick started around the car for the other door but Cindy reached over and locked it. Pauley grinned at Thad, "Come on Thad get the lady into the back seat. Either you share her or we take her. Share her and at least you get a little taste too."

"Hey Pauley this one's a real winner, she's going to be good for the rest of the night." Pauley started past Thad to have a look in the car and never saw it coming. Thad was burning with rage and had stopped thinking and just started reacting.

"You bastards," the blow caught Pauley on the back edge of his jaw. The force of the blow broke the jawbone causing Pauley to scream in pain. Thad had learned some things from the beating in the alley. The second blow caught Pauley in the left kidney causing his knees to buckle. Patrick was dumb struck to see his brother slumping to the ground, but recovered quickly lunging toward Thad.

"You fucker, you're a dead man!" Patrick ran square into a straight right hand thrown by Thad. The blow crushed his newly healed nose from the fight in the alley. The follow-up left hand knocked him out. Thad turned and faced Pauley trying to get up from the ground. He took one step and kicked him under the chin breaking his jaw in a second place. There was no more fight left in the Harrington boys. Thad grabbed Pauley by the front of his jacket and snatched him to his feet.

"You hear me Pauley?" Pauley nodded his head, his face screwed up in pain.

"You mess with me or mine, ever, and I will break every bone in your body. You understand me?"

Pauley nodded his head and tried to mumble something but it was unintelligible. Thad threw him sideways into the bushes. He walked over to the Olds, removed the key and threw it into the bushes. Thad looked at the Ford and saw Cynthia's frightened eyes looking back. She unlocked the door as Thad walked up. He got in and hit the starter. The Ford popped to life and Thad let off the brake.

"Oh Thad are you alright? I was scared to death. I didn't know what they were going to do but I knew it wasn't going to be good."

Thad's body was shaking. He put his arm around her and pulled her close.

"It's alright now love, they were going to rape you. I'm so sorry that I put you through this. I will never let anything happen to you. I will always be here to keep you safe."

Thad wiped Cynthia's tears, kissed her gently, put the car in gear and turned around heading back down the road.

"We will never give anyone the opportunity to do that again Cindy."

Cindy cuddled up against him. Thad kissed her forehead, "right now we need to find O'Shay. I need to tell him about this and see what I should do. I hurt both the boys back there and Daddy is not going to be happy about it."

Cynthia straightened up, "I know where he is. He's not working tonight and will be at the slipper with Aunt Maggie."

Thad parked in the alley and they went through the back door. Emil, the bouncer, greeted them as they came in, "Evenin' Missy Cynthia. Hi Thad, how you feelin'?"

Thad smiled at Emil, "Good! Thank you, have you seen O'Shay?"

"Sho-nuff, he be up in the parlor with the boss lady havin' dinner."

Thad and Cynthia went up the stairs. As they entered the parlor O'Shay greeted them.

"Hi kids how's it going? You two look tired."

It was Maggie who sounded the alarm.

"Thad, what happened to your hands?" Thad looked at his hands and for the first time realized that there was blood on his knuckles from abrasions caused by the punches.

"Oh no!" Cynthia almost yelled it before she hurried to get something to clean him up.

"We need to talk Bob. We ran into the Harringtons under bad circumstances. I know they were going to rape Cindy, the way they were talking and all. I left them laying in the bushes."

O'Shay looked at him hard. "Are they alive Thad?"

Thad smiled, "Yes, I think I broke Patrick's nose again. He was trying to get into the car after Cindy. I also knocked him out. Pauley may have a broken jaw and will pee blood for a few days, I know what that feels like. I threw their car key in the bushes and if they don't have another, they are probably still there."

"Where's there, Thad?"

"The dead end road on the south side of Portage Bay."

"I know where that is. I'm not going to ask you what you were doing there, but it's not a good place to be. There's been a number of assaults up there. Never any suspects, I wonder if it's the Harringtons." O'Shay got up, "I have to make a call."

He hurried out of the room. Cynthia and Maggie came back with a basin of water and towels.

Maggie looked at Thad with gratitude and anger.

"Thank you for saving Cindy, but don't you ever take her any place like that again."

Thad dropped his gaze to the floor.

"I'm sorry Maggie. We just didn't think anything like this could happen. It won't happen again, I promise."

They were cleaning Thad's hands when O'Shay came back.

"I'm having them picked up. They may well be our rapists. If they're still there, they'll be brought back to the jail and be booked as suspects. Now tell me exactly what happened."

Thirty minutes later the questioning was completed.

"Can either of you think of anything else?"

Thad and Cynthia looked at each other.

Thad answered, "No that's everything that happened. I wasn't going to let them attack Cindy, they would have had to kill me first."

Maggie chimed in, "It wouldn't have happened at all if you hadn't been there."

Thad nodded his head in agreement as Cynthia took his arm and leaned up against him.

"I think we have enough for an attempt rape charge." O'Shay was going over his notes.

Maggie put her hand on O'Shay's arm.

"Is that going to do any good? The old man will just buy their way out of it won't he?"

"Most likely that's exactly what he would do, but that's not the point." O'Shay leaned back in his chair.

"It sounds like you did a number on them Thad. John Harrington is not going to like that. I can see him trying to file assault charges against you. We'll beat him to the punch and charge the boys, that way he'll have to settle. I'll call on him tomorrow and explain his options. I'm sure he'll be reasonable."

Emil poked his head into the doorway.

"Offica' O'Shay, phone for you."

O'Shay left and Cynthia finished cleaning Thad's hands.

"I need to finish med. school just to take care of you Thad." Cynthia smiled at him and then kissed him.

"Thank you Thad, you were so brave."

O'Shay came back from the phone.

"They were still there. Patrick was trying to hotwire the car and Pauley was kicking it, looked like he kicked in all the doors. They claimed they were assaulted and robbed by you and an unknown female. They are now safely behind bars in the county jail. That was good thinking coming to me Thad. If you hadn't the police would be at your house looking to arrest you. Nice going."

Thad took a deep breath.

"I had better go home and tell my parents before they get a call from John Harrington and are fed lies."

Cynthia walked him down to the car. She wrapped her arms around and he kissed her.

"I'll call you in the morning, love. Don't worry it'll be all right. I will never put you in that position again."

"I didn't mind what we were doing Thad, I was enjoying myself. We just need to find a better place next time." Thad smiled and kissed her again. She slipped into the back door and Thad headed for home.

***

Thad and his father sat in the parlor quietly discussing the ramifications of what had taken place. Depending on what John Harrington did there could be consequences, business wise, for his father. Chadwick had initially been upset with Cindy and Thad for being where they would be vulnerable to such an attack. Then he remembered the barn in Vermont so many years ago and relented that it was a matter of life.

"What did Bob O'Shay say to you Thad."

"Not a whole lot father. He took a report and said that the Patrick and Pauley were in jail. He also said that their father would most likely get them out and they would lie that it was me who assaulted and robbed them. Before I left Bob said that he would contact John Harrington and use the report as a bargaining chip. He doubted that the boys would ever be charged and that John Harrington would not file charges against me. I just worry that this may disrupt your business arrangement with Harrington and the bank."

Chadwick looked surprised.

"You have been listening. I wondered if you even knew what I did, let alone who was involved. I'm surprised and pleased."

Thad leaned forward and looked intently at his father.

"Well father, what do you think?" Chadwick took a deep breath.

"Thad, business does not always take place with people who like or even totally trust each other. Business is business and has nothing to do with how well you like the other person. Hodge, the bank president, is my buffer between John Harrington and me. Harrington is a wheeler-dealer who is always looking for a fast buck. Hodge keeps him on the straight pathway. I really don't think that this is going to interrupt our business dealings. You, however, need to watch your back regarding the Harrington boys. They are not going to take this lightly, even if they are not formerly charged with a crime. They're going to be looking for revenge. Be careful son." Chadwick reached out and patted his son's hand. "If the boys recognized Cynthia she may also be in harms way."

Thad did not sleep well that night. Anger still lingered over the actions of Patrick and Pauley. *They would have raped Cindy if I hadn't attacked them. I know now what I have to do. Others need to be protected from the likes of these two. Policing is the answer. I will be a police officer and I will try my best to get people like the Harrington's off the street to protect others.*

Chapter 7

By 1910 Seattle was starting to change physically as well as financially. Built on seven hills it became quite clear to the city fathers that for Seattle to become a commercial success it would have to be easier to get around. It was also clear that although the mud flats to the south of downtown had been filled the waterfront still lacked easy access. The bluff running along the water's edge restricted commerce. The project to level things out had begun in an effort to remove the hill called Denny, in an effort to re-grade the street levels and to fill the waterfront areas. This would facilitate greater access and smooth traffic flows for commerce. Opportunities would abound for Chadwick to assert his presents in the financial community. Things were happening so fast that it was difficult to obtain enough money to complete many of the projects being considered. One misstep in investing and his whole world could come crashing down.

"It's not good right now, John. We're just spread to thin." Chadwick, Herrington and Hodge had been bickering for almost an hour.

Herrington sighed, "Chadwick we have to move now. Jim agrees with me. If we don't capitalize on the opportunities as they arise we'll miss out. You don't really think that George Frye, Denny, Joshua Green or any of the others are worried about being spread to thin do you?"

Chadwick sank into the soft leather chair, "Look John, if you and Hodge want to finance the city construction job, you go ahead. I just can't put up anymore money until the re-grade job is done. I just can't afford to extend myself any further. Our little streetcar company is just starting to make money. That will get better as soon as the North Seattle re-grading gets completed. Add to that the fact of my having to move my family as they continue to cut the hill down."

Hodge perked up, "I made an offer for you on that property on Queen Anne Chadwick. I think they're going to accept it. You could build two houses on it if you wanted."

"That's another thing John. I'm going to build one of the finest houses on the hill and that's going to take capital. I just can't get involved in this one. The one I want is the county street and sewer project next year. That will be the capper project for us, be patient."

Chadwick got up and headed for the door.

"Chadwick," Harrington had gotten up from behind the dark mahogany desk that dominated his office.

"On a personal note, are your son and his lady friend going to press charges against my boys?"

Chadwick suppressed his rising anger.

"I think the police officers who talked with you worked out a just agreement John. Your boys stay away from them and no charges will be pressed. I think you have enough to worry about with the three charges against them already.

Harrington puffed on his cigar, "I have obtained the services of one of the finest defense attorneys in the state. I think we will be okay there, don't you?"

The smirk on Harrington's face irked Chadwick, "I have no idea what happened in the other incidents, but I do know what happened in Thad's case. If your boys did what the others say, they deserve what they get. I don't want our personal lives to mix with business John. In the future let's stick to financial matters."

Chadwick spun around and left the office. John Harrington took another drag on his cigar, *pompous self-righteous son-of-bitch*, "Hodge if that kid of his causes me anymore grief, I'll bust his balls."

Jim Hodge just nodded; *my God does Chadwick know who he is messing with? I should tell him, but I owe Harrington a great deal and he could hurt me too.*

***

The old police station sat at the corner of Third and James next to the new county courthouse and sheriff's office. The relations between the two agencies had been strained for some time since the miners strike in the Renton coalfields south of Seattle. With the county government supporting the mining companies, county officers were sent to keep the peace by allowing newly hired workers, or scabs as the unionists called them, to enter the mines. The more liberal thinking city government yielded to pressure from the unionists and socialists. Officers were sent to the mines to protect the interests of the strikers. It was inevitable that the two law enforcement agencies would tangle. As Bob O'Shay put it, "It all went to hell in a hand-basket."

On the third day of the strike, as a group of scabs attempted to break the line of unionists and strikers, shots were fired. No one knows for sure who fired the first one, but after the firing stopped, three scabs were dead and two county deputies were wounded. On the other side, four strikers lay dead and one police officer was wounded. Both sides would blame the other and the animosity between the two agencies would last for years.

The police station was a two story wood building that looked more like an eye sore rather than a police station. The entry was on the second floor and stairs went up to the entrance from both ends of the building. The architecture looked like something out of an old book of castles. That was probably why the citizens fondly called it the 'Katzinjammer Castle'. Inside were the administration offices of the police department which were jammed into small dingy rooms. The largest of the rooms was for the assembling of the officers who were getting ready to go out on the street. Thad stood against the wall of the assembly room. O'Shay had gone to the locker room to put on his uniform. The officers were drifting in, stopping at a large bulletin board at the end of the room. There seemed to be information that they were reading and some gathered sheets of printed material folding it neatly and putting it into their tunic pockets. Their pants were dark blue with a white stripe running down the sides. They wore white shirts and most had a cross draw holster and gun on their pants belt while handcuffs hung on that belt or went into the back pants pocket. They all carried a baton, or as most of the officers referred to them, night sticks. As Thad watched they started putting on their calf length tunic with shiny copper buttons and a Silver Star badge. They carried their domed helmets with a silver insignia on the front. It reminded Thad of pictures he had seen in school of British police officers. Thad felt awkward and out of place. Almost every officer looked him over as if studying him.

"Mitchell isn't it?"

Thad looked quickly in the direction of the voice, Officer Blackwell had been standing across the room trying to figure who the young man was leaning on the wall of the assembly room. He knew him from somewhere but could not quite make the connection until he moved closer and the incident on First Avenue popped out.

"Yes," Thad was startled that the officer had remembered his name.

Blackwell extended his hand and Thad took it in a firm handshake, "What are you doing here Mitchell?"

Thad felt more comfortable now that he at least knew someone else.

"I'm here with Officer O'Shay. He's going to take me out on patrol with him."

Blackwell looked a little surprised, "Really, well if you're with an officer, O'Shay is the one that I would pick to go with. He broke me in when I first came on. You thinking about it?"

Thad was feeling more relaxed as the other officers saw him talking to Blackwell, "Yes, and Officer O'Shay said he would show me around."

Blackwell looked Thad over assessing him.

"You're fortunate Mitchell. O'Shay doesn't do that. He must like you or think you have potential. I'm just getting off shift so I better go change. Good luck!"

Thad watched Blackwell stride away toward the locker room; he was stopped at least three times along the way by other officers who took a good look at Thad after talking with him.

O'Shay came striding through the door, larger than most of the others, he was an imposing figure in his uniform. Several officers stopped him and they talked briefly. Finally he walked over to Thad, "Well you feel a little intimidated Thad?"

Thad looked at O'Shay with a shy grin, "Yes, it's strange to be the only one in the room who is different. I feel like I have two heads or something."

"Get used to it. If you become a police officer, you'll be the only one out there who looks different in a crowd. The difference is that you're the one with the authority and the others know it."

Thad noticed that the other officers were starting to form two loose lines the length of the room facing one of the long walls that had a podium near it.

"They're getting ready for roll call Thad. I better get in line." O'Shay got into the back rank of men with the other taller officers.

Thad noticed that on average he was as tall as most of the other men and at least as substantially built. He was becoming more comfortable in his choice. Two men had taken up a position at the podium in front of the officers. One had the stripes of a sergeant and the other had a silver bar on his collar. Thad assumed he must be a lieutenant. He was not that familiar with military rank. The officers were standing in line talking and moving around a little when the sergeant gave a command. The process mesmerized Thad. To him it was almost mystical although to the officers he was sure it was much less.

"Atteeenhut," the word was slurred together with an emphasis on the last part. The officers seemed to stiffen, hands at their sides, heels together standing straight and tall, looking straight ahead. No one spoke. Thad was impressed. The sergeant almost muttered the next command, "at ease men." The officers relaxed, but did not move around or talk.

The lieutenant stepped up to the podium.

"Got some complaints from the downtown merchants north of the line, they have some transients and drunks sleeping in the doorways and on the steam vents. It seems that these undesirables are taking care of their bodily functions in other than the proper places."

A voice came out of the ranks, "Somebody take a crap on the mayors door step lieutenant?" A chuckle went through the ranks, which the lieutenant ignored. "Officers south of the line, be looking for those same folks. The weather is getting colder and the transients could die of exposure. The missions are open and have some room. If they fill up try to keep em movin."

Another voice from the ranks chimed in, "Isn't that like messing with natural selection sir?" Again the chuckle went through the ranks. The sergeant frowned and the chuckling stopped.

"Sergeant, call em out," the lieutenant stepped away from the podium.

The sergeant started calling out names and when answered gave a cryptic message.

"Johnson."

"Here."

"Box 24."

"Wilson."

"Here," "box 12 and your own."

"Bake."

"Here."

"You're in the hole."

"O'Shay."

"Here."

"Box 8 and you have an observer right?" the sergeant looked directly at Thad.

I feel like I'm in a glass jar being studied, "Right Sarge."

The sergeant continued until everyone had been called and assigned, then he simply dismissed them. Officers milled about and then started heading for the doors. Thad was watching the men disperse when he realized the sergeant was walking directly toward him.

The sergeant stuck out his hand.

"MacAfee, Bob tells me that you are thinking of becoming a policeman."

Thad shook his hand, "Yes…sir," Thad was unsure how to address him.

"Sergeant will do son. Well look around. It's a very select group of men. If you're lucky enough to make it, you'll be joining a very close knit family. O'Shay says you have potential. That's a big step towards making the grade. O'Shay is one of the best we have."

The sergeant abruptly turned and headed for his office.

"You ready to go Thad? I'm sure that you have a million questions and we'll get to them later, right now let's go get a cup."

Thad followed O'Shay out the door, *a cup, what in the world does that mean and what's the hole?*

Thad soon learned that a cup meant a cup of coffee. They walked down to a place that they both knew well. It was cold outside and Thad was glad to go inside the Silver Slipper for a cup of coffee. Plus he would get to see Cindy. They entered through the alley door, Thad felt that creepy feeling that he got whenever he went down this alley. The beating that he had experienced here came back in flashes. *I was lucky to not be killed or crippled out here.*

Marco got them each a cup of coffee and Maggie and Cynthia came down and joined them.

"You promised to take good care of him tonight Bob." Cynthia was still a little concerned about Thad's well being.

Thad felt a little embarrassed, "I'll be fine Cindy. Please don't worry."

"O'Shay put his hand on Thad's shoulder,

"I promise Cindy. I'll bring him back with most of his pieces still intact." Maggie frowned, but O'Shay just grinned.

"What's the hole Bob?"

"I guess that does sound a bit strange. Let's see if I can give you a short answer to a complicated question. Most of the officers walk a foot beat. That's the boxes that the sergeant calls out at roll call. Remember when Blackwell went to the box on the pole and called the station for his arrest?"

Thad was captivated as were Maggie and Cindy.

"Yes I do."

"Well that's a box and each one has a number. That box number tells you where you're working. Ours is box 8. That's the one Blackwell used on the corner of 1st and Washington. We also have another box at 2nd and Jackson. Now when you call on that box, let's say you have an arrest, well the officers in the hole are the ones that will come get the suspect in the wagon. The hole crew also take reports at the station from people who walk in. They run errands and if there are situations that call for a patrol car to go out then the hole crew are the ones drive it to a call for services. They don't have to do that much downtown because there are so many beat officers here. In the outer precincts, there are fewer beats and the hole crew is larger and responds more."

It was Cynthia who asked the question, "Who gets assigned to the hole Bob?"

"Usually it will be a mix. There will be some new officers, officers working relief and some old timers who volunteer for it. The old timers usually rule the hole, which means when there are errands to run the newest officers do it. The same applies when there are calls that a beat officer can't get to and officers in an automobile are needed to respond."

A thought hit Thad, "What do they do when there is nothing going on."

"Well there's paperwork to file, phones to answer, reports to be taken and when all else fails they play cards. Let's take a walk Thad. There are things to check and people to see."

Thad jumped eager to go. He kissed Cindy on the cheek and headed for the door. O'Shay gave Maggie a peck on the forehead, "Slow down Thad this isn't a foot race, we take it slow and easy. There's more to see and hear when you take your time. We'll go out the front door, that way the folks in the lounge will see that we are around and that has a tendency to stop problems before they happen."

Outside it had gotten colder, but had not started to rain. That was always a blessing for a beat officer in Seattle. They started the patrol by going to the call box and ringing in. As they approached the corner the light on the top of the box suddenly began to blink.

"Looks like the station wants to talk Thad. That could mean that they may have a message or a call for us."

O'Shay produced a large brass key and opened the box. Thad got his first look inside. There was what appeared to be a phone that O'Shay picked up waited a few seconds and then started talking to someone. There was other stuff there too. It looked like an arc with numbers from 0 to 9 with a pointer and a small handle. *I'm sure that Bob will explain that to me at some point.* The light on top of the box had stopped blinking when O'Shay made contact with the station.

"Got it," O'Shay hung up the phone and wrote some information on a note pad that he kept in his shirt pocket.

"Well Thad, here we go. It looks like we have a couple of characters causing a problem at one of the houses over on Jackson. Jake from the Chinatown beat is going to meet us there. Look if we get into a situation there I don't want you getting involved. You're not being paid to hang it out and I don't want you getting hurt, do you understand?" Thad was disappointed but he understood what O'Shay was saying. They walked at a fast steady pace the three blocks to the Golden Eagle. The Chinatown beat officer was waiting just inside of the alley next to the building.

"Hey Bob, talked to a guy coming out. He says that there are at least two seamen in there that have a mean streak a mile wide. They're ready to fight anything and have challenged half the bar. They already took out the bouncer with a sucker punch. He's in the back with a broken jaw. I already unlocked the box on the corner, just pull it open if you need to. How do you want to handle it?"

O'Shay let the information sink in, "You go in the back door, I'll give you to the count of 15 after I see you go in; then I'll go in the front and draw their attention. Get an angle on them and move in slowly. I'll try to get them to leave peacefully. If they won't we always have the assault to arrest em' for and we'll just take em' out."

O'Shay pulled his nightstick from its ring and nodded to Jake who hurried down the alley and into the back door. "Thad, I want you to stay outside on this one."

O'Shay headed for the door and moved in quickly. Thad's heart was beating so hard that he thought it would pop out of his chest. He could feel it throbing in his temples. He had to take just a peak inside of the door.

Thad cautiously slipped in the box house and moved to the left just inside of the door, his back to the wall. O'Shay had his back to the door and was in front of two men dressed as though they may be seamen from one of the ships in the harbor. Both were loud and one was arguing with O'Shay. The other was encouraging with loud comments and bravado. O'Shay was standing his ground and Thad saw Jake slipping through the tables approaching from the back. Thad was so excited that he thought he was going to throw up when suddenly the man closest to O'Shay lunged at him. The second man was more observant than Thad had thought as he spun and lunged at Jake who had moved in closer. They were grappling with the two men and the outcome seemed obvious, both officers were using their nightsticks effectively. What they had not seen was the third man getting up from the table behind O'Shay. His hand was going into his pocket. Thad had been so intent in the struggle that he did not notice until the man's hand was coming out of his pocket. The glint off of the knife blade caught his attention. The man was moving fast toward O'Shay the eight inch blade pulled back at his waist his arm starting forward to run the knife into O'Shay's back. Thad exploded off of the wall. *I've got to stop him, he's going to kill O'Shay.* The knife was coming forward and only inches from Bob's back when Thad collided with the man knocking him sideways, grabbing the man's right wrist and hand holding the knife, he twisted it up and away as the assailant tried to turn to face his attacker. Both of them crashed onto a table crushing it. The seaman had at least twenty pounds on Thad but their height was about even and Thad had surprise in his favor. The knife hand now was stretched up and away. The man was trying to bring it to bear against Thad. They landed on the floor, the assailant on his back and Thad on top causing the air to rush out of the assailant. Instinctively, Thad raised up and drove his knee as hard as he could into the man's groin and then followed that with two more strikes. The assailant screaming in pain, but was still trying to bring the knife down to cut Thad. The blow was swift and sure. Thad saw the nightstick smash against the back of the man's hand. He heard the bones break and he let go of the wrist. Almost immediately a second blow shattered the assailant's wrist. The man made no sound, which Thad thought strange. Everything was happening in slow motion. The assailant's eyes bulged like they would pop right in Thad's face and then rolled up as he passed out from the pain. Thad tried to get up, but couldn't seem to move. Suddenly O'Shay's big hand grabbed the back of his jacket and he was jerked to his feet.

Jake was handcuffing the other two as O'Shay spun him around, "Goddamn it, I told you to stay outside, now get there."

Thad stumbled out the door and put his back against the wall to steady him. It suddenly hit him that it could have turned out differently. He wasn't armed in any way. What if he had not been able to control the man? He would have been stabbed and most likely killed. Thad stumbled to the curb and vomited into the gutter.

Jake had gone to the box and made the call. It was only a short period of time until the wagon came chugging around the corner the officer jumped down and hurried into the box house. Jake, Bob and the transport officer brought out the suspects. Bob had the man who had tried to stab him. It was obvious that the man was in dire pain. His broken hand and wrist was cuffed behind him and was screaming in pain. He tried to twist away from O'Shay who in turn gave the handcuff a turn and the assailants knees buckled, he slumped to the ground.

O'Shay grabbed the man's collar and snatched him to his feet. "Do as you're told or I'll tear the damned hand off!" The suspect settled down, "Get the doors Thad."

Thad hurried to the back doors to the wagon and opened them and stepped back and the officers started loading the suspects. O'Shay's went in without incident, but the transport officer's suspect turned before making the second step into the wagon and kicked out at the officer. His punishment was sure and swift. The officer side stepped the kick and then punched the man in the lower abdomen followed by a blow to his nose causing the man's head to snap back followed closely by his body as he landed flat on his back on the floor of the wagon. Thad could see that the man's nose pushed over at a strange angle, blood running down the side of his face and onto the wagon floor.

Thad could not believe the power of the punch and looked at the gloved hand of the transport officer who looked at Thad with a stern face, "loaded gloves." He held up his fist and Thad could see the bulge in the glove across the knuckles.

Jake's prisoner went into the wagon without any trouble, as he stepped over the unconscious body of his friend.

The transport officer turned to O'Shay,
"Is that right?
That scum bag tried to put that boning knife in your back?"
"Ya, damned near got me."

The transport officer climbed into the wagon. Jake cranked it for him and it fired to life.

"Maybe this crew needs a trip around the block O'Shay."

"Take em' straight in John, I want em' in one piece for the prosecutor."

"Hell O'Shay, they got two days to heal before court."

"Straight in John."

"I'll go in with him and help unload Bob," Jake climbed into the front seat of the vehicle. "You guys want to ride in on the back step?"

"No thanks, we'll walk, I want to talk to this young man."

O'Shay looked intently at Thad who was afraid of what was going to happen. *This is not going to be a pleasant walk.*

They walked for about a block, neither saying a word. It was O'Shay who broke the silence.

"If you really want to be a police officer, one of the first things you have to do is learn how to take orders. I told you to wait outside, why on earth did you come in there?"

O'Shay didn't wait for an answer, "You didn't even have a weapon! What were you thinking Thad?" O'Shay was shaking his head in disbelief.

"I…I don't know Bob. I was excited and just wanted to take a peek. I thought I could stay out of the way. I just wanted to see you guys work."

"That's no excuse, you should have stayed where I told you." They had walked another block.

"I would have stayed on the wall and not gotten in the way Bob, it was just…when I saw the knife and him coming at you from behind I just reacted, I…I couldn't just stand there and let him stab you. I'm sorry I didn't follow orders."

"You could have been killed Thad."

"I know."

The two walked another block in silence.

"Thanks…so could have I." O'Shay said nothing the rest of the way into the station.

***

The process seemed endless. Booking sheets had to be filled out on the three suspects. The suspects with the injuries had to be screened by a doctor in the city jail before they could be booked. Reports and statements had to be completed. Thad and the transport officer took the two injured suspects to the city jail where the doctor taped the nose of one and set the hand and wrist of the other, then cleared them for jail, and more paper work. Back in the write-up room and holding area, the two were placed into holding cells while the booking sheets were filled out. O'Shay worked on the report while Jake and the transport officer took the suspects over to the county jail. The charges on these three would be felonies and as Jake explained, all felony prisoners go to the county jail, misdemeanors to the city jail.

Thad could not believe the amount of paperwork that had to be completed for an incident that took only short time to take place.

"What are all of these reports Bob?"

"These reports are where you make sure that the suspect goes to prison. The better you are at writing these things, the easier it is for the prosecutor to put together a case for trial and get them convicted."

O'Shay pulled out a number of reports and gave them to Thad.

"What you have there is the paperwork that would be used for this incident. There's an incident report. Because this was a felony there is a statement that each officer must do. There are the booking sheets and the form clearing them for a cell from the doctor. These all have to be completed before we go back out. Take them into the break room and get familiar with them and have a cup of coffee while I finish up, Hungry?"

Thad hadn't thought about it and suddenly realized that he was.

"Yes."

"Good. Soon as I'm done we'll go see Maggie and get some dinner."

Thad got a cup and sat down at a table in the break room. He started to sift through the paperwork studying each carefully. He was aware that someone had come into the room. He looked up to see the sergeant getting a cup of coffee and studying him carefully. The sergeant walked over, sat down and looked at the papers Thad was going through.

"Lots a stuff huh." Thad nodded.

"I've been at this job for 17 years now. There didn't used to be so much paperwork. Believe it or not, but there was a time when you just arrested em', made a quick report and locked em' up. Now it seems like every year they come up with some new piece of paper we have to fill out. They call it accountability."

Thad took a drink of his coffee, "How long have you been a sergeant MacAfee?"

MacAfee looked a little surprised, "Remembered my name did ya? Not a bad attribute for a police officer. How old are you now son?"

"I'll be nineteen in two weeks sir."

Sergeant MacAfee shifted in his chair.

"Word has it you saved the life of one of my officers tonight."

Thad felt uncomfortable, "Did the word also tell you that I didn't follow orders and stay outside like I was told?"

"No…but you just did and that's what's important. How'd you feel about what happened Thad?"

Now Thad was surprised that the sergeant remembered his name, "Didn't think about it until it was over; then I got sick and threw up." Thad looked embarrassed.

MacAfee looked at him and chuckled, "We've all been there son…we've all been there." MacAfee suddenly turned serious.

"Thad, if you're serious about it take this," MacAfee slid a form over to him. "I'm sure that O'Shay will be more than happy to help you fill it out. If you really want to be a cop this is the first step. You have some good support and we do need officers. Your chances are pretty good. List me as a reference." MacAfee walked away.

The rest of the night was uneventful for O'Shay, but for Thad it was an eye opener. They made the rounds of the box houses in the Tenderloin several times. They were all busy with men coming and going. Every place they entered people would stare at them. Thad was more than a little uncomfortable.

"Do people always look at you that way Bob?"

O'Shay smiled and waved at one of the bartenders.

"Yes Thad, you're an authority figure and you have to remember that these folks are feeling a little guilty about being here. You get over that feeling of being exposed after a while."

Thad watched as the "girls" worked the crowd.

"Are these people doing something illegal?"

O'Shay tilted his head, "Technically yes. Gambling and prostitution are illegal in the county, but the politicians in the city tolerate it for the time being. The vices have been tolerated in Seattle for a long time now…just as long as it stays below the line. We just kind of ride heard on it and keep the problems in check."

As they walked through a box house toward the back door, Thad watched as one of the girls headed up the stairs with a gentleman in tow. By the time she was halfway up, she already had her dress opened and off of her shoulders and her breasts exposed. The two disappeared around the corner at the top of the stairs and he heard her give a little shriek and then a laugh.

"Do you ever go upstairs Bob?"

O'Shay was very nonchalant, "Not unless there's a problem."

Outside in the alley O'Shay stopped and looked intently at Thad.

"Thad this kind of activity has been going on forever. It had always been illegal in this society and in some others it's not illegal. I can see changes coming and there could be a time when another more pious administration will think that this conduct is terrible. They'll demand enforcement against it. We don't make value judgments about what these people do. We just do our job and leave reforming to the reformers, the churches and the courts. If a new administration gets elected, I'll guarantee you we'll be upstairs and we'll be pulling folks out of the beds and arresting them."

O'Shay started off down the alley, "The changes are coming Thad."

***

"Cindy, it was the most exciting thing I have ever done in my life." Thad could hardly wait to call Cynthia and had to force himself to wait until a decent hour.

"Thad you could have been killed last night." Cindy sounded upset.

"Things are happening so fast, I can't keep up. My life is changing and it scares me. I have made some decisions about school and I want to talk to you about them. It will affect both of us and we should discuss some things. Can you come down tonight?"

"Cindy, I can come down right now if you need me."

"No not now, I'm just about to leave for school. Tonight about six, we'll have dinner here and talk. I love you Thad."

"I love you too Cindy. I'll see you at six." Thad looked down at the application sitting on the table. It was all filled out and ready to be turned in. *Cindy is having a problem with this. Maybe I had better wait until after we talk before I turn it in. Whatever I do, its gong to impact her and she should have a say in what happens in her life. What if she can't take my being a police officer? Bob's ex-wife left him for that very reason. Could I give up Cindy? Would she make me give up the job? Cindy is right. We need to talk.* The time until six o'clock would be an eternity for him.

"Bob did what? He didn't say a thing about it last night."

They were sitting in private dining area of the Silver Slipper getting ready for dinner. He had only been there five minutes. Thad arrived at the backdoor of the Slipper at six sharp, full of foreboding and his heart beating like a drum. Emile greeted him as he came through the door.

"Evenin' Mr. Mitchell, Miss Cindy's in the parlor."

"Thank you Emile, is she alright?"

Emile looked at him quizzically, "She look fine sir…right as rain."

Thad hurried to the parlor and Cindy met him at the entrance.

"Cindy are you….," he did not get another word as Cindy put her arms around his neck and kissed him long and hard pressing herself against him. Thad forgot what he was going to say and just lost himself in the touch, the feel and the smell of her. Thad pulled her closer.

Cindy loosened her arms from around his neck and whispered, "We have to talk Thad."

Thad tilted his head back and groaned. "Are you sure you want to talk?

Cindy gave him a quick peck on the mouth, "I know what your thinking, but we have to talk."

It was then she told him about Bob and Maggie.

"I'm shocked Cindy. They're going to get married?"

"Not only that Thad, but Maggie is going to sell the Slipper and she and Bob are going to buy a house up on Capital Hill."

"What about you Cindy? Where will you stay while you finish school?"

Cindy looked suddenly serious. "That's not a problem Thad. They said that I can stay with them while I finish school and that brings up another question. I'm seriously thinking of changing my major to nursing. I already have the majority of classes that I'll need. All I will have to do is my practicals at the new county hospital up on the hill and I can get my RN."

Thad sat quietly listening.

"Are you sure that's what you want to do Cindy?"

"Will it bother you if I don't go on for my MD? Thad I don't think that I can wait that long. It will be another four years before I can complete school. Do you want to wait that long?"

Thad took a deep breath, "Cindy does this have anything to do with my becoming a police officer?"

Tears filled her eyes, "Thad you could have been killed last night. I almost lost you once and now this." She took hold of his hands, "I couldn't live, if I lost you Thad. I know how much it means to you to be a police officer. You know that I'll accept whatever you feel is best for you and will make you happy."

Thad kissed her hand.

"Thad, that's only part of it. I don't want to wait another four years to start our lives. I want to start that now. I want to enjoy waking up with you every morning and going to bed with you every night."

Cindy pressed her face against Thad's chest and wrapped her arms around his waist clinging to him as tightly as she could.

"Thad please tell me what you're thinking."

Thad cradled her face in his hands and tilted her face up,

"If you want to go into nursing that's alright with me. I need to know if you can take me being a policeman? It's important that I know Cindy. I love you and I want to marry you."

Tears flooded Cindy's eyes and she fairly jumped off of the floor to kiss him.

"Oh Thad I love you and you can be whatever you want as long as I have you.

"Is that a yes Cindy?"

"Oh yes, yes, yes."

They were locked in an embrace when they heard Marco in the doorway.

"Ahem, excuse me Miss Cindy, but your dinner is ready."

"Let's eat Thad. I can hardly wait to tell aunt Maggie."

Thad was a little concerned.

"I hope she will be as happy as you are."

Cindy took his hand as they walked into the parlor.

"Are you happy Thad? Why wouldn't Maggie be happy for us?"

Thad pulled out her chair and she sat down.

"Cindy, Maggie is very protective of you and she might think we're too young."

Thad sat down and Cindy placed her napkin in her lap.

"Thad, it's not like we're getting married tomorrow. I have to finish school and you need to get established on the police department. We do have some time you know. Aunt Maggie will be delighted. Let's eat."

Maggie and Bob walked into the parlor as Thad and Cindy were working on desert. "Thad, did Cindy tell the good news?"

Bob dropped down in a chair and poured a cup of coffee.

"Yes, when is this supposed to happen?"

"As soon as we can get a house and sell the Slipper."

Maggie sat down on his knee, "I already have an offer on the Slipper from the Considines and we found the most beautiful Victorian up on Federal Avenue. It's perfect, Cindy you'll just love it."

Cindy smiled and put her hand on Thad's. It will only be for awhile Aunt Maggie. Thad and I have talked it over and we will be getting married when I finish school and he has his probation completed on the police department."

Maggie stood up and looked at both of them.

"Are you sure you want to do this?"

Thad kissed Cindy's hand.

"Never more sure of anything Maggie, we're going to tell my parents tomorrow morning right after I turn in my application to the department"

Thad looked over at Bob O'Shay who gave him a wink.

Chapter 8

The job had not started off as exciting as Thad had thought it would. He remembered the exciting times walking the skid road beat with Bob O'Shay. Oh, the swearing in was exciting. Cindy, his mom and dad and, of course Maggie and Bob had been there when Chief Bannick had sworn him in as a new police officer. The three days of indoctrination went quickly and getting all of his gear made him feel like he was a real officer. Although that was true, there was a great deal more to learn. He was now a rookie and would be on probation for six months. He started in the lowly hole running errands for the brass and everyone else, answering the phone, taking reports at the counter and filling, what seemed like, a ton of paperwork. Occasionally he was allowed to drive the new Ford panel wagon to go on errands and to pick up arrests that had been made on the street. Booking the prisoners was often interesting and allowed him the opportunity to deal with a wide variety of criminals. Bringing the prisoners down for the shift change show-up broke the monotony at least once a day.

Those men arrested in the past 24 hours would be brought down stairs and sat on a bench to one side of the assembly room. In front of the podium there was tape on the floor in the shape of a box. Prior to roll call Thad would bring the prisoners down and seat them. A list would be given to the duty sergeant. The sergeant would call out for the next prisoner and Thad would escort him to the box, facing the officers. The list given to the sergeant had the man's name and offense on it and the sergeant would use it to address the officers.

"This is Mr. Michael Jenkins, he's a petty thief and drunk roller. He was arrested last night south of the line at 1st and South Jackson. Turn sideways Jenkins! He's five feet 10 inches and one hundred sixty pounds. Face the officers Jenkins! He has an extensive record. Keep an eye out for him. Go sit down Jenkins, next prisoner."

The process would start again.

Every day there was something new to learn and the grisly old station sergeant never let him forget it. The man's voice sounded like it came from the heavens after a flash of lightning. "Never let 'em know your scared son. They don't know unless you let em'. You got the power and they fear it. Remember the only one you can trust out there is another uniform. Don't expect some citizen to jump in to help if you're getting your butt kicked. Gonna be another copper that saves your hide. Any time you do anything that may be controversial, you write paper on it. Nobody can cover your tail like you can, always remember CYA...cover your ass."

Those nuggets of information were imbedded in Thad's mind. Sometimes he would wake up in the middle of the night hearing Sergeant Guzman's words of wisdom.

O'Shay made sergeant and was transferred to the east precinct so he was close to home. Thad hoped that he would be able to work for him but he first had to complete his probation; four more months and of course his time in the hole. It seemed like an eternity what with planning for a wedding and finding a place for he and Cindy to live. Cindy was almost done with nursing school and had been doing her practical at the new county hospital on first hill. They liked her so much that they had already offered her a job when she graduated. There were some nice homes near there, but Thad feared they may be out of their price range. *I think maybe I should talk this over with dad. With his head for business he may be able to figure out a way for us to swing it.*

Most of the time, when it was slow, he would sit and watch the "Old Timers" in the write-up room pay cards. Something called "Tonk" seemed to be the favorite and small amounts of money changed hands. Although he was catching on to how it was played he knew better than to ask to sit in, and in any case he would most likely lose his money. Night shift offered a little more excitement. Even though he was inside there were problems that came in from the street. On weekends there was almost a steady procession of people who wanted to report crimes and Thad would take the reports at the counter. Mostly it was petty thefts, minor assaults and drunks wanting to be arrested so they would have a place to sleep for a few hours. Occasionally something different or exciting would wander in off the street.

"Excuse me officer" Thad looked up from the desk. The man standing on the other side of the counter looked to be in his forties, his hair, slightly graying, it was nicely cut and he sported a neatly trimmed mustache and goatee.

"I would like to report a theft."

Thad got up from the desk and walked to the counter. *This is a man who is obviously, from his appearance and dress, from North of the line.*

"Certainly sir, I'll just grab a report."

Thad set the report form on the counter.

"Name?"

"Do I have to give my name?"

"I'm afraid so sir, your name and address are needed for the report." Thad filled in the pertinent information needed to start the report.

"Officer, could we move this along a little faster, I am getting a bit chilly."

Thad looked around, *it has to be at least seventy in here, and it's not particularly cold.*

"Okay sir, I'll speed it up. Exactly where did this theft take place?"

The man looked around seemingly embarrassed by where it happened.

"Well officer, it was in the alley west of First Avenue. You know the one that runs south from South Washington Street."

Thad looked at the man again, *what was he doing in the alley in Skid Road?*

"Okay and what was taken?"

The man's face became redder, "Look officer can we do this somewhere else I'm uncomfortable standing here like this."

What's with this guy, "Uncomfortable with what sir?"

Suddenly the man stepped back from the counter, "Well see officer, she got my pants."

Thad looked down to see that from the waist down the man was naked.

"She got my pants the bottom of my long johns and my wallet. Can we go into an office or something before someone else walks in?"

Thad finished the report in one of the interrogation rooms after getting a blanket to wrap around him.

"Just how did she get your pants and long johns from you sir and who is she?" Thad was now trying to keep a straight face. *Cindy is not going to believe this.*

The man looked at the floor, "It was a prostitute officer, flaming red hair and huge ti…well you know, they were big. She was going to give me a blow-job in the alley, but she wanted me to take my pants off so she could…this is embarrassing officer, and must I go into all the details?

Thad was trying not to think about a red headed hooker with huge breasts.

"No sir, I think you've given me enough to finish the report. We'll get some officers to check the area and see if they can find your pants. I'm afraid you wallet is most likely gone.

"Thank you officer and thank you for the blanket to wrap around me…"

"No problem sir, would you care to use the phone to have someone come and get you?"

"I think that would be nice, thank you"

Thad led him to a phone and went back to the counter to finish the report. As he was just finishing the man poked his head around the corner.

"Officer," Thad looked up.

"Yes Sir, did you get someone?"

"Oh yes, my wife is coming down to get me. Could you…um…do me a little favor?"

Thad smiled, "Not to worry sir, I won't tell her what happened"

"Well thank you officer, but that's not it. Could you punch me in the face before she gets here?"

What did he say,

"Excuse me sir, did I here you right? You want me to punch you?"

"Yes please, I told her that I had been having dinner with a business acquaintance and I was jumped by some thugs as I left the restaurant."

"I won't tell her what happened sir, but I won't punch you, sorry."

"Oh it's alright officer, I thought it was at least worth a try. Good night, I'll wait for her downstairs."

The wagon calls were a welcome break from sitting in the station. Most of the time, they were pick-ups for drunks. It was a toss-up as to which was worse, sitting in the station bored or handling drunks who were most likely smelly, dirty, foul mouthed, angry, combative or had urinated in their pants or worse. Even those became routine after awhile. Occasionally, however, they also got interesting.

Sergeant Guzman's gravelly voice bellowed down the hall. "Pick-up at Occidental and South Washington, Mitchell, grab the keys and go."

Thad cranked the engine over and hopped into the open front panel truck used to haul prisoners and chugged down toward the Tenderloin. He saw the beat officer flagging him down as he turned down Occidental.

Ed Blakey walked up as Thad pulled the wagon to the curb.

"Hey Mitchell, Guzman take you off leash?"

Thad bristled at the remark of being controlled and watched because he was a rookie.

"Yeah, I guess so Blakey, is that a problem?"

Blakey smiled, "Nope just unusual that's all. Guzman usually keeps a tighter rein on new officers longer than this. Got a couple of winners for ya' ta' haul up to the station."

Thad could hear the female voices getting louder around the corner.

"You want me to pull around?"

"Nope, we'll walk em' around." Blakey strolled around corner, "Okay ladies lets go…your chariot awaits"

Thad got out of the van and opened the back as they came around the corner.

"You ass holes, this is bullshit and you know it. Disorderly conduct fighting is a bunch a crap arrest." The first one looked to be in her thirties and hard as nails. Her top had been torn off, her breasts were hanging loose and her left eye was starting to darken, where someone had punched her.

The second one was giving Blakey all hell.

"Come on Blakey you know this is shit. If I was humpin' some guy in the alley I could see it, but Christ, for fightin' with Nancy, that's shit."

Blakey just smiled and kept leading her toward the van.

The first one reached the step to go in and looked away from the beat man to Thad who had taken her arm and was attempting to help her into the van.

"Oooow…a baby one, a brand new baby one. Hey Margo look what we have here, a baby policeman. I'm Nancy honey, tell you what, you let us go and I'll give you a blow job. Hell if you can get it up twice, Margo'll give you one too." Nancy shook her breasts back and forth, "You can even rub my tits while I do it. Whata ya say honey?"

Thad let go of her arm like it was on fire and stepped back. Margo chimed in, "Aw Nancy, now ya scared em." Margo grabbed her crotch, "I got somethin' right here for ya baby, beats hell out of a blow job."

Blakey stepped up and forcefully took Nancy by the arm and herded her into the wagon, "Leave the man alone ladies, you want to give the place a bad reputation?"

He winked at Thad as Margo climbed in, blowing Thad a kiss.

Blakey shut the door and Thad dropped the locking pin in place. "Put em' in a holding cell Mitchell. We'll be up in about twenty minutes. You can take em' up on their offer if you want, but don't turn em' loose." Blakey started to walk away, "Oh yes, if you're actually thinking about it, keep in mind that these two probably have diseases that the doctors don't even know about yet."

Blakey gave him a big toothy grin and walked away.

Thad put the van in gear, *I don't think I'll tell Cindy about this one*. He headed off to the station with Nancy and Margo in the back singing bawdy songs.

"Mitchell," Guzman's voice thundered through the corridors of the precinct. "Get the wagon we're goin to give em a hand below the line."

Thad grabbed his hat and hurried to the wagon parked in its stall in front of the station. Guzman was already there.

"You drive kid, down to the waterfront at Yesler. The beat has a problem that needs attention."

Guzman cranked the siren as Thad made a u-turn in the middle of the street and headed down Cherry toward the waterfront. As they neared the wharfs, Thad could see that two officers were in a confrontation with several rough looking men that appeared to be seamen. There had already been a physical confrontation and both the officers and the seamen had superficial wounds. They had reached a standoff and it was up to Thad and the sergeant to equal the odds. Thad was about to learn several lessons in police work. There were seven of the seamen and only four officers.

Thad pulled on the emergency brake as Guzman hopped out of the wagon and approached the men.

"All right you men up on the wall and I mean now.

The sound of Guzman's voice startled even Thad. He could see that the sergeant and the officers had their night sticks out and Thad pulled his as he hurried along after him. The seamen looked startled at the presence of the fierce sounding man in uniform who was striding toward them.

One of the other officers growled the same order, "On the wall now."

Several of the men realized that discretion was the better part of valor and turned toward the wall. A couple of the men, however, decided that no one was going to take them to jail, not without a fight. The closest one to Guzman turned toward him reaching out to grab him and Guzman clubbed him to the ground for his trouble. A second man had come at Guzman from the side and was about to grab him when Thad took careful aim at his wrist and brought his baton down with all the strength he could muster. He remembered how effective it had been when O'Shay had done the same thing to the man in the tavern with the knife. Thad could hear bone snap as the baton found its mark just above the wrist. The man's knees buckled and his scream startled Guzman causing him to jump sideways. The man grabbed his arm and rolled on the ground crying out in pain, the men who were not already on the wall, got there as quickly as they could.

Guzman cut the man's sleeve open and took a look at the grisly mess that once was a forearm. The blow had enough force behind it to cause a compound fracture. The bone was protruding out through the skin and bleeding profusely. Guzman tore the man's shirt and made a tourniquet out of it and cut off the blood flow.

"Well, looks like this one will have to go to the hospital." Guzman shook his head and looked at Thad.

"Son you aren't cuttin' down trees. A little less force next time might be good. You probably crippled this one. Although, he most likely got what he deserved." Guzman slapped Thad on the back, "You passed boy, now help load em' up."

Thad opened the back of the wagon and the officers started loading the men. As Thad was assisting the third man into the wagon and feeling good about himself, he got careless. Feeling bad for the man with the shattered arm who had just been hauled away to the hospital by the second wagon, Thad was assisting the prisoner to get in so that he would not be injured. He never saw the elbow coming that struck him directly in the nose.

"Oh shit!" pain shot through his face down his neck and it felt like it exploded out through his toes.

"Damn" Thad grabbed his face as he backed away, his eyes filled with tears, he couldn't see and he could feel the blood, his blood, running through his hands and onto his uniform shirt. *What the hell happened.* His eyes were starting to clear and he saw an officer pick up the now unconscious man and throw him into the wagon.

"Get in the wagon son, I'll drive." Guzman steered him to the passenger seat.

"Put your head back and use your handkerchief over it. It'll slow the bleeding, just relax. You give them the opportunity and they'll assault you. That badge don't mean shit to some folks and they would like to push it where the sun don't shine…if you let them. You gotta' always expect the worst in people until you find out otherwise."

Thad held his aching, bleeding nose. *Another Guzmanism, another lesson.*

Cindy was in the ER and near the end of her shift when two officers brought in a man who had been injured in a fight. The man was in agony as the ER doctor removed the towel from around the patient's forearm and Cindy stepped up to assist him. *He looks like one of those men from off of the ships in harbor,* what she saw made her stomach churn, *my God the bone is sticking straight out of his arm.*

The doctor studied the arm for a moment, "How did this happen?"

The man clenched his teeth, "Goddam cops, grabbed me for no damned reason and smashed my arm. They're gonna pay for this."

The doctor looked at the officers placidly standing nearby watching their prisoner.

"Officer how did this happen?"

"Nightstick Sir. He was attacking our sergeant and an officer hit him on the forearm with his nightstick, just before he made contact with the sergeant. this going to take long? We have to watch this one. If it's going to take a long time we can get someone from the hole to take over."

Cindy knew that Thad was working the hole and it might be him that came up to watch the prisoner.

"Would the officer from the hole be Thad Mitchell?"

The officer looked surprised then smiled, "You know Thad?"

Cindy knew she was blushing, "Yes. I was just wondering."

"Don't think Thad will be the one to watch the prisoner but he may be up anyway, he got hurt in the fracas."

"How badly was he injured?" Cindy kept her voice steady, determined not to panic.

"Oh not serious, you might say he got his nose bent," the officer had a little grin on his face and it irritated Cindy.

"Do you think that it's funny, officer?" There was a definite sharpness in her tone of voice.

The grin was suddenly gone, "Oh…no ma'am, I just remembered the lecture he got from the sergeant after the incident. That probably hurt more than the broken nose. We've all been there ma'am, it's just part of the job."

Now Cindy was concerned, "Broke…he broke his nose?"

"Yes Ma'am, he may or may not be up. Sarge is pretty good at fixin noses, but this being his first, he'll most likely come here. I know I did the first time."

"How many times have you broken your nose officer?"

Cindy couldn't believe what she was hearing. *Good lord broken noses are an occupational hazard?*

"I think it's been four maybe five times. I think we better call the station. Is this going to be long doctor?"

"Cindy, give this man a shot of morphine and send him up to the OR. Yes, officer this is going to take awhile and he will most likely be here for some time."

"Okay Thad, let's take a look at your beak."

Guzman was being gentle but didn't sound like it. He had put a hot towel on Thad's swollen face and now it throbbed like it was going to blow up. *I think I need to see a doctor.*

"What we can do is get it good and warm and then straighten it out with your fingers and put a piece of tape on it, works most of the time."

Most of the time, what does it look like when it doesn't work? I still think I need to see a doctor.

Thad removed the towel and looked into the mirror.

"Geez sarge, it looks terrible"

Guzman had a grin pasted on his face, "Aw don't worry about it kid, it gives you character."

Thad could see that the swelling was starting to close his eyes and he was starting to turn black and blue. *Oh man I don't need this shit and it's really starting to hurt.* The last thing Thad needed was another joker.

"Hey is that my old friend Thad Mitchell or is it a raccoon?"

Bob O'Shay sauntered into the locker room.

"Hey Guzman, looks like one of your lesson times."

O'Shay stepped around in front of Thad and took a better look at his nose. There was actually empathy on his face and in his voice.

"Ooow Thad…you looks like hell, you really got whacked."

Guzman chimed in, "Ah…couple of hot towels and some tape and he'll look like his beautiful self again."

Thad felt forlorn. *Good lord, I feel like a damaged specimen in a comedy show. I need to see a doctor.*

O'Shay took another look, "Nah Frank, this is his first and it does look like it could use some professional help."

"What do I look like, chopped liver?" Guzman feigned having his feelings hurt, "I got the hands of a surgeon O'Shay."

O'Shay laughed out loud, "Those meat hooks of yours are made for ripping parts off of a fried chicken not sculpting the fine features of this lad's handsome mug. I'll take him up to the hospital. I know several ladies who would take me to task if I let his face fall apart."

"Hey Mitchell," one of the officers from the hospital entered the locker room.

"Ouch, you look terrible, I bet that hurts."

Oh man, I need to see a doctor.

"Oh yes, there's a very attractive nurse up at the hospital who's very concerned about your well being. I thought she was going to rip my heart out for thinking your broken nose was funny."

Oh man that's the last straw, now Cindy knows. This is not going to be a good day. Never again will I step in front of an elbow or anything else. Guzman's 'Laws of survival.'

It took the doctor three painkiller shots and forty five minutes to put Thad's nose back into reasonably good shape. There had been some surgery and a pin inserted to help it heal straight.

"Cindy, tape him up and take him home."

The doctor gave Cindy a wry smile, "Your policeman is going to survive. When the swelling goes down he'll most likely look just like he did before someone tried to rearrange his face."

Cindy had not said anything about the incident while Thad was being treated. In fact, she had not said anything at all. *Oh man she's upset and angry and I'm going to get a lecture about how dangerous my job is. She is not going to want me to be a police officer and it's going to get ugly.*

"Cindy, say something, anything, I'm sorry if I upset you."

Cindy stared into Thad's swollen eyes. She leaned down with her mouth next to his ear and whispered.

"I'm going to take you home and just hold you. My poor baby, you're going to need a whole bunch of TLC and I'm just the person to give it to you."

Thad relaxed. *Maybe this is not going to be such a bad day after all.*

O'Shay had dropped Cindy and Thad at his parent's house. He had called ahead so that Chadwick and Becky would not get all crazy about Thad's injuries. *After all cops get their noses busted sometimes, it goes with the job.*

Thad was a little wobbly on his feet from the medication. Chadwick and Cindy got him inside where Becky had turned down his bed. They got him undressed and tucked in. Everything was a little hazy to Thad, but he was asleep almost before his head hit the pillows. Cindy made sure his head was elevated on several pillows and he had fresh ice on his nose, as she practiced her nursing skills.

Becky was more than just a little distressed, "Cindy is he going to be okay?"

Cindy tried to reassure her, "Yes Becky, the doctor did a great job rebuilding his nose. It should be just like new when the swelling goes down. It was scary though, it's more personal when it's someone you love."

Becky saw the tears welling up in Cindy's eyes.

"Its okay honey and I want you to stay here with us until he gets better. Chad will take you home so you can get some things you'll need here. It'll also give us a chance to talk about the wedding."

Chad looked in on his son with his bandaged face sleeping soundly and then down the hall at Becky and his daughter-in-law to be hugging in the drawing room. *Yes this is a good match. Our family is growing, life is good and all is right with the world.*

***

Two days after the pin came out there was only a small amount of swelling remaining and the black and blue marks had turned to green and would soon fade. They were almost gone and Thad was still enjoying the TLC he was getting. Cindy moved back with Maggie and Bob but stopped by regularly. They had even gone to dinner last night. By his calculations, Thad figured that he had about 4 days left on his sick leave and then it would be back to the hole where he would be relatively safe. The call from Guzman changed all that.

"So how is the nose coming kid?" Guzman had called almost every other day just to check on how he was doing. *Interesting guy that Guzman, he really did care about his people.*

"Looks like your sick time and your probation have been shortened. They're short handed in the east precinct and you're being transferred there. You passed kid, you're a full fledged police officer now, congratulations!"

Thad was dumbfounded, "When do I report sarge?"

Tomorrow and you'll be working Third watch for O'Shay. He'll keep you out of trouble and don't forget what I taught you. Don't forget the old Sarge. Let me know how it goes and take care of yourself."

"Thanks Frank, I couldn't possibly forget you and I'll stay in touch."

Guzman hung up the phone. *Good kid, we need more like him. Had my son lived, I would like to think he would have turned out the same.* Guzman cleared his throat, *well who's the new guy in the hole,* "Mulrooney, my office."

Chapter 9

The new house on the south side of Queen Anne hill was more spectacular than anything build before. Becky had problems giving up her spacious home on 2nd and Lenora, but the physical shape of Seattle was changing rapidly. The regrade was nearing its completion and the hillside south of her beautiful house was slowly being washed away to fill in the water front. Almost two blocks were being added from the bottom of the bluff out into the shallows of the bay to a rock pile known as Ballast Island. Much of the Denny area had been transferred to the Back Bay shallows south of Jackson Street. The old stilt box houses were now gone and although the Tenderloin south of Yesler was still intact; it was smaller and more concentrated.

The new house on the side of Queen Anne Hill was so grand it was almost embarrassing for Becky. It was built on a triple lot that was now landscaped with sweeping flower beds and lush shrubs. Great expanses of lawn surrounded the house that faced south overlooking the bay and the city. On clear days Mount Rainier filled the horizon like a huge ice cream cone. At the entrance to the property a massive brick arch straddled the drive that veered to the right as it looped counter clockwise past the front of the home and through a sally port. It then continued looping around until it intersected itself in front of the entrance gate. At the head of the drive the sally port was supported by two massive columns on either side of the entrance to the two story brick home. To the left of the home was a three car garage. It was in the same design as the home itself. The exterior of the home was brick and wood in a Tudor design. The massive eight foot oak door opened into a large foyer. To the left of the foyer was the den and library. To the right was a sitting room. Through the foyer led into a hallway that accessed the dinning room, living room, kitchen and a guest room at the end of the hall. The covered veranda that opened off of the living room ran across the entire back of the house. It allowed the family to sit in the afternoon and gaze out over the one hundred and eighty degree view. To the left they could see lake Washington and the Cascade Mountains and looking all the way to the right they could see the bay, the sound and the Olympic Mountains. The master suite and two other guest rooms were located on the second floor at the top of a curved staircase that started just past the foyer. Becky had stood on the lot before the building started and was awed by the grandeur of what would become her view from the new home that Chad would build for them.

Now as the contractors did their finishing work she walked from room to room and realized that this was not just another house, this was a mansion. This was a symbol of what Chadwick had accomplished since arriving here from the gold fields. It was assuredly larger and grander than Harrington's and that seemed important for Chad. Standing in the large dining room, that would hold a dinner party for at least 20; she realized that she had only a short period of time to get things ready. Within two weeks they were scheduled to move everything from the old house to the new. An associate of Chadwick's had purchased the old house and would start moving it to the lake side of first hill. The hill it stands on would then be washed away to the waterfront. There would be no sign left that her grand house once stood there. With the city reimbursing Chadwick for the property and the sale of the house, Chadwick was able to totally finance the new one.

The last thing that Chadwick had removed from the house was the metal boxes that he had carefully stashed in the hidden alcove of the basement. He had put it there before Becky had arrived and now he slid it into a compartment he had built in the basement of his new home. As he slid the panel over the opening of the compartment, he felt assured that no one could find it without knowing where the panel was and he was the only one who did.

Things were happening so fast it was hard to keep up with what was gong on. Maggie and Bob had gotten married. It was a wonderful wedding in their home on Federal Avenue. The police officers did get a bid rowdy at the reception but nothing got broken. Maggie had been more than a little concerned about damage. The big beer keg in the back yard just off of the porch seemed to be the gathering place. Becky and Maggie were on the porch watching the high jinx's of the seventy guests.

"They're getting a bit loud and rowdy aren't they Maggie?"

Maggie looked away from the crowd toward Becky.

"Ah, it is a rowdy bunch they can be. They work hard and they play hard.

Not to worry. They would not want to suffer the wrath of Sergeant O'Shay should they go too far. The neighbors won't mind. They're here in the middle of it all."

Becky looked a bit perplexed. Maggie just smiled and patted her hand, "Remember Becky, when you give a party with policemen, invite the neighbors. It saves a lot of headaches in dealing with complaints."

Becky relaxed and folded her arms, "Well we have an empty lot to the East of us and the new mayor lives next door. He is a bit pious, so Thad's wedding reception may be a new experience for him."

"What's he like Becky? I know that he ran on a law and order platform. Word has it that he is going to shuffle the police department and shut down the Tenderloin. Sure glad I sold the Slipper when I did."

Becky leaned closer to Maggie, "I've only met him twice while the house was being built. I've had more contact with his wife whose been dying to see what our place looks like. I think that she keeps an inventory of the building materials and furniture that go in. The marble and slate must have really tantalized her."

"What's she like?" Maggie was looking for some smut.

"I think she's rather churchy. That doesn't surprise me at all, after listening to her husband's fire and brimstone speeches during the campaign."

"Okay what are you two up to, over here whispering to one another? I'm sure that someone is being raked over the coals."

Bob O'Shay thumped up the steps to the porch.

"Mrs. O'Shay, would you care for another beer before those rowdy 'coppers' drain the last drop from the keg? How about you Becky? Chadwick has bet Thad that he can out drink him and I do believe that he's going to make it."

Maggie fairly glowed as O'Shay dropped himself down on the porch swing beside her.

"Now isn't he a prize Becky? Big as a bear and as cuddly as a stuffed toy" Maggie snuggled up against him as he put his arm around her.

"What do you know about the new Mayor, Bob?"

Bob suddenly got serious.

"Things have been running pretty fast and loose for a lot of year's ladies and there are some forces on the department that are more than a little uncomfortable about the new administration's agenda. The Tenderloin crowd, no offense Maggie, have had free reign for as long as I can remember. They make a pretty good living providing more than what a few people want. They're not going to stop wanting those things that the Tenderloin provides. If we enforce against it, the activity will either go underground or find a way to keep the law off of their backs."

Becky was wide eyed and totally captivated.

"How would they do that Bob? They wouldn't hurt the officers would they?" Fear for Thad's safety was creeping into her thoughts.

"No, that would be bad business Becky. Policemen get more than just a little defensive when folks start striking out at their fellow officers."

"They buy them off Becky, at least the ones that can be bought off."

Maggie just blurted it out as a matter of fact.

Becky could hardly speak, "But who…how…how do you know who can be bought off?"

Bob dropped his voice.

"You don't Becky. It can start at the bottom or at the top and can permeate the whole department or just part of the department. The administration of the department controls who and where it happens. The attitude is that everyone has a price. I don't believe that, but that's what the crooks believe."

Becky pressed on, "What do you believe Bob?"

"I think that those who can be bought off are in the minority. Coppers who have gotten themselves in financial binds and can rationalize the taking of money for looking the other way are few and far between. We all have had financial problems. My ex-wife cut me a new one. Sorry, but she did. I had to work a couple of jobs to get out of debt, but I could never rationalize taking money, but I know that some have."

Maggie leaned forward to be closer to Becky, "When I bought the Slipper we had just changed administrations from closed city to open city. I know for a fact that the previous owner was paying the beat officers money to keep him out of trouble with the law. It broke him and that's when I came along to buy it. It's happened before and it will happen again."

O'Shay took Becky's hand, "Becky, don't worry about Thad. He's a good kid with a lot of smarts. You've done a wonderful job with him and his values are sound. It will be an easy job, but I'll make sure that he's never tempted."

With that O'Shay leaned back and kissed Maggie's cheek.

"Mrs. O'Shay we have a celebration to attend."

Becky looked out at the crowd and watched Thad fall backwards off of a bench onto the grass and Chadwick laughing so hard he had tears running down his face. He tried to pick him up and then just lay down beside him. Cindy looked up at Becky on the porch with a bewildered look on her face and they both started laughing.

"Maggie, I think it's time that Cindy and I took our beer soaked men home."

Maggie laughed, "We could load em' into the paddy wagon but I don't think the new Mayor would think that was a good idea. I'll have Bob and some of the boys load em' into your car. If you can't get them out once you get home just leave em' in the car. They'll come out eventually." Maggie waved at O'Shay,

"Bob would you help these two ladies load their men into the back seat of the car and get it started for them."

O'Shay looked over at the Mitchell's on the ground and when he was through laughing grabbed a couple of more guys and stuffed Thad and Chadwick into the Ford. As they rode home, Thad and his father were in the back seat singing some bawdy song that Chadwick had learned in Alaska. Cindy looked warily into the back seat, "Do you think they'll be alright Becky?" Becky just shook her head; *I think I'll just leave them in the car.*

Thad and Chadwick sat at the breakfast table not looking well at all. Even the shower had not helped either of them. Chadwick had called his secretary and told her to reschedule today's appointments. Thad holding his head was thankful that O'Shay had told him to take today off. *I am in no shape to go into work today. How the hell do the drunks I deal with all the time do this? If I live through this God, I swear I will never drink again.*

Cindy brought in breakfast. The toast looked great but the eggs and sausages caused Thad to jump up from the table and rush to the bathroom to relieve his churning stomach. Stumbling back to the table he discovered that his father had managed to eat some toast and keep it down. Thad began to nibble at the toast when they both became aware that Becky and Cindy were standing in the doorway of the dining room.

"Did we have a nice time last night gentlemen?" The look on Becky's face spoke volumes about her displeasure.

They looked at each other and began to giggle, then outright laugh which of course caused them to grab their heads because of the throbbing pain.

Becky and Cindy looked at each other knowingly with little smirks on their faces.

"Cindy, remind me not to have kegs of beer at your reception, although a little white wine might be nice."

***

It didn't take long for the changes in the department to start. A new chief was appointed and the old one decided to retire rather than be demoted back to captain. That would leave the door open for a changing of the administrative staff. The mayor made it quite clear, at the swearing in of the new chief, that this was going to be a new police department that enforced all of the laws not just some of them. Things were going to change south of the line and anyone on the department that could not go along with that should look for a new place to work.

The raids started almost immediately. Squads of officers would routinely swoop down on establishments in the Tenderloin arresting the prostitutes as well as the customers. Gambling joints, pool halls, and dope dens were also targeted. For the sin merchants it was roll over and die or fight. Some went out of business, others decided to fight and they would fight the way they knew best. They would use cash as their ammunition. Used wisely and discreetly they would find that they could be above the law.

More and more raids were coming up empty. It was as though the targets knew the police were coming and were able to look respectable by the time they got there. The mayor and the chief of police touted the reason as being that of control. The tactics that were being used had stopped the illegal operations south of Yesler Street. Crime was down in the Tenderloin and it was all due to the programs generated by the mayor and his new chief. The public bought it, but there were officers who knew better.

The realization came a year after the new administration had taken a firm hold on the reigns of the city. Gambling and prostitution was still prevalent but discreetly practiced in the old Tenderloin. It was less so in Chinatown. The backrooms of oriental markets, barbershops and laundries were converted into gambling halls. Recessed doorways in alleys opened into sub-basements where one could lose his money or virginity if they chose to. The mayor's constituency was not happy, which of course meant that the mayor was not happy.

"Chief, what are we doing about the Chinatown problem?"

Chief Severyns squirmed in his chair,

"Mayor I have my best men working in it. These guys are straight as an arrow and if anyone can attack the problem, they will. We should start seeing results soon. Be patient. It will take some time. The problem is ingrained in the community and it's going to take a great deal of pressure to eliminate the problem." The mayor leaned across the table looking squarely into the face of the chief.

"I don't have the time to be patient Pat. I need results now there are folks who backed me and they want to see things happen now." He straightened up, "Make it happen chief or I'll find someone else who can."

Chief Severyns did not like being threatened.

"It will happen Mr. Mayor. I've placed a number of good officers in Chinatown and the sin merchants will be starting to feel the bite real soon.

The Chinatown beat officers were not happy when the orders came down transferring them to other beats. They had earned the right to walk that beat and now it was being taken away from them.

"Sarge, what the hell's going on? Whose idea was it to pull us off the beat?"

Sergeant Bratten looked around furtively in the restaurant to be sure that no one could hear.

"Look guys, it's the new Chief. I know that it'll put a dent into our finances but we aren't the only ones getting hurt. The money goes up the chain and it's going to be up to those at the top to do something about the changes. Give em' a little slack. You'll get your beat back."

O'Shay's squad relished the reassignment to China town. They were eager to start moving on the gambling joints and prostitution in the area. As a result of intelligence gathered by the officers raids started within a week. The business men's clubs called Tongs were hot beds for gambling and each Tong, a business association, were the first to feel the pressure. Teams of police officers were kicking in doors of known gambling operations, arresting the patrons and seizing the proceeds of gambling and prostitution.

It would start as minor harassment.

"Hey Sarge," it was Casey Martin, Jerry Blackwell's partner.

"Look what we found stuffed into the call box at Maynard and Jackson just now." O'Shay took the note, *"To whom it may concern. We will no longer put up with the enforcement practices in China Town. It would be safer for you and your families to work in some other area in the city. You have been warned."*

"What the hell's going on?" O'Shay jumped up out of his chair.

"Any idea who put this there?"

Martin shook his head, "If I did I'd bust his head for him."

"Take it easy Martin, that's what they want you to do. That gets you in trouble and then they have a hammer over you and reason to move you out."

O'Shay carefully put the note into an envelope, "I'll write it up and send it up the chain. The brass needs to be aware of the problem. *It's started, the subtle threats and pressure to back off. Next it will be transfers for all of us.*

"O'Shay, I got the memo and the threatening note."

O'Shay had responded to Captain Bagley's office as requested.

"I realize that you and your squad have been making a lot of arrests for gambling and prostitution. There are going to be some who would like you to stop."

O'Shay pulled a chair over and plopped done next to the desk.

"I also want you to know that we have been receiving complaints regarding your tactics and the use of force by your officers. You and your men may need to slow things down a bit and let it cool off. In the meantime I'll take this to the next staff meeting and we'll discuss it there. You have anything to say?"

O'Shay looked steadily into the eyes of his captain.

"You askin' me to tell my squad to back off? It was my understanding that we were put there to take care of business and that's what we've been doing."

The captain had his best public relations grin on his face.

"Now sergeant, I would not ask you to go against your orders, but it might be wise to let things settle a bit. I'll take it up at staff and get back to you."

O'Shay stood up quickly, pivoted and walked out of the office.

Captain Bagley picked up the phone and dialed.

"Mike, we have a problem and it might take a bit more work. O'Shay and his crew are not going to go easily. I think an example will need to made and a case for removal be formulated. I'll come up with the rational for transfer. We need to meet with the rest of the players, you take care of that." Bagley hung up the phone and began making notes. *We need to move fast before they do any more damage to our arrangements.*

The squad meeting was held where O'Shay knew no one would know about it or listen in.

"Okay guys here's how it is; We can sit back and go out with a whimper or we can go out kicking and screaming. They have the power and can break us up or move us anytime they feel like it, depending on how deep this thing goes. So, here's what I'm proposing. We take down one or two joints a night and hopefully get the attention of those who are not involved. Any one got any suggestions?"

Thad chimed in almost immediately. Martin and Blackwell have all the information that we need to kick some butt Bob."

Blackwell threw a folder onto the table.

"Our informants have identified five places that are running hot gambling operations this week. Three of those have whores for the asking and their services are being well used. I've put them in order. I think that we should start at the beginning and work our way through the folder. We can hit the top two tonight because the informants tell us they're operating now. We'll confirm the others for the next two days."

O'Shay looked at the names of the targets.

"These are big operations. Both of these Tongs are major players. This will cause some interesting ripples, anyone not in agreement?" All eyes were riveted on O'Shay, "Okay let's do it.

Blackwell did the briefing.

"Okay, Miller you do the door with the ram, Mitchell, Martin, Wilson and Baker you're the entry team. Cameron and I will pick up the pieces that the entry team leaves behind. Sarge you follow in and direct once we get it controlled. I don't expect any problems except at the door. There are two body guards and they may be armed. Entry team, as you go in, if they give you any problem take em' out and leave em' lay. Get everyone on the floor and we'll regroup and take it from there. Any questions? Okay, get familiar with the layout of the place. There's a drawing on the blackboard."

O'Shay stood up, "Okay guys, we go in twenty minutes. We'll meet at 7th and King in the alleyway. The place is just down the block, so we'll go on foot and move in fast. I'm not going to alert the whole crew or the watch commander. We'll let it be a surprise." O'Shay grinned at his men, then he looked directly at Thad, "Entry team, be especially careful of the body guards at the door. Locate them quickly, assess their threat and take appropriate action, be careful."

No talking car to car on the new radios. Especially if you're talking about the raid, these things are monitored. We don't want the crooks getting an anonymous call about our coming. O'Shay started to walk away then turned.

"Martin, I know they're a pain in the ass, but I want at least two cars with the new radios in them at the raid cite."

"You got it Sarge."

Thad could feel his heart beating in his temples. *No matter how many times we do this the rush is still there.* The entry door to the club cracked like an egg shell when the ram struck it. It crumbled away as the entry team burst through.

All were yelling, "Police, Police."

The guard to the left immediately threw his hands in the air screaming, "Don't shoot, don't shoot!"

The guard to the right came off his stool grabbing at his belt under his coat, Thad was only two feet away, *Christ he's going for a gun.* Thad already had his revolver in his hand and he swung it hard against the side of the guards head. The guard dropped to his knees and Thad kicked him in the chest. The guard fell backwards onto the floor, his gun skittering across the floor and against the wall.

They continued into the room, "On the floor, on the floor."

There was pandemonium as some went to the floor immediately and others looked for a way out. There was none, they were trapped and ultimately went down with the rest. A table had gotten tipped over, there were chips, cards, dice and money scattered everywhere. Men were moaning, crying and some had urinated in their pants. Thad looked around delighted, *this has to be the biggest raid we've done. There must be ninety guys in here.*

At the back of the hall other members of the entry team were herding naked and half dressed men and women through the doors from the back rooms. *They look ridiculous with their hands up and no clothes on.* Thad could not help but chuckle to himself.

It was clear that this would be the only raid they would do tonight. It had taken nearly two hours to identify the people who had been arrested. O'Shay seemed to be everywhere.

"Okay we're going to be selective about who goes to jail. Good ID and they'll be identified in the report for the prosecutor to deal with. No ID and they get booked."

It was amazing how many people suddenly had ID on them and were more than willing to tell the police who they were, no one wanted to go to jail although for a variety of reasons several did. O'Shay's voice boomed across the room, "Thad you and Martin do the count."

Officers had been scooping up fistfuls of cash and a box full of cash and checks were found on a back table. Thad separated the checks and began to add them up. *Oh shit I know these people. They work in the mayors office.*

"Hey Bob."

O'Shay sauntered over, "Whatcha got Thad."

"Look at these checks Bob, recognize the names?"

"Sure do, I was just lookin at the faces that go with em. One of them, that one," O'Shay pointed to one of the checks, "told me that we were in big trouble."

"Are we Bob?"

"Don't know Thad, but this raid is going to cause quite a stir. It's gong to be interesting as to what the county prosecutor does with this one."

O'Shay gave Thad a wink and walked away.

Captain Bagley and a lieutenant came through the door.

"O'Shay, what the hell is going on here? I heard you call for a wagon for multiple arrests, what the fuck do you think you're doing?"

"My job captain, just my job."

"God damn it O'Shay you were told quite clearly to back off."

"I don't recall that as being an order captain. In fact you said you wouldn't give me an order like that. I did back off, we're only doing one raid tonight."

Captain Bagley's face turned beet red. Thad could not believe how red it got, *damn, he's so puffed up it looks like he'll explode.*

"Ummph," it just kind of emitted from Bagley's throat and face.

"O'Shay, you son of a bitch, you're going to hear about this."

Captain Bagley spun around and barged out the door, the lieutenant scurrying along behind him.

O'Shay watched him leave and muttered to himself, "Fuck you captain."

The next morning it hit the papers. Banner headlines screamed; "PUBLIC OFFICIALS, PROMINENT BUSINESS MEN ARRESTED IN GAMBLING AND PROSTITUTION RAID."

Thad began to stir. He was all warm and cozy snuggled under the down comforter; he smelled coffee. *Mom must have put a fresh pot on. No she should be gone to her club meeting this morning.* He crawled out of bed and noticed that his clothes that he normally threw over a chair were neatly folded on the chair. He looked at the clock, *man it's almost one o'clock. I should have been up hours ago.* Thad caught a movement at the bedroom door out of the corner of his eye and turned to find Cindy, dressed for work, in the doorway with a sly grin on her face looking him up and down.

"Cindy what are you doing here?"

"Well right now I'm admiring the man I'm about to marry, not bad. Take a shower and humanize yourself. I have food and coffee waiting for you. Oh yes, the paper is full of your escapade last night. There's going to be fallout over that one, you guys scooped up a lot of big names."

Cindy turned and started down the hall.

"Cindy, what are you doing here?"

Cindy stopped, and looked back at him with a grin on her face.

"Well…I knew that everyone would be gone this morning and thought you might want to practice for our honeymoon. Just couldn't bear to wake you though."

Her smile got wider and she turned and walked down the hall emphasizing the swing in her hips. During breakfast Thad told her about the raid and the humorous things that had happened when the door came down. She especially enjoyed the half dressed men and women standing with their hands up.

"Will there be any problems for you guys over this one?"

"Don't know, O'Shay got into it with the captain at the scene. Bagley was pretty hot when he left. I guess we'll find out when I get to work."

Cindy looked at her watch.

"Thad, I have to be at work in thirty minutes I have to get out of here." She jumped up from the table and gave Thad a kiss.

"Maybe I should have gotten you up. Shoot, if I had I would have never gotten to work." Cindy grabbed her coat and ran out the front door.

Thad watched Cindy drive off and then called O'Shay.

"Haven't heard a thing Thad, I expect if there is any fireworks over it we won't hear anything for a couple of days. Come in a little early for work in case there is damage control to do."

That'll work out just fine; I can have dinner with Cindy on her lunch break and then go into the station.

"You there Thad?"

"Ya, that'll work out fine Bob, I'll see you there."

"All's quiet on the western front Thad."

O'Shay was sitting at his desk sipping a cup of coffee.

"No memos, phone calls or get your butt up to my office orders, nice and quiet."

Thad grabbed a cup and began to fill it.

"Are we doing another one tonight Bob?"

"Nope, Martin and Blackwell are going to do some recon tonight and see if the other games are going. We might set one up for tomorrow night."

O'Shay leaned back in his chair. He had a silly grin on his face.

Thad sipped his coffee, *he's up to something I know that look.*

"What's going on Bob? You know something I don't and you're busting to tell me. Are you gonna make me guess?"

"Sergeants exam results came out this afternoon."

O'Shay waved the list just out of Thad's reach.

Thad popped out of his chair.

"How'd I do Bob? Come on let me see the list."

O'Shay handed him the list, "You finished number one Thad, but that was really no surprise to anyone."

Thad sat back down in his chair and read the entire list.

"Wow Bob, number one on the list. I could make sergeant any time. Am I ready?"

"You'll do fine Thad, your more than ready. In fact the rumor mill has it that you could get tapped for the new dry squad. The county already has one and the legislature has already passed a no booze law. Congress will pass one just like it within the year. It looks like prohibition is here Thad. If they offer it to you take it, you'll be good there."

"I don't know if I want to leave the squad Bob."

"Not enough room for two sergeants here Thad. I have this feeling that it won't be too long before they break this squad up and scatter it to the winds. We don't play their game and they know it."

O'Shay took a long sip of coffee, "It's a fact of life Thad, and I've seen it before. You make note of who's involved in executing and initiating the orders to break us up. They'll most likely be up to their necks in corruption. Identify those folks and then watch your back."

The squad assembled in the day room for roll call, got their assignments with the rest of third watch. They left the building and reassembled in the back room of the Greek restaurant owned by officer Demotopolis's father.

O'Shay once again held court.

"Blackwell and Martin are already out making contact with one of their informants. There's supposed to be a big game tonight at one of the underground joints. We think it's the one in the alley off of Jackson Street between 6th and Maynard. As soon as they know, we'll hold a briefing and kill some time until the thing gets going good. Stay near your car radios for the next couple of hours. You won't hear a call for you but I'll contact Demo here and ask him to return to the station. That's the signal to get your tails into the station to form up. Any questions?"

"Yeah Sarge," it was Bradley, the newest member of the squad.

"What if Martin and Blackwell come up empty?"

"Guys, if it's a no go, I'll notify Demo to call his Dad. We'll wait for another night to stir the pot."

O'Shay had a wicked grin on his face, "Okay, hit the bricks."

Thad and Buck Jones, Thad's new partner, had handled a minor disturbance at one of the restaurants in Chinatown and a larceny at one of the small stores down on Dearborn Avenue. It was actually very quiet in Chinatown and they kept their ears glued to the radio in the car. The radios were a new addition to the patrol cars and left a lot to be desired. There were dead spots where the radio could not receive or send and when they were working they were scratchy but they were better than nothing. It had been almost three hours since hitting the street when the call came in.

The dispatcher's voice sounded hollow and the transmission was scratchy but it was understandable.

"Chinatown units we're getting a report of shots being fired somewhere around Maynard and Jackson. Car Three-twenty-one, check the area."

Buck grabbed the mike, "Three-twenty-three will head that direction also, any other information?"

"Three-twenty-one in the area, nothing here."

"Three-twenty-one and Three-twenty-three, we're getting another report that they thought the shots came from 7th and King Street."

"Three-twenty-three, we're at 7th and King nothing moving."

"Seattle Police Radio to all Chinatown units. We are receiving a call of an officer involved shooting in the alley off of Jackson between Maynard and Seventh Avenue."

Thad accelerated to the King Street end of the alley and popped out of the car.

Buck gave a quick message, "Three-twenty-three at the south end of the alley and out of the car," and then followed Thad.

Thad was against the outside wall beside the alley, and gave orders in a hushed tone, "Buck, take the other side don't go in yet."

Peeking down the alley it was difficult to see anything. There were no lights, and the garbage cans were stacked everywhere along with cast off junk piled here and there. Nothing moved. There was no sound except the sound of his heart thumping in his ears.

Standing near their car they could hear the radio crackle to life.

"Three-twenty-one at the north end of the alley. Thad hold your position, we're entering."

"All units, sergeant is responding from the station."

There was no response all eyes and ears were concentrated on the alley.

Thad and Buck braced their arms against the interior wall of the alley, revolvers up at the ready, silently cursing the darkness and staring through it to the other end of the alley where the crew of one-twenty-one was making entry to search it. Thad caught the movement of them moving into the alley. *Damn they're exposed in that back light.* They quickly disappeared as they moved to the sides of the alley into the darkness. Thad could hear rustlings from time to time but could not tell exactly where they were.

The flashlight popped on startling both Thad and Buck. It illuminated a dumpster laying on its side.

Miller screamed down the alley, "Oh shit, Thad, get an ambulance. It's Blackwell and Martin. Oh Christ hurry with that ambulance!"

Buck ran to the car and grabbed the mike, trying to keep the panic in his voice under control.

"Three-twenty-three emergency, we have officers down, need ambulances, make em' fast."

"All units stand, by Three-twenty-three, location."

"Tell em' to come in from the Jackson street end of the alley between Maynard and Seventh."

"How…how many do you have down Three-twenty-three."

"Two." Buck dropped the mike and turned away from the car gasping for air the lump in his throat hurt to badly to talk any more.

Thad moved up the alley checking the doorways as he went. *Can't relax the shooters may be looking for more targets.* He felt reassured as he saw the police car slid to a stop and the huge frame of O'Shay get out and start for the alley.

Thad and O'Shay reached the officers about the same time, both froze.

Baker leaned on the wall of the alley with a blank stare, his eyes locked on Martin, laying in a pool of blood his eyes bulging from his face, a bullet hole between his eyes.

Miller sat in the blood of Officer Blackwell, cradling him in his lap, blood soaking into his uniform as he gently rocked back and forth. There was a bullet hole between Blackwell's eyes and the back of his head was blown away.

Miller looked up at Thad, tears streaking his face, his voice cracking with emotion.

"They executed em Thad, the bastards executed em."

Thad felt his knees go weak. Bile rising in his throat. He closed his eyes and thought of First Avenue and Blackwell saving him from the street thug years ago. He strained to fight back the tears and was snapped back to reality by the angry growl of O'Shay's voice.

"The informant. Who was the fucking informant they were supposed to meet him here."

Thad's mind raced, *who did they meet, Blackwell mentioned his name, what was it…Chin.*

"Chin, Bob, it was Lee Chin. He keeps a room at the Maynard hotel."

Thad looked down the alley. Not twenty feet away was the back door to the Maynard hotel. Thad lunged down the alley grabbing the handle on the door, *damn, locked.*

O'Shay rushed past him toward the South end of the alley.

"Grab your partner Thad we need to talk with mister Chin. O'Shay almost ran over Buck coming up the alley.

Thad turned him around as he went by.

"Come-on Buck we got work to do."

The clerk got out of his chair slowly as the three officers approached the front desk of the rundown hotel. He stared at them almost resentful not saying a word.

O'Shay leaned against the counter, "Chin, Lee Chin, what room is he in?"

The clerk got a crooked grin on his face exposing his yellow teeth, "You only cause me trouble. Why should I tell you anything?"

O'Shay reached across the counter grabbing the clerk by the front of his shirt and snatching him off his feet and halfway across the counter.

O'Shay's voice was low and menacing, "Because if you don't tell me right now, I'll split your fucking face like a melon and stuff your balls in the hole where your brains used to be."

The clerk's arrogant look was gone. No more crooked smile and his once piercing eyes were now filled with fear and dread. O'Shay threw the clerk backwards bouncing him off the wall behind the counter.

"312...room 312." He couldn't get the words out fast enough before assuming a fetal position in a corner behind the counter.

O'Shay glared at the clerk, "Be here when I get back if you know what's good for ya'" the clerks eyes grew larger and he just nodded his head.

The three headed for the lift when Thad veered off toward the stairs.

"Bob, give me two minutes the go up. We don't want any surprises when you get there. It could be a trap."

"You got it Thad," O'Shay looked at his watch. "Don't do anything stupid Thad, just secure the hall."

Thad bounded up the stairs. As he took them two at a time he could almost feel the musty dampness of the old hotel. The years of cigars, cigarettes, booze and urine gave the place a unique odor that seemed to permeate everything that entered. Thad checked the second floor as he reached the landing. A hooker was coming out of one of the rooms, but seeing the police officer with his gun drawn, caused her to silently scurry back into the room. She pushed the door open as she entered, banging it against whoever was on the other side. The door slammed shut. As he reached the third floor landing he could hear the lift starting up from the lobby. Thad took up a position so that he could see down the empty hall, revolver pointed, if anyone popped out with a gun they were dead meat. The lift door opened and O'Shay motioned for Thad to follow him and Buck. At room 312 they took up positions on either side of the door. O'Shay stepped partially in front of the door, raised his foot and kicked forward. His heel slammed into the door just above the knob and below the deadbolt lock. The door jamb shattered as the locking pins tore through it. The door swung open at tremendous speed, smashing against the wall on the far side of the frame.

Thad and Buck, guns pointing scanned the room. It was small, dark and smelled bad. The light hanging by a cord over the small table and two chairs was swaying from the force of the door opening. The swaying light cast eerie shadows around the room as it swung to and fro. Thad scanned past the electric hot plate and dishes stacked in the filthy sink. The broken down overstuffed chair had holes in the fabric and what was left of a couch had a blanket thrown over it as if it was a shroud. His side of the room was empty.

"Shit" Buck said it softly and Thad turned to his left to see the body on the bed.

O'Shay walked past them into the room and toward the bed.

"He didn't go easy."

Thad walked over beside O'Shay who turned to Buck, "Bucky me boy go get that piece of shit clerk and bring him up here. I want him to see this before we have a little conversation."

Thad looked down at the bed. Lee Chin was about 5'2" 120 pounds soaking wet. His hands were tied behind his back and his feet were tied together and drawn up to be tied to his wrists. He was on his back, naked, his legs spread wide. The bare wires of an electrical cord were taped to his testicles. There were cigarette burns on his chest and his throat was cut from ear to ear. There was a ten dollar bill stuffed halfway into his mouth.

O'Shay stepped away from the bed shaking his head, "Nope he didn't give up easy. He protected Blackwell and Martin as long as he could. Where the hell's Buck and that clerk."

"I told you to back off O'Shay, I told you, but oh no you had to pull the tiger's tale."

Captain Bagley came striding into the room, Lieutenant Reynolds scurrying along behind.

"Well look what it got you. This is your doing O'Shay. You got two of your officers killed and this man tortured to death. I hope the hell you realize what you've done."

O'Shay spun around and started for the captain whose eyes suddenly filled with the same fear that Thad had seen in the desk clerk. Bagley began back pedaling as O'Shay came at him. Thad grabbed his arm stopping him doing harm to the captain and ultimately himself.

"You don't scare me O'Shay," every one in the room knew that was a lie. Bagley began to bluster again.

"This squad is through. I'm going to scatter it to the winds and you; you're going south where you can stay out of trouble. Now clean up this mess and see me in the morning, I'll have your orders for you." With that Bagley carefully backed out of the room not taking his eyes off of O'Shay and was gone.

O'Shay leaned against the wall, he looked tired.

"I didn't think they would go this far Thad, not killing two of their own. Maybe this is my fault. maybe I..."

"Bull shit Bob." Thad felt his own anger rising, "We all agreed, we knew what the dangers were and we accepted them. There isn't or wasn't anyone in this squad that would have done it any differently. What goes round comes round Bob. We'll get our chance, but we just have to wait."

The resolve in Thad's voice was obvious. There would be a payback.

O'Shay looked up at Thad and smiled.

"You're going to make a great sergeant Thad and I want to be here when you drop that other shoe. Come on, the dicks and the newspapers are going to be all over the place. We have paperwork to do and friends to bury."

"It's done..."

"No, it wasn't too drastic. It needed to be done this way..."

"A message needed to be sent and it gave us the reasons we needed to move the crew don't go soft on me, you know damned well it had to be this way..."

"Don't worry. I'm reassigning the old crew back to Chinatown and Skid Road. We're back in business and your cut will be right on time, as usual."

Captain Bagley hung up the phone leaned back in his chair and lit up a cigar.

***

The wedding cheered everyone up after the funerals for Blackwell and Martin and the sweeping changes that had taken place with the Chinatown squad. O'Shay was sent to the Georgetown Precinct and was working day shift. He would have preferred the action of nights, but in the south end it was about as quiet on the night shift as it was on days. With the new administration, cost cuts were being made. Since all of the police cars now had radios there really wasn't any need for a precinct in West Seattle. The community was not happy about it, but the precinct was closed down and moved to Georgetown in the old town hall. The rest of the squad had been scattered around the city.

The Mitchell wedding turned out to be the event of the summer with any body who was anything vying for an invitation. Chadwick was recognized as one of the leaders in the community and there were a great many folks who wanted to be seen at anything he was involved with. Becky and Cindy had decided to have the wedding in the park down the street from what was now called the Mitchell house on Queen Anne Hill.

O'Shay, who had been the best man, felt uncomfortable in his tuxedo and wished that there was a keg stashed somewhere on the grounds. Maggie and Becky were busy hustling around making sure that everything was perfect and the caterers were doing their job. Cindy was hanging on the arm of Thad and looked radiant in her wedding dress, even the 'coppers' were behaving themselves. Thad looked over at O'Shay and rolled his eyes.

He excused himself and wandered over to where O'Shay was looking out over the city.

"It's changing Bob. Every day it seems that there's something new going on."

O'Shay put his hand on Thad's shoulder.

"Yeah, yesterday it was gambling and hookers, now its booze. It's going to be interesting to see how that all shakes out. Heard anything about a promotion and a new assignment?"

"As a matter of fact, I got called up to his highness the chief's office. Apparently when Cindy and I get back from our honeymoon I'll get my stripes and go to the dry squad. That reminds me where did you come up with the champagne for this gala event?"

"Ha, mister dry squad honcho, wouldn't you like to know. Just because prohibition is in effect doesn't mean they poured it all down the drain. It seems that my bride kept a number of cases when she sold the slipper. I think that this was a good way to get rid of it, don't you think?"

"Think about what O'Shay? I haven't seen any booze that would be illegal."

Both men laughed and watched the sun sinking behind the Olympic Mountains.

"Thad, I think it's time for you to grab that beautiful wife of yours and slip out of here. Have a good trip to California and then get back here and help hold this city together."

O'Shay looked over at Maggie, Becky and Cindy,

"I don't know whose glowing more your mom, Cindy or Maggie but I'll tell you what, I'm takin my bride home and lighting up her life tonight."

Chapter 10

11:00 PM Ludlow Bay. No lights were visible anywhere. Even the stars were covered by a thick overcast. Ludlow Bay came off of the Admiralty Inlet and ran in a southwesterly direction for approximately a mile. It was a quarter of a mile wide at its widest point and it made an abrupt right turn about half way down. Huge cedars and firs, some of it old growth, covered the flats and ridges surrounding the bay. It was very sheltered, extremely dark and bone chilling cold. The lumber mill loomed large and dark on the north shore. Even the buildings and the small hotel were unlit adding to the mystic of this secluded body of water that lent itself to the smuggling of alcohol from Canada just a manageable boat ride across the Straight of Juan De Fuca.

The fog had started to drift in, not thick, but in wisps like ghosts dancing across the water. They carried with them a dampness that seemed to soak into your very soul. Thad pulled the collar of his wool uniform jacket tighter around his neck in a vain attempt to keep the cold dampness out. He had been on the Dry Squad for six months. Most of the time they were raiding the gin mills in Seattle and some of the "shiners" that set up their stills in any isolated wooded area they could find. A few times they had boarded boats in the bay as well as some of the fishing boats that called Ballard their home port. It was now much more profitable to bring in liquor than to haul fish. This was the first time they had gone outside of their jurisdiction and they were staking out Ludlow Bay across the sound on the Olympic Peninsula. This was one of the hottest smuggling spots on the Sound. Thad had attempted to take his squad into the county on several occasions, but it was made quite clear that the County Sheriff controlled what took place in his county and no municipal department was welcome. The sheriff may have had other reasons, but at least part of it was the gun battle between county and city officers during the labor strikes at the coal mines. It had turned out to be a sore point that would not heal.

Ludlow Bay was perfect for the bootleggers who were bringing in illegal alcohol and it was outside of King County. It was a straight shot down from Canada, it was isolated and law enforcement on the Olympic Peninsula was almost non-existent. The few people that lived around the bay were there for the logging and the commercial fishing. The company store and the mill were quite at night. If there were any guests at the hotel they were in bed long before the bootleggers arrived. On nights like this they turned the lights out and locked the doors until the bootleggers had unloaded and left. It was after all, safer that way. The less you saw the longer you lived.

Thad looked around at the rest of the crew packed into two Chris Craft speedboats. The boats themselves were fast. There was no doubt about that, but they were open and cold. He wished that they had brought the departments steam driven boats, they at least had a covered cabin although they were not much for speed. Since the federal agents had been brought into this operation they dictated what equipment would be used and they liked the speed and flash of the Chris's. In his boat there was John Appleby and Frank Hanson, both veterans of the Dry Squad. They had been assigned as soon as the State had passed Prohibition. There had been some animosity when Thad, a brand new sergeant, was put in charge of the unit. The mayor and the chief had gotten a good deal of positive press out of Thad making sergeant so young and being put in charge of the dry squad.

O'Shay had taken him aside and whispered in his ear when Thad was getting tired of all the hoopla.

"Look Thad, you're the chief's and the mayor's golden boy right now. Use it to your advantage. The guys in the squad will ease off once they get to know you."

Of course, as usual, O'Shay was right and the squad worked well as a team.

Two Federal Revenue agents were also on board and Thad did not like either. They always seemed to act like they were better than the locals, as they put it. They made it clear that they were the ones in control and that the "locals" were just there to assist. Thad knew that wasn't true. He and Buck Jones, who was supposed to be in the other boat, had done the work-up on this load of booze that was being smuggled in from Canada. It was Buck's informant who had given him the tip needed to develop the information that a large shipment was coming in tonight. *Buck's been sick for two days with the flu. It's too bad he'll miss all the fun.* When he had requested permission to go beyond the jurisdiction to intercept the shipment, the feds had gotten involved and ultimately took over the case. Thad would have sooner gotten the Coast Guard involved, but the revenue agents had determined that ten officers and two boats would be sufficient to handle the vessel bringing in the liquor.

Thad snuggled himself down deeper into the large collar of his heavy police jacket. Even the extra sweater that he wore could not keep the cold out. *Becky's off tonight and all warm and toasty in our bed.* Both of them working nights had been working out well. They could spend the days together loafing in bed if they wanted or visiting the new house being built near his parent's home. *The house should be completed in another month then we can get out of the rental we're in.*

A thump drifted across the bay bringing him back to matters at hand. It was hard to tell exactly where the sound came from and he started into the darkness searching for movement. There was no breeze at all, the water was like glass and the only movement was the wisps of fog that floated by. The engines of the boats had been shut off and silence was the order of the night. Any sound generated from the boats either mechanical or voice would carry across the water and would possibly alert those who had come to take possession of the shipment. The two boats were anchored on the south side of the bay close to shore where they were hard to see. The drop would be across the bay at a point of land that stuck out into the bay next to the logging complex. Thad fingered the safety on the Thompson sub-machine gun he was carrying. The shipment was late, and it should have been here by now. Somewhere out on the Sound he thought he could hear the muffled exhaust of a boat motor. Bill Weaver, the leader of the Federal crew, tapped his partner on the arm and pointed out toward Admiralty Inlet at what appeared a small light that blinked on and off three times. There was an answer from the point of land on the North side of the bay. Thad's pulse quickened, *how long have they been there? I didn't hear them arrive, they're being as quiet as we are; do they know we are here?*

The engine noise had increased and Thad began to make out the vessel entering the bay its bow slicing through the thickening fog like a large knife. It appeared to be a cargo vessel with no running lights, about 80 feet long and it was headed toward the point of land. This was it, the plan was to move in and intercept the boat before it could make landfall. Agent Weaver looked at detective Appleby and nodded to start the engine on the Chris. As the engine came to life Thad heard a tremendous roar from deeper in the bay. His and the companion boat had started to move toward the cargo ship when it became obvious that they were not alone in the bay. The two fast speedboats came out wide open from a small finger of the bay directly behind them. The two boats were on them before they had time to react.

Thad turned to face the threat, *My God, they knew we were here, they were ready for us, how did they know?*

Almost simultaneously two bright spotlights clicked on and gunfire erupted from the attacking boats. Bullets began tearing into the fragile wooden hulls of the Chris Crafts, tearing them apart. Automatic weapon fire, "Jesus they have Thompson's" were the last words agent Weaver would ever say as he took a round through his forehead that knocked him out of the boat.

The boat Thad was in jerked to the right, as Appleby was hit, causing Thad to loose his balance and fall into the bottom of the boat. He could hear bullets snapping past his head as he fell. He landed on the second ATF agent whose chest was torn apart by multiple bullet wounds. Thad struggled to his feet kicking off the safety on the Thompson, Hanson was gone, Thad's mind was racing; *He must have been knocked overboard.*

There was still fire coming from the attacking boats, but it was now concentrated on the second police boat. Their attackers were now abreast of him as Thad frantically sprayed bullets at them from his sub-machine gun. The attackers seemed surprised that there was anyone alive on the boat and Thad saw several men go down as he fired. Concentrated firepower now turned toward him and Thad knew he was about to die. Dropping the Thompson, Thad threw himself into the icy water of Ludlow Bay just as his boat was torn to pieces and sank.

Diving deep Thad struggled to get his heavy jacket and sweater off so they wouldn't pull him down. As he came back to the surface he saw that the second police boat was gone and the attackers were circling for survivors. Thad heard a splash off to his right. The attackers heard it too and spotlights converged on the lone swimmer in the water. It was Hanson headed for shore as the boats moved in closer. He heard someone give an order and two rounds from a shotgun ended Hanson's life. Thad stayed as still as possible in the icy water. He fought the fear that welled up inside him. His stomach churned and he fought the urge to vomit. His friend had just died a horrible death and he was next. Thad was some 50 yards from the attackers and prayed they would not see him in the darkness. The spotlights played across the water and in doing so silhouetted the attackers' leader in one of the boats.

He was shouting orders to the men, "Make another pass to the south. Biggs, you move along the point. Kill anyone you find, I want no survivors."

Thad could barely believe his eyes, *Drago*, even from here Thad could see the cold gray eyes, and fear griped him. He remembered those eyes from the alley so long ago. They were the gray dead eyes of the man who was trying to stomp him to death. He had to survive, he had to make it to shore, and he had to kill Drago. The boats moved closer, the spot lights dancing across the water. *I have to get to land. Maybe the sound of the engines would muffle my swimming noise.* As quietly as he could Thad began to move toward land, the sound of the boats kept getting louder as he struggled not to break the surface of the water.

"Over there to the left, I think I heard something."

The spot light slashed across the surface of the bay and swept past him. *Oh please God don't let them see me.* Thad tried to stay as still as he could.

The spot lights now were sweeping back and forth,

"There, there's one floating in the water right there."

The roar of the motors and the sound of a sub machine shattered the stillness of the night. Thad could feel the 45 slugs thudding into the water around him. The spots converged on his position, *this is it, Cindy I love you.* Drago's boat was 20 feet away coming at full speed. Thad could see the man on the bow, shotgun poised.

Cindy had bolted upright in bed at 11:00 at night. *She had only been in bed for about 2 hours. Something's wrong, Thad's in trouble I just know it.* She turned on the light and fumbled with the phone. A groggy sounding Bob O'Shay answered the phone.

"Bob, it's Cindy, something has happened to Thad, I think he's in trouble or hurt. Who do I call to find out?

O'Shay was suddenly wide awake,

"How do you know Cindy, have you heard something, where is he?" The questions were rapid fire and he didn't wait for answers.

"Have you called the station and what did they say?"

"Bob stop, I had a dream and there was gun fire and boats and screaming, I just know something has happened to Thad."

There was a pause on the other end of the line.

"Look Cindy, I know that Thad's job scares you, but he's a good cop and can take care of himself. I'll call the station and check, but I am sure that he's just fine. You go back to bed and get some sleep I'll call you as soon as I find out anything."

Cindy settled back down in bed and soon drifted off into a sound, but troubled sleep.

The knocking on the door woke her and Cindy scrambled out of bed grabbing her robe. She glanced at the clock as the knocking continued, *oh it's 9:30, Thad must have lost or forgotten his key.* Opening the door her heart sank when she saw O'Shay and Maggie standing there. Bob looked grim and Maggie had been crying. *Oh my God, Thad.*

Maggie began to sob as Cindy's knees buckled and she fell into the arms of Bob O'Shay, her face ashen and tears flooding from her eyes.

Cindy's voice came in gasps between sobs, "Oh…Bob…is Thad…dead." She choked on the last word and her body began to shake.

O'Shay wrapped his arms around her as Cindy buried her face in his chest.

"We don't know Cindy. Word has it that they were ambushed while trying to stop a liquor smuggling operation on the peninsula. As far as we know right now there weren't any survivors, but that doesn't mean he is dead. There is always hope until they identify him, I'm so sorry Cindy, I'm so sorry."

Bob's voice began to crack as he thought about the young man he had taken under his wing.

"There's a team on the way over there right now. Jefferson County deputies are already there and they aren't saying much. Maggie and I will stay here with you; I left this number with the department."

Cindy had become quiet, "I dreamt about it Bob. I saw it all, the shooting everything. He can't be dead, he just can't be!"

Cindy went on auto response as she started doing what she knew she had to. The call to Thad's parents was tough, but she got through it and it was comforting that they were on their way over to her home. They would all need each other for support if the worst came to pass. By the time Chadwick and Becky arrived Cindy had made coffee for everyone and sat staring at her cup as they all tried to talk about everything except what was tearing them apart. They all started and then stared at each other when at 12:30 the phone rang.

Bob O'Shay jumped up, "It must the department with news."

As he reached for the phone, a cold hard voice stopped him, "No Bob, it's going to be about Thad, I'll answer it."

Cindy was already moving to the phone and picked it up.

"Hello?"

Thad dove deep and felt rather than heard the pellets from the shotgun slam into the water where he had just been. He swam under water toward a wooded point of land that stuck out in the bay. There was heavy brush and trees that came right down to the water. His lungs ached and he could still hear the sound of the boats moving across the water searching for his body. *I need air, I can't go any farther without air, it's either drown or be shot.* At that moment, bottom and eel grass, he was there. Thad blew out his last breath, took one last stroke and thrust his face out of the water gasping for air. *Dear God don't let them be here.* The boats had moved to his left about 20 yards. Voices drifted across the water.

"Any sign of em?" It sounded like Drago

"No, the shotgun should have finished em', the crabs will do the rest"

Thad could hear another boat coming across the bay, motor wide open.

He lay on his back there in the shallows and the reeds, not moving trying to catch his breath without making any noise or rippling the water surface. *I've got to get out of the water, I must find cover.* Thad rolled over and staying low in the shallows moved toward the shoreline. Reaching solid ground Thad crawled into the brush and lay there shivering. The two attack boats had now been joined by a third that had come out from the point where the liquor was being unloaded. The boat came along side the boat with Drago in it. A man in the third boat was angry, "God damn it Drago you weren't supposed to kill them all. There'll be hell to pay."

"Screw you George," Drago was his usual arrogant, righteous self. "I don't like witnesses and as long as I'm running this show we'll do it my way. If you don't have the stomach for this, then get your ass back to Seattle and let me do my job."

The man was adamant, "Bullshit Drago, Harrington is not going to like what took place here tonight. It's going to bring heat down on everyone."

Drago's voice got a sharp tone to it, "Yeah well you certainly haven't said no to the money and you'd be singing a different tune about killing them if they had seen your ugly face."

Thad shifted his position slightly to see who the man was, *that voice is familiar, I've heard it before, but where?* What he saw angered him beyond belief, *George Bagley, Captain George Bagley Seattle Police watch commander. That's how they knew the Dry Squad would be here tonight. I have to survive.*

It seemed forever as Thad lay there in the woods waiting for the hunt to end. The crew in the boats had fished out the bodies that were floating in the bay.

"Weight em' down men, dump em' back in and the crabs will take care of em'. Couple of weeks and nobody will know who they are." Thad thought of the end for his friends and tears welled up in his eyes. The knot in his throat hurt and made it hard to breath. The anger, however, was overwhelming. Someone would pay for this and despite the cold and his wetness, the all-consuming anger seemed to warm his body.

***

The boats were silent and only the rumble of the trucks and cars leaving the area echoed through the otherwise silent woods. The cargo ship had pulled out and was headed back to Canada. Thad moved further into the woods away from the bay, he had to find shelter and dry off or he would die from the cold. He had seen the results of over exposure in seamen who had jumped ship in the days when it was a common practice to shanghai seamen.

Stumbling through the thick underbrush Thad thought that he could see the outline of a small log cabin. There were no lights, but maybe, just maybe he had found his salvation. Thad pulled out his revolver hoping that the salt water had not soaked into the bullets. There was no fire in the stone fireplace so chances were good that no one was asleep inside. Thad tried the latch and to his surprise the door opened.

"Is anyone here, hello."

Thad slipped inside and moved around the door frame and against the wall staying low. The last thing he needed was to be shot by an alarmed resident after escaping the carnage in the bay.

The cabin was small, all one room. It smelled of fireplace smoke and dampness. There was a table, wood stove, bed and a small fireplace. It was cold, but it was dry. Thad fumbled around in the area of the stove and found matches allowing him to light a small oil lamp. There was a fire set in the fireplace; *someone was intending to come back.* Thad lit off the fire and relished the heat that began to seep into his battered body. He got out of his wet clothes and dressed in a pair of work pants and shirt that he found hanging near the bed. Suddenly he realized just how tired he was. He sat down on the bed and placed his revolver under the pillow. He lay back and was sound asleep almost instantly. Thad's dreams were filled with the horror that he had just experienced. Machine gun fire, bodies flaying about, floating corpses and Drago drifted in and out. At the sound of a hammer coming back on a revolver, Thad's eyes flew open and he was wide awake.

"You move mister and I will blow your head off," the voice was cold and menacing.

Thad looked slightly to his right and found he was staring down the barrel of a 45 caliber revolver. Thad stiffened, "I'm not moving, and I'm not a threat to you."

Thad's mind raced, *what are my chances of getting to my gun under the pillow, slim to none came back the silent reply in his head. It's time to talk.*

The barrel of the gun was steady. This man was not afraid and most likely would shoot if challenged.

Thad cleared his throat, "Look, I'm a police officer, we got shot up tonight, I needed a place to hide and dry out."

There was no sound from his captor, then, "How do I know you ain't one o them shiners that slip in and out of here."

Thad allowed his eyes to drift slowly away from the barrel of the gun and up to the face of his captor. He was older maybe late fifties; his eyes were clear and his hand steady. This was not a man to try and con or overpower.

"Look I lost friends last night when the shiners ambushed us in the bay. I need to get in touch with my department and let them know what happened"

The man's voice was softer, "How bad you shot up?"

The question startled Thad, he had not even thought about being hit by the gunfire.

"I…I don't know." Thad turned his head and saw the blood on the pillow.

"I was cold, tired and in shock when I found your cabin. All I wanted to do was lay down, close my eyes and get warm."

The side of Thad's forehead stung and his left arm hurt up near the shoulder. When he looked back the muzzle of the gun was gone.

"Well let's take a look son, bullet wounds can go bad on a man real fast if they ain't taken care of."

The man was walking back to the bed with a box in his hand. A quick check showed that the two wounds were superficial. Two grazes, one on the left side of Thad's head and the other a little deeper, but still a graze on his upper left arm.

The man expertly dressed Thad's wounds, "You were lucky son, what were they using, these are pretty wide gouges."

Thad's mind drifted back to the horror of the night, "Sub machine guns, Thompsons I think. Where did you get your doctoring skills? You a doctor?"

The old man smiled, "Nope, medic during the war to end all wars. Now that's a joke. We'll always be fightin a war somewhere. You fought one last night and God knows we're always fightin with somethin in our selves."

Thad sat up and turned on the edge of the bed putting his feet on the floor. The old man put his hand on Thad's shoulder, "Not to fast son, that bullet put a nasty whack on your head and you might want to take it easy for awhile."

Thad did feel a bit shaky, "Who are you?" Thad looked over at the man now starting to make some coffee.

"Names ain't important son, I don't want to know yours and you don't need to know mine. Life's a lot simpler that way and most of the time a lot safer."

The man put the pot on the old wood stove turned and looked intently at Thad.

"I got to go out for awhile, there ain't no phone here, but you could find one over to the company store across the bay. We get a boat from Seattle once a week. It was here day before yesterday so unless someone comes lookin' for you, you're gonna have to find someway to get up to Port Townsend. They get one every day most of the time."

The old man grabbed a jacket and started for the door.

"You're clothes are dry, I really don't expect to find you here when I get back. I'd like it better that way."

He was starting out the door when he suddenly turned around, his eyes softer than before.

"Son, be careful who you call. They knew you were here. Think about it." With that he was gone.

Thad dressed, the old man's words and thoughts raced through his head. *Who do I call, who can I trust, I need to go down to the bay and see what's there.*

Thad left the cabin and followed a trail back to the bay. The sky had broken clear and when Thad reached the bay it was calm and as flat as a mirror. There was not a hint of the carnage that had taken place the night before. Something did catch his eye at the waters edge about twenty feet to his right. Something was floating in the reeds that hugged the shore. Moving closer he was expecting the worst, but instead realized that it was a police raid jacket floating there. Using a long stick he retrieved the jacket only to discover that it was his. He looked around, but found no sign of the sweater he had slipped out of. From the jacket he recovered his badge and ID. What he needed now was a phone. He had lost his watch and didn't know what time it was, but by the angle of the sun it must be somewhere near noon and Thad suddenly realized that he was hungry.

Thad walked around the edge of the bay toward the little settlement by the lumber mill. As he approached the settlement he could see a pier that jutted out from the saw mill on the point. *That must be where they unloaded the liquor last night.* It was then that he saw the police boat tied to the pier. On the back side of the point he looked down on three Jefferson County police cars. There were four bodies laid out on the grass with blankets over them. A small crowd had gathered to watch what was going on. Thad went down the hill and quietly moved to the back of the crowd. The three Seattle Police uniforms stood out from those of the county sheriffs at the scene. Chief Severyns, Asst. Chief Branson and Capt. Witherspoon were there.

The face of the Chief was pale and grim, "So this one is a federal agent and we can't identify the other two. Did you find any of my people, we had six here?"

The county captain shook his head, "Sorry chief, we made a number of passes and didn't find anyone else."

Thad started to move forward when a fourth police uniform walked through the onlookers from the water side.

"Chief, this looks like it. It doesn't appear that anyone survived."

Captain Bagley, the bastard had the balls to come over for the investigation. Anger welled up in Thad. He wanted to charge through the crowd and put a bullet into that bastard Bagley's head, but common sense stopped him. *Is this all a charade? Is the chief and the command staff all involved? I have to find a phone, but who do I call? I can't reveal myself, not yet or I might never leave this place.*

Slipping away from the crowd of curious people Thad headed for the lumber company store to find a phone. *By now Cindy must have gotten word that something terrible had happened. I have to call her.*

Chapter 11

Her voice seemed calm when she answered the phone, but Thad could hear the tenseness. "Cindy, it's me Thad," he heard Cindy gasp and then break into racking sobs.

"Oh Thad, oh Thad, your alive, are you hurt?"

"Cindy, I'm fine, get control I'm in trouble and I need help. I wanted you to know that I was alive, but don't tell anyone that you have heard from me. I'm going to call Bob and try to figure out what to do next."

Cindy pulled herself together. Everyone in the room was throwing questions at her. She held her hand up and they stopped.

"Thad, what do you need me to do. Do you want me to come and get you, I will do anything."

"Cindy, listen to me. Just stay where you are and if anyone asks if you have heard from me, tell them no. I'm sure that someone from the department will be contacting you. Don't trust them, do you understand? Do not trust them. I have to call Bob, I love you Cindy…"

Cindy cut him off, "Thad wait don't hang up, Bob and Maggie are here and so are mom and dad and I love you too Thad."

With that Cindy turned to O'Shay, tears streaming down her face and held out the phone to him.

"He needs you Bob. He's in some kind of trouble. No one is supposed to know that he called." Cindy scanned the group.

"That means everyone in this room. No one must know that Thad's alive."

Bob O'Shay took the phone, "Thad, what the hell's going on?"

O'Shay listened for a full twenty minutes before making any comment.

"You're sure about Bagley and which Harrington are we talking about? I don't trust the old man and both of the boys are dirt bags. Any one of them could have set this thing up, but my money's on Pauley."

Thad looked around to be sure no one else could hear the conversation, "I'm positive about Bagley. I don't know about the others or who else in department might be involved. As for the Harringtons it could be anyone of them, but most likely Pauley. Bob…Drago was running the show."

The door to the store opened and Thad watched two deputies walk in and go over to the counter.

"Bob I'm not safe here. If they find me, I could be very dead. I'm going to try to get a ride to Port Townsend. There's a boat to Seattle everyday. When I make connections I'll call you so you can pick me up at the dock when I reach Seattle."

"Thad, I'll start making contact with some folks who owe me and don't worry I won't let anyone know about you. Call at my home, either Maggie or I will be there all the time."

"Tell Cindy I love her Bob and that I'll call her when I get somewhere safe."

Thad hung up the phone and turned to find a deputy walking toward him. Panic griped him and his mind told him to run, but his instincts told him to wait.

The deputy stopped and looked quizzically at him, "You okay mister, what happened to your head, you look a little pale."

"Oh it's all that stuff down by the bay. I've never seen a dead man before. It kind of shook me up. As for my head I was chopping wood yesterday and a chunk flew up and hit me."

The deputy broke into a grin, "Well ya seen one stiff you seen em all, we get used to it." With that bit of bravado the deputy looked past Thad, "You done with the phone"

Thad nodded and moved away and made for the door.

"Hey mister," Thad froze, "This yours?"

The deputy held a piece of paper that was laying by the phone. Thad shook his head and slipped out of the door. Deputy Mike Winters looked at the doodling on the paper. He could make out a boat, water, trees, and two names worked into some kind of pattern, Cindy and O'Shay, but no numbers.

***

After making the calls to Cindy and Bob Thad settled back on the Motor Vessel Vermont as it steamed out of the Port Townsend harbor and headed south toward Seattle. The ride up from Ludlow and been pleasant enough. Although it struck him as interesting that although helpful, the people here did not want to know anything about you or give up anything about themselves. Could that be a product of the liquor smuggling that was prevalent on the

Peninsula. He decided that he would have to lock that piece of information away for future use. Thad wedged himself into a corner and closed his eyes. The first stop on the trip would be Edmonds some 90 minutes away. That's where he would meet O'Shay. It made no sense to go into Seattle and having someone recognize him. Plans had to be made and strategies had to be worked out if he was to survive.

Just as he expected, no matter what he had told her, Cindy was waiting on the dock with O'Shay as the boat pulled in. Waiting at the rail he could see the look of chagrin on Bob's face when they made eye contact. *Poor Bob, he suffered the wrath of Cindy trying to talk her out of coming along.* Thad gave O'Shay a reassuring smile.

Cindy jumped in the middle of his chest as he reached the bottom of the gang way. She buried her face in his neck and sobbed.

"It's okay Cindy. I'm fine I'm sorry it scared you"

"Oh Thad I though that I lost you, it was unbearable," Cindy pulled her head back and looked into Thad's eyes. The tears had stopped and there was a flash of anger that now emanated from her eyes.

Uh oh here it comes, it'll be the lecture about the job and how it's not fair to her. Thad would be surprised.

"Who did this Thad?" Cindy brushed her finger tips lovingly over his battered face. "We need to find who was responsible for this terrible thing and make sure they never do it again."

Thad looked past her as she kissed his cheek, the look of surprise must have been obvious as O'Shay had a smirk on his face and he rolled his eyes.

"Come on folks, we need to move out of here before someone recognizes Thad and the wrong people get word that there was a survivor."

O'Shay hustled them away from the dock and into his car.

"Thad I checked out the chief, he's clean. He took it real bad that he lost six of his people in the ambush. He's threatened to contact the governor and call out the militia to combat the problem, he wants vengeance. The US attorney is on board, they are not happy about losing the revenue agents. King County prosecutor wants a task force put together to investigate what happened. You are about to become a very popular and unpopular guy Thad. Oh, by the way, you look like shit son."

Thad pulled Cindy closer. *It's going to go fast and furious once the meetings start. I wonder what changes will happen in my life. Will I be ostracized in the department when they find out that I am going to the prosecutors? I can't let that stop me, these people have to be stopped and Drago needs to disappear forever.*

"Are you sure about Bagley, Thad?" The Chief looked distressed when Thad had told the events that had taken place that night.

"I'm positive chief. I was not more than 30 feet from him when he was arguing with Drago."

Vince Davis, the US Attorney perked up, "That's the place to start. If we snap him up before anyone knows what has happened we very well may be able to move on these people before they have a chance skip out or start covering their tails."

Thad was feeling a little intimidated by all the authority in the room, but some things had to be said.

"Chief I'm more than just a little concerned about involvement of others within the department. If Bagley was involved there must be others that must have known even though they didn't take part in the actual ambush they must have known."

Thad shifted uncomfortably in his chair.

"Once they find out I survived I could be dead meat"

Davis Chimed in, "What if we make this whole thing a joint operation, Federal and Local. Thad could be assigned to the task force. These guys were killing police officers. How much offense could the other officers take at him trying to bust cop killers?"

Chief Severyns looked intently at Thad.

"How do you feel about that Thad?"

Thad looked over at O'Shay who Thad had insisted be there. Bob gave a quick nod.

"Okay Chief, I think that I would enjoy being a part of the investigation."

"Oh you'll be more than part of it Thad. I'm promoting you to Lieutenant you're five on the list and you're going to need some horse power so I'm pulling you up out of order. You'll head up the departments side of this investigation. At this time it will be a temporary assignment, but could be permanent in the future, time will tell. I'll assign a good investigator, Franklin I think. What do you think O'Shay, got anyone else in mind"

O'Shay smiled at Thad, "I think he would be a fine addition."

Thad looked quizzically at the chief and then O'Shay. Chief Severyns smiled, "O'Shay's been onboard from the git-go Thad. Apparently he doesn't like anyone messing with his family. O'Shay will be your point man. He knows people and can smooth the playing field for you and he can open doors that might be closed to you. You pick two others that you think you can trust and we'll be up and running by tomorrow."

"I've got two federal agents on standby." Vince Davis got up and walked to the window, "We don't want to take over the investigation, but we do want the thugs who shot up our guys. This has to be a team effort. No secrets from one another and the resources of all. The Justice Department has office space in the new Hoge Building. We'll turn that over to the task force. How about we all meet there at 7:00 tomorrow morning and work out some strategies. You can't miss the place; it takes up the whole 14th floor"

***

Drago sat with his back up against the wall so that he could take in the whole room. He didn't want any surprises and Harrington and Bagley were late. He relaxed a little when both Bagley and Patrick Harrington strolled in.

"Well gentlemen glad you could make it. Have a drink to a very successful endeavor. We should get top dollar for this shipment, its good stuff."

Drago slid a bottle across the table. Patrick opened the bottle and poured some into a glass and took a sip.

"Well Drago the liquor has a better taste than the one you left in everyone's mouth over the way you handled the delivery. Was it necessary to kill them all?"

Drago got that nasty tone in his voice, "What's the matter Patrick, Captain gutless here been whimpering to you and your brother?"

Bagley's face turned red with anger and his eyes narrowed. *Who the hell does this two-bit thug think he is? I don't have to take this shit.*

"Bullshit Drago, it's your boneheaded move that has put this whole operation in jeopardy. The rumor mill has it that the Chief is meeting with the US Attorney to form a taskforce to solve the murders."

Drago leaned across the table menacingly

"So what 'gutless', they can look at it all they want. There ain't no one to tell tales. No body survived so who can finger us. You two make me sick. I got a sizeable chunk of money coming so cough it up so I can go out and get some air.

Patrick slid a thick envelope across the table.

"Here's your money Drago, count it cause it's the last you'll get. You're a loose cannon and we won't be needing your services any longer."

Drago grabbed the envelope, jammed it inside of his coat then reached across the table and grabbing Patrick by the front of his jacket with his left hand. In his right hand, he held a 9 inch filet knife.

"So this is why your chicken shit brother isn't here in person. Afraid I might slice up his pretty little face. Did he send his stupid brother to get his sliced up for him?"

Patrick's eyes fairly bulged as they locked on the razor sharp shiny blade as it inched closer to his face. Drago had no intention of actually cutting Patrick, at least initially, but now it seemed like a little blood couldn't help but make a point.

"Want to find out how much it hurts to have your mouth enlarged Patrick my boy."

Drago froze when he heard the hammer come back on Bagley's police revolver.

"I think we've have had enough of you Drago. Unless you want to be carried out of here with only half a head, you'll put the knife away now.

"Your 45 will make a great deal of noise in here Bagley. How you gonna explain why you shot a man and in the presence of a witness."

"Trust me Drago, I'll manage."

Drago slid the knife back into its sheath.

"I won't forget this you two, watch your backs." Drago grinned and walked out.

It was Patrick who finally spoke.

"That's got to be the scariest guy I have ever met. I think that maybe he's outlived his usefulness. That taskforce you were telling me about, maybe they would like to know where Drago is? I would expect that you would be close enough to assure that Drago doesn't live to be captured. It would be worth a great deal to both my brother and I."

Bagley leaned forward in his chair, his forearms resting on the table.

"Just how worth it would it be to you Patrick?"

"Let's just say that the number of ten thousand comes to mind when we got the news."

"I'll see that it happens." Bagley left the room heading for the station.

***

"How'd it go Pat?" Pauley got up from the oversized leather chair. He poured Patrick and himself a shot of whiskey.

"Here's to further success little brother. Let's toast to our new office space and the operations that are going to make a great deal of money." He poured the drink down. "Now tell me about our friend Drago."

"It went just fine Pauley. Drago called you chicken shit. He said that you didn't have the guts to go down to see him in person. That true Pauley?"

Pauley leaned across the desk menacingly,

"What do you think Patrick? You think I'm chicken?"

"Don't know Pauley" Patrick stood his ground. *You're not intimidating me this time, you sent me down there.*

"I almost got my throat cut by that bastard Pauley. Bagley saved my butt. That why you sent me down there, so you wouldn't get hurt?"

Pauley exploded around the desk grabbing Patrick by the front of his jacket.

"What are you saying piss ant." It wasn't a question, but rather a statement.

"You've never had the brains to handle any of the stuff we've done. It's always me, I'm the leader and you follow like a goddamned puppy. You're expendable Patrick, better for you to get roughed up than me cause without me you're nothing."

Pauley's eyes were wild, his pupils almost pinpoints. Patrick, for the first time was truly afraid of his brother.

Pauley shoved Patrick backwards propelling him up against the wall.

"You do as your told Patrick and remember that you are not indispensable."

Pauley got that nasty crooked grin that Patrick had seen too many times when Pauley was about ready to hurt people. *I'm indispensable am I, well so are you dear brother. I ordered a man killed this afternoon, it was easy and I could do it again with you. You won't throw me to the wolves, not again.*

Patrick straightened his jacket, "Okay Pauley, you don't have to get nasty with me." I told Bagley to take out Drago before he brings the roof down on all of us including you."

"And what did our friend the crooked cop say?" Pauley turned and poured himself a drink.

"Ten thousand and it's a done deal"

Pauley spun around, "T...t...ten thousand dollars, is he crazy? Who the hell does he think he is for Christ sake? Ten thousand my ass, I'm not paying him that kind of money for a lousy hit."

"It's worth it Pauley. We're not talking about some street punk here, we're talking Drago. He's crazy and dangerous. It won't be easy and he's not happy with his cut. He could do us a lot of damage Pauley."

Pauley took a sip of his drink and turned toward Patrick.

"So could Bagley Pat…so could Bagley. We may just need to take care of our cop friend. He just might have to be the victim of a terrible accident. That would be the end of the line of anyone that could tie us into the shooting in the bay. Yes…a nasty accident would be a fitting end."

The phone startled both of them. Patrick reached for it,

"Who knows this number and that we would be here?"

Bagley shifted from one foot to the other.

"Come on, come on, answer the damned phone."

He recognized the voice immediately, "Patrick, they know."

"What are you talking about Bagley? Who and what do they know?" Patrick was not comfortable with the panic in Bagley's voice.

"The department, the feds. all of em' know about Ludlow. They know that Drago was involved in the shooting at Ludlow. They've set up a task force and they are going after Drago.

Pauley saw Patrick pale, "Who is that Patrick?"

Patrick held up his hand to quiet Pauley.

"What about us? What about you? Do they know everything?"

Bagley looked quickly around to be sure he was alone.

"I don't believe they know about us or they would have sucked me up at the station. My source said that they just discussed Drago and finding him."

Patrick was holding the phone so hard his knuckles were turning white

"Take him out Bagley, take him out now."

Bagley couldn't help, but smirk, *I've got em now, and they're squirming big time.*

"No problem Patrick, but you can tell your brother that the price just went up to fifteen thousand. No agreement, no hit. Tell him."

Patrick put his hand over the mouthpiece as he turned to Pauley.

"Some how the cops know about Drago and the shooting, someone must have survived. They're out looking for Drago and if they find him it's all over."

"Shit, tell him to kill him before they find him."

"I did Pauley. He said he will. He said he wants fifteen thousand or no hit. He's robbing us Pauley."

Pauley's crooked grin spread across his face.

"Tell him no problem Patrick. Tell him no problem and to come here as soon as it's done. Yeah, have him come here for payment."

"Okay Bagley, Pauley agrees to the fifteen. When you get it done, come to the office and we'll have your money."

Bagley laughed out loud.

"Fuck you Patrick. Fuck you and your brother. When it's done I'll call and you can deliver my money. Don't screw with me Patrick. I can do you a lot faster and better then you can do me. I'll call when it's over." Bagley hung up the phone.

Pauley was staring at Patrick, "What did he say. Is he coming here?"

"No Pauley, he isn't. We have to meet him after he gets it done. It would seem that our friend Bagley doesn't trust us. I can't understand why, can you?"

Bagley picked up the receiver. He had a very important phone call to make. *Things are working out well, it should all come together very well, fifteen thousand and the other coppers will do my job for me, very nice.* He started dialing.

The meeting had gone well. Everyone was enthusiastic about the project and eager to start the ball rolling. By dinner time, a strategy had been formulated and all agreed that they should start with Bagley. It was agreed that Thad should not be involved in Bagley's arrest just in case something went wrong no one would be able to say that he over reacted.

Thad got up and stretched.

"What say we all go down to the waterfront for some fish?"

As they started for the door the phone rang. Agent Williams answered.

"Yeah it is." There was a long pause while he listened. "Who is this? Don't hang up." Williams looked over at Thad.

"Drago is staying at the Seattle Hotel room 214. The guy wouldn't give his name and hung-up."

Thad took charge, "We're moving on this one, he won't stay in one place long."

Captain Bagley hung up the phone. A sly smile eased across his face, he felt pretty good about himself. *There, the brand new taskforce knew about Drago and exactly where he is. All I have to do is wait until they try to take him, he'll fight and they can kill him for me. Or, they'll flush him out and he'll make for the waterfront where I'll kill him and everyone will think I'm the hero of the day. Either way I win and collect some cash from those scum Harrington brothers.* Bagley stepped out of the phone booth on First Avenue and eased up to the corner where he could watch the hotel. *From this distance, in the dark with my uniform on they will never see me. They're going to be too busy to look around for anyone. All they want is to get in there and get Drago. This couldn't be any better even if I had planned it myself.*

The Seattle was one of the better hotels in town until recently. When built it was the place to stay for business men and affluent visitors. It was close to downtown and the offices of the commercial center moguls. Time had not been good to the Seattle. Its ornate façade and gothic lines had gone out of style and the business center had moved uptown away from the docks and skid road. The Seattle, once the center of commerce, was now perched at Occidental and Yesler streets just across the red line from the Tenderloin. Cheap rooms and hookers were the order of the day and young boys ran numbers between the hotel and the Britannia Tavern across the street. Its location was good for Thad and the new task force, however. It was only three blocks from the Hoge Building.

It was already dark when they left their office and headed for the hotel. A hasty plan had been thrown together. Thad and one of the federal agents would take the front lobby. The detective and one police officer would take the back to assure that Drago did not slip out that way. A police officer, Bob O'Shay, the other detective and an agent would go to the room. They were all in plain clothes and all were concerned with what any uniformed officers might think and do if gunfire broke out, but there simply was not time to notify the watch commander. Bagley watched as they entered the front door, O'Shay was the first up the stairs. *So Bob O'Shay has a piece of the action on this one, There goes Mitchell, the others I don't recognize, might be 'Feds', there must be others gong in the back. Wait, Mitchell, he's on the dry squad. He had to be at Ludlow. Christ he survived, they do know what happened there. Do they know about me? Don't panic, don't panic, they would have arrested me already if they knew. Some how they know about Drago, but they don't know about me.*

Thad controlled the desk clerk to assure that he didn't call up stairs to Drago and warn him. Thad also checked to make sure that Drago had picked up his key and went up to his room. Finding that he had, he gave thumbs up to the arrest team who started up the stairs. On the second floor, they started toward the room. As they came abreast of the lift, the doors opened. A prostitute with her hand down the pants of a grinning business man in a three piece suit saw the men in the hall with their guns out. Before they could stop her, she let out a scream that was immediately muffled by O'Shay's huge hand. However, the damage had been done. The door to room 214 came open a crack and then slammed shut. The men rushed the door. As they came up to it there was gunfire inside and bullets came crashing through the door narrowly missing the agent. O'Shay kicked the flimsy door open and all four fired into the room. O'Shay emptied his 45 revolver. *Screw taking this asshole alive, he's just too dangerous.* As O'Shay reloaded the others made entry ready to shoot anything that moved. Drago was not there. The window was open, the wind blowing the curtains.

The agent yelled, "The fire escape, he's gone down the fire escape."

It didn't take long, Bagley heard the gun shots echo out into the street and almost immediately he saw a figure pop out the window, clamor down the fire escape and drop to the ground. *Shit they missed him. Its okay, come to papa Drago I have a present for you.* Bagley drew his pistol and watched intently to see which way Drago would go. He was startled to see the man burst out of the front door of the Hotel and run in Drago's direction. *Damn he's between Drago and me. Drago has to go south.* Just as he predicted Drago ran straight south into the Tenderloin with the other man after him. Two shots rang out from the fire escape and men began to scamper down. *Drago will still go to water, one maybe two blocks down, but he'll head for the water front and I'll be there waiting.*

In the lobby they heard the gunfire, "Shit we have a firefight," the agent with Thad started for the stairs.

Thad grabbed his arm, "Hold your position we don't know where Drago is."

They heard someone yelling about the fire escape. Thad turned toward the front door, "Watch the lift and the stairs and don't take any chances."

Thad crashed out of the front door of the Seattle Hotel and turned to his left around the South side of the building. As he rounded the corner he saw Drago hit the ground running south. Men were clambering out onto the fire escape.

Someone on the second floor fired two shots at Drago who was now running south from Yesler Street into the Tenderloin, both missed. Drago continued to run south on Occidental Street with Thad in close pursuit.

O'Shay had finished reloading his revolver as a Fed and a Detective started out the window yelling "He's getting away."

On the fire escape landing both men took aim at the now running suspect.

O'Shay slipped past them as they fired. He saw Thad run across the street in pursuit of Drago. "Don't shoot, Thad's in your line of fire."

O'Shay scrambled down the two floors, dropped to the ground and began running after Thad and Drago. *Damn, they have a block and a half on me. Feet don't fail me now.*

Captain Bagley headed south on First at a trot, he had to stay between the water and Drago. At Main Street Drago fired one shot at his pursuer cut to his right down Main and then darted to his left down a dark alley. Thad swerved to his right as Drago fired a wild shot at him before ducking into the alley. Thad stopped short of the entrance of the alley. *I'll be back lighted when I enter. It will make a good target for Drago, but I have to go.*

O'Shay started to run he could barely see them in the darkness, but enough to see that two blocks ahead they turned right toward the water front. As O'Shay came to the end of the first block he turned toward the water. *Maybe I can cut him off if he tries to double back.* Midway down the block he heard the gunfire. *God no, they've faced off in a firefight and Drago has the advantage.*

Thad had entered the alley quickly staying as low as possible and using an alcove as cover. The alley was pitch black and Thad had to let his eyes adjust before he could move. *I can't let Drago get away.* Thad moved down the side of the building. He was sure that the beating of his heart could be heard all the way down the alley. His eyes were riveted into the darkness anticipating the movement of Drago. He envisioned those cold gray eyes seeking him out, waiting and looking for the opportunity to terminate his pursuer. Thad was aware of the sweat running down his back, soaking through his shirt. He was conscious of his sweaty hand wrapped around grip of his 45 Colt revolver, his indexed finger along the trigger guard and its muzzle pointed steadily down the alley into the darkness. He tried to relax his forearm to avoid cramping caused by the weight of the weapon.

Thad's breath caught, he heard the movement before he saw it, faint, barely discernable. Again, there it was his finger curled onto the trigger pad pressing ever so slightly. The attack would come quickly and deadly, he had to be ready, *no panic, stay loose and be smooth.* He moved further down the alley. Garbage was strewn everywhere. There was a sickly sweet smell of rotting things, he didn't want to think about what he was walking through, *stay focused, the only thing that matters is Drago.*

The empty tin clanked out from behind the garbage pile followed closely by a large gray wharf rat. Thad tried not to look at it or several others scurried past him snarling menacingly at being disturbed by the men who had crept into their territory. No matter how much he loathed the filthy things, he could not allow them to distract him from the danger in the darkness ahead. The last rat darted toward him snarling as it came. That instinctively kicked it sending it sailing across the alley squealing loudly in pain. He almost missed the movement just forty feet away. Thad threw himself to his right as the flare and report of the small caliber pistol shattered the darkness. He felt the sting on the left side of his face as the bullet missed its main target, but caught his left cheekbone. The roar of his 45 resounded down the alley drowning out the second report of the smaller weapon. Thad heard the bullet snap past his head. Thad's first shot went wild into the darkness, but the flash from Drago's second shot gave a telltale location. Just prior to hitting the pile of rotting garbage, Thad fired two more times. As he landed on the pile he heard Drago cry out in pain. Thad landed hard, unable to break his fall, the wind was knocked out of him. He sucked air hard. The smell of the garbage filled his nostrils and mouth making his stomach churn. *Maintain control, Drago, where's Drago.* Thad came up on one knee leaning against the wall. *A footfall, Drago's running, is he attacking or fleeing.* Thad brought up the muzzle of the 45 to bear down the alley. Rising up he could see into the darkness, *away, Drago's running away.* Thad rose up as Drago fired again, wildly; the bullet struck the alley wall and ricocheted away harmlessly. Thad aimed purposefully and squeezed off a shot. Drago, silhouetted against the light at the alley opening was, but a shadow. He jerked to the right and cried out in pain as he exited the alley turning right he disappeared. Thad was up and running, now becoming aware of the pain in his left cheek and realizing that Drago may still pose a threat. *What if Drago's waiting for me to run up*, the report of the pistol caused Thad to dive to the left against the wall, but he saw no flash, *who fired?* Thad took cover in a recessed doorway waiting for his target to reappear. It seemed like an eternity and Thad started to inch his way toward the mouth of the alley feeling vulnerable. At the alley entrance he peeked around the corner. The dim streetlights partially illuminated the sidewalk area, Drago was gone. *Wait, there up the street a body laying in the gutter*, Thad peeked again then stared at the form laying there. *It's not Drago, it's a police officer*. Thad broke into a cold clammy sweat.

As O'Shay ran he could here the pop, pop, of Drago's smaller weapon and then the thunder of Thad's 45 as he returned fire. *It sounds like the kid is holding his own, for now at least.* O'Shay was sucking air as he reached First Avenue and stopped before turning the corner. He peeked around the corner just to be sure that Drago was not there. He was now sure that two blocks farther down the street Thad was in a fight for his life.

O'Shay started moving down the block staying in the shadows. He heard another pop that was answered twice by the booming report of the 45. *By the sounds of the gun fire, they're in the next block, maybe at the other end of that. Hang on kid I'm comin.* O'Shay broke into a run when he caught a movement at the end of the next block. *Damn shadows. Was that someone moving at the other end of the next block? Could it be Drago? No, it was going the wrong way, it was moving toward the fire fight.*

Captain Bagley followed the sound of gunfire staying in the shadows. *They're in the alley in this block and moving south.* He reached the corner and moved toward the alley entrance. *Come on Drago, I have a surprise for you.* The sound of the 45 was almost deafening, he heard someone yell and Drago came limping out of the alley. Bagley moved to the street and leveled his revolver. "Drago over here," he wanted to see Drago's face when he dropped the hammer on him.

"You bastard," Drago recognized Bagley immediately and understood only now what had taken place.

It happened so fast that Bagley did not have time to react. Drago fired from the hip hitting Bagley right between his bushy eyebrows. The bullet punched a nice neat hole and then scrambling his brain as it tumbled around inside his skull. Bagley dropped to the gutter like a sack of grain. Drago, staying in the shadows, his leg bleeding badly ran across First Avenue toward the waterfront.

O'Shay crossed onto the next block, he heard the 45 roar again, followed shortly by a pop. *I've got to get closer to the next intersection. Drago could come running around the corner and I can't see in the darkness. Wait, was that someone moving toward the water? I thought I saw something, maybe not, need to be closer.* O'Shay picked up his pace again and stopped at the corner. He had not seen anyone exit the street. He peeked around the corner and saw someone with a gun in his hand standing over a body laying in the gutter. O'Shay leveled his revolver. "Police, don't move," *please God don't let it be Thad laying there.*

"It's me Bob" Thad turned toward O'Shay.

"Did you see Drago run across the street?" *Damn that was someone I saw in the darkness.* O'Shay spun around and looked toward the waterfront, but no one was insight. Drago had slipped away again. *It would take an army to find him amongst the freight and warehouses on the piers.*

O'Shay turned back toward Thad, "Who's that on…"

"It's Bagley Bob," Thad sounded perplexed, "What the hell is he doing here?"

"No good most likely." O'Shay moved up and took a closer look at the body of a man he once trusted.

"Who shot him Thad?"

"I don't know Bob, my last shot was at a shape going out and away from the alley." Thad's hand holding the 45 began to tremble.

O'Shay put his hand on Thad's shoulder.

"Don't worry about it son, it'll be okay, put your gun away."

Thad shakily holstered the gun, "Never killed a man before Bob, not like this, will it really be okay?"

The whole world began to arrive. It seemed that people were coming out of the wood work to see the body in the street. Uniforms appeared out of no where, beat cops and motor officers came rolling in to the shooting. O'Shay made sure the area was cordoned off so the crime scene could be investigated. A team of detectives from the homicide unit showed up to take over the investigation and as requested. Thad turned his 45 revolver over to them. The Feds were going to go back to the office and button it up for the night. They looked at the Captain laying dead in the street and then back at Thad.

"See you in the morning?" Thad just nodded his head. *If I still have a job you'll see me in the morning.*

Come on Thad. O'Shay patted him on the back, "Let's get up to the station, we have some paper to write. Try not to worry, it'll get sorted out. Bagley was a dirt bag, a crooked cop and he got just what he deserved."

Thad turned and looked back at the now covered body of Bagley, "Yeah, but I may have shot a cop Bob. How is that going to play to the rest of the department? We needed him and the information that he had."

O'Shay put his arm around Thad's shoulders, "Okay so had some info we needed. We still have Drago. We need to find Drago. He has the same info and most likely more. He is the only one who can tie in the Harringtons. We'll find him. There are twenty officers down on the docks now looking for Drago. There was blood in the alley Thad, you hit em' at least once and he's bleeding. He has to get medical attention. We'll find him."

Chapter 12

The headlines screamed the news in large bold letters: "Police Captain Brutally Murdered by Fleeing Criminal."

The article went on to declare that Captain Bagley was a hero of the first order when he joined in the pursuit of the criminal who, when confronted, coldly shot him in the head.

Thad wadded the paper up and threw it into the fire. So that was to be the departments and the city's position when dealing with crooked cops.

"Damn it Cindy, the city should have gone up front with this. Bagley was a crooked cop and he was shot by one of his cohorts in criminal activity."

"It isn't going to do any good getting yourself all worked up when you knew all along that the city would take this position. The mayor doesn't want any waves regarding police corruption during his time in office."

Cindy slid her arms around him and laid her head on his chest, "At least they haven't shut down your unit so you're still free to continue with that investigation."

Thad kissed her on the forehead, "Trust me Cindy the only thing that will keep that going is the 'Feds' being involved. If it wasn't for them who ever's involved in the corruption at the administration level would be trying to cut us off. They have to be getting concerned that we may find them out. Drago is still out there somewhere and I'm sure they don't want him found, at least alive."

The distinguished looking man with the graying hair watched closely as the finishing touches were put on his shoes. "Ah, nice job Jimmy, nothing makes one feel better than newly shined shoes."

"Yes suh, an I takes good care of yours."

He handed Jimmy a healthy tip, "And I do appreciate it Jimmy." Slipping on his top coat and derby he walked confidently out of the cigar store at second and Yesler where Jimmy's shoe shine stand was located in the tobacco shop. At the deli on Yesler he stepped into the phone booth and dialed.

"It's me! You read the morning paper about Bagley? Are we involved in that mess in any way other than it was Bagley who got his brains blown out?"

He looked around to see if anyone was close enough to hear the conversation.

"Good, I'm glad to hear that. That means he may have actually been trying to do his job, which I doubt, or it was a rogue operation."

He listened intently, "I would agree, Bagley always was a little greedier than I cared for. Any idea who ran the operation?"

He watched as a beat officer walked into the deli, smiled and waved at him as he passed the phone booth. He smiled back, "Okay, There's nothing we can do about the unit investigating the deaths of the dry squad members, not with the feds involved. There's no telling though how much this new lieutenant Mitchell knows. If his unit starts to get close to us, he may have to suffer the same problem as those two beat cops in the alley in Chinatown. Am I making my self clear? Keep an eye on him."

He hung up the phone, straightened his derby and stepped out of the booth.

"And how are you today officer?"

The beat officer was standing at the counter talking to the owner of the deli.

"I'm fine sir and yourself."

"Right as rain officer, keep up the good work." He walked out the door, *officer's shoes could use some polish. I might mention that to someone.*

It was not a pleasant time at the office of the Harrington brothers.

"A hero my ass, the dumb son-of-a-bitch got himself killed trying to rip us off for some umpteen thousand dollars."

Pauley was beside himself.

"Now that thug Drago is out there somewhere and is only too aware that we were the ones who set him up. Well don't just sit there brother dear, say something."

Patrick shifted in his chair, "All I can think of is that damned fillet knife inching toward my face and that icy cold look in those dead gray eyes. Pauley, he's one scary man. I don't ever want to look into those eyes again."

Pauley sat down and looked intensely at Patrick, "Pat what do we know at this point?"

"I made some calls this morning early. There was a tip on the location of Drago. I am assuming that Bagley did that and hoped that the cops would kill Drago for him. Drago escaped and a running gun battle took place. I think

Bagley tracked the foot chase to where he confronted Drago coming out of an alley. We have no idea what took place between the two, but Drago was faster than Bagley and shot him dead between the eyes. He then escaped down the waterfront."

Pauley tilted his head back and looked at the ceiling, "Jesus, he has to know it was us and I am sure that we can expect a visit somewhere in the near future."

"There is some good news Pauley. They found blood at the scene that couldn't belong to Bagley."

Pauley looked back to Patrick, "Why not?"

"There was a trail of it going to the waterfront. The cops lost the trial about a block north."

Pauley smiled for the first time, "So Bagley did get a piece of him."

"Nope, there was blood in the alley too. Our old buddy Thad Mitchell was the one chasing Drago. It seems that he got a piece of Drago in the alley and as Drago went out of the alley."

Pauley took a deep breath, "How good is the info Pat?"

"It's very good! The source is in a position to review all of the paperwork and interview people involved. Its good information Pauley, Drago has a couple of holes in him. With any luck he'll die."

"Well for our sake dear brother, let's hope he dies quietly and quickly." Pauley walked over to the humidor, pulled out one of the Cubans and lit it up,

"That would certainly simplify our lives."

Doc Martin took a pull on the whiskey bottle to steady his hands. It was not uncommon for this 65 year old doctor to discreetly tend to those who would rather not have their names or their injuries divulged to the police. These people wanting discreet medical care always paid well and always in cash. He had seen this man before and as before he was frightened of him.

"Well sir, I see we have some wounds to bind." He carefully studied the gouge on the left leg and the through and through wound under Drago's left arm.

"These should clean up real well. That one in your side, under your arm is a nice neat hole. Yep in one side and out the other. I'll need to take a couple of stitches, but you will be fine."

He grinned at Drago bearing his tobacco stained, decay filled teeth and the receding gums that held what was left of them in place. His breath reeked of alcohol and his eyes, bloodshot and watery, were surrounded by puffy pink sagging flesh that had spider veins running through it. The unkempt gray hair added a touch of macabre to his whole appearance.

Drago looked with disdain at this disgusting and pitiful human being. *What the hell am I doing here with piece of crap cleaning my wounds?* But he already knew the answer. This poor excuse for a doctor was the only one he could trust not to call the police as soon as he walked out the door. For the past 40 years this doctor had tended to the criminal element not caring about names or the hows of the injuries he treated. He made a good living at this practice and the alcohol and drugs helped stop the pain of who he was and what he did for a living. The city of Tacoma had provided a perfect place in which to ply his trade. It had always been years behind Seattle and the corrupt government, both county and city, had allowed his business to flourish. Things had slowed down a bit, but there were always those people who, like gray eyes here, were willing to pay the extra money for the anonymity.

Doc Martin reached for the bottle before starting the stitching.

"No more booze Doc, I don't want to look like a crazy quilt when you're done sewin' me up." It was not a request it was, rather, an order.

The doctor hesitated then picked up the bottle.

"Mister, if I don't take a pull on my friend here, you would look like a crazy quilt."

The Doc displayed his teeth again and Drago turned his head away.

"Just get on with it Doc, I don't want to be in any one place for very long."

Doc. Martin to a long pull off the bottle and picked up the needle. He hacked a wet, rattled cough as he started to put the stitches in place.

"Be done here in just a minute."

The doctor surveyed his handy work and pronounced it complete.

"The bandages should stay in place for a couple of days. You can take the stitches out in about a week. Same thing as I told you last time. Keep em' clean and if they get red and swollen come see me."

Drago reached into his pocket, "The same Doc.?"

"Nope this was a little more work. It'll be three this trip."

Drago peeled off three one hundred dollar bills and jammed them in the Doc's. dirty, stained smock pocket. He looked at the wad of bills and thought about Patrick throwing the envelope across the table and telling him that was the last of it. *There will be more you little puke. You and your brother are going to pay dearly for this!*

Drago turned and started for the door, "See ya next time gray eyes." Drago froze and then spun around.

"That could get you killed Doc. don't press your luck."

The doctor was feeling a little more boozy than usual and displayed his teeth one more time.

"And who's gonna sew you up next time gray eyes? You think discreet doctors grow on trees?"

It happened so fast that the last words had barely passed over the doctors puffy lips. The filet knife seemed to come out of nowhere. Doc Martin barely caught the glint off of the blade just before it caught him on the left side of his throat just below his ear and slashed horizontally across his throat to the right side exiting just below his right ear severing muscle, windpipe and carotids. There was no pain, just the sound of air whistling out of the severed wind pipe. He dropped to his knees then slumped to the floor, his life being pumped out by his now racing heart. He died very shortly after Drago had walked out of the room shutting the door.

***

Everyone was present for the staff meeting on the fourteenth floor of the Hoge Building. Thad had called and notified them that he and O'Shay would be just a couple minutes late. Thad had picked O'Shay up and rather than going directly to the meeting they had stopped at the park just a couple of blocks from O'Shay's house.

"Why we stoppin Thad?"

Thad stared for a moment at O'Shay, "I've got this problem Bob. I think we may have a leak in the unit. It dawned on me after the killing of Blackwell and Martin and then…"

"Whoa. Whoa. Whoa." O'Shay held up his hand, "Let's start at the beginning and walk through it."

Thad took a deep breath.

"After the murders of Blackwell and Martin I got to thinking. How did who ever killed them know that they would be in the alley. The only way they could have known is from the snitch, Lee. You triggered it when you said that he didn't give em' up without a fight, or something like that."

"Yeah, I remember that."

"Anyway I started thinking about it later at home and realized that the only people who knew about Lee were you, me and some of the squad. Let's assume that it was Bagley that made the phone call to the office telling us where Drago was."

O'Shay was concentrating on every word, "Okay I think that would be a good assumption."

"Now Bob, the question is how he knew where we were. We had been in the Chiefs office when the thing was set up. We notified the people who were going to be on team right after that meeting and told them not to say anything to anyone."

"Okay I'm still with you."

"So between the time that we notified everyone and then met in the office in the Hoge Building, Bagley finds out where we are and what's going on. It has to be someone in the new squad that fed Bagley the information."

"Jesus Thad, who's the leak."

"We need to find the common denominator, who knew before the murders and who knew about the new unit."

"Thad, there are only four that meet those requirements. You, me, Bob Miller and Buck Jones."

"That's what I came up with too. You and I were together after the set up so that clears us and leaves Miller and Jones."

"So it has to be one of them who tipped Bagley."

"It can only be one of them. Bob Miller didn't know, only Buck knew because he was with me when Blackwell told me where they would be and who they were meeting with. Buck has to be the leak. The greater question is, however, what did the department corruption have to do with the dry squad massacre? Buck called in sick that night."

"First things first Thad, how do we prove that Jones was the leak? Word of mouth could have gotten to someone else who tipped Bagley. We'll need some kind of proof that Jones is the weak link."

"Let's get to the meeting. We'll work out the details later at my house after."

Thad began his briefing.

"Okay, here's where we are. We've lost one of our prime sources of information. There's no doubt in my mind that if we had gotten Bagley alive he would have rolled over on the corruption that led to the deaths at Ludlow Bay. Unfortunately, we'll never know for sure. Here is what we do have however. Drago is still out there somewhere and until we find his cold lifeless body he is still a source of valuable information. The other thing that we know is Harrington. One or all of them are involved in the booze run. The problem is which one or is it all three. What we need now is information. We need to beat the bushes and dig up any information that will help us. Let's take the next three days and start digging. Put some pressure on all of your sources and don't limit yourselves to just the city and the county. Branch out and dig everywhere. Miller, don't you have a brother on the Tacoma PD?"

"Yeah Thad I do. I'll contact him today."

"Good, I'm sure that Drago has to be doing business in more than just this area. Have him check with hospitals and doctors. I got a piece of him in the alley and I may have hit him twice."

Thad took a deep breath and looked around the room.

"We've got a lot of work ahead of us guys and not a great deal of time to fit it into. Anyone got any questions?"

"Yeah, I do" Miller stood up and perched himself on the edge of a table.

"How hard are we going to be able to lean on the Harringtons? The old man has lots of clout in the city and seems to be able to pull some pretty heavy strings when the going gets tough. I dealt with that family before on some rape cases and watched them walk away."

Franklin chimed in, "Lieutenant, old man Harrington has been buying his way out of problems for years. Are we just spinning our wheels here when we go after them?"

Bob Davis the federal supervisor was leaning against the wall.

"He doesn't have pull with the federal government guys. We lost people in that Ludlow deal too and the US Attorney isn't going to back down on filing charges for the murder of those agents. I don't care who the suspects are."

Buck, sitting near the back of the group stood up.

"Thad, are we going to be leaning on the Harrington boys soon?"

"No Buck, at least not right away. We want to be sure that we have sufficient information before we make any moves. We don't want to tip them off or give them anything they can use against us if it comes to a court fight. Everybody, check and double check your information. We want to build a solid wall of probable cause before we move or it could come back to bite us you know where. Anything else… Okay you have Bob's and my numbers if you need anything. We'll meet back here in four days, same time, unless notified otherwise."

As everyone was filing out Buck walked up front.

"Thad…uh…Lieutenant, when we start moving on the Harringtons, I really want to be involved. The younger ones especially are bad actors. We need to take them down and make it stick so anything I can do to assist I would be more than happy to get involved."

"Thanks Buck, I appreciate your eagerness to help. Shake up your informants and get us the information we need and when it comes time you can be guaranteed that you'll be right in the middle of it."

Thad shot a sideways knowing glance at O'Shay as Buck walked out of the door.

"You've got the twinkle in your eye Bob, save it we haven't got him yet.'

***

Thad made a fresh pot of coffee and sat down at the table with O'Shay.

"We probably could have discussed this at the office after everyone left, but I just feel more secure here."

"You've got a really nice place here Thad, great view, nice grounds and by the look of it a gardener. I bet the mayor wonders how the cop next door is able to afford all of this."

Thad smiled, "Got any other digs to make Bob? I feel very fortunate that my parents let me build my house on one corner of their three lots. It's not as grand as theirs, but it's better than the rental we were living in at the bottom of the hill, and oh by the way it doesn't hold a candle to your place up on Federal."

"Yeah Thad, but I do my own lawn."

Thad sat down pulled out a piece of paper and started scribbling on it.

"Bob we have to find some way to get Buck to tip his hand. I think that I've figured a way to do it. Do you have any ideas?"

"I think if we can get a piece of information that the Harringtons would want to know about and slipped it to Buck so that he was the only one to know about an operation we could monitor him and see if he goes to the Harrington Boys."

O'Shay learned back in his chair seemingly pleased with himself.

"Bob I wouldn't want to try and monitor him. He may make us and the show would be over, but what about this? We feed him information on an operation involving the Harrington's and see if they act on it.

"That's good, but how do we feed him the information?"

"I don't know yet, but we have a meeting in four days at the office and hopefully something will come up that will help us."

Thad looked down at his scribbling and it germinated a plan.

Everyone scribbled down notes and the bits and pieces came floating in from each of the squad members. Everyone had a little something, some good some not so good, but at least everyone was contributing, even the 'Feds'.

Finally it got around to Bob Miller. "I've got a bit of news. It seems that one of my informants helped unload a shipment of liquor into a warehouse down in the industrial area south of skid road. I started checking on the owners of the building in hopes of finding out who had rented the location and I found out that it is owned by Lightning Distribution Inc., which I later found out is owned by Peak Construction, which is owned by the Harringtons."

Thad continued to scribble on his doodling pad.

"Can we clearly show that the liquor is under the control of the Harringtons Bob?"

"Not for sure yet Lieutenant, it will take a little time to be sure that there isn't some one else renting the place."

Agent Davis interjected, "We may have enough to get a federal warrant Thad I can check with the US Attorney tomorrow."

"Would you do that for us and let me think about it, I don't want to jump into anything before we're ready and loose it in court due to a technicality. Let's see I don't think we can move on this until next week or so and even then we still may not be able to. Okay anything else? Let's go get some Chinese for dinner. Does that sound good to every one?"

Everyone agreed that Chinese sounded good and headed for the door. Thad ripped off the doodling page from the pad of paper and threw it into the waste basket and they headed out the door. O'Shay was the last one out and started to lock the door.

"Wait a sec Sarge. I forgot my pen in there."

O'Shay looked sideways at him, "It'll keep till the morning."

"Come on Sarge, it's my good pen. It was a present from my Mom."

"Geez, okay Jones go get Mommas pen."

O'Shay unlocked the door and Buck slipped in. O'Shay stepped over to the hinged side of the door where he could look into the room. Buck burst back out through the door.

"Thanks Sarge, I got it. Meet you over at the restaurant."

With that Buck bounded down the stairs.

"Well, did he get it Bob?" Thad leaned against the rail of the stairs.

"Yep, sure did. Went right over to the waste basket and pulled out your doodling."

Thad smiled, "Well aren't we happy with ourselves. Now let's see if it works. It's almost midnight now so I would imagine he'll make his call tomorrow, let's eat, I'm starving."

Pauley picked up the phone on the second ring. "Import Export, can I help you."

"Pauley it's me, Buck," he looked around just to make sure there was no one near the phone booth.

"We need to talk. It's important and it's going to cost you a little more this time."

Pauley rolled his eyes at Patrick sitting across from him.

"How much Bucky and why will it cost us more?"

Buck's voice tightened, "I told you before Pauley, I don't like being called Bucky, the price could go up if you fuck with me."

Pauley smiled, he loved it when he knew he got under someone's skin.

"Okay…Okay Buck…how much this time."

"Four Thousand Pauley, it's worth it."

"Four…Four thousand, who the hell are you trying to con. Do I look stupid to you Buck?"

It was Bucks turn to smile, "If you don't get this information Pauley you'll look stupid and a dumb as well. Meet me at Interlaken and bring the money."

Pauley glared at the wall, "When Buck"

"Now Pauley, I'll be there in 10 minutes." Buck hung up the phone and looked at the doodling on the note book page.

Buck Jones watched as Pauley and Patrick pulled into the Interlaken park area. He had checked the area and was sure that they would be alone. He watched as they entered the park and drove up the narrow lane to the parking area. No one had followed them so for now at least they were safe.

Pauley slammed the car door as he got out looking angry.

"For four thousand this had better be good Buck."

"Let me tell you a little story Pauley."

"I don't need no fuckin' stories Buck."

"You need this one cause it will save your ass Pauley. It seems that our lieutenant has a bad habit."

"You talkin about that ass hole Mitchell?"

"The very same, it seems that when he's talking he has a habit of drawing little pictures and designs on a piece of paper. He works ideas and thoughts into the designs as he talks or listens."

"Big deal Buck, lots of people doodle when they think."

"True, but I recovered the doodles from the meeting last night and they concern you and your little operation."

"Come on Buck give, what's worth four grand."

"The money first and then you get the info."

"Screw you, half now and the other half if it's worth it." Pauley pulled two thousand out of an envelope and handed it to Buck.

"Fair enough, take a look at the paper. See the design at the bottom of the page? Look closely, it says raid the Harrington warehouse night after tomorrow."

Pauley looked at Buck,

"What warehouse is he talking about Buck?"

"I'll take the rest of the money now Pauley."

Pauley handed over the other two thousand.

"What warehouse Buck" Pauley sounded concerned.

"It seems that one of the members of the unit has an informant that unloaded booze into a warehouse south of skid road, familiar with anything like that Pauley?"

Pauley's face turned pale as he looked at Patrick,

"Shit Pat that's everything we have. That shit Mitchell is going to hit it tomorrow night."

Patrick and Pauley started for the car then Patrick stopped.

"Any way you can stall em Buck?"

"I'll try, but I can't promise you anything. We'll all be together tonight and maybe I can lead them in another direction, what can you give up."

"The personal stuff Pat, give em' the personal stuff at the office. We can talk our way out of that by saying it was left over from before prohibition and we were just storing it. We've got, what, two cases of scotch there. Give em that for Christ sake."

"Okay, the scotch it is. I'll tell em I have a snitch who knows where it is and we do your office." Buck walked across the parking lot to his unmarked car and got in feeling good about the money in his pocket.

It had been a nice dinner on the Harringtons. It had been a good day for officer Buck Jones and he was feeling pretty good about himself and the world in general as he started the car.

"Sam 26, Sam 26 do you read radio."

"Sam 26 copy"

"Jones your lieutenant has been trying to reach you. Meet him back at the office ASAP."

"Received radio, Lieutenant Mitchell at the office."

Bob O'Shay was sitting at his desk his feet propped up on the window ledge listening to the radio monitor on top of the file cabinet.

"Well he's on his way Thad, this should be an interesting evening."

Thad took a sip from his coffee,

"It will be Bob, but it's not going to be enjoyable if it works out. He was, after all my partner, I trusted him."

"Think of Blackwell and Martin Thad and you won't feel quite so bad I'm sure. Come on, it's getting dark. Let's meet him downstairs, we can go in my car."

Buck parked his car and walked over to O'Shays.

"What's shaken"

Thad looked into the back seat as Buck got in.

"You said that you wanted to be involved if we were going after the Harringtons. Well we're going to do some surveillance on them this evening."

Buck took a deep breath, "Good, but I have some good information from an informant that's as good as gold. He's very reliable and can place the boys in possession of some booze. Go down to first and take a right. Go uptown to first and Lenora where there's a two story office building. The Harrington boys have an office and small storage area there. My informant says that they have cases of liquor in the storage area."

Thad looked over at O'Shay,

"It's only six thirty, let's go take a look Bob. You say it's first and Lenora Buck?"

Buck was so pleased with himself he could hardly stand it. *This should mean more money from the Harrington money tree.*

"Yeah, First and Lenora."

The building was located mid-block south of Lenora. Bob stopped the car about three quarters of a block away.

Buck was already starting to get out.

"It's dark enough let's go take a look at what we got." Buck led the way down the street.

O'Shay spoke in a hushed whisper, "Remember Blackwell and Martin Thad. I don't think we're dealing with the same folks, but be on your toes."

O'Shay pulled out his pistol as did Thad as they approached the building.

"Looks pretty dark Buck, don't think anyone's home tonight."

"It's just like the snitch said that's the office and there is access through the office and from a loading dock behind. I verified that the Harrington boys have rented the space so the information from the snitch is verified. We should get a warrant, call in the crew and crack this place open. We can at least get them for possession of alcohol, what do you say Thad, let's do it."

"Good job Buck."

Thad and O'Shay scanned the area to be sure that they were all alone.

"Let's go back to the car and formulate a plan before some one spots us and the whole thing goes up on smoke."

Back at the car Buck couldn't stop talking about getting the warrant.

"As soon as we get back to the office I'll write up the affidavit and search warrant while you guys get the squad together. When I find a judge I'll get it signed and meet you all back at the office. I'll do a briefing and we can go get some action, look out Harringtons here we come."

As they drove down Second Avenue Thad listened to Buck rattle on. *He is trying his best to make sure that we're at the wrong location when we need to be.* He looked over at O'Shay and smiled. *Yes this was going to be interesting and afterward there will be some very hard questions for Officer Buck Jones.*

"Hey, where you goin Sarge? You just missed Cherry Street." Buck sounded a bit concerned as they continued past Yesler,

"Where we goin, we're losin time on getting that warrant for the office."

Thad half turned toward the back seat.

"It's okay Buck, we'll get that warrant. This will only take a minute. We want to take a look at something else south of here."

O'Shay turned at Forest and then right on sixth, dumping the lights as he did. He stopped the car a block from the warehouse where they could see the loading doors. The warehouse was a two story building with no second floor just very high ceilings. It covered about half a block in both directions. There were two loading docks on each end and they were very busy.

"Bingo Bob I do believe that there's a party goin on." Four trucks were backed up to the loading docks and four more were standing by for their turn to load up.

Bucks voice had gone up about an octave as reality started to sink in.

"What the hell is going on here?"

Thad turned in the seat and faced Buck, his pistol was aimed precisely between his eyes.

"You son-of-a-bitch, now you know how Blackwell and Martin felt in that alley. You twitch and I'll blow your brains all over the back seat of this car. Give em' the word Bob, take em down." Thad reached inside of Bucks coat and pulled the revolver out of its holster.

Lights were coming on every where, red lights, spotlights, headlights. Marked and unmarked police cars converged on the warehouse as paddy wagons came rumbling down the street to haul off those arrested.

Tears streamed down Bucks face, "How…how…did you know, how did you know?"

Thad put on his best grin as he looked into Bucks eyes, "You told us Buck. You told us and you're going to tell us a whole lot more before this evening is over."

***

"The Feds are out picking up the Harrington boys, as we speak."

Thad sat across the table from Buck Jones. Jones had been taken to the unit office in the Hoge Building directly from the warehouse. The lights were off on the 14th floor except for the back corner where they sat. Buck knew that others were there, but he couldn't see them. He was alone, he was intimidated by his ex-partner now his lieutenant, and he was afraid.

"I…I'm sorry Thad, but…"

Thad cut him off,

"Don't call me Thad! You don't have the right."

Buck felt as though he had been slapped.

"Jesus Tha...lieutenant, it's a lousy liquor violation here and I didn't even steal the liquor."

"How long have you been whoring yourself to the Harringtons, Buck? They pay you a lot of money for screwing your friends?"

"I didn't screw you guys! I just gave them some information that allowed them to have a head start on the squad. How the hell did you figure it out?"

"I don't think the how matters Buck. What matters is that we did. You tip them off about the raid operation at Ludlow?"

Buck's face drained of blood and his breath caught in his throat,

"Lieutenant...shit...I didn't have anything to do with the mess over at Ludlow. I didn't even know that was going down, that was all Bagley. I swear lieutenant I didn't have any part of that mess. Please believe me, cops got killed there, I didn't have any part in that."

Thad wanted to reach out and slap Buck, but he maintained a calm exterior.

"Oh, you draw the line at killing of police officers, is that right Buck?"

"I swear lieutenant I wouldn't do that."

"Really! How much did you get for serving up Blackwell and Martin in the alley."

"AAAAGH" Buck threw himself back in the chair,

"Oh God...oh God." Tears burst from Bucks eyes and his fists pounded on his legs.

"I didn't know, I didn't know they were going to kill them. I thought they were going to do the snitch, I thought Martin and Blackwell would wind up in the alley all by themselves when the snitch didn't show. Oh God I didn't know." Buck put his hands to his face and sobbed.

Thad could almost feel the pain that was racking Bucks body and mind. *You poor bastard, that had to be eating you alive if it's true. Who needed the information, certainly not the Harringtons, we're talking a whole different group here.*

Thad looked into the darkness and in a hushed tone talked to some one else in the darkness. "Get a prosecutor over here it's going to hit the fan big time."

There was shuffling as someone moved away to a phone.

It took the prosecutor 20 minutes to get to the Hoge Building from being sound asleep in his bed. The magic words, "police corruption" had gotten him moving. Thad had gotten Buck settled down and had not asked him any other questions.

The federal supervisor, Jack Davis, got Thad off to the side as O'Shay got Buck some coffee.

"Look Thad, you're not bound by the Amendments to the Constitution like we are so you don't have to advised him of his rights."

"Can you still use the information that we've discovered?"

"Supreme Court in 'Silver Platter' doctrine says that we can, when it's received from the local jurisdiction. You also have a state court prosecutor so he can use the evidence also. What we will need is Buck's cooperation and testimony."

"Buck," Thad put on his most sympathetic voice, "I need to know. I need to know who you told about the meeting in the alley. Were the Harrington boys part of that one?"

Buck had been looking down at the table, then suddenly looked up at Thad, his eyes cold and hard.

"That's your problem Thad…Mr. Idealistic and Mr. Clean! You just can't envision that there may be corruption going on in the department. They could spit in your face and you wouldn't know it. We beat our heads on the wall, everyday. We hang our asses out, everyday. We take physical and verbal abuse every fucking day and they pay us shit. The citizens criticize us for everything we do and the press tells us we aren't doing our jobs and crucifies us at every opportunity. It doesn't make any difference if they're right or wrong, as long as it sells papers. Well where do we get ours Thad, tell me, where do we get ours? I'll tell you…we don't! So what difference does it make if we take a little for us. We're not greedy, just a little for us to off set the low pay and all the crap that goes with this job."

Buck took a deep breath and looked at the ceiling. He looked back at Thad.

"Screw you Lieutenant Thad Mitchell. I don't think you have a need to know. You already think I'm crap anyway. Remember I worked with you, I know how your mind works, and it's not going to make any difference what I tell you. I'll still be crap to you. So you tell me why I should give you shit."

Buck stared at Thad with a nasty grin on his face.

Thad leaned across the table, his voice low and menacing, "We lost five good cops and four Federal agents at Ludlow Buck. They didn't do anything to you, but you sold out to the people who killed them. You fed them information, you took their money and you tried to throw us off the track probably for more money. You sold your soul to other crooked cops so you could benefit from the deaths of two good men who you worked with. Those men trusted you and wanted nothing more than to be your friend, watch your back and make sure that you went home in one piece every night. You gave them up for money. You gave them up for your own well being. The snitch was a hundred times the man you are Buck. He died trying to protect Blackwell and Martin while you pocketed the blood money. Buck you are crap and I'm through with you."

Buck's face was ashen and the grin was gone. Thad stood up and turned away from the table facing the darkness.

"Mr. Prosecutor, he's all yours, have your way with em'."

Thad walked into the darkness of the room.

"Thad wait, I'm sorry, I didn't mean all those things about you, please, Thad…Lieutenant. It was Bagley and Major Wooten. They told me they just wanted the snitch, Lieutenant I swear!"

Thad's voice floated from the darkness.

"Tell it to the prosecutor Buck, he's the man who can help you or hang you."

Buck felt naked and alone. He looked at the man now seated across from him, King County Prosecutor Richard Shilling. He was a bulldog in court and Buck had seen him turn witnesses into mush on the stand.

"Can we make a deal sir? I don't want to go to jail. please, I know we can work something out."

Shilling folded his hands on the table.

"Let me tell you where we are Mr. Jones. On the Ludlow Bay thing, I will charge and convict you of aiding and abetting aggravated first degree murder at least after the fact and quite possibly during the fact. On the Chinatown incident I will charge and convict you for aiding an abetting the aggravated first degree murder of two police officers. Either of these charges will get you at the least a life sentence in this state. Add to that the US Attorney will want to speak with you regarding the deaths of those Federal agents and that could get you life also. It's not a matter of if you'll go to prison…it's a matter of how long you'll be there. We could place you where no one knows who you are or we can place you in a prison with advanced notice of exactly who you are. I am sure you know what happens to police officers who go to prison. It isn't pretty Mr. Jones. Now what would you like to tell me about?"

Thad put on his coat, "Miller, you and Fredrickson stay with em'. Book him when the prosecutor is done. Write it up and leave it on my desk. Take the morning off and I'll see you here tomorrow afternoon. You ready Bob?"

O'Shay walked past him to the door and opened it, "You look tired boss." The comment startled Thad and he looked questioningly at O'Shay who smiled and winked.

"You earned the respect of every man in this room tonight Thad. You earned that bar, you did good son.

Chapter 13

It was almost mid-night when Cindy heard Thad drive in. She always felt that great sense of relief when he got home and she knew that he was safe for another day. She met him, as she always did, with a hug and a kiss. That was the nice thing about working comparable shifts. This morning, however, was different.

"Thad you look awful! What happened?" She wrapped her arms around him and tightly.

Thad returned her hug and kissed her on top of the head.

"Buck Jones."

"Your partner? Is he okay? Did he get hurt?"

"No Cindy, it was worse. I had to arrest him tonight. He's been on the payroll of a group that's been smuggling liquor and I think he's involved in graft within the department. The prosecutor has him right now and a couple of the guys will book him when the prosecutor's done."

Thad slumped down in an overstuffed chair in the living room,

"I'm bone tired honey, I just want to close my eyes and sleep for a week."

Cindy kissed his cheek, "What can I get you? Have you eaten?"

Thad pulled her down onto his lap, "No all I need is you wrapped around me and all your love soaking in. I just need to remember how good life really is. I never want to forget that or lose this wonderful feeling I get just holding you. You bring everything into perspective. How was your day?"

"It was good. Maggie came over and we had a little tea party with Mom until I had to get ready for work. The hospital was quiet tonight, but it usually is during the week unless there's a full moon."

Cindy shifted in his lap and kissed him.

"Are you sure you're not hungry?"

"I'm positive Cindy."

"Well, now might be a good time try and make a baby." Cindy got a smile on her face, Thad stood up picking her up as he did and carried her toward the bedroom, "You got it lady we police officers always try to please."

"It's agreed then." Chadwick signed off on the corporate papers as had Harrington and Hodge. They all shook hands and Harrington poured everyone a scotch.

"This, gentlemen, is good stuff from pre-prohibition, not that cheap crap coming in from Canada."

Chadwick took a sip, *my son was almost killed over that cheap crap from Canada that your boys most likely smuggled in, you pompous ass. This is the last deal I will ever need you for.* He put down the glass and never touched it again.

"Well Chadwick, how does it feel to be in control of the new company?"

"Good Jim. The pooling of our money has given us the base we need to file for the public works project with the county. With the matching funds from the county, we'll have more than enough capital to complete the job and get a great return on our investments."

"Here's to success partners." Harrington was pouring another round. "You've hardly touched you drink Chadwick, anything wrong?"

"No it's fine John, just a tad early in the day for me."

Chadwick got up and picked his coat off of the rack.

"Well, I'll have my attorney file these papers. Jim, if you'll open that corporate account that we discussed, I'll drop by tomorrow and deposit my share in so we can get started. There are also some legal papers that my attorney is drawing up for the county to show that we're financially sound and ready to do business."

John Harrington got up from behind his desk.

"This is just the beginning Chadwick. There are big things coming down the road and we'll be in the perfect spot to get big chunks of the projects.

Harrington stuck out his big hand and Chadwick shook it, *you're right Harrington, but on those we'll be bidding against each other.* He shook Hodge's hand and headed out the door.

Chadwick was feeling on top of the world as he walked into his office in the Pioneer Building.

"Have you seen this mornings Star!" Janet had been his secretary since the day he opened the office.

"Have you seen this Mr. Mitchell?" She was carrying the morning paper as she walked toward him.

"No Janet I haven't had time this morning to read the paper. What's all the fuss?"

Janet held up the paper so Chadwick could read the banner headlines.

"Seattle Police Special Investigations Unit Raids Liquor Warehouse"

Chadwick took the paper and started to read the article.

"That's not the best part Mr. Mitchell, the Harrington boys got arrested by the Government Revenue Agents that have been in town. Does this have anything to do with that shootout over at Ludlow Bay a few weeks back? I'll bet it does, those Harringtons are a bad lot if you ask..."

"Hush Janet, I can't think with you rattling on like that. I'll be in my office. what time is it?"

Janet's eyes were big and round. She wanted to know more about this situation.

"It's a little after noon sir."

"Oh, good, would you ring up my son for me?" Chadwick turned and headed into his office, shutting the door. *Patrick and Pauley got arrested; Thad must have had something to do with all that. I wonder why Harrington didn't mention it. Maybe he didn't know.*

The intercom buzzed,

"Mr. Mitchell, Thad's on the line."

"Thad what's going on with that raid and the arrest of the Harringtons?"

"How did you find out about the arrests Dad?"

"The paper Thad, haven't you read the paper yet? It's all over the front pages. Was that one of your operations?"

"Yes, we raided their warehouse last night. We think that they were connected to the Ludlow thing, but we don't have any hard proof yet. There's a man out there who can tie them in, but we can't find him. If we do the Harringtons will do some serious jail time. I hope this doesn't interfere in your dealings with their father."

"Don't worry about that son. After this project we're working on I won't be doing any more business with him."

"Well watch yourself Dad, I don't trust any of them. I've got to go read the paper and find out if there is anything I need to tend to. I'll call you later."

Thad scanned the article and found what he had hoped would not be there. *Damn someone leaked the arrest of Jones. He could be at risk sitting in a cell in the county jail.*

Thad quickly dialed the phone, "King County Jail, Williams."

"Williams, this is Lieutenant Mitchell Seattle Police. Who's the jail supervisor today?"

"That would be Sergeant Jackson sir. Do you want to talk to him?"

"Yes, please."

"Jackson, what can I do for you lieutenant?"

"I'm checking on the status of a prisoner that was booked in last night by the name of Buck Jones."

"Hang on lieutenant… Yeah, he was booked in at two o'clock this morning and was put into solitary."

"Sergeant, has anyone requested to see him since he was checked in?"

"Well no one till about an hour ago when Sheriff Tennant checked him out."

Thad tried not to panic, *shit what in the world would the sheriff want with my prisoner and where did he take him.*

"Sergeant, when the sheriff checked him out did he put down where he was taking him?"

"No sir, sorry he didn't say, just took him out and left with him."

"Was anyone with him when he did that?"

"Look lieutenant, I'm not sure that I want to get into the middle of this. It's between you and Sheriff Tennant and maybe you should talk to him. All I can tell you is that he showed up with two deputies and they took the Jones guy out."

"I can appreciate that sergeant. I'll give him a call. Thank you."

Thad hung and redialed, "US Treasury Department Abbott, can I help you?"

"Is Davis in yet?"

"Yes Special Agent in Charge Davis is in this morning. May I tell him who's asking?"

"Sorry, this is Lieutenant Mitchell, Seattle Police."

"Just a moment please."

"Thad, what's going on?"

"May need your horsepower Dick, the Sheriff has checked our prize witness out of jail and I'm not sure where he's taken him or what's going on. I'm calling O'Shay and going down to the Sheriffs office."

"Jesus Thad, why would the Sheriff check him out?"

"Dick, there has always been bad blood between the sheriff's office and the city. What ever the reason I'm sure that it's politically motivated. Can you meet us at the sheriff's office? I think we may have to put Buck in federal custody."

"I'll meet you outside on the steps in about 45 minutes. Let's move fast on this Thad. We need this guy's testimony."

Thad hung up and dialed O'Shay and explained the situation,

"Bob I'll swing by and pick you up on the way."

"Thad, what's wrong?"

Thad spun around to see Cindy standing in the doorway with a worried look on her face.

"Its okay honey, just some politics going on and we're going to put a stop to it."

Cindy began fussing in the kitchen.

"It's going to be alright Cindy," Thad slipped his arms around her and held her tight.

"I just worry about you Thad. You get so caught up in these things that you hardly have time for us anymore."

"Well, except for last night…that was very good." Cindy looked up at him, her cheeks pinked.

"You have little devils In your eyes Mrs. Mitchell." Thad kissed her on the neck.

Cindy pressed against him, "How would you like breakfast in bed this morning?"

"I would love it, but O'Shay would be waiting for me for a long time. Can we think about it for desert tonight?"

Cindy bit his ear, "Sure, get my hopes up and then run out on me. Thad Mitchell you're a beast, but I don't have to work today. Come home as early as you can, I'll have a dinner that you won't forget for awhile." Cindy kissed his ear.

"Now Lieutenant Mitchell, go do you your police stuff and don't forget what's waiting for you at home."

Thad picked her off the floor and kissed her, then set her back down.

"That's so you don't forget what's coming home to you."

Thad let her go, grabbed his coat and headed for the door.

"Be careful Thad."

"I will Cindy…love you."

With that Thad hurried out the door. *What the hell is going on downtown?*

Should I notify the chief or wait until I have a handle on it. O'Shay will know what's best.

They stood in the outer office of the Sheriff. The secretary had effectively stopped them from entering the inner office unannounced. "Lieutenant, do you have an appointment to see the sheriff?"

"No I do not, but it's a matter of the greatest urgency."

"Well Lieutenant, there are others ahead of you and the sheriff is in a meeting at the moment. I am sure that he'll be tied up for most of the day. If you would like to have a seat with the others I will try to work you in."

"Okay lady," Agent Davis had had enough. "I know you're just doing your job so let me give you some advice. You get on that intercom and tell Sheriff Tennant that Treasury Agent Davis and two others are out here and demanding to see him now. You can also tell him that if he refuses, I will leave and be back in 10 minutes with a Federal Warrant for his arrest for tampering with a federal witness. Now, get on the intercom and if you refuse I'll be back with a warrant for your arrest as well."

The secretary jumped up and scurried into the inner office. O'Shay looked over at Agent Davis.

"Damn Dick, I think she may have wet her pants." *Thad just smiled, now that's the horsepower that we needed. Let's see if it worked.*

It only took two minutes to find out. The secretary reappeared through the door, her eyes still large and round and her complexion seemed pale.

"The sheriff will see you now."

All three moved quickly through the door. They noticed a side door to the office was just closing as they entered. Sheriff Tennant was seated behind his rather large mahogany desk.

Agent Davis started immediately,

"Sheriff, if that's my prisoner going out the door you had better get him back immediately."

"Agent Davis I don't recall any federal hold on Mr. Jones."

"Well there is now Sheriff and I want him back here now, unless, of course you want to face a Federal Judge and explain all this to him."

Sheriff Tennant got up from behind his desk, "Don't threaten me Davis! I'm the appointed head of law enforcement for this county. This is my jurisdiction and I do as I please."

Davis snatched the phone on the Sheriff's desk, "Fine Tennant, let's see what the US. Attorney and the judge have to say about it." Davis started to dial.

"Okay Davis, you hold the high cards, this time." Sheriff Tennant took the phone and re-dialed.

"Brad, bring the prisoner back up here. Yeah, bring the prosecutor too, we might as well get this out in the open."

"Happy now Davis, who the hell are these two guys" Tennant slammed the phone down.

"Sorry Sheriff didn't have time to introduce them. Davis got an evil grin on his face, "Lieutenant Mitchell and Sergeant O'Shay, Seattle Police."

Sheriff Tennant made no effort to shake their hands, but rather scowled at them.

"I don't see any need for their being here and I am telling them to leave." It was Thad who jumped in this time.

"I don't think so Sheriff. It's my unit that made the arrest and raided the warehouse. This is my prisoner as well as the US. Treasury's."

Sheriff Tennant straightened himself up to stand a little taller, but he still could not come eye to eye with Thad.

"Your department is precisely what this is all about lieutenant and I don't want you near, or any part of this discussion, now leave."

"No can do Sheriff. You can call my Chief if you like, but we're working directly with the United States Attorney on this and we are going to stay."

Sheriff Tennant's face started getting red.

"Who the hell do you think you are…Lieutenant? You can't come in here ordering me around. This isn't Seattle PD and you don't have any authority here. I'm the boss and you do what I tell you to do."

Tennant kept getting closer to Thad who took a step toward the Sheriff. *If this son-of-a-bitch wants a fight he'll get it.*

O'Shay moved quickly, *Thad's going to drop him and that'll only mean trouble for him.* He stepped between Thad and the sheriff, just his sheer size startled Tennant who stopped immediately. The sound of O'Shay's voice caused Tennant to take a step back.

"Okay gentleman that's enough, this is not productive. Look Tennant, I remember when you were Chief of Seattle. You were a square shooter and kept the department clean. The Lieutenant here survived Port Ludlow and two of his close friends were killed in Chinatown. He's one of the good guys Sheriff."

"I would agree with that gentleman." Jack Garrett, the County Prosecuting Attorney had come through the side door with two deputies and Buck Jones.

"I think that we all need to sit down and cool off. Lieutenant I'm assuming that you have a problem with us taking your prisoner out of jail."

Thad looked over at the Prosecutor.

"Yes sir I do."

"Well I can understand that Lieutenant." The County Prosecutor turned to the two deputies.

"Officers, please take the prisoner back over to the jail and put him in solitary."

The deputies took Buck by the arms and walked him toward the door. As they passed Thad, Bucks head was bowed as he looked at the floor. Thad almost felt sorry for him. *Jeez he looks terrible, what a waste.*

Buck suddenly raised his head and looked at Thad. His eyes were soft and filled with tears.

"I'm sorry Thad, I really am sorry." The deputies led him out the door and closed it behind them. Everyone was staring at the door. It was the prosecutor who broke the silence.

"Okay gentlemen, shall we move to the conference room and discuss why we are all here and ready to fight? Agent Davis, it's been awhile, how have you been?"

"Good Jack, and you and the family?"

"Couldn't be better." They led the way to the conference room table.

"I am assuming that we are all here for the same reasons." Garrett looked around the table. "Davis, why don't you start it off!"

"Glad to, I'm here because of the Ludlow Bay incident. We lost agents and Seattle lost officers. I'm part of a task force set up to determine who was behind it. With the arrest of Buck Jones, I think we have the link to punish the brains behind the operation. I would differ to the Lieutenant here." Davis looked directly at Sheriff Tennant.

"Who by the way, is the Taskforce Commander. It was his work that led us to Jones…Lieutenant!"

"It's a little complicated, Thad took a deep breath, but it's basically this. We were hitting the gambling joints in Chinatown. Because we were hitting them hard, two of our officers were murdered in an alley where they went to meet with an informant. That was almost two years ago. The crime was never solved and the squad was broken up and transferred all over the place. The reason given was that we were too controversial and heavy handed. Basically, administration decided it was our fault that the two officers had been murdered. We speculated that it was either the Chinese or someone in the department. We never were able to come up with an answer until the Ludlow thing when someone tipped off the bad guys and that got some officers killed. We deduced that Buck Jones was the common denominator in both situations. He was my partner in Chinatown and was assigned to the task force looking into the Ludlow shootings. We fed him information that only he knew and he passed it on to the Harringtons, which culminated in the warehouse raid. I didn't think that the Harrington boys were involved in the Chinatown thing, which meant that it had to be someone on the department. After all that I'm here to protect Jones. We need his testimony regarding the Ludlow operation and for the department corruption. We now have at least two names regarding the murder in Chinatown, but we need Buck to put pressure on the command officers behind it. I was concerned that the Sheriff's department was about to taint our prize witness."

Prosecutor Garrett leaned back in his chair.

"Well I can tell you that the reason we took Jones out of the jail, was to question him regarding the police department. We're all after the same thing. We want to convene a Grand Jury to hear the information and start charging officers with corruption."

Thad glanced over at Sheriff Tennant.

"Mr. Garrett, my concern is that there are hidden agendas, political in nature, which could get in the way and taint the whole thing."

"What makes you think that Lieutenant?"

"Well Sir, I know that Sheriff Tennant was Chief of Seattle until two years ago when the new mayor bounced him and replaced him with Chief Bannick. Vendettas will only complicate what we're trying to do and that's cut out the graft and corruption in the department." Thad looked over to find the Sheriff glaring at him.

Garrett glanced at the clock, "Well it's almost five. Let's call it a day and I'll make this suggestion. We're going to convene the Grand Jury and Davis I think we need one of your people in on the discussions and strategizing. Mitchell we need the same from you. That way everyone is on board and we have no secrets from one another. This should be a group effort. My office will be the contact point so have your representatives' get in touch with my office. I'll keep everyone notified as to when we'll have meetings. Is everyone okay with that?"

Everyone around the table nodded and Thad chimed in,

"We need to keep a lid on this. I don't know who leaked the information to the press, but in doing so they jeopardized the whole thing and put our witness in a bad situation. The enemy has been alerted, so they'll be looking for a way to quiet the witness."

Davis cleared his throat, "I want the witness to be locked in solitary and checked every fifteen minutes."

Thad turned to O'Shay, "Bob will you take care of that before you go home?"

"No problem Lieutenant, I'll take care of it as soon as we leave here. Oh...you don't have to take me home. My bride is picking me up and we're going to dinner downtown."

As they filed out of the office, Sheriff Tennant put his hand on Thad's arm.

"Would you step into my office for a minute?"

"Sure Sheriff. Bob I'll see you tomorrow at the office." O'Shay looked at the Sheriff and nodded his head as he went out of the door.

"What can I do for you Sheriff?"

"Just a word is all, Lieutenant. It appears that we are on the same side, but that doesn't excuse what took place in here today. We will work together, but don't ever challenge me again. Do we understand each other, Lieutenant?"

"No I don't think we do. I am not a yes man and if I think you are wrong I'll tell you so. I will freely express my opinions and expect the same from you. I would expect that we would treat each other with respect and I do not expect that you will ever get in my face again like you did this morning. Now we may...understand each other."

Tennant took a long look at Thad, "Okay Lieutenant you've got a deal. Good luck on charging and convicting the Harringtons. They're a slippery lot and the old man will spend whatever it takes to get them off."

"Thanks for the words of encouragement Sheriff." Thad stuck out his hand and Tennant shook it vigorously.

"Lieutenant I think this is going to work out just fine."

Thad walked out of the office and was surprised to see O'Shay waiting for him.

"Thought you left Bob."

"I did, but I got outside and decided to come back in to be sure that you were okay. Are you?"

"I'm fine Bob, we found mutual ground and everything's going to be alright."

"Look Thad, why don't you get Cindy and have dinner with Maggie and me?"

Thad though for a minute and remembered how Cindy had chewed on his ear before he left.

"No can do Bob, not tonight, Cindy is preparing a very special dinner for me at home and I better get there if I want any of it."

O'Shay started to walk away.

"Well you have a nice dinner tonight, and by the way, you won't see me at the office tomorrow, it's the weekend, see you on Monday.

My God Cindy's right I get so wrapped up in the job that I even forget what day it is. That has to stop. I have to spend more time with Cindy. I wonder what's on the menu tonight.

Thad opened the front door and walked in. The house was dark except for a small fire in the fireplace.

"Cindy?"

There was no response and the house was quiet. Thad quickly surveyed the den, dining room and kitchen. Nothing was cooking and the lights were off.

"Cindy?"

Still there was no response. Thad felt a knot forming in his stomach and fear beginning to creep in. *Something is wrong Cindy should be here. Could those bastards who killed Blackwell and Martin have come to my house?* Thad drew his revolver and quietly moved through the house. *Wait, a noise. A noise from the bedroom, soft, barely audible.* Thad eased up to the bedroom door, barely ajar, he gently pushed it open, afraid of what he might find.

She turned from the window somewhat startled, the light from the full moon shone through the window and silhouetted her from behind causing her sheer gown to disappear. Thad holstered his revolver before stepping into the room.

The front of the gown was open exposing her nakedness.

"You're late for dinner darling. But not to worry I kept it warm for you."

She glided across the room slowly allowing Thad to get a good look at her.

"You're way over dressed for dinner my love. We'll have to do something about that."

Thad stripped off his shoulder holster and dropped it on the floor. Cindy's mouth closed over his as she unbuttoned his shirt. Thad did not remember removing his shoes. *Dinner had never been better.*

He leaned forward in his high-backed leather chair, the phone receiver pinched between his ear and his shoulder as he poured himself a brandy, carefully placing the crystal decanter back on the desk and putting the glass stopper back in it. Leaning back, after taking a sip, he continued his phone conversation.

"How long were they in the Sheriff's office?"

"Who all was in the meeting?"

"Did Jones give them any names?"

"Well, God damn it find out. Get some one on the inside. We need to know how much they know…"

"I agree, if Buck turns around on us, they could start working right up the chain and we would all go down. I think that Mr. Jones needs to meet with an unfortunate accident…"

"I'm glad you agree. Make it happen and call me when it's done. In case I'm contacted I may need to make an appropriate response."

He smiled as he hung up the phone and pulled a Cuban cigar out of the humidor on his desk. He started to strike a match to it. *Damn I need to go out on the veranda. Isn't this a bitch when a man can't even enjoy a cigar in his own house? Oh well, Emily will stay happy, it's a wonderful evening, and everything is under control.* He took a deep pull off of the cigar. It tasted sweet after dipping the end of it into his glass of brandy. *The question is, what will I do with Mitchell and company? We have to neutralize them without being obvious. Loosing their information source will keep them away from our door for the short term, but further action may be necessary.*

Thad lay on his back staring at the ceiling. The window was open and the warm night breeze caressed his bare skin. It had been too warm to pull up the sheet to cover them after their love making. Cindy laid on her side cuddled against him her leg over his. It was nice to feel her nakedness pressed against him. Her breathing was slow and steady as she slept, twice, had been quite enough for both of them tonight. *Maybe tonight will be the night that something happens. Having unrestricted sex is good for a couple of reasons. We can have sex whenever and however we want and hopefully one of these times we'll be pregnant. Oh well, I think we have both resigned ourselves to not having children. Even Mom has stopped asking. God knows it isn't like we haven't been trying for the last 12 years.* Thad moved his arm that had gone to sleep some time ago trying not to wake Cindy. She mumbled something unintelligible and rolled over while pulling up the sheet. Cindy was in a fetal position on her side and Thad pressed himself up against her back pulling his knees up under hers. He slipped his arm over and around her. Cindy snuggled in tighter against him and he listened as her breathing became deep and steady again. He kissed her on her neck, laid his head back and drifted off to peaceful sleep, *how lucky am I.*

Bob O'Shay sat on the porch swing gently rocking, nursing his beer and staring at the stars. It was so quiet you could hear your heart beat. The screen door squeak caused him to turn toward the door as Maggie came out. Damn, *she is one good looking woman.*
"You're awfully quiet out here Bob whatcha' thinking about?"
"Oh I'm a little worried about Thad." Bob took a pull on his beer.
Maggie snuggled up against him on the porch swing.
"Is Thad okay?"
"Oh, I guess so Maggie. He just puts so much of himself into the job that I hope he takes the time to loosen up once in awhile. This job will kill you if you try to do it 24 hours a day. Sometimes you just need to leave it in the locker room. I may have to take him aside and have a little talk. I hope he's taking care of business at home. I wouldn't want him to screw up his marriage because of this job. A lot of 'coppers' have done that. They forget that their other job, the important one, is at home."
Maggie took the beer from O'Shay, took a sip and set it on the floor. She put her hands on either side of his face and turned his head towards her planting a long passionate kiss on him.
"Thinking of taking care of business at home, Mr. O'Shay, have you ever made love on a porch swing?"
Bob grinned at her, "Well Mrs. O'Shay, can't say that I ever have, but I am a quick learner."
It was a warm quiet night; the sound of the silence was broken only by the

buzz of the crickets and an occasional giggle from the back porch swing of the O'Shay home.

***

Every one was seated around the conference table on the 14th floor of the Hoge Building.

"Okay let's see where we are." Thad was standing at the head of the table. "Miller, let's start with you."

"Checked with my brother in Tacoma and they're investigating a homicide of an underground doctor."

Agent Davis chimed in, "A what?"

"An underground doctor, Dick; This guy specialized in treating injured criminals, cash on the line and no questions asked."

"What does that have to do with our situation?"

"It seems that the last customer the doc was known to treat was some guy built like a tank, graying at the temples and witnesses described his eyes as death gray."

"Drago…that has to be Drago!" Thad sat down.

"I think so too, Lieutenant. This homicide took place a day after the alley shooting. I would assume that our friend Drago is alive and well. Oh yes…the homicide. Well he cut the doctors throat from ear to ear, clean, front neck muscles, windpipe, jugulars and carotids everything with one swipe. I bet the doc hardly knew what hit him."

One of the federal agents spoke up, "Shit, we really needed to hear that just before lunch."

His remark was met with soft chuckles from the group.

Thad got up and moved to the window looking out on Elliot Bay.

"Well he's had plenty of time to heal up. If I were him, I would be looking for the guys who set me up. Anyone disagree with that?" There was no response.

"We need to beat the bushes. He's either in or on his way to Seattle. I think that it's pretty clear to even the most casual observer that the Harrington boys set him up using Bagley. If I were them, I'd be glad that I was sitting in a cell instead of on the street."

"That brings up something else Thad." It was the Deputy Prosecuting Attorney assigned to the task force.

"It seems that Daddy bailed them out yesterday afternoon."

Thad spun around to face the table.

"I thought because of the ambush murders they were in with no bail! What the hell happened?"

"You know the Harringtons Thad. Three of daddy's attorneys showed up with a Writ out of Pierce County for their release. Judge had to set a reasonable bail, turned out to be five hundred thousand each. We tried to stay the writ, but failed so they walked."

Thad took a deep breath, "We need some good news. Franklin, how's it going on the Sheriff's group?"

"Not much to report Lieutenant. Buck now has an attorney and has decided he doesn't want to talk to anyone from the Federal side. We can still talk to him, but he isn't saying much. We have the names of the two admin guys that he blurted out that first night and we've turned that over to the county. They're doing backgrounds on them now. Buck's weakness seems to be the murders in the alley. He chokes up, whenever, we bring that up. I think if we are going to get him to crack, it will be on that point. He keeps saying no matter what happens, I'm a dead man. That and every time we talk to him, he always ends the conversation with, 'please tell Thad I'm sorry'. We'll keep working on him lieutenant. Maybe, just maybe, he would spill his guts to you. If I feel its right, I'll bring it up with him."

"Okay, let me know. Anyone got anything else?" The room was quiet, "All right beat the brush. We need to find Drago."

The meeting broke up and Thad went back to his office.

"Thad?" He looked up at O'Shay in the doorway.

"Come on in Bob. You were awfully quiet out there today, you Okay?"

"Other than being worried about you I'm fine."

"Why me Bob?"

"Let's go get a cup Thad. We need to talk about this job."

"Ah, I think I already know what you're going to say. But I think lunch would be better. Let's go down to the waterfront. That sounds peaceful."

"You got it boss." O'Shay jumped up with a grin on his face, "Peaceful is what you and I both need right now. Let's try that new fish place at pier 52."

They sat out on the dock at Ivar's Fish and Clam House. The warm summer sun reflecting off of the small chop on the bay made it look like dancing diamonds. It felt good to feel the breeze off of the water and smell the salt air, not to mention the fish and chips they were digging into.

"Bob, did it ever bother you not to have kids?"

"Oh, a little I think, but Carol and I never had any. She didn't want kids. Maggie and I can't so I guess I just accepted it. I've heard it's not all it's cracked up to be anyway. Course, Maggie has Cindy and she's like her own daughter. I got to experience some of that, why?"

"Cindy and I have been trying for some time now and it just hasn't happened. We've kind of resigned ourselves to the reality that we may not have any kids, but we still keep trying."

O'Shay got a big grin on his face,

"Yeah, but Thad, that's the fun part, don't knock what you enjoy doing. That brings up a point about this job Thad."

"I know, it dawned on me the other day when I didn't know what day it was. I've been working too hard and too many hours. I decided that I need to spend more time in my private life than I do at my job."

"Good, now I don't have to give you a lecture about it."

"Well I started this last weekend. Cindy and I spent most of it in bed, it was great. We're thinking about taking a little trip next weekend."

"That's a great idea Thad, but a whole weekend in bed?" O'Shay got a sly grin on his face, "The whole weekend, trying to make babies?"

"None of your damned business, Sergeant O'Shay"

They both laughed and started walking back to the office.

"Ya know Bob I would sure like to catch Drago alive. I bet he would be fascinating to talk to."

"Oh, I would think so, as long as he was chained to the wall like the animal he is."

***

The trip to Victoria by boat had gone off without a hitch. Thad wanted the skipper to take them off the shipping lane and do a side trip to Ludlow Bay so he could show Cindy where the ambush had taken place. Thad could get no closer than the one hundred yards off the mouth of the bay before he told the skipper of the boat to turn around.

"I just can't do this Cindy. There are too many ghosts in there, it's just too soon."

Cindy wrapped her arms around him as the boat made its turn, "Its okay Thad, I understand. Sometimes we see too many things that we shouldn't and it takes time to deal with them."

Cindy held his hand and they walked the deck. The rest of the trip was a relaxing joy. They had spent the night at the Empress Hotel, had tea and crumpets in the hotel atrium, and just generally relaxed. As they turned into Elliott bay, they were both amazed at how the city was growing.

"It looks so different from here than it does when you're in it." Cindy was hanging onto the rail scanning the shoreline.

"Look, up on the hill, you can see Mom and Dad's house, and you can almost see ours."

Thad scanned the skyline, "The Smith Tower looks so tall from here and see how much lower the hills are since the regrade."

Thad took a hold of the railing on either side of Cindy and she leaned back against him.

"It all looks so peaceful Thad."

"I know Cindy. You would never think that anything bad would ever happen there. We both know it does, and that's why I do what I do."

Cindy spun around and grabbed his face kissing him, "I know Thad and I love you for it."

The boat approached the waterfront and others began to line the rail to get a glimpse of the waterfront from the bay side. Thad could remember the first time he saw the bay with the masts of ships looking like a forest. Since steam power, he seldom saw a sailing vessel in the bay. It seemed kind of sad.

"Oh look Thad there are two policemen on the dock. I wonder what they're doing."

"I would say by the look of them, they're most likely working on something."

Thad had a feeling of apprehension creeping into him and his concern was verified when one of the officers spotted him at the rail.

"Yep, they're working alright. They're looking for someone." Thad patted Cindy's hand.

"Who would they be looking for Thad?"

He gave Cindy's hand a squeeze, "I'm afraid they're looking for me. I think our weekend has just come to an end."

The officers were waiting for them as they walked down the gangway to the pier. Other passengers were looking at them funny as one of the officers gave a smart salute, more for public show than protocol, "Lieutenant, sorry to bother you, I realize that you're on holiday. The department has been trying to find you all weekend. There's been a development that requires your attention. We have a car standing by to take your wife and luggage home. They would like to see you at headquarters as soon as you arrive."

"Cindy I…"

"It's okay Thad at least I got you for this weekend. I understand, I'll see you at home. Now, which of you nice officers is going to take me home?"

"Thanks Cindy, I did have a wonderful weekend, I'll be home as soon as I can get there." He gave her a hug and a kiss before she marched off down the pier with an officer in tow. Thad watched her go, *yep she's a goodun.*

"Okay officer…" he glanced at the name tag, "Taylor, what terrible thing has happened. I don't know it all sir, it involves an explosion at some office and people saying that the police are trying to kill them."

I'll be damned, Drago's back in town.

The officer notified radio and he was bringing Thad in. He turned on the overhead emergency equipment and hit the siren once to clear traffic as he pulled out of the parking lot.

"Is this entirely necessary officer, I mean lights and siren, we're only going five blocks."

"Sorry sir, they said get you there as fast as possible"

As they rounded the corner on Yesler, Thad could see a crowd out in front of the police station. On the steps as they got closer he could see Patrick and Pauley Harrington with whom he assumed was their attorneys and a crowd of press. As they approached the building, he could see Pauley pointing at the patrol car and yelling.

"That's him, that's the crooked cop who's trying to kill us. He's the one who set us up and bombed our office."

The officer started to pull over, "Taylor, take it around the block and into the garage from below."

"Are you sure that you…"

"Now Taylor, do as you're ordered"

"Y…y…yes sir"

Looking out from his office window he could see the crowd gathered in front of the police station.

"Well let's see how Mr. Mitchell handles this little dilemma. I have a feeling that this will keep him busy for awhile and out of my hair."

"Wouldn't it be simpler just to let me kill em? After all I owe him a couple."

He turned and looked at the stocky powerfully built man graying at the temples whose cold gray eyes gave the impression that he could kill at the drop of a hat.

"You'll do exactly what I pay you to do and no more. This has to be low key…a hit would be too obvious. I must admit that the bomb in the Harrington office was a nice touch"

Drago smiled and leaned back in the cushy leather chair. *Of course I will…as long as it suits me.*

"I still have a bone to pick with the Harringtons. They tried to have me killed and they have a payback coming."

He pulled a cigar out of the humidor and looked at Drago.

"What ever you do in that matter, comes after you finish with my business. Do we understand each other Drago?"

Drago simply nodded his head.

"You want a press conference, a press conference, are you crazy?" O'Shay jumped out of his chair.

"Thad, this is the press, they want your head in a basket."

"I know Bob." Thad turned to Chief Severance, "Sir I think to get the press into your conference room gives us a home field advantage. We need to reassure them that neither I nor anyone else on the department had anything to do with the bombing of their office. As for setting them up, we can lay it off onto the prosecutor's office who is reviewing the case against them. What do you think?"

"I don't know Thad maybe I should clear this with the Mayor before going that far."

"I'm sorry Chief, but we don't have the time for conferences. It's either a go or no go and it's your decision."

Severance looked over at O'Shay and Special Agent Davis. Davis jumped in, "he knows more about this situation than anyone else Chief."

"You thought enough of him to make him an out of order Lieutenant Chief, have you lost that faith in him?" Everyone in the room turned toward O'Shay looking very serious.

"No, I haven't, let's do it. Barker, invite the press to my conference room for a press conference."

Thad was headed for the door and stopped, "Barker, make sure that its press only. We don't need a circus in there with everybody yelling and trying to get printed space with their name in it."

"That's my boy." O'Shay gave everyone his best grin as he followed Thad out the door.

Thad had followed the Chief in making a statement to the press and was finishing up.

"And let me assure you that no one on the department had anything to do with the bombing of an office or any other structure in this city. As for the allegations that I, or this department set up the Harrington brothers are ridiculous. While I can't discuss the evidence of a pending case, I can tell you that the probable cause arrests of both brothers were based on solid evidence attained after a lengthy investigation by this department. The County Prosecutors office is, at this time, reviewing the evidence and will present the appropriate charges based on that evidence, not just my word or the word of other police officers. As Chief Severance stated before, if it is discovered that any officer on this department was, in anyway, involved in that bombing or forged or lied about evidence, I would personally arrest them. I cannot discuss a pending investigation, but be assured that when the investigation is culminated; we will make full disclosure to the press." Thad did not take questions, but rather turned and left the conference room.

"Well how did it go Bob?"

"You were great Thad. I was proud of you. Who'd a thought that pile of broken bones, vomit covered, bloody piece of crap that I picked up in the alley would have turned out this good."

Both of them laughed. Thad headed for the door and O'Shay stopped him.

"Oh Thad, did you see Guzman in the back of the conference room?"

"No I didn't, I would have liked to say hi to him. I never forgot his lessons. I hope he thought that I did okay in there."

"Oh I think he thought you did great, he had tears in his eyes."

Thad choked back the lump in his throat and headed out the door. *I just need to get home and hold my wife.*

Chapter 14

It was as though everything had ground to a halt. Thad sat in his office sipping on a cup of coffee feeling less than useful. *I hate this time in a case. I know things are going on. The prosecutor's office is trying to put together the case on the Harringtons and any hopes for a grand jury hinge on whether or not Buck decides to talk to them. We have enough to send him away for aiding and abetting the alley homicides, but we can't tie anyone on the department to the crime. Damn we need his testimony and something else to corroborate his testimony against Major Wooten. With Bagley dead and Buck not talking, the damned Major just may walk away from this one.* He sighed, put his feet up on his desk and took a sip of his coffee, which by now had started to get cold, and stared at the ceiling.

"Is there anywhere around here that a girl could get someone to buy her lunch?" The female voice caused him to start and almost spill his coffee.

Thad spun around to find Cindy standing in the doorway. *Make a note; turn my desk around so I can see the door.*

"Cindy...what a surprise," Thad looked at his watch and realized that it was almost one o'clock.

"Of course you can. I know a guy who would love to buy you lunch. Want to go anywhere special or do I get to pick?"

"Some place quiet would be nice." Cindy took his jacket off the coat tree and held it for him while he put it on.

"I know just the place and it's only two blocks away. What a surprise. I'm so glad to see you."

"Oh I'm just full of surprises." Cindy gave him a hug.

As they walked out of the office, the new Otis elevator doors were opening and O'Shay came rumbling out.

"Thad...those goddamned weak-kneed sons-a-..." a startled and surprised look came over O'Shay's face. "Oh, Cindy, I didn't see you there.

Sorry…uh…sorry about the language. We don't get many female callers up here."

"Oh really Bob, how many do you get up here?"

O'Shay's face was red and he kind of shuffled his feet, "Well, actually none. What's going on?"

"Thad's taking me to lunch."

Thad was grinning at O'Shay and his beet red face, "I'm going to take her down to Cleo's Place, wanna come along? You don't mind do you Cindy?"

"No…uh…no that's alright."

She seems a little hesitant.

"Are you sure you don't mind Cindy? Maybe you just want a quiet lunch with Thad here and don't need a grizzly old sergeant draggin along."

"No, no Bob, I just came down to surprise Thad. Please come with us, I'd enjoy that." *What I need to say can wait till later.*

"My only request is that you two don't talk shop."

"You got it lady," O'Shay offered his arm and Cindy took his and Thad's as they headed for the elevator.

After lunch Thad walked her back to her car.

"Are you okay Cindy you hardly touched your lunch."

"I ate most of it Thad. I just thought it would be fun to see you this afternoon since I was already downtown." She started to get into the car and stopped turning around she gave Thad a hug and a kiss on the cheek.

"I love you Thad, I'll see you at home for dinner." Thad helped her into the car and started to shut the door.

"Cindy, I love you too, are you sure you're all right?"

"I'm positive, I'm just great! See you at home."

Thad watched as she drove away. *Something's wrong, something is going on, I can feel it.*

Thad came through the door and found O'Shay, detective Franklin and a prosecutor waiting for him. Franklin was grinning from ear to ear.

"Good news lieutenant, Buck cracked. You want to tell him Bob?"

"No go ahead, you made the breakthrough."

Franklin perched himself on the edge of a desk.

"I started leaning on him about the graft in the department. He kept telling me that I was wasting my time and to just leave him alone. I was just about to give up for today when I told him how hurt and disappointed you were in him.

Out of the blue he starts blubbering like a baby. It took me totally by surprise. I just sat there dumbfounded. He cries for about five minutes and then tells me that he wants to talk to you. I tell him that you don't have time for chit chat and he says that he'll tell you everything. I called the prosecutor here and he comes up to the jail and we talked with Buck. It seems that he will only tell you, but said that it would be okay if O'Shay comes along."

Thad looked at the prosecutor, "Your thoughts Jim?"

"If it was you alone, I'd say it wasn't good, but the two of you will be alright. However, he has one other stipulation. He doesn't want to do this during the day. He doesn't want a whole lot of folks around. He says after the evening meal around six or seven would be perfect. He's concerned about others in the department knowing what's going on. I would suggest that we tell him it's a go and spend the rest of the afternoon figuring out what we need from him."

O'Shay had been soaking everything up.

"If he spills his guts to us tonight I think we had better move him somewhere else. Once the crooked cops find out he's turnin' on em', his life won't be worth a wooden nickel. A safe house, we need a safe house to keep him under wraps."

Thad leaned back in his chair.

"It can't be a department safe house. I don't think a county location would be good either. No offense Jim, but the county is just too close. I'll call Davis over at the Federal office. I'm sure they have at least one that we can use."

I've got to call Cindy and let her know that I will be late and to hold dinner."

Thad went into his office and called.

"Cindy I'm sorry, but I won't be home for dinner. Something has come up regarding Buck and I'll be working late."

There was a long pause on the other end of the line.

"What time do you think you'll be home Thad?"

"Most likely around eleven or twelve if everything goes well." *She just doesn't sound well.*

"I'll be up when you get home and can heat your dinner if you want."

"That's not necessary honey, I'll just grab something before I go see Buck."

"I'll be up Thad, we need to talk." *He needs to know.*

"Cindy, what's wrong, please tell me." *I knew it, I could just sense it today something is wrong.*

"Not now Thad, it can wait until tonight. Everything is fine and we'll talk when you get home. Now go and do what we citizens pay you for. I love you Thad."

"Cindy…"

"No Thad, hang up and go to work. It's okay bye."

Thad hung up the phone and sat back in his chair. *God please let her be alright.*

Thad and O'Shay walked into the jail at precisely six thirty. They locked their weapons in a gun box pocketed the key and buzzed for entry. The jailer behind the booking counter looked out at them.

"ID gentlemen…oh, not you O'Shay, I know who you are! How bout you?"

Thad held up his badge, "Lieutenant Mitchell."

"Oh sorry Lieutenant, I didn't recognize you without your uniform."

There was a loud buzz and the barred door slid open so they could enter the holding area.

The jailer looked to be the only one on duty as he smiled out from behind the booking counter. "How you doin O'Shay, it's been awhile. What can I do for you two?"

"I'm fine Pete. We need to talk to one of your prisoners."

"Oh yeah…who?"

"Buck Jones."

"Jeez, didn't you guys get the word? The jailer looked surprised. He's dead…hung himself bout two hours ago. They hauled him out of here in the meat wagon not twenty five minutes ago."

Thad was dumbstruck.

"H…How the hell did he hang himself?"

"Bed sheet Lieutenant. Tied it to the steam pipe on the ceiling and stepped off of his bunk."

O'Shay's voice dropped to a growl, "Pete, where did he get a goddamned bed sheet. He was in solitary and on close watch he didn't have bed sheets."

"Don't know about that Bob, I came on just after it happened. They were just cutting him down when I got here. You're gonna have to talk with the day shift and the 'dicks'. They were all here including the watch commander and the Major. It seems like the only person not here was the Chief, but I think he's out of town."

Thad leaned against the booking counter trying to control the rage burning inside of him.

"Tell me Pete…" Thad's voice had a nasty tone to it that O'Shay had never heard before and it surprised him.

"Who was the Major that was here when you arrived?"

At the sound of Thad's voice the jailer took a step back from the counter.

"It was Major Wooten Lieutenant."

"Fuck!" Thad exploded; he kicked a waste paper basket across the holding area scattering papers as it bounced across the room.

"Those dirty bastards murdered him right in the goddamned jail. Those sons-a-bitches."

Thad was almost out of control and O'Shay moved in to settle him down.

"Thad…Thad damn it… Listen to me…Thad. This ain't gonna help…Thad." the last word sounded like it came from heaven and Thad froze.

"Take a deep breath Thad and calm down. We can't change what happened. We can only try to work around it. We lose control and they win. Let's get out of here. Open the gate Pete."

They picked up their weapons and left the jail. By the time they reached the Hoge Building Thad had calmed and started thinking again.

"Tomorrow morning Bob, I want you to go to homicide and get everything they have on this. I doubt it will be much. We'll call in everyone on duty in the jail and we'll have the prosecutors office issue subpoenas if necessary. We'll need to get Davis and the US Attorney on this also. We need to take this department apart piece by piece if need be. If we don't stop it here it will only get worse."

"Okay Thad, we'll start first thing in the morning. Right now we both need to go home and think about it. Thad I don't think they'll go this far, but watch your back and don't take any chances. I'm sure that you and our unit are becoming a thorn in their side."

Thad nodded, "Okay Bob, let's go home."

Thad started to open the door of his car then stopped. He looked underneath just to be sure that there were no surprises.

He picked up the phone on the second ring.

"Yes…"

"What a shame he hung himself you say…"

"It must have been his connection to the deaths of those two police officers in the alley in Chinatown. I'm sure that he felt a great deal of guilt…"

"Oh yes, I will have an appropriate response if I'm asked. Thank you and goodnight."

He pulled one of his Cubans out of the humidor lighting it up as he walked out onto the veranda. *Yes, this does call for a good cigar.*

Thad pulled up the drive and parked. *How could things get this bad? There has to be an answer out there somewhere. I just have to find it.*

***

As he walked into the entryway he heard Cindy coming from the den where she had been sitting in front of the fire. She was wearing her pink rob and fuzzy slippers.

"Thad you're home early…I'm so glad you're here." She threw her arms around him and hugged.

Thad could feel his body relax as he put his arms around her.

"I can't begin to tell you how good this feels."

Cindy looked up at him and then stepped back.

"Thad what's the matter? What's happened?"

Tears of sorrow and anger filled Thad's eyes.

"They murdered him Cindy. They literally murdered him in his cell. I can't believe they did that… I just can't believe it. Poor misguided Buck didn't have a chance."

Cindy led him over to the couch where they sat down. She put his head to her breast, held him and rocked him. *Oh he's in such pain.*

"Cindy they hanged the poor bastard right in his cell."

The tears flooded out, some out of frustration, some out of compassion, and some out of anger.

"Oh Thad, I'm so sorry." She held him tight and rocked as he wept. All the frustration seemed to drain out of him at one time.

Slowly Thad regained control, the release had felt good.

"I'm sorry Cindy, it just kind of all came out at once. I shouldn't bring this stuff home to you, it isn't fair."

"No Thad, this is exactly where you should bring it. Here with me you're safe and you can say what you think and what you feel. That's what our marriage is all about."

"You said we needed to talk, I thought it was about my job or you were having a problem. What is it Cindy?"

Cindy opened her robe exposing her abdomen.

"Put your head here Thad." She patted herself.

"Cindy…I…"

"Just put your head there Love."

Thad laid his head gently upon her.

"Now Thad, just below my belly button, give me a kiss"

"Cindy…what's this all…"

"Please Thad…just kiss me right there."

Thad gave her a kiss just below her navel.

"Cindy what are…"

"Shush Thad, we have a baby growing there." She felt the tear drops falling warm against her skin. This time they were tears of joy.

***

Chadwick Mitchell leaned back and looked around his conservatively appointed office in the Pioneer Building. Not even in his wildest dreams did he ever think that he would become this successful and wealthy. The new corporation that he had formed with Harrington would dominate the construction for both the city and the county. With this sweetheart deal they would have to contract with the corporation. Their first job was about to begin and the way things were growing in the area there would be many more jobs to come. With his 60% interest in the company he was in the driver's seat and the bulk of the profits would go to him. He had made it. He was now a player in the power and politics in the Puget Sound basin and particularly Seattle.

It would be any day now that he should hear back from the bank where he had made an anonymous offer on his Father's land holdings. How could they refuse, those dirt poor, bible thumping sod busters would jump at the opportunity. The bank would forgive the two outstanding loans they had and they could still live on the land as tenants. He could hardly wait to see their faces when he achieved his revenge. It had to be right though. Things had to be worded just so for the maximum effect. He had composed it in his head a hundred times. It would go something like…*you never supported me, you stood by and watched as this poor excuse for a human being beat and demeaned me, now it's my turn to show you the same compassion that you showed me. Yes, that would do it for my unfaithful siblings. For my father, there should be a special hell. I want to see the anguish in his eyes when he hears the words, 'you bible thumping hypocritical bastard, you beat and humiliated me for years and told me that I would never amount to anything and that I would wind up in Hell. You threw me out screaming at me to get off of your property and never come back. Well you old bastard, I am back. I own it and you have one day to get you and yours off of my property. Yes it will be gratifying. It will make the hurt go away and make me whole again. Life will be good.*

The ruckus in the outer office brought him sharply back to reality. Janet's voice was strong and firm.

"You can't go in there; Mr. Mitchell is not to be disturbed by anyone."

The deep, loud, aggressive voice startled Chadwick.

"Tough lady this badge says I can go where ever I want."

Chadwick started around his desk as the door burst open and a very large aggressive looking man burst into the room as if he owned it. Two strides into the room his left hand came up to eye level holding a leather case with a bright gold star in it.

"Detective Knox,…King County Sheriffs Office, you Chadwick Mitchell?"

The man's voice sounded like it was following a bolt of lightning, loud, booming and forceful, it made Chadwick's knees tremble, "Y…y…yes I am." Chadwick hated this feeling of helplessness and lack of control. He drew himself up, looked sternly into the detective's eyes, "What's the meaning of this?"

The detective thrust a folded paper into Chadwick's chest, "A little present from the prosecutor's office. They expect you to be in court on the date indicated inside to answer charges."

"What are they?" Chadwick could feel himself loosing ground again.

The detective glared at him, "Something about fraud and theft. You steal something or cheat someone?" The detective looked around the office and grinned, "By the looks of this place, I'd say they're probably right."

Chadwick felt rage surge through his body,

"This is ridiculous you tell them they can damn well talk to my attorney."

Chadwick didn't like the grin that tugged at the corner of the detective's mouth, "Hey your choice. Just remember that if you don't show, I'll be back and I won't be nearly as nice as I've been this time."

The detective wheeled around toward the door where Janet, was standing. He never broke stride, giving her a once over with his eyes, he stormed out as confidently and he had stormed in.

"Is everything all right Mr. Mitchell, are you all right sir?" Janet was wringing her hands and her voice was etched with concern.

"I'll be fine Janet. Get my attorney on the phone and place a call to Ned Johnson. He's the county prosecutor who signed this."

Chadwick slumped into his chair and began to read the charges. Filing a false affidavit of net worth and embezzlement of county funds.

Chadwick's mind was racing, *this is crazy, and the money is in the bank in the corporate account.*

The intercom voice box crackled to life.

"Mr. Mitchell, I have the prosecutor on the line."

Chadwick had meet Ned several years previous when he made an unsuccessful run for county prosecutor. Chadwick had backed his candidacy for prosecutor with campaign funds and even voted for him.

"Ned, what's this about charges?"

Ned's voice was distant and cold.

"You can't con the county any more Mitchell, we've checked your accounts and you lied to us about your resources and the counties matching funds are gone. I will not discuss this with you over the phone and I will see you in court."

A wave of nausea swept over Chadwick as the phone went dead in his ear. His mouth had a foul taste and sweat beaded up on his face.

"This can't be happening to me." He punched the button on the intercom, "Janet, call the bank and ask for Jim Hodge."

Chadwick still sweating leaned back in his chair trying to control his nausea.

"Mr. Mitchell," Janet's voice came over the intercom, "I have the bank on the line."

Chadwick grabbed the phone from its cradle.

"Jim," the voice on the other was not familiar.

"No sir, Mr. Hodge is not in at the moment. I'm Frank Cross senior vice-president of the bank, may I help you?"

Chadwick felt his frustration welling up inside him, "Yes, please check both of my accounts." Chadwick rattled off the numbers and waited while the accounts were checked.

"Mr. Chadwick, I have the information for you. Our records show that you closed your private account when the money from it was transferred to the new corporate account. We have a letter from the corporation, of which you are President and Chief Financial Officer, authorizing the closure of the account and the transfer of all funds to a bank in San Francisco."

Chadwick felt the nausea creeping over him again.

"What bank were they transferred to?" The man sounded a bit confused, "I don't have that information sir, Mr. Hodge handled the transaction."

Chadwick quickly hung up the phone, *the moneys gone.* He fought to control the nausea. Anger and then rage quickly replaced the nausea. He slammed his fist onto the top of his desk. *Hodge, anyone, but Hodge, my friend, my confidant how could he do this? Harrington, he had to be at the bottom of this whole thing. He set me up.*

The rage now boiling inside of him Chadwick opened the desk drawer and retrieved his 38 caliber revolver, the same one that he had used to kill the thieves in Alaska in what seemed like a hundred years ago. He jammed the gun into his waistband and putting on his suit coat, slipped quietly out of the side door of his office. Someone was going to pay for this. Accounts must be settled and he knew where his enemies could be found.

"Mr. Mitchell," Harrington's secretary was coming from behind her desk in an effort to block his path.

"Mr. Harrington is in conference and cannot be disturbed."

Chadwick was having none of it.

"Out of my way Agnes, I don't give a damn what he's doing." He pushed her roughly aside and barged into the office.

Harrington sat at his desk, a cigar in one hand and a glass of champagne in the other. Seated across in much the same condition was Jim Hodge. Chadwick slammed the door in Agnes's face.

"Having party gentlemen?" Acid dripped from each word. There could be no doubt that Chadwick Mitchell was not a happy man.

"Would you care to tell me what the hell is going on?" Chadwick appeared on the surface to be icy cold and in control, but on the inside he was in such a rage that he could hardly control himself.

"I was served by the prosecutor with charges today, the money from the corporate account is gone, both mine and the counties. I'm being charged with crimes, talk to me…now." His hands were shaking now and he was having difficulty breathing. Seeing these two together was almost more than he could take.

"Calm yourself Chadwick," it was Harrington who spoke first. "I'm sure that we can explain and you of all people will understand."

Hodge was visibly pale and had to set his glass down to keep from spilling his champagne.

"Chad, we've been friends for a long time now, you don't know all that has happened and and and…"

Hodge looked as though he was going to have a heart attack.

"It all fell apart, we had to do something, we had to cover ourselves…we had to do something."

"Shut-up Hodge Harrington stood up, Quit whimpering like a goddamned woman!"

He turned toward Chadwick, "Okay you got screwed. There was no way we could cover the costs of all the construction for the sewage job. I would have gone bankrupt and Hodge here most likely would have gone to jail. Your low man on the totem pole old buddy, so you take the heat."

The rage was building inside of Chadwick that he thought his eyes were going to explode. Harrington stepped up beside Hodge who was shaking in his chair and starting to weep. Harrington placed his hand on his shoulder to calm him.

"You have to understand Chadwick; we've been leaders in this community far longer than you. We have reputations to uphold and families who should not have to live with the shame. You're new here. You're just starting to build a reputation. You'll get a short sentence and be out in a year, I promise we'll take care of your family while you're gone," *especially that pretty little wife of yours.* Harrington's face had brightened and he flashed that toothy grin of his.

For Chadwick there was no control. His mind was operating on just adrenaline and rage. Thoughts flashed through his mind so fast he could hardly understand them. *Their families, their reputations, my god what about Becky, what about my family. What about Thad, he's a policeman? What about me?* Chadwick was totally out of control staring at Harrington's grin and Hodge sitting there, weeping.

"What about me?" the words burst from deep inside, from some where Chadwick had never experienced before.

"You Bastards!!"

The first round from the 38 caught Harrington in the center of his forehead just above his big bushy eyebrows. It happened so fast that Harrington had no time to react. His jaw dropped leaving his mouth agape as blood and gray matter exited the back of his head. Before he could fall or make a sound the second round struck him through the heart. As Harrington was dropping to the floor, the third round struck Hodge in the throat as he was starting to scream. That scream was snatched from his lips and died in a hissing gurgle as the bullet tore his throat apart. The fourth round struck Hodge in the left temple causing blood to coarse out through the neat round hole. Harrington had sagged to the floor a blank dead stare in his eyes and Hodge slid out of his chair to a crumpled heap on the floor next to him. It was over in less than 5 seconds. The air smelled of cordite, sharp…biting, stinging the senses. Chadwick remembered hearing the shots not as bangs, but as dull thumps. The sound was well muffled by the bookshelves, furniture and oak paneling. It happened so fast, it was so sudden, there was no longer any rage; there was only a strange kind of peace. Chadwick put the gun back into his waistband, straightened his jacket and tie. He exited the office by the private side door. *Its four o'clock, Becky will be getting dinner, I should go home.*

Agnes looked up at the clock, *goodness it's almost five o'clock. I wonder if I should let Mr. Harrington know that I am going home. No he's been in this meeting for quite awhile now and he doesn't like to be disturbed. I'll just leave a note and slip out.* Agnes put on her coat, gathered her things and quietly slipped out of the office.

Becky was finishing dinner as Chadwick came through the door promptly at five.

"Did you have a good day Chad? Cindy was over today, we worked on a quilt for the baby. Can you believe she's already six months along? The Kids are so excited and so am I, it doesn't seem like we are old enough to be grandparents. Oh dear I am just rattling on and you haven't had a chance to get a word in edge wise." Becky dried her hands and put her arms around Chadwick's neck kissing him.

"I love you Chad, how was your day?"

Chadwick held her close not wanting to release her. Wanting only to loose himself in her warmth and not think about what he had just done to their lives. Chadwick picked her up and started up the stairs to the bedroom.

Becky clung tightly to him her arms wrapped around his neck, her voice husky, "Chad my love, dinner..."

"It can wait Becky. We can enjoy dinner after we enjoy each other."

He carried her up the stairs, totally oblivious to the carnage just fifteen blocks away.

***

Pauley Harrington poked around through the burned remains of the office and warehouse. *It has to be that damned Drago who did this. He knows we set him up and he is going to make our lives miserable. Well guess what Mr. Drago. I can be just as nasty as you can. You may have just bought yourself more trouble than you can handle.* He found what was left of the desk and his big leather chair. *Damn, I really liked that chair. Oh well, I can get another just as soon as we settle this stupid liquor violation. The attorney doesn't think we'll get any time, even though it's a felony. We'll just plead guilty to a misdemeanor and get a slap on the wrist. That bastard Mitchell needs a lesson too. Dad will know what to do.* It was starting to get dark and Pauley was starting to talk to himself.

"Where the hell is Patrick with the flashlight?" He turned to start out of the office.

"I don't think you're going to need it asshole!"

Pauley spun around found himself looking into the cold gray eyes of his worst nightmare, "Drago!"

His mouth dropped open as he was grabbed and slammed against the wall so hard that it knocked the wind out of him.

"You bastard, you set me up to be killed. To bad for you, that you sent someone who was incompetent."

Pauley started to say something and it froze in his throat when he saw the long boning knife in front of his face.

"No Drago it wasn't me. I swear it wasn't me. It was Patrick who set you up. I told him, Patrick don't do that it will just piss him off. I told him Drago, I told him, but he wouldn't listen. I'm not your enemy Drago, don't hurt me, I'm on your side. Listen to me Drago! *Oh God Patrick, get here, somebody get here, somebody help me.*

Drago sneered at Pauley pinned against the wall, his eyes pinpoints in the fading light. He laughed out loud when Pauley's bladder released and the wetness spread down the front of his pants.

"You lying piece of shit. Patrick doesn't take a crap unless he asks you first."

Pauley tried to scream as the tip of the knife sliced under his left cheekbone, across through the bottom of his nose and under his right cheekbone. Before the scream could eminate, Drago slammed his finger tips into Pauley's throat and all that came out was a gurgle. Pauley's eyes bulged and Drago could almost smell the fear.

"Oh we're just getting started Pauley. You didn't think I would do you quickly, did you?" The sound of the car door slamming drew Drago's attention away from Pauley.

"Pauley…Pauley you here?"

Pauley could hear his bother calling. The pain of the slice across his face had not hurt that much, but he could now taste his own blood. *Oh thank God, it's Patrick. I'm not going to die.*

Drago turned back to Pauley.

"Well, the fun's over you piece of crap." With a single swipe Drago laid Pauley's throat open all the way to the back neck muscles and let him fall to the charred floor his severed arteries pumping copious amounts of blood onto the wall as he slid down.

Patrick did not come in.

"Pauley? It's getting dark Pauley, are you here? Come on Pauley, stop kidding around, I got the light…Pauley?"

Later for you Patrick. I want you to find your brother and think about it. Drago wiped the knife off on Pauley's shirt as Pauley lay twitching on the floor. He quietly slipped away out the back through the warehouse.

***

It was hours later as they lay exhausted under the covers of the big feather bed. Becky, relaxed, her arm draped over Chad laying on his back, her face wedged into his neck his arms wrapped around her, Chad allowed his mind to return to the events of the afternoon. He loved the softness of her naked body pressed against him and the thought that this could be the last time he ever felt her was almost more than he could bear. *They'll come for me, but when. I'll be locked up like the common criminal that I now am. There'll be shame brought on my family. God help me what will I do? I can't face going to prison for killing a man who lied, cheated and deserved to die. I have only one alternative and that's to leave and never return. I must end it here and* bring no more or shame or hardship to my family. It'll break Becky's heart and destroy mine as well. Oh what have I done to us?

Around midnight Chad quietly slipped out of bed and gathered some of his clothes and things that he would need and he slipped downstairs. In the basement he went to the back room and slid back the panel to remove one of the metal boxes that he had so carefully placed there. He removed only two of the fifty pouches in the box, closed it back up and put it away. In his study he carefully wrote a note to Becky which he left on the kitchen table where she would find it.

"*Becky my Love: I have done something terrible that will bring shame upon our house and family. Everything was so right for us and I have put all of that in jeopardy by acting in a fit of anger. You will hear terrible things about me in the coming months. Please know that I would not plan such a thing and I cannot bear to face neither the anguish that I have caused nor the shame that I have brought upon you and our family. For all of your sakes I will remove myself from this world that we have created. Do not look for me, although the police will. By the time you read this Chadwick Mitchell will no longer exist in this world. Please forgive me and know that what I do now is out of my love for you.*

Chadwick."

Having done that Chadwick composed a second note and placed it by the phone. Where he knew she would go after discovering the first note.

"*My Darling Becky: Show this note to no one, even Thad unless you feel you must. Know that I was lied to and cheated out of our fortune. My love I have created a back-up plan for just such an occasion, do not fear that you are left with nothing. Although you never told me, I have always been aware that you did not sell all of our property in Vermont. You wisely set aside enough to keep you and Thad if for some reason it did not work out with us here in the Northwest. I have always thought how wise you were to do so.*

I have provided for you well. In the back room of the basement there is a panel in the wall in the Northwest corner of the room. Slide it to the left and inside you will find two boxes. Do not divulge the existence of the contents as there will be those who will try to claim it for themselves. Use the contents as you see fit and know that it was placed there out of my love for you.

Chadwick.

Having placed the notes Chadwick carefully packed his meager belongings and slipped out of the house.

Agnes opened the office as usual in the morning. She was surprised to see Mr. Harrington's coat and hat still on the coat tree in the outer office. *He must have forgotten them when he left last night.* Opening the door to his office she discovered that he hadn't forgotten them at all. The grisly sight of Harrington and Hodge caused her to go numb. She was shaking so badly she had to sit-down. Collecting herself she stumbled out of Harrington's office to her desk where it took her three tries to call the police and even then she had to look up the address of the office. In a few short minutes there were police officers everywhere. Everything was a blur for Agnes, she could hardly remember her own name let alone answer the questions that were coming at her a mile a minute. It would not be until noon before she was calm enough to sit in the office of the homicide detectives and answer questions. She went through the day including the afternoon when Hodge came in and then later when Chadwick came in angry.

The detective perked up at Chadwick Mitchell's name.

"Are you sure that Mr. Mitchell was still there when you left?"

"No he could have left by the side door out of Mr. Harrington's office."

"No I didn't see them alive after Mr. Mitchell may have left."

"Yes Mr. Mitchell was angry when he arrived and he barged into Mr. Harrington's office."

Detective Sergeant Miller left the questioning and picked up the phone.

"Lieutenant Mitchell please... Thad, Bill Miller in homicide. I think you better come over here and listen to this interview. It concerns your father, he may be in trouble."

Thad hurried from his office in the Hoge Building running the four blocks to the police station and then up the stairs to the homicide unit.

"Bill, what the hells going on?"

Miller carefully explained what had happened and the information that they had received from Agnes.

Thad sat dumbfounded as Miller relayed the information to him.

"Have you arrested him yet?" *That sounds so dumb, we're talking about my father here.*

"No, not yet, but I think that the prosecutor will agree that we have probable cause to do that."

"Did anyone see him do it." Thad tried to keep his hands from shaking.

"No, but we can place him at the scene about the time that the homicide occurred."

"So our probable cause is weak until we can talk to him, is that right?" Thad knew he was reaching.

"Technically your right Thad, we do need to talk with him and soon."

"Hey Mitchell," Ashcroft strolled into the office.

"Glad you're here, I've got an item of interest for you."

"Be gentle Bob this had been a tough morning." Thad turned to the detective.

"Well, this should cheer you up. You've been working on the Harringtons right?"

"Yeah, we think they're good for the mess over at Ludlow."

Ashcroft smiled and threw a file onto the desk.

"It seems that someone didn't like Pauley Harrington. They sliced up his face and cut his throat from ear to ear. We've been over at their burned out office, processing the scene. The brother is a basket case and scared to death that he's next. He says that it was some guy named…let's see," Ashcroft reached for the file.

"Drago." Thad put his hand on the file, "Yeah, that's it, Drago. He says Drago is going to kill him too."

"Well that's quite possible Bob."

"Well here's the best part. The brother, Patrick, he gets into a police car and demands that he be taken to the prosecutors office. He goes in and tells the prosecutor he wants to plead guilty to the liquor violations and be put in jail. He thinks he'll be safer there than out on the street with this Drago guy."

Thad plopped down in a chair. "I'll be damned. Did he say anything about Ludlow?"

"Don't think so, just the liquor thing."

"Lieutenant your wife is on line two and says that it's important."

"Dear God, now what!" Thad grabbed the phone, "Cindy?"

"Thad come home, Mom has gone to pieces. There is something terribly wrong and Dad is gone."

"Hold things together Cindy, I'll be right there." Thad's heart was pounding, he hung up and turned to Miller.

"Bill, he's been home and gone. I'm headed to his house now and I think you had better come with me. If he's there I can't arrest him and you'll have to do it. If you want you can bring some one else with you."

"It's okay Thad, I feel safe with you. Let's go."

Arriving at the Mitchell house was an experience in itself. The gates stood open and they drove through the archway and up the circular drive. A drive took off from that which led to Cindy and Thad's house some seventy-five yards away. The drive went under the front portico to the steps leading up to the front door. Cindy was standing in the doorway as Thad and Miller arrived.

Cindy looked with suspicion at Miller as she hugged Thad.

"Mom's sitting in the library Thad. She's very fragile. Please go easy on her."

"Where's my father Cindy?"

"We don't know Thad. He packed some things and he's gone. He did leave a note." Cindy looked at Miller and Thad could tell by her eyes that she was holding something back.

"Miller you can come with me if you want, but I do want to talk with my Mother."

"It's okay Thad. I'll wait at the library door while you talk to her."

Becky was sitting in one of the wing backed chairs staring out the window. She looked up as Thad walked in and her eyes filled with tears. She made no sound as she turned away and continued to stare out the window.

"Mother something terrible has happened."

"I know Thad," Becky drew a deep breath, "I've lost my love and my heart is broken. I don't know what I'll do without him. I feel so lost and alone."

Becky abruptly got up and threw her arms around Thad. She buried her face in his chest and began to sob uncontrollably.

It wasn't until an hour later that she was able to answer questions about Chadwick. Cindy had made tea and they sat around a table, Becky, Cindy, Thad and Miller, softly talking and looking at the note that Chadwick had left.

"It was as though nothing was wrong when he came home," Becky was watching a couple of tea leaves float around in her cup. "In fact he was quite amorous." Her cheeks pinked, "When I woke this morning he was gone and this note was laying on the table."

Miller jotted in his notebook, "He didn't say anything about what had happened, or that anything happened at all?"

"No detective, not when he came home he didn't. I didn't know anything was wrong until I read the note. I was not even aware of what he was talking about until I just now talked to Thad. It's just awful. There must have been something dreadful that these men did to cause Chadwick to commit such a crime. Are you sure that it was Chadwick who did this?"

Miller glanced over at Thad, "Not for sure Ma'am, but everything points to Mr. Mitchell. I'll have to take the note as evidence, I know it doesn't say what he did, but we'll still need it for the prosecutor."

Detective Miller carefully placed the note in an envelope, sealed it and put his initials on the sealed flap.

"Thad does you father own a gun? It looked like they were shot with a large caliber firearm."

"Bill I don't know if he had one or not. I'm sure he must have when he prospected in the Klondike, but I've never seen one and he never mentioned it. Mother, it's important, do you know of a gun that father may have had?"

Becky stared at her coffee cup slowly shaking her head then suddenly looked up. "I remember that he once told me that when his mining partner was killed in the Klondike he had to shoot the men who tried to rob them, but I don't remember him ever having a gun."

"Well if you find one ma'am I'm sure that you will let either Thad or myself know about it." Miller looked directly into Becky's eyes, "Mrs. Mitchell is there anything else that you should tell me about this incident?"

"No detective, you know everything that I do."

"Well if you do think of anything else, please call me and let me know."

Thad sat back in his chair watching his mother and his wife carefully. *It's in both of their eyes, Miller most likely doesn't see it, but I know both of these women very well. There's something else, they're both holding back something.*

Miller got up and picked up his coat.

"Thank you very much for the tea. I think I have everything I need for now. Thad do you want me to drop you at your car at the station?"

"No that's okay Bill, I'll have Cindy run me down later to get it. Thanks for…well thanks, I'll drop by you're office in the morning."

Thad watched detective Miller walk down the stairs and get in his car. As he pulled away Thad closed the door and turned to look at his wife and mother.

"Okay ladies, what are you holding back, and don't tell me nothing, because I know you both too well."

Cindy was holding Becky's hand, "There's a second note Thad."

"Damn Cindy, that's important we should have shown it to Miller."

Becky's voice was calm and sure, "Stop Thad, it doesn't implicate him in anything. It's for us and no one else." She held the note out to Thad.

"What is he talking about Mother? What property and what's this panel and boxes all about?"

"Calm down Thad, come into the den and sit, I'll tell you all about it."

Settled into the den Becky began her story.

"Thad when you and I came out here it was the hardest thing I have ever done until now. I wasn't sure how you and I and your father were going to get along. I wasn't even sure that I still loved him. He told me to sell the business and all of our holdings in Vermont. It broke my heart to sell my fathers business. Although, it was a business that Chadwick had built. I sold everything associated with the business and held out on the property that he had invested in. We still own a couple of hundred acres in Vermont and on the coast of Maine. I held that out just in case I got out here and it was a dismal forbidding place with Indian attacks. It was also my insurance in case I found that there was no love left between your father and I."

"I'm sorry Mother I never knew." Thad took his mother's hand.

"I know Thad. I didn't want you to know how confused I was and I didn't want you to worry. When we arrived I knew that I still loved and adored your father and quite frankly I forgot about the property."

"What's this about boxes behind a panel? What's in the boxes?"

"I don't know Thad, Cindy and I decided to wait until you were with us and we were alone before we tried to find the boxes. Please don't be angry with us dear, it was just what your father asked."

Thad took a deep breath and collected his thoughts.

"Okay let's go find out what's in the boxes."

In the basement Thad followed the directions in the note and found the panel. It took several tries to figure out how to slide the panel aside. Sliding it open he found the two metal boxes, removed them and Becky opened them. One of the boxes contained forty-eight and the other fifty leather pouches.

Each pouch contained two pounds of high grade gold. Thad slumped down into a chair, "Mother there has to be a couple of hundred pounds of gold here. At today's rate these have to be worth hundreds of thousands of dollars, maybe even a million, you're a very rich women."

Becky began to cry, "No I'm not Thad. My heart and my life are gone. The love of my life is gone and he may already be dead. I think he is going to kill himself."

Both Thad and Cindy were stunned. Cindy responded first, "Wha…what makes you think that Mom, why would you say that?"

"Cindy think of the first note, think what it said, he's no longer going to be in this world, what's that say to you Thad?"

"Oh no," Cindy began to cry as she took Becky into her arms and they hugged.

Thad choked back the lump in his throat, *Come on you're a professional think about it.*

"I don't think so Mother. Listen to me, both of you. I don't think that he is going to commit suicide, I think he's buying time."

Becky looked at him wide eyed, "How…why…what makes you think that Thad?"

"Look at the boxes. This one has fifty sacks in it. Knowing my father the other box should have fifty also. He's taken two sacks out of this box to sustain him where he's decided to go. He's not dead mother, he's disappearing."

"Where would he go Thad?" Cindy was wiping the tears away.

"I don't know, Mother you know him better than anyone, do you know where he is?"

"I don't know Thad, I really don't. From the note, Hodge and Harrington have cheated him Thad. Find out what they did; clear his name of what ever they did to him. He's a good man Thad, help him, he's your father after all."

Thad took his mother in his arms, "I'll do what ever I can Mother."

Chapter 15

No one had heard from Chadwick. The police had wanted teletypes scattered all across the country but no response from anyone regarding his whereabouts. Even though Thad had assured her that it wasn't happening, Becky was sure that there was someone listening to her phone calls and tampering with her mail. Actually even Thad wasn't sure if anyone was or wasn't.

Word was that Congress was about to throw out Prohibition. The State Legislature had already started discussion on a new bill that would lift the prohibition on alcohol and Thad had already observed the shuffle within the department as detectives started jockeying for positions in other units.

The mayor had been re-elected for a third term and was still pressing his law and order agenda. It was going to be harder for him to maintain that stance now that liquor would be available. The church backers of the mayor's agenda had managed to hang onto some restrictions regarding alcohol by not allowing sales on Sunday. Basically no one could buy a drink or a bottle of anything with alcohol after midnight on Saturday until midnight on Sunday. Just one more thing for the police to try and enforce, most thought the "Blue Laws" were a pain and stocked up on Saturday or found a taxi driver and paid inflated prices during the Sunday closure.

Thad had bigger fish to fry. There were loose ends to tie up on Ludlow and what was left of the Harringtons. Both Pauley and the old man were buried on the same day and two days later Patrick was sent to the reformatory at Monroe having been given five years for the liquor violations. Thad knew that he would not serve more than two with good behavior. There was also the graft on the department to deal with. With the death of Buck Jones, they were pretty well dead in the water and if Drago wasn't found the investigation would be all but over. The county prosecutor wasn't a great deal of help but was at least trying to do the best he could.

"We just can't press charges against Patrick Harrington for the homicides at Ludlow Thad…" Ned Johnson shifted in his chair.

"I know that you're adamant about what you heard that night but the comment made could have referred to any one of them or all of them. The old man is dead, thanks to your father I might add. We think your prime suspect killed Pauley Harrington and we just don't have enough to charge Patrick, at least not for Ludlow."

Thad walked over to the window and stared out at the bay.

"Well at least he went up for the liquor violations."

Johnson got a smirk on his face.

"I wish you could have been here Thad. He came in begging to be put in jail. He laid it all out and pled guilty before anyone asked him to. Everyone in the office was watching and remembering when the smug little bastard would always get off when he did something wrong.

"At least that's something Ned. I just didn't want to see him walk away clean."

"If your team could only have found Drago, it might have been another story. We also have another little problem however. The defense attorneys are appealing the guilty plea. They're going to try and convince the court that you had a personal vendetta against the Harrington family since your father was cheated by the old man and killed him. They're going to say that the only reason he plead guilty was because he was afraid of you." I don't think that it will work, but there was the homicide."

"But Ned, we can show that they cheated him and it was them, not my father, who took the money."

"I know Thad, you did a good job of clearing your fathers name on the fraud and embezzlement charges, but there's still the homicide."

"God, that's so frustrating Ned. If he hadn't written that note and fled it would have been difficult to get a conviction on him for killing Harrington and Hodge."

"Well Thad, we'll probably never know. We can't find him anywhere, it's like he disappeared off the face of the earth. You think he's dead?"

"I don't know the relationship that he had with my Mom… I would have expected that he would have contacted her by this time if he was still alive. I think that it's at least a good possibility that he took his own life. My mother is convinced that he did. She's thinking seriously about moving back to the east coast now that our baby is born and things are starting to smooth out. She took this whole thing really hard. It's as if her spirit was broken. There just isn't any fire in her eyes like before."

"Well, I'm sorry Thad. This was really a mess for you and us. We had high hopes of cleaning up the graft in your department, but without Jones we had to drop the idea of convening a grand jury."

Thad took his coat off the rack.

"Well we did what we could do for now. I have an appointment with the Chief in an hour. I think that he is going to drop the squad and transfer folks around. He's already breaking up the dry squad. Let me now if you'll need me for court on the appeal."

Thad shook Johnson's hand and headed out the door. *Well I wonder what new and exciting thing is coming around in the Chief's office.*

Thad walked down the hallway for the administration offices. *I wonder how many of these men are on the take and how do they keep it from the Chief?* As he walked by Major Wooten's office the door was shut. *This son-of-bitch is at the very least a conspirator to murder and he's getting away with it.* The Chief's office was at the end of the hall. Thad walked through the open double doors and up to the Chief's very capable gate keeper Margaret Scotts. No one saw the Chief without first getting by Margaret. If they were not expected, either in person, or by phone they don't get past Margaret.

Margaret looked up as Thad walked into the outer office.

"Good morning Lieutenant. He's on the phone. I'll let you know when he's ready for you. Please have a seat. I'm sorry about that thing with your father and I hope your mother is doing well."

Thad walked over and sat down against the wall.

"Thank you Margaret. Mother is hanging in there."

Margaret went back to her work as Thad watched her. *Interesting woman, not married, late thirties, not gorgeous, but not unattractive. Chief brought her on board when he took the job and the rumor mill has it that when he isn't at home with his wife, he's in bed with Margaret. I don't think I want to know one way or the other.*

Margaret was suddenly on her feet coming around her desk.

"He'll see you now Lieutenant." She brushed past him and opened the door to the inner office and ushered Thad in.

Chief Severyns was seated at a large conference table, paperwork scattered around him.

"Morning Lieutenant, have a seat," he was pointing to the chair across the table from him. "Margaret would you get us some coffee please."

"Of course sir," she straightened the papers next to him and hurried out of the room.

"Well Mitchell you've had quite a time this last year. How's the new baby?"

"Fine Chief and yes it has been quite a year."

Severyns straightened some papers.

"Well as we speak the Volstead Act is becoming history. Never did like that one, to hard to enforce, look what it did to those officers in Ludlow Bay. In any case Mitchell," the door opened and Margaret came in with the tray of coffee.

"Will there be anything else Chief?"

"No, this will do nicely Margaret," Severyns patted her hand and her cheeks pinked. "Thank you." Margaret hurried out.

Maybe there is something to those rumors I've been hearing. Thad picked up his coffee and took a sip.

"As you were saying Chief."

"Oh yes, I think that the investigative unit we formed for Ludlow has reached a point where...well there's not much more you can do at this point. I think we should shut it down." The Chief looked over his coffee cup, "What do you think Mitchell? Can we expect much more from the unit?"

Damn I just had that feeling. Thad set down his cup, "Chief I think that as far as Ludlow, without Drago we're at a dead end. There's still the question about graft on the department. We could work on that end of that problem."

Chief Severyns put on his best political smile.

"I think that the Bagley thing was an isolated incident Mitchell. One cop gone bad does not corruption or a scandal make. The problem is gone now and things are under control."

This is bullshit.

"What about Major Wooten Chief? It appears that Bagley was not alone in the corruption. Two police officers were killed."

"Now Lieutenant...Thad, I've spoken with the prosecutor, the Mayor and Major Wooten. There is no way that it can be proven that he was or is involved in any kind of corruption. The Mayor agrees with me, we don't have enough to take any action against Major Wooten. I hope that this issue is not going to be a problem for you. I have big plans in the works for a man of your caliber. There was some concern when I appointed you to Lieutenant out of turn, but you've proven that the skeptics were wrong. You've proven that you're up to a good challenge and I have one for you to tackle," the chief intently locked eyes with Thad, "so, where do we stand on this?"

So it comes down to this, well let's see what we can get. "I'm for whatever's best for the department Chief. If you think that we should move on then I'm there. What's the challenge sir?"

Severyns face broke into a wide grin almost in relief.

"I'm forming a new detective unit. It's going to be devoted solely to vice and I want you to run it. If you remember, your rank was temporary and I'll make it permanent if you accept this new assignment. The new vice unit will be responsible for enforcing gambling, prostitution and narcotics. You'll be able to staff it with your own people."

So I get my own unit within the department and permanent rank, that's the payoff for looking the other way. Well guess what chief I'll still be working on it.

"I think that'll be an enjoyable challenge Chief. Thank you for considering me, I know that I can do a good job for you and the department. Who's the boss?"

"Well I'm sure you know that Tennant lost his job as Sheriff. The newly elected County Executive decided to replace him with his own man. Tennant has agreed to come back to Seattle in his old position as Chief of Detectives, he starts tomorrow, I understand you two know each other, is that right?"

Thad smiled remembering the encounter in the Sheriff's office.

"Oh yes we are well acquainted."

Chief Severyns stood and stuck out his hand.

"Glad we see eye to eye Mitchell. We all work as a team here." Thad shook his hand, "when do I start, and where are my offices Chief?"

"See Margaret on your way out, she has all the info you need," Severyns walked to the door with him opening it as they got there, "I know you're up to the task Mitchell, I know we…I've made the right choice on this one."

After picking up everything he needed from Margaret, Thad headed out of the building and to the nearest private phone.

"Bob, Thad, let's meet some where, we need to talk."

"Really, why is Maggie over at my house? Is everything okay?"

"Oh I see, she just can't keep her hands off of Amos. Poor unloved child won't know who his actual mother is between Maggie and Mom. I'll be right up and we can talk at your place."

Thad stepped out of the phone booth and looked around. A man was smoking a cigarette halfway down the block and abruptly turned away looking into a store window, but Thad had already picked him out. *That's twice I've seen that guy, in front of the station and now here. Am I being followed or am I getting paranoid, time will tell.*

I know that you're thinking of retiring Bob, but I need you for a couple more years. We both know we can trust one another and you know where all the skeletons are buried. Come with me and honcho the Vice Unit. If they leave us alone we can still work the Chinatown thing on the sly. We just might make a difference you and I."

"Jesus Thad, I shoulda' left you laying in the alley that night. My life would be a lot simpler. I promised Maggie I'd retire so you gotta' Thad took his mother's hand, tell her not me."

"Okay Mr. tough guy, I'll tell your wife you can't retire just yet." Thad sat back and smiled. Both men laughed as the phone rang.

"Hello…"

"Maggie slow down, what's wrong?"

"Yeah, he's still here. I'll tell him."

"What's going on Bob? What is it?" O'Shay hung up the phone.

"It's your Mom Thad, she just dropped a bomb and tipped over the apple cart. It seems she is moving back East to Maine. Our ladies would like you to come home now. I'll go with you."

"I will not change my mind Thad" Becky straightened in the chair and picked up her coffee.

"I've already contacted a friend of mine back in Vermont and he's sending me pictures of the piece of waterfront property I own on the shore in Maine."

"Mother," Thad was persistent, "you'll be all by yourself there, who'll look after you? Anyway your family is here."

"Thad, Cindy, Maggie and I have talked about it and they agree with me. I need a new start. This terrible thing with your father has absolutely stunned me. I need time, I need to get away from here and get my bearings back."

Thad reached out and put his hand on her arm, "Mother I…"

"No Thad, it has to be this way"

"Okay, Thad took a deep breath and sighed.

"Okay, but promise me that if you're lonely or need help you'll come back here."

"I can do that Thad."

"Promise me Mother"

"Okay Thad, I promise"

"When do you plan to go back Mom?" Cindy had tears in her eyes, "Will you be here for awhile at least"

"Yes honey it will be several months before the cottage is renovated." Becky sipped her coffee and realized that her heart was beating faster and she felt a thrill of excitement run through her. *This is something I haven't felt since Chadwick left, this is a new start.*

"I also have loose ends to tie-up here before I leave. Thad, I'm signing the house and property over to you and Cindy. The rest of the estate…"

Becky paused and looked and Maggie and Bob.

"You know Thad! I'm taking part and leaving the bulk to you, and, of course, Cindy and Amos."

O'Shay shot Thad a questioning look, but didn't say anything.

Thad looked down at the floor then at his Mother, he was obviously uncomfortable, "Mother, I have to ask, please understand, it's what I do, but this sudden move, does it have anything to do with Dad?"

"Well yes it does Thad, he's gone. I need to move on with my life."

"No Mother that's not what I mean, and there's no easy way to ask this so I'll just do it. Have you heard from him Mother? Do you know where he is?"

"No Thad, I haven't heard from him. That makes me believe that he's no longer with us. We meant the world to each other and if he was still alive he would have contacted me by now." A tear escaped down her cheek and she wiped it away as thoughts of Chad flashed through her head.

"That's why I need to move on with my life Thad. It helps me forget the pain of not having him with me any longer. Everything here reminds me of him and sometimes, it's more than I can bear. This beautiful house needs love and joy in it and I can't provide that any longer. You and Cindy and Amos should be here now. I'll be just fine back east."

Thad walked Bob and Maggie down the steps to the circular drive. The air was fresh, clean and crisp. It was another beautiful spring evening with the scent of newly opened flowers drifting across the yard.

Thad put his arm around Maggie's shoulder.

"I know that you're not happy with me Maggie, but I really do need him. It'll only be for another year or two at the most. Please don't be angry with me."

"Oh damn Thad I'm not angry with you or even Bob. I know how much he loves the job and just like the old harness bull that he is, he just loves to pull that old wagon. You have to promise me that you'll keep him out of trouble. If you let anything happen to him out there, I will beat you within an inch of your life. Are you hearing me Thaddeus Mitchell?"

Thad smiled and gave her a hug, "I heard you Missus O'Shay, and thanks for letting Mr. O'Shay come out and play for a little while longer."

Thad glanced over at Bob who was looking up at the moon with a slight twinge of a grin on his mouth.

"Humph," Maggie shrugged Thad's arm off, "I'll play alright Thad, if anything happens to him I'll play you like a drum." Maggie stepped into the car as Bob held the door.

Bob closed the door and started around the car whispering to Thad.

"You silver tongued devil you, I really didn't think you could pull it off." O'Shay stopped and turned toward Thad.

"What estate was she talking about Thad…Never mind, it's none of my business. See you tomorrow at work. We have an office to set up and staff."

Thad watched as they drove out of the gate. *Things are happening almost too fast what with Mother leaving and the department evolving. We need to put the brakes on and assess where we're at and what's going on…and the graft. We need to get a handle on the graft. That damn Drago has the key, we need to find him and make him cough it up.*

Drago sat in the overstuffed chair, legs crossed, drink in hand, savoring the large Cuban cigar. *Ah, this is more like it. This is the way life should be and soon will be for me.* He looked around the plush library. Rows of dark mahogany bookshelves, pieces of art work interspersed around the room. The carpet thick and plush, the double entry doors that went from floor to ceiling, the six foot teak desk in front of the bay window that looked out over the city and Elliot Bay. Behind the desk was a large leather chair where his employer sat looking very serious as he puffed on his cigar.

"Drago, we may have a problem with this new Vice Squad thing that the Chief has set about putting together. As you know I have interests that are not going to like the police poking around in their endeavors in the areas of prostitution and gambling."

"Who are these interests?" Drago straightened up hoping for some tidbits that he may be able to use later on.

"You don't have a need to know who they are Drago. Just know that they have promised to keep the operations low key so as not to ruffle the feathers of the church folks who think that they run this town." He got up from the desk and turned to the bay window.

"Our old friend Thaddeus Mitchell has been anointed to run the new squad." He paused and puffed on the cigar, "he came close to doing a number on us with that Bagley thing and we barely averted disaster. We can't allow him to get that close to us again."

Drago felt a twinge of pain in the old bullet wounds that Thad had inflicted on him during their last encounter.

"Do you want him taken out? I would be more than happy to do that, I owe him."

His employer spun around, "That's the last thing we need to have happen, although…it's always an option. Drago I'm paying you a great deal of money to take care of certain matters for me. You do as you are told and don't go off on your own personal vendetta. It will only screw things up and you're not being paid to do that.

Drago was stung by the rebuke. *One day Mitchell, I will get the opportunity to inflict some serious pain on you and maybe even yours. But for now.*

"I understand, what do you want me do?"

"I'm not sure yet, but we need to find some way to intimidate him into backing off. He obviously doesn't need the money so that will not be an avenue we can explore. Maybe, just maybe, if we could find a way to make him afraid to make any moves against our interests that would be a better approach."

Drago took a sip of his scotch.

"Now that's an intriguing thought. I've seen him and his very attractive wife. I think messing with her mind would be rather fun. It would surely get some kind of response from Mitchell if he knew his lovely wife might be in jeopardy…if he tries to do anything." *I wonder how she would look naked, with panic in her eyes.* He felt himself begin to stir at the thought.

"Yes she is beautiful and he would be very protective of her. That may be the way to go."

"Be careful Drago. We don't want to have him over react either. Between him and that bull of a Sergeant that's always with him…"

"Oh yeah, the big guy with the whore wife. Now there's a combination for you. I did some work for her years back. She's a hard nosed bitch as I recall."

"Well we don't want them both on our cases at least until we see how things are going to shake out." He walked back to the window stubbing his cigar out as he went.

"Tell you what boss, I'll think about some ways to cause mild intimidation and get back to you on what I am going to do." Drago started toward the big double doors.

"Drago, don't do anything without letting me know first and use the side door over there." He pointed to an almost invisible door that led to the outside of the house.

"I would rather not have people see you coming and going. There may be questions that would be difficult to answer."

Drago felt the sting again, *you pompous bastard, okay for now I'll go out your side door and sneak away, but it won't be long before you accept me in your house as a guest whether you like it or not.*

"Sorry boss, I forgot where I was," Drago headed for the door, "I'll get back to you in a couple of days." As he went out the door he patted the thick envelope that he had been given. *There's enough money here to keep me for quite awhile, so tonight it's a nice place to stay and a whore to play with. I would rather be doing Mitchell's wife, but a whore will do for now.* The door shut quietly behind him and Drago melted into the night.

He pulled out another Cuban and lit it as he walked out onto the veranda and looked at the lights of the city. *It's growing bigger by the month. The opportunities are endless if I can keep a lid on the police department. Drago's a piece of shit, but I need him right now. As soon as his work is done, so is Drago, permanently.* He took a deep breath and smelled the scent of the spring flowers. *Ahh, I love this time of year, everything is new and fresh, the cycle begins again.* He thought of Drago and Mitchell's wife, it made him shudder, he took another drag on his cigar and went back into the house.

***

Thad showed up early at the new offices of the Vice Unit in the Hoge Building. The office wasn't as large as the feds had two floors up. There was only room for his conservative office and eight desks. He was pleased that all of the furniture had been put in place complete with file cabinets and telephones. *This is where we start anew and try to crack down on the gambling, drugs and prostitution in our fair city. If they think that I'm not going to keep working on the department graft, they will be sadly mistaken. I'll have to be a lot lower key than before, but we will be working on it.*

Personal items had already started appearing on desks. Thad smiled. Some of the detectives, who had been assigned to the unit at his and O'Shay's request, had already been into the office and selected the desks that they would be using. *Well at least it looks like they're ready to go.*

Thad started to pick up his box for his office, but the sound behind him caused him to spin around.

"Chief!"

Chief of the Investigative Division, ex-Sheriff John Tennant stood in the doorway.

"Morning Mitchell, in early I see. I like that in my command staff." Tennant walked in and looked around, "Not bad, I would rather you were over in the Flat Iron Building with the other units, but there just isn't any room. This office is better than you would have over there so you're better off, but I'm not comfortable with it." Tennant walked over to the window and looked out across Third Avenue.

Thad dropped his box in his office, "Why's that Chief, don't you trust me?"

Tennant never turned around.

"Oh, I trust you Mitchell. I've liked you since that 'to do' we had over in the Prosecutors office. You stood your ground and didn't back off when I blustered. No I trust you. It's just that I learned long ago that if there's going to be a problem in a police department, it's going to be with booze, dope, gambling and women. Think about it Mitchell, your unit handles all four and all four can cause corruption in any department. That's where the money is so there will be some temptation. I hope you took that into account when you selected your people." Tennant turned from the window and stared at Thad.

"I'm aware of graft and corruption Chief and I picked my people very carefully. I don't want another Bucky on my hands. I'll put checks and balances in our system to assure that there is accountability all the way up including myself."

"How'd you feel about him dying in the cell like that?" Tennant's eyes softened.

"I think it was crap Chief. He didn't commit suicide. He was murdered in that cell. He sent for O'Shay and me. He was going to lay everything out for us. The murders of the officers, Ludlow, gambling, whores, the whole works including the people pulling the levers. By the time we got there he was already dead. Oh…I know about corruption Chief."

Tennant pursed his lips as he listened intently, "Well I know corruption too Mitchell and I don't tolerate it in my Division. We'll see each other a great deal. I like to know what's going on and I expect that you will keep me informed." Tennant pushed his 5'7" 200 plus frame off of the desk he had been leaning on. "I think that we'll get to know each other very well."

Thad watched the Chief stride out the door; *I wonder where he actually stands? Is he part of this whole corruption thing or can I count on him if I need help. Time will tell.*

As soon as one very large man left the room another came thumping through the door carrying two boxes of stuff to be jammed into his desk.

"Hey Thad, saw Chief Tennant getting on the elevator as I was getting off. What's goin on?"

"Just a, 'your on notice that I'm watching visit', I think." Thad took one of the boxes from O'Shay,

"Geez Bob you've got enough stuff here for two desks, you moving in here? Did Maggie chuck you out of the house for not retiring?"

O'Shay dropped the other box on the desk just outside of Thad's office.

"Nope, I just figure as long as I'm going to be here for another year or so, I'm going to be comfortable. I even brought my own hot plate and coffee pot."

The rest of the squad was drifting in and putting their stuff away. O'Shay turned and faced the squad room.

"Listen-up, meeting in one hour in the back conference room, be there." He turned and smiled at Thad,

"That okay with you lieutenant" Thad smiled back.

"We got a conference room Bob?"

"Yep, right through that door next to your office"

"Oh, I thought that was the john and I had the space closest to it. Where's the john O'Shay?"

"It's out the door and down the hall Thad just like upstairs. I thought you were a trained observer."

Thad grinned and went into his office and started unpacking.

***

Cindy put Amos in the stroller and wheeled him down the drive toward the front gate. There wasn't a cloud in the sky as she turned right and headed for the little park that overlooked the city. The birds were making a racket in the oaks that lined the street and there was the steady hum of the bees in the pollen laden flowers. The breeze was warm and she hit a steady stride that made Amos squeal. He liked to go fast; the faster the better he was definitely his father's son. It was six blocks to the park and at this pace she would begin to feel it by the time they got there. She could take a short rest while Amos played in the grass and then back to the house where Amos would be ready for his nap. She made this trip to the park three times a week and it seemed to do the trick in getting off the extra weight she had put on during the pregnancy. She was almost back down to her normal weight. It had taken almost a year to get serious about a schedule that would begin dropping the weight. Thad had never complained about the extra pounds, but he seemed a little more physically attentive now that her figure was almost back to normal and she certainly felt better.

As she entered the park, she noted the man sitting alone at one end of the small park. She also saw Thelma and her new baby near the middle. She had met Thelma several weeks ago when she had brought her baby to the park. Cindy came up to bench where Thelma sat watching Tony her nine month old.

"Hi Thelma, whew...I think that I set a little faster pace than usual this morning. I'm a little winded."

Thelma's head snapped around and she looked startled.

"Oh I didn't hear you come up Cindy, deep in thought I guess."

"Is everything alright Thel?"

"Oh yes, I'm glad you're here though. I was a little concerned about the man at the other end of the park. When I got here he was real intent on watching me, then looked away as if disinterested. Have you ever seen him here before?"

Cindy took a good look at the man seated on the bench at the end of the park.

As she turned her head to get a better look she saw his face turn away. *He was staring at us and averted his eyes when I looked at him. Oh it's just my imagination, with a policeman for a husband I get paranoid.*

"No I haven't seen him here before; he probably lives in the neighborhood and just wandered down to the park. He looks harmless."

Amos had plopped himself down on the grass next to the baby's blanket and was inspecting him. Cindy leaned back on the bench and let the warm sun soak into her. She was almost drifting off to sleep when Thelma stirred causing Cindy's eyes to pop open.

"I have to go Cindy." Thelma was gathering up the baby's stuff and putting him in the stroller.

"Will you be here the day after tomorrow?"

"As usual Thel unless it's cold or rainy, you never can tell about Seattle."

They both laughed and Thelma headed out of the park. As she left Cindy looked up to see what the man would do. He watched her leave and then looked back toward the city leaning his head back to the sun hit his face. *Don't be so suspicious Cindy it's only a man in the park enjoying the sun.*

Amos had been running in circles in the grass in his bare feet and was running out of steam.

"It's time to take you home for a nap mister."

Cindy began to gather toys and attempting to get Amos's shoes back on. As she loaded him into the stroller she looked up and discovered that the man was now gone. *When did he leave? It must have been at least 20 minutes after Thelma. Oh well he's gone and I'll most likely never see him again.* Cindy wheeled Amos out of the park and started for home. She had only gotten to the corner when the man from the park came around it.

"Hello…I couldn't help noticing you in the park. What a fine young man you have, he seems to be very well behaved. How old is he?"

Cindy was startled that he had spoken to her and took a closer look and him. She didn't sense any danger, not here on the street where a scream would bring people out of their houses. Thank you. He's a little tired now and will get cranky soon enough. He's 14 months and is starting to get around too well."

Cindy continued past the man keeping an eye on him.

He turned toward her as she passed.

"Oh, tell Thad that his friend from downtown said to say, hi."

"Is there a name I can give him?" Cindy kept moving away.

The man was now moving away.

"No, just tell him it was an old friend from south of the line. He'll know who you're talking about. Please give him my best."

With that the man continued walking back toward the park. *Damn she is beautiful; I will have her, but not now. In time, when it's right, I will have her.* Grinning to himself Drago walked past the park to where he had parked the car. *This should shake up our friend nicely. Let the games begin Thaddeus Mitchell.*

Thad hung up his coat just in time to catch Amos who toddled down the hall toward him.

"Well tiger what kind of day have you had lounging around the house?"

Thad gave Amos a kiss on the cheek and a hug.

"And where's mommy Amos?" Amos's eyes lit up as he pointed to the kitchen. Thad gave him another hug as he wiggled out of his arms.

While Amos trundled into the play room, which sometimes substituted as a library, Thad headed for the kitchen and the wonderful smell emanating from it. Cindy was busy at the stove stirring the good smelling thing in the pot.

"Ummm, smells like spaghetti with some of your homemade sauce." Thad slid his arm around her and kissed her on the cheek.

"Amos seems happy, how was your day?"

Cindy let the spoon sit and turned putting her arms around his neck.

"We had a good day, and this makes it a very good day." She kissed him gently.

Thad straightened up looking into Cindy's eyes, "Well we should have more days like this," he pulled her closer.

"Not now Detective Lieutenant Mitchell, the sauce will scorch." She extracted herself from his grasp and stirred the bubbling pot.

"Wash up, Thad and put Amos in his highchair I'm dishing up. They ate quietly laughing at Amos who was getting more on him, than in him.

"We went to the park today and it was so pretty. Cindy wiped Amos's face. Amos got to play in the grass and I talked with Thelma. Amos was interested in her new baby but it didn't do much so he was happier just running around in circles. How did it go at the new office?"

"Tennant was there bright and early to lay down some ground rules. He doesn't like us being in another building away from the rest of the CID units.

I guess I can't blame him, I wouldn't be happy either. I expect I'll be seeing a great deal of him."

"Oh that reminds me…I had the strangest encounter today at the park."

"Oh really, like how" Thad twirled spaghetti onto his fork.

"Well there was this man there at the far end of the park. He seemed to be watching us. He left after Thelma did and I didn't think much more about it. But on the way home about a block from the park he came around the corner in front of Amos and I."

Thad had the fork poised to go into his mouth, "Did he say anything to you?"

"He did."

"What did he say Cindy?" Thad paused.

"He said to say hi to you, that he was an old friend from south of the line. Does that make any sense to you? I asked his name but he said you would know who he was." Thad frowned, "What did he look like?" Thad shoved the fork full of spaghetti into his mouth.

"His hair was dark and greased with a curl in the front and he was graying at the temples. Oh yes, he had a nasty scar on his cheek and he walked with a slight limp, but probably the most telling feature was his eyes…cold gray."

Thad choked on the spaghetti spitting most of it back onto his plate.

"Thad, are you alright, did you take too much?"

Thad's stomach churned and he felt like a bolt of ice had just run through his entire body.

"I know who it was Cindy. It was Drago."

Cindy stared blankly at him,

"Drago? Thad, who is Drago? You're upset, who is this Drago?"

Thad wiped his mouth, *oh my God he's found me before I found him.*

"He's a killer Cindy and now he knows where my family is." Thad pushed himself back from the table, *stay in control, this can be handled, but who can we trust?*

O'Shay and Maggie pulled up in front about thirty minutes after Thad made the call.

"What the hell's going on Thad? Is this the first time she had seen him in the area?"

"Yes Bob. He showed up at the park where Cindy takes Amos several times a week. He knows her. He knows where we live. The question is why

Bob, it has to be more than just a running gun battle in an alley. What the hell is he up to?"

O'Shay leaned up against the wall, "I'd say it's your new assignment Thad. Whoever's pulling the strings on the corruption in the department and the sin on the street is making a statement. He's using Drago to do it."

Thad sat down in the den looking at O'Shay. The look in his eyes sent a shiver through the grizzly old sergeant.

"I don't like that look Thad, what are you thinking?"

Thad took a deep breath slowing his heart rate down.

"The rule book just went out the window Bob. You and I are fair game but our families are out of bounds. They break the rules, we break the rules."

O'Shay looked at his protégée for a moment and saw the eyes of a stone cold killer.

"Be careful Thad, and anyway where would we start?"

Thad got up and walked across the room.

"We start with the weakest link Bob. We start with Wooten and we start tomorrow."

O'Shay took a deep breath.

"Anything you say boss." *Now this could be fun. At least we won't go down without a fight.*

Chapter 16

Thad and O'Shay had met in the office to figure out how they were going to attack the weakest link in the corruption system.

"I don't think there's any question that the Major is the one we need to start with Bob."

"I don't either, it has to be Wooten." O'Shay took a drink of his coffee.

"If we can get him to crack the whole system comes apart. With any luck, we get the guy at the very top."

"Ah yes, the head of the snake." Thad grinned,

"The head of the snake, what do you mean?"

"Look…think of the whole corruption thing as a snake. We can chop of the tail of the snake, those and the bottom of pecking order, and the snake just grows a new tail. If we can get the head, the whole snake dies." The phone ringing cut off the thought.

"Vice, Lieutenant Mitchell…"

"Hi Jim, what's going on over at the prosecutors office?"

"No kidding, it's not as much as I hoped for, but better than nothing. Thanks for letting us know." Thad hung up the phone.

O'Shay was on the edge of his chair.

"What's going on Thad?"

"That was the prosecutor's office Bob. A judge just threw out Patrick's appeal on the liquor violation. With good behavior he'll be out in two and a half years."

"Well that will keep him out of our hair for awhile." O'Shay took another sip of his coffee.

"Well what do you say Thad. Shall we make a run on Major Wooten? I know right where he will be in just about an hour."

"Why are we sitting around here?" Thad looked out into the office. "Carlisle?"

"Yes Lieutenant."

"You going to be around for awhile?"

"Yes Sir, I've got a ton of paperwork to take care of."

"Good, if anyone calls, O'Shay and I are going to be out working on something."

"You got it Lieutenant."

O'Shay grabbed their coats.

"Let's go out and commit law enforcement Thad."

***

Major Wooten lifted his bulk out of the chair in his office and walked over to the coat rack. *Time for a little lunch, my stomach's growling like a lion. I'm not getting enough exercise and it's probably time to go on another diet.* At six feet two he now tipped the scales at two hundred and seventy two pounds. His girlfriend, Wendy, had mentioned the extra weight a couple of times after lovemaking. His wife was always trying to get him to eat healthier as was his doctor. *Damn got to lose some of these pounds but a couple of cabbage rolls at Irene's Diner sure sound good right now.* He almost had his jacket on when his private line rang. *Shit..., oh hell, I better get it, might be important.*

"Major Wooten...," he recognized the voice on the other end immediately.

The man leaned back in his chair and took a drag on his Cuban, "Wooten, I just wanted to check with you and see how our friend the lieutenant is doing with his new assignment."

"How the hell should I know? I'm not his boss and the last person I would talk to about it is Tennant. That straight arrow son-of-a-bitch would start grilling me as to why I had a need to know. We're gonna have to watch that one. He could really cause us problems."

"Take it easy Wooten, he's not a problem and our friend the Lieutenant just got his first wake-up call."

"Wake-up call? What the hell are you talking about? What wake-up call?"

"Our friend 'D' made a friendly little contact with Mitchell's wife. I would imagine that Mitchell was pulling out his hair and got the message very clear when he found out."

"Mr. D? Are you talking about Drago? That bastard is really scary. He's a loose cannon and we should have cut our losses and got rid of him long ago. Can't you see that?"

"Not to worry Major, He will be taken care of when the time is right. For now, you keep an eye on Mitchell and let me know if he starts screwing with any of our clients. We don't want him messing with our bread and butter now do we?"

"Yeah, yeah, I'll watch Mitchell but you had best be careful with him. He's a bulldog and he does have the ear of the county prosecutor. He follows the rules but I'm not sure if he isn't above bending them a little when it comes to his family, just you be careful."

"I'll worry about the good Lieutenant and you do the job I pay you for, alright?"

"You get your moneys worth out of me. I'm going to lunch." Wooten put the phone back in the cradle a little harder than need be. *Pompous ass-hole, tell me how to do my part. I hope I busted his fuckin' eardrum.* Wooten went out the door headed for Irene's Diner.

Thad and O'Shay sat in the car at the other end of the block from Irene's Diner.

"You're sure he'll show up Bob?" It was the third time Thad had asked him. O'Shay sighed, "Yeah Thad, he'll be here. He's running a little late but he's like clock work. He goes here every day to fill that fat face of his. I just hope we can take him down before he has a heart attack or stroke." *You fat assed bastard where the hell are you?*

"Bob thanks for letting Cindy and Amos stay at your place until this thing is over. I do worry about Maggie and Cindy being alone though."

"Not to worry Thad Maggie has a shotgun. Short barreled, chopped down stock, nasty little thing, 12 gauge, breach load, double barrel, has buck shot in it and she knows how to use it. First round makes a guy company and the second makes him a crowd. She ran a box house, remember. She kept it behind the bar."

"Damn did she ever have to use it?"

"Nope, I guess she hauled it out once or twice but anyone seeing it decided that they didn't want to mess with her."

"Jesus Bob, where did Maggie get something like that?"

O'Shay laughed, "Remember Miguel the little Mexican bartender she had? He was with her until she sold the place. He made it for her. He said she needed something to make her bigger than the bad guys."

They both spotted him at the same time trudging around the corner at the far end of the block.

"There he is Bob."

"Yep, just like clock work. You can't miss that lard butt. I don't care how big the crowd is."

Thad took a deep breath. His heart was beating faster as he got more excited about what they were going to do.

"Does he always go to the back room Bob?"

"Yep, he's a creature of habit. He goes into the back room where it's private so he can eat his lunch in peace and have a couple of cocktails while he's in uniform. Come on we'll slip in the back door and give him a little surprise."

They got out of the car and headed down the block as soon as Wooten went in the front door.

"Could there be anyone in the back room with him?" Thad's heart was really starting to pump now.

"No he goes in shuts the door and no one else goes in. Sometimes his chippie Wendy meets him here and he gets a little afternoon delight. But I checked, she's in Spokane visiting her folks. I don't know what the hell she sees in that tub of lard. She's actually kinda cute so she must get something out of it."

They reached the back door.

"Hang on, it's always locked but I got a key."

"Where'd you get a key to the back door of Irene's O'Shay?"

"You forget I used to walk this beat here. I have keys to most of the joints down here." O'Shay quietly unlocked the door and they slipped inside. The smell of cooking cabbage hit them like a wet towel.

"Umm, must be Thursday, that's cabbage roll day." O'Shay led the way down the darkened hall. Thad thought he saw some movement at the other end then he felt O'Shay's huge hand on his chest and he was suddenly pulled into a darkened recess.

O'Shay's voice hissed in his ear, "Quiet, the waiters bringing Wooten's afternoon slop to him. Must be a rough day he's got a glass and a bottle."

Thad's voice was suddenly calm and cold.

"He doesn't know it but his day is about to get a lot worse."

Once the hallway cleared they made sure no one else was around as they stood in front of the door to the back room. Thad and O'Shay looked at each other and O'Shay wrapped his hand around the knob. Thad nodded his head.

Wooten was draining a shot glass of whiskey when he heard the door open as Thad and O'Shay made entry.

Wooten pivoted in his chair; "I'm not to be dist…" he choked on the rest of whatever he was going to say.

Thad led the way in as O'Shay shut the door and closed the bolt.

"Afternoon Major washing down a little cabbage roll are we?" Thad's voice had the edge of razor blade. There was no mistaking the animosity in it.

Wooten stood up from his chair, "What the hell do you thi…"

Thad cut him off, "SHUT UP Wooten and sit down."

"Bullshit Mitchell, you don't tell me wha…"

Thad leaned into Wooten's face his voice nasty and cold, "I said sit Major"

Wooten started to protest but he felt a pair of very large hands slam down on his shoulders driving him into the seat of the chair.

"Do as you're told Major you might not like the alternatives."

There was no mistaking the voice or the hands. Wooten tried to talk but nothing came out except one word, "O'Shay?" He tilted his head back a looked up into the smiling face of Robert O'Shay.

The sound in Thad's voice snapped his attention back.

"Listen up Major…I am about to do you one hell of a good turn."

"W…what's going on Mitchell? What do you think you're doing?"

Thad held up his hand silencing Major Wooten.

"Wooten, you've had a pretty good thing going here but it's all about to come crashing down on you." Thad paused for just a second to let that soak in, "That includes the death of two police officers in Chinatown and six officers at Ludlow Bay. We're going to hang it all on you Major."

Wooten was overwhelmed by what he was hearing.

"I…I…I didn't have anything to do with Ludlow Bay Mitchell that was a rogue operation pulled off by Bagley. You can't hang that on me; I wasn't involved!" There was now a note of panic in Wooten's voice.

"That's not how the Feds see it Major, they want to hang it on someone and you're the one we're going to give them."

Wooten tried to muster his confidence, "You ain't got shit Mitchell, you can't touch me and you know it"

Thad smashed what confidence level Wooten may have had, "Guess again Major, you remember Bucky? You ordered him killed in the jail, well guess what Wooten, Bucky left paper."

Sweat popped out on the forehead and upper lip of Major Wooten, his face blanched noticeably and he started licking his lips as his mouth dried out.

"Paper? He left paper?"

"Did you realize that the Feds had a hold on good old Bucky when you had him killed? Do you want to know what happens to cops who kill federal prisoners Major? They send them to a federal prison and somehow the inmates find out who the cop is. Save your butter Major cause you're going to be everybody's love toy in prison."

Wooten was tearing up and trying not to cry, "I didn't do Ludlow guys. I swear I didn't do Ludlow, don't hang that one on me."

"You may get a good lawyer to get you out of that one Wooten, but two cops and a federal prisoner…that will get you enough time."

Wooten was now in tears, "Jesus, oh Jesus, I don't want to go to no federal prison. Please guys."

Wooten felt the large hand on his shoulder.

"Easy Major, we've known each other for a long time. Why, I remember you when we worked the street. I was a rookie and looked up to you." O'Shay's voice was soft, warm, even comforting.

"I think that I could talk Mitchell here into cutting you some slack."

"Bull shit O'Shay, I'm not cutting this bastard anything, three cops Bob, he had three cops killed. The only thing he needs is to have someone cut his fucking throat."

Wooten looked into Thad's eyes and saw cold, stark, hate. The look in Thad's eyes told him he was a dead man.

"Cool down Lieutenant. Let me talk to the Major maybe we can work something out."

"Jesus Christ O'Shay all I want is to see this bastard in prison with 40 cons waiting their turn to make love to the cop."

"Come on Thad, be reasonable; let me talk to the Major."

Thad jumped up out of his chair knocking it over, "Well make it quick cause I'm going to be calling the Feds."

Thad stormed across the room and with his back to O'Shay and Wooten and stared at the wall. He bit his lip to keep from laughing about what was taking place.

Bob O'Shay sat down across from Major Wooten and poured him a drink.

"Here ya go Major this will help calm you."

Wooten slugged down the drink and looked at the bottle.

"No, not now Major, we need to talk and I think fast. My young friend there isn't happy at all. It seems that his family has been threatened, but I expect that you knew that already. You know how the cops feel about that."

"I told em' Bob, I told em' that wasn't a good thing to do. I just knew it would set Mitchell off, I told em' so."

"That's just it Major, who did you tell. Who's bringing all this down on you. You don't really think that they're going to help you, do you? They're going to expect that you'll be a good soldier and take the heat for em'. They don't really care what happens to you in prison as long as you don't connect them."

Wooten's head hung, he couldn't look into O'Shay's eyes. He started rocking in his chair, "My God Bob they'll kill me I know they will"

"Not if we protect you Wooten. You help us and we help you. We may even be able to get you out of serious jail time, if you cooperate. You know how it works, you've been there. We need names Major and we need your help and we need it soon. We have to talk to the Feds, they're going to want assurances or they'll scoop you up like a seagull on a beached fish."

"Give me a little time Bob," Wooten was now pleading. O'Shay could see the panic in his eyes. *Jesus, he doesn't know that we can't hold him, use it.*

"I don't know that I can do that Major it's going to be up to the Lieutenant."

"Talk to him for me Bob, I don't want to go to jail but I think that they'll kill me if I tell who he is. The guy at the top has the power Bob, he gets things done. All I want to do is get things in order before I give you the names. Buy me some time, please."

O'Shay got up from the table he saw the small 38 in its holster on Major Wooten's belt.

"I'll take that Major, I don't want you to do something stupid and it wouldn't make any difference. If anything should happen to us, the material we have goes directly to the Feds and the prosecutor." O'Shay pulled the short barreled revolver out of its holster and walked over to where Thad had been listening.

"Well here we are can't hold him, afraid to let him go."

"He's as much as confessed to Chinatown and Bucky Bob. If we let him go there's no guarantee that he will stick around." Thad thought for a minute.

"Okay let's let him go and give him a short leash. He has to be in the prosecutor's office tomorrow morning or we turn the hounds loose."

Thad turned and walked over to Major Wooten who was at the table pouring himself another drink.

"We have the stuff we need Wooten, you're done, it's just a matter of if you'll spend time in jail as somebody's bunk muffin. You have until tomorrow at ten to be in the prosecutor's office. If you're not there we turn the hounds loose and they hunt you down like a dog and you go to a federal prison that'll make hell look good. If you're there, we work a deal. You got that?"

Wooten nodded his head, "Thank you Mitchell, I'll be there I promise."

"You don't have to promise me Wooten, you just be there or you know what'll happen. Your cooperation will do wonders for you with the court."

Thad nodded at O'Shay and they walked out the door.

Wooten poured himself another drink. *They're right, he won't help me. He'll feed me to the Feds and gloat to the press how the police finally caught the cop killer and leader of the corruption on the police department. I don't have a choice and I don't have a chance unless he does know a way to get me off the hook.*

Major Wooten was now feeling the whiskey as he stumbled out of the back door and headed for a pay phone.

He picked up the private line phone on the first ring a little annoyed that someone would be using it. After all, everything was moving along just fine and an unexpected call usually meant trouble.

"Yes…" he switched hands with the receiver and pulled a cigar out of the humidor.

"Wooten, slow down," *he's been drinking and I think a lot*, "What do you mean they know everything, how could they?" *Christ, do they have Drago? How much do they know?*

"God damn it Wooten stop, take a deep breath what are you talking about?"

"Paper? What do you mean they have paper? What paper are you talking about?"

"My God, that cop in jail wrote things down and they have it?"

"Did Mitchell mention my name?" *How much do they know, did they get my name, I've got to calm Wooten down, he's hysterical, he could implicate me if he cracks.* "Listen to me Wooten…Listen to me damn it. I have the contacts, I'll protect you. You can trust me on this one. Where are you now?"

"You know that Flat that I have in the Benton Building?

"You know the one, I let you use it with that girl friend of yours, what's her name, Wendy."

Yeah that one, I'll call the manager and he'll let you in. Stop blubbering, you're not going to jail and what the hell is a bunk muffin?"

"Hang up Wooten and get your tail over there. Lay low, don't go out for anything and don't answer the door unless it's me or Drago. You got that Wooten? Good, go sleep it off. I have to make some phone calls and I'll get back to you, now go." He set the phone gently into the cradle and lit his cigar as he walked over to his office window. He stood for a moment gazing out over skid road. *They haven't got me yet, I still have an Ace or two up my sleeve and I'll play Drago first.*

Thad and O'Shay sat in the car watching Wooten stumble out of the alley from the back of Irene's.

"Paper, Thad where did you ever come up with paper."

"Is there something wrong with that Bob?"

"No, it was brilliant, I don't think he would have cracked if you hadn't brought up paper and made him believe that Buck had written the stuff down that he was going to tell us."

Thad straightened up in the seat.

"There's the good Major and it doesn't look like he's headed for the office. Wouldn't it be nice if he led us right to the big guy."

"No such luck Thad, he's going to that pay phone. Man I wish there was some way for us to find out who he's calling. What're you doing Thad?"

"Writing down the time, we can check with the phone company. Maybe they can tell what numbers were called from that phone at this time. I remember reading somewhere that they were working a new system. It's at least worth a shot."

"Where's he going now? It's not in the direction of his office. Let's tail him on foot." O'Shay popped open the door and stepped out, moving down the street. Thad jerked out the keys and climbed out hurrying to catch up with O'Shay who was picking up his pace.

"Come on Thad we don't want to lose him now."

Wooten hung up the phone wiping tears from his eyes. The thought of going to prison was more that he could bear. *Protect me, protect me my ass. All that ass hole thinks about is himself, what am I gonna do? He knows right where I am and will be until he tells me different. Don't answer the door unless it's him or Drago. Jesus, Drago, if he shows up there would be only one reason. That bastard is going to have me killed, that son-of-a-bitch. Well guess what, I can get him before he gets me.* He turned the corner and realized that he was in front of the Benton Building. *I'm not goin' in there like a lamb to slaughter. I have to get the super to let me in the flat, but I don't have to stay there. That way he won't know I'm not there when he sends Drago to do his dirty work. I may be drunk, but I'm no Bagley, you scum bag.*

Pleased with himself, Wooten entered the building and knocked on the managers door. He had no idea that standing outside watching him through the glass doors were Thad and O'Shay. They watched as the building manager and Wooten got onto the elevator and the doors closed. Thad slipped inside and watched the dial over the elevator door move up through the floor numbers. O'Shay came through the door behind him,

"Top floor Bob, they went straight to the top."

"I know the manager Thad, let's wait till he comes back down."

As they stood there the needle started back down.

"Come on, let's get out of sight and see who gets off." They stepped in a recessed alcove and watched the needle continue down.

The door opened and the manager stepped off and started for his office. O'Shay stepped out behind him, "Brad."

The manager spun around and a smile lit up his face.

"O'Shay, how the hell are you? It's been awhile."

"I've been great Brad, can we talk?"

"Sure come on in." The manager opened the door to his office and started in. O'Shay and Thad followed close behind and Thad shut the door.

"What can I do for you guys?"

O'Shay got right to the point.

"Need a favor Brad…you just took a guy up to the top floor, who rents the room?"

"It's actually two rooms, more like a suite. I'll get you the card on it." Brad walked over to a file drawer and started flipping through the cards.

"This official O'Shay or just curiosity"

"A little of both Brad, just checking some things out."

"Ah, here it is." Brad handed the card to O'Shay.

O'Shay looked at the card and a shocked look appeared on his face. He handed the card to Thad.

"You're not going to believe this."

Thad looked at the card, "Shit, you're right Bob."

"Anything wrong O'Shay?" Brad sounded a little concerned.

"No, just surprised I guess, no everything's fine, no problem." He handed the card back to the manager.

"Thanks, I appreciate the help Brad, it's no big deal, but I would rather you didn't mention our little visit to anyone."

"Hey, I owe you big time O'Shay. I wouldn't have this job if it wasn't for you. They would have never hired me with my record if you hadn't dropped a good word for me. I always appreciated what you did. As far I'm concerned, you were never here."

"Thanks again Brad." O'Shay and Thad left the office and headed for the elevator.

"Well Bob, I think we should pay our friend Wooten another visit." The elevator started its climb to the top floor.

"You know where the room is?" Thad could feel his heart racing as they passed the ninth floor."

"Yep, it's to the left, down the hall and around the corner. It's a corner room overlooks the Bay."

They stepped off the elevator and started down the hall when they heard a door open and close around the corner. They both stopped short of the corner and waited to see who would come around it.

Wooten watched the manager leave after letting him in and he shut the door and locked it. *I feel nauseated and my guts are churning.* Wooten headed to the bathroom. *I'm not gonna be here long enough to let that crazy bastard Drago come and kill me. He won't find anything but an empty room when he gets here.* He felt a little better when done and walked over to the window and looked across the bay to West Seattle. *Mexico sounds pretty good right now. With the money I've put away I can live there for a long time. I won't have to slog through another Northwest winter for awhile.* He unlocked the door and walked out.

Walking around the corner in the hallway his heart seemed to stop and he froze in his tracks.

"Going some where Major?"

"H…how did you guys know where I'd be?"

Thad put on his most wicked smile, "We know it all Major."

I'm trapped, there's nowhere to run. Oh my God. Wooten's whole body seemed to wilt.

O'Shay stepped up and put his hand on Wooten's arm. "I really think now would be a good time for all of us to go talk to the prosecutor Major."

"They'll kill me Bob. I know they'll kill me if I talk."

O'Shay tightened his grip on Wooten's arm.

"I think you're a dead man either way Major. You need us to keep you alive. Let's take a little walk up to the courthouse, it's only four blocks. Fresh air will do you good." He guided Wooten down the hall and onto the elevator.

***

This was the fourth time he had called and with each attempt he became more agitated. His cigar had gone out long ago and he was chewing on what was left.

Come on, answer the God damned phone you crazy bastard.

"Drago, where the hell have you been?"

"I don't have the time, we have a situation and it needs your immediate attention."

"I don't care, I have two tasks for you and they need to be done now."

"Don't give me any crap. First the good Major Wooten is in my flat in the Benton Building. He's been told to stay there until contacted by you. Get him out of there and then kill him. Make his body disappear. Okay?"

"I thought you'd like that. The second thing is even better. Our friend Mitchell didn't heed the first warning. He's launched a full investigation into our operation. He needs a graphic wake-up call. His wife Drago…she's yours. Do what you will with her but don't kill her. Mitchell needs to see everyday what happens to people who mess with us."

"No I don't care what you do. Just make sure it's brutal and obvious. Do you have any questions?"

"No need to thank me, get it done and have fun." He hung up the phone and lit the stub of a cigar he had been chewing on. *Well Lieutenant Mitchell, let's see how long you're investigation lasts after this eye opener.* The thought of what was going to happen to the beautiful Mrs. Mitchell sickened him, but only for a moment. After all it was necessary.

Drago set the phone down and closed his eyes visualizing Cindy, naked, laying under him with fear in her eyes and a scream on her lips. The image made him start to get and erection. *Screw the Major, he can die anytime. The woman comes first. The time is right Mrs. Mitchell, you're about to be violated in more ways than you can imagine. I'm looking forward to a couple of days of pure sexual gratification. Oh yes, the time is right.*

"Maggie, where ever did you get this ugly looking weapon? It's a shotgun isn't it?

"Yes Cindy it's a shotgun, I used to keep it behind the bar at the Silver Slipper. It was just in case. Bob laughed when I showed it to him and told him I had never fired it. He took me out in the woods and taught me how to use it. That was before we got together and my heart fluttered even then when he was near me. The big lug never had any idea what was going on. Sure glad he finally figured it out."

"Thank you for letting Amos and I stay with you. I'm more worried about the guys than I am for me. I really don't think that they would do anything to me but Thad and Bob could be in danger."

"Don't you fret about those two, they know what they're doing and they watch out for each other."

I missed not having Becky around to talk to after she left for the east coast. It's nice being able to just sit, have coffee and talk with you."

"How is she doing back there Cindy"

"Oh she's fine. A little lonely but starting to make friends. I guess New England folks are a bit standoffish to newcomers. But Becky has a way about her that puts people at ease and she still has the Vermont twang. I guess the property is right on the ocean and the cottage that was there has been totally redone. Most of the work was completed before she arrived and they are just doing some finishing stuff so she was able to move right in."

"Does she write regularly?"

"Oh yes, we get a letter almost every week. I write back and I've sent some pictures of Amos, Thad and I. I'm glad you're here Maggie. I don't know what I would have done if it wasn't for you. My life would have been so different if you hadn't taken me in. I guess I would have married Billy Marshall. I'd be living on a farm herding a passel of kids and milking cows."

"Billy Marshall? Oh yes, that would have been the teary eyed young man on the station platform in Kansas. Wonder whatever happened to him. I certainly hope that he's not still waiting for you to come back. You ever think about him?"

"You know I really haven't. I wouldn't trade what I have for anything else in the world, I'm so happy."

"Well honey you've made my life full of sunshine and flowers."

"Oh Maggie, I need to run over to the house. We left in such a hurry that I left a bag packed with clothes for Amos. I really need to go get them."

"No Child," Maggie was firm. "Thad and Bob said that you should stay here and not go out unless one of them was with you, and they know best."

"Oh Maggie, the bad guys aren't going to do anything to me, that's crazy stuff. I'm not the one in danger, it's Thad."

"And I'm telling you no, don't go back to the house till Thad says it's okay. Talk to him when he gets home tonight. Maybe he'll take you over to get the clothes this evening. I know, give him a call and he can pick them up on the way here."

"Oh, that's a good idea I'll give him a call at the office."

"Cindy honey, I have to run to the store. You stay put right here till I get back. That gun is easy to use, just point it at the target and pull the trigger. Pull the trigger again and the second barrel goes off, just hold it tight. I'll be back in about an hour."

Cindy could hear Maggie driving off as she dialed Thad's office.

"Vice Unit, Carlisle can I help you?"

"Carlisle, this is Mrs. Mitchell. Is my husband there?"

"No, I'm sorry Mrs. Mitchell, he's not here right now and I don't know when he'll be back in. He and the Sergeant are working on something. Can I take a message?"

"Just tell him that I called and that I'm going over to the house to get some clothes for Amos."

"Clothes for Amos got it ma'am. I'll give it to him as soon as he comes in."

"Thank you" Cindy hung up the phone. *I do need those clothes. They're not going to bother me. I'll drive over, zip in and zip out. I won't be there more than two minutes. What could happen in two minutes?*

"Come on Amos, we're going for a little ride." She grabbed some things, scooped up Amos and headed for the car.

Thad had stopped at a pay phone on the way to the prosecutor's office to let them know that they were bringing Wooten in. He also called, now special agent in charge, Dick Davis.

"Yeah Dick, I think that we have what we need to take down the boss of the corruption in the department. I'm not so sure about the Ludlow thing but at least it's a start. We're headed up to the prosecutor's office now to sort it out…thanks Dick, I'll keep you in the loop."

Thad hung up the phone and looked at Wooten. Head down, red eyes rumpled uniform, messed up hair. *You sorry looking piece of crap.*

"Okay let's finish our little walk."

Prosecutor Garrett was waiting for them when they entered the office.

"This way gentlemen." He headed for the conference room and shut the door after they were all in. For the next hour Wooten laid out the structure of the corruption within the department. He laid out the levels and the names while a stenographer reeled off page after page.

The secretary stuck her head in the door, "Is Sergeant O'Shay in here?"

Thad turned and looked at her, "No he went for coffee, can I help?" Thad got up from the table and walked to the door.

"Well I don't know, I have his wife on the line and she seems very excited."

Thad stepped out of the room, "I'll take the call."

"You can use the phone on that empty desk. Thad picked up the phone, "Maggie?"

"Oh thank God I found someone. I've been calling everywhere. Thad, Cindy and Amos are gone. I just got back from shopping and they and the car are gone. I'm afraid she's gone back to the house to get some clothes."

"Shit, I'm headed there now Maggie." Thad hung up the phone and turned to the secretary.

"When Sergeant O'Shay comes back tell him Cindy may be in trouble and I'm headed to my house. You got that?"

"Yes sir I'll let him know as soon as I see him."

Thad sprinted down the stairs and across the park to the police station. On the parking deck he spotted a patrol car with the keys in it and jumped in. He started it as an officer came out of the patrol office.

"Hey that's my car, hold it right there." Slamming it into gear, he roared off towards home.

Cindy drove through the front gate and up the circular drive stopping in front of the stairs leading to the great stone entrance.

"Come on Amos let's go get your suitcase," she picked him up, grabbed the large diaper bag, cradled him on her hip and went up the stairs getting out the front door key as she went. Amos was wiggling and it took her two tries to get the key in the door and turn the lock. The door popped free and she pushed it open with her elbow as she entered the house. She turned to the door and pushed it closed. As she turned to walk down the hall her world exploded.

Drago sat in the den looking at the toys scattered around and the books lining the shelves. He had found the brandy and poured himself one and sat down to wait. He was now on his second when he heard the car drive up. Peeking out the window a smile creased his face as he watched Cindy get Amos out of the car, plant him on her hip and start up the stairs. *Come to Papa missy, I've got a big surprise for you.* Drago put down the Brandy and moved to the doorway into the den. *This is perfect, she can't see me and I'm just two strides from the front door. This is too easy.* When Cindy turned her back to him to shut the door he stepped out, as she turned toward him, he slammed his open right hand along the side of her face while grabbing Amos with his left. Cindy's body bounced off of the wall then slumped to the floor in a heap. Drago stood over her looking at her bare legs where her dress had slid up when she fell. *Now it begins my dear.*

Cindy's eyes fluttered open, everything was a blur, the room was dark but as her eyes cleared she realized that the drapes were pulled and she was in the bedroom at the end of the hall laying on the floor. *What happened, my face is on fire, Amos, where's Amos.* She looked around beside the bed her purse and the diaper bag were there. She stood up and had to grab the dresser, her legs were wobbly.

"Amos, where are you Amos."

"He's right here and for now he's fine," the man's voice came from the far side of the room. Drago turned on the table lamp and Cindy gasped. Amos was seated on Drago's lap and at his throat was Drago's boning knife. The light from the lamp glinted off of the blade making it look even more hideous.

"My baby, please don't hurt my baby. In Gods name don't hurt him."

Drago laughed, "In Gods name is it! Well the only God here is me. I have the power of life and death that makes me God." Drago's face broke into a big smile.

"I have no intention of harming your baby, that is, of course, as long as you do exactly what I tell you to."

Cindy's heart froze and a cold chill ran through her body. *Oh my God, he's the man in the park and he's going to rape me. I should have listened to Thad, I'm so stupid.*

"Now if you don't do what you are told, I'll cut this baby's throat so fast it will make your head swim. Do you understand me Mrs. Mitchell, or should I call you Cindy? I think it'll be Cindy, that sounds much more personal now, doesn't it."

Cindy's mind raced, *how can we get out of this? What can I do to stop this madness...nothing, I can do absolutely nothing.*

"Come closer Cindy" Cindy took three steps closer to Drago who was now about ten feet from her. Her eyes were locked on the knife at Amos's throat and he was whimpering softly.

"There, that's better; now take off your dress."

"Please don't do this, please!!"

Drago's voice was firm, hard and cold.

"Don't tell me what to do Cindy, just do as you're told or the baby dies. Take your dress off, now."

Cindy unbuttoned her dress and eased it to the floor. She now had only her bra and panties on.

Drago looked her up and down. It made her want to vomit. *Amos, think of Amos, dear God help me.*

"Ah yes, more lovely than I ever imagined. Now the bra Cindy, take it off."

Cindy reached behind her and undid the catch. She pulled the straps over her arms and let it fall to the floor. She could not look at Drago any longer and stared at the floor. She could hear his breathing quicken.

"Come closer Cindy, closer, move closer." She stepped toward him and was now within arms reach. Still, she looked at the floor. She looked up when she realized that Drago had put Amos down. She looked straight into his eyes, cold gray and lifeless. They were the eyes of a killer.

"The child lives for now Cindy, make no mistake you do something stupid and the child dies. Do you understand?" Cindy stared blankly at him.

His voice hardened, low and menacingly.

"Do you understand Cindy?"

Cindy nodded her head.

"Say it Cindy," her voice was not much more than a whisper and she choked back the fear.

"I understand."

Drago smiled at her as he ran his hands over her body caressing her breasts. *Oh God make him die, please make him die.* Cindy tried to concentrate on the ceiling and close her mind to Drago's hands exploring her body, fondling her, his hands running down her back to her buttocks and into her panties and then pushing them down till they too fell on the floor. She heard the change in his pocket jingle as his pants fell to the floor. She looked at the ceiling not wanting to look down, afraid of what she would see, his hands still touching her. He was no longer breathing now, it was a pant. *Oh God let him Die, Please God strike him dead.*

Suddenly he snatched her off of her feet and threw her down on the bed climbing on top of her.

"It's now Cindy, the time is right now, spread your legs." He was rubbing his hardness against her pubic hair.

"Spread your legs damn it!"

"No, please don't do this"

"Damn you bitch, I said spread them!" Drago slapped her hard on the side of her face.

Stars flashed in Cindy's vision, her face felt as though it had just burst open she was slipping fast into semi consciousness as she felt her legs pulled wide apart. Her ears were ringing and she did not hear the front door burst open and Thad calling her name. She just knew she was about to be violated. Cindy slipped further in unconsciousness and did not feel Drago jump off of her.

Damn it's Mitchell, that bastard, he's a dead man. I'll kill him and his kid, then I'll do his wife.

Drago didn't bother to put on his pants he grabbed his jacket and snatched out his revolver as Thad came running out of the den where he had first gone. As Thad entered the hallway Drago could see the revolver in his hand. Thad turned toward the bedroom just in time to see Drago, wearing only a shirt, aiming a revolver directly at his head from some twenty five feet away. Thad tried to bring his weapon to bear on the half naked man in the bedroom doorway but could not do it fast enough. He saw the flash rather than hearing the report of the shot. He felt as though his head had been hit by a large club. His knees buckle and slammed into the hardwood floor as his body crumpled downward. His head was the last thing to bang onto the floor as he went over backwards. Bright stars flashed in his brain along with flashing lights then blackness.

The blackness began to clear, *am I dead? No I'm still alive.* Thad opened his eyes, his head throbbed and his vision was blurred. He blinked trying to clear it, someone there standing over him looking down. The ringing in his ears lessened and he could hear laughing, he blinked again and his vision cleared. The half naked man, Drago, standing astride of his head, laughing.

"Take a last look Mitchell, you're looking at the best part of the best man. I win, I get the last shot. Think of me on top of your wife Mitchell."

Drago brought the revolver up from his side and aimed it directly between Thad's eyes. The explosion rocked the hallway.

Tears streamed down Cindy's face as she saw Thad go down in the hall way. She shook her head to clear it. *The diaper bag, where's the diaper bag.* She rolled off the bed remembering she had seen it there. Two snaps and it popped open, inside she grabbed the cut down double barrel she had brought with her from Maggie's house. *He killed my husband, the bastard, he killed my Thad.* Her head now clear, she stood up and started down the hall. Drago was looking down at Thad and laughing, his revolver pointed at Thad's head. She brought the weapon up to waist high and remembered Maggie's words, "Hang on tight and pull the trigger."

Cindy tightened her grip and pulled the trigger. The blast was deafening and a cloud of acrid smoke belched out the left barrel of the shotgun. The gun jumped back toward her causing her to stagger slightly but she pressed on as she saw Drago's stomach turn to jelly as the buckshot slammed into him knocking him backward into a sitting position against the wall.

Thad saw Drago's stomach explode as he was taken off of his feet and knocked backward. Thad, in his fog, could not believe what he was seeing, *is this a dream? Maybe I am dead, I don't understand.* Thad looked down toward the bedroom and saw Cindy walking down the hall, naked, carrying Maggie's double barrel shotgun, smoke coming from one of the barrel. She did not look down as she stepped over Thad's body walking in the direction that Drago had been knocked.

She walked past Thad afraid to look down as she might lose her concentration. Drago was still breathing but it was labored, his right hand laying on the floor still held the revolver. His face was frozen in shock and disbelief as he looked at the naked woman standing there with the shotgun.

Slowly she brought the muzzle of the gun in line with Drago's face. She wanted him to see what was coming and it felt good to watch his eyes follow the right barrel until it stopped aimed at his face.

Cindy remembered Maggie's words again.

"Pull the trigger a second time and the other barrel goes off." Cindy tightened her grip and looked into Drago's cold gray eyes, "Die you bastard," she pulled the trigger a second time and Drago's head exploded splattering blood and gray matter over the wall.

The front door crashed open as O'Shay charged through it revolver in hand. The bizarre, surreal scene of blood, brains and nakedness was almost mind numbing. The pain in Cindy's voice snapped him back. Her face was screwed up in anguish and tears flooded from her eyes, "Oh Bob he killed Thad, he killed my Thad."

It was only too clear that Drago, or what was left of him, was no longer a threat. O'Shay jammed his revolver back into its holster and tore off his jacket wrapping it around the almost catatonic Cindy. He pulled her close to him and she buried her face in his chest sobbing. Gently, O'Shay removed the shotgun that was dangling from her hand at her side.

When he had removed it Cindy wrapped her arms around him and sobbed uncontrollably.

In the distance O'Shay could hear the patrol cars responding to his help the officer call he had made when he heard the shotgun go off.

In between sobs and gasping for air Cindy could only manage, "I'm so sorry Bob, I'm so sorry, I got Thad killed, I'm so sorry.

O'Shay sat in the hospital waiting room chair in an alcove off the main waiting room. He was leaned forward, his forearms resting on his thighs, hands clasped, talking as quietly as he could. There was no sense of letting others waiting there know what had taken place.

"Cindy's resting quietly. The doctor gave her a sedative to calm her down. Exam showed that she was not raped, but the trauma of killing her attacker like she did and seeing her husband shot, pretty much freaked her out. She was a blubbering mess when they brought her in. The doctor said she'll be just fine and she's a tough one, having worked here in the ER as long as she has, not much she hasn't seen and already dealt with. How are you doing?"

"My head feels like there's a hornet's nest in there. Thank God he hit me in the head at an angle and it was a small caliber gun." Thad smiled, then grimaced as it pulled at the stitches.

"You always said I was a hard headed SOB, now I guess you have proof. Where's Amos is…he alright?"

"Oh yeah, he's just fine Maggie took him to our place and he went right to sleep after she fed him."

Thad straightened up in the chair, "What a mess this is! What kind of shape are we in?"

O'Shay sat up in his chair, a big grin on his face.

"We got the warrant and we've kept a lid on the thing. All we're waiting for is you to clear your head so we can go arrest him. We felt that we owed you that after the work you've done on this. Whenever you give the word boss, we take him down. Doctor says Cindy will be out for a few more hours and you can leave anytime you want."

"Well Sergeant O'Shay what the hell are we doing here. Let's do it so that I can get back here and sit with my wife who just saved my life."

The news had been trickling in all afternoon. Big shoot out at a police officer's home. One dead, two injured no details forthcoming from the police as to exactly what happened. He was chewing on an unlit cigar and talking on the phone.

"Any details come out yet on what happened?"

"Well if any further information comes in let me know so that I can make an appropriate response if asked."

"Yeah, well either way it looks like a couple of my problems have been taken care of. I'd rather that Drago removed Wooten before playing games with the woman, but I should have anticipated that he would go for the lust first. With any luck Drago's dead and now Mitchell's gotten the message to back-off."

He hung up the phone, struck a match, as he gazed out the window onto Elliott Bay and Skid Road, and lit his cigar.

Thad, O'Shay and two detectives got off the elevator on the top floor. The waiting room was rather austere which fit the persona that the man wished to present to those who entered his domain.

"May I help you gentlemen?" The secretary was brusque, business like and as austere as her surroundings.

Thad led the group toward her desk. She looked a little taken aback by the man with bandages on his head and fresh bruising on the right side of his face.

"Is he in?"

In her best gate keeper voice she stood her ground.

"Do you have an appointment?"

"No we do not, but he WILL see us."

"If you don't have an appointment you'll have to leave. He sees no one without an appointment, please leave."

Thad smiled, turned and started for the short hallway to the man's office.

"It's alright he'll see us."

"I'm calling the police." she picked up the phone and started to dial.

O'Shay grabbed her hand as she reached for the intercom button. "It's okay lady, we are the police."

Her eyes grew wide as O'Shay flipped open his badge case so she could see the shiny Detective Sergeant badge inside.

"It is okay and he will see us."

Her bluster was gone as she slumped, eyes wide, into her chair.

O'Shay smiled at her, "Now close you mouth Miss...uh" He looked at the name plate on her desk, "Baker, you might catch a fly in it." He turned and followed Thad down the hall.

He could hear faint voices in the outer office. *Damn are the reporters here already? I don't have all the answers. When Janet calls me on the intercom I'll just give her the signal to stall them until I can get more information.*

Thad had not bothered to knock. He opened the door and walked in.

"You can't just barge in here whenever you want to. You men get out of my office!" He keyed the intercom, "Miss Baker, call the police." There was no response.

He took another look at the men walking toward him. "Wait I know you, you're…"

Thad cut him off, "Yes you do you two faced son-of-a-bitch."

Thad put on his best 'I win grin' and didn't care that it pulled the stitches and hurt like hell.

"Mr. Mayor I have a warrant for your arrest for murder, conspiracy to commit murder, graft, corruption and several other things that we'll think up later. I am going to get a great deal of joy watching you drop through the trap door with a rope around you neck. Hands on the wall, feet back and spread-em', you're under arrest."

***

It was a celebration of sorts. The grand Jury had handed down a seven point indictment against the Mayor and fifteen other law enforcement officers. Prohibition had been repealed and the booze was once again flowing freely except in Seattle on Sundays and most importantly Sergeant Robert O'Shay had finally retired. The one hundred plus guests were beginning to depart after an afternoon of beer and barbecue on the huge lawn at the home of one Lieutenant Thaddeus Mitchell and family. Thad sat with Amos on his lap and Cindy leaned against him holding his arm. Maggie and Bob sat next to them and they all were quietly watching the sun set behind the Olympic Mountains.

Thad broke the silence Just as the sun went down and the sky looked ablaze. "Ya know folks it doesn't get any better than this.

Epilogue

The gust of wind shook the whole house causing Becky to start. *I thought the storm was about blown out but obviously I was wrong.* The banging of one of the shutters caused a terrible racket as it slammed against the house. *I had better secure that or it will break apart.* Donning her rain gear she went outside struggling against the biting cold wind and driving rain. The waves sounded like small explosions as they slammed into the rocks near her beach. She could envision the plumbs of white foam arching into the air off of the rocks as the ocean threw itself against the seemingly immovable obstacles. It took only a minute to secure the loose shutter and she started back toward the front of the cottage. *What was that? Did something move out there in the trees? The storm is playing tricks on me, I must be getting old.* She shut the door and engaged the dead bolt. *Why do I have this creepy feeling? Being alone is not a good thing, especially during one of these Atlantic storms.*

Becky settled back into her overstuffed, tapestry covered chair, facing the crackling fire and retrieved the letter she had received from Cindy and Thad. She had already read it at least 4 times but each time she felt closer to her loved ones.

Dear Mom:

Sorry we have not written for awhile, but we have been busy redoing the house. Thad is finally working days again and is now a Precinct Commander. We have decided that he will go a couple of more years and then retire. Money is not a problem, thanks to you, and with Amos established in the police department and on his own, maybe we can do some traveling.

Becky's mind jumped back to the plans that she and Chad had made to see the world. Either he was busy with business or there were other things going on that kept them from following that dream. That dreadful thing with the Herringtons brought everything to and end. She felt the now familiar lump in her throat rising, pressing until the tears ran down her cheeks. Her world was shattered that day, her only love was gone.

How many years has it been..., almost twenty five now and still I feel as though my heart will break.

Becky lay her head back against the soft chair and let the warmth from the fireplace seep into her aching body and waited until the tears subsided. She dried her eyes and went back to the letter.

You wouldn't recognize Seattle, everything seems to be changing. Old familiar buildings have been torn down and new taller ones have taken their place. With the Asian trade, we have become the major city in the state and the primary port for any commerce to the West. The harbor is busy all the time and business is booming. The Navy presence at the new piers at Innerbay and the airfield at Sand Point does have an effect on crime here. So I guess all of the advances are not good. Thad says that if we didn't have the Navy at pier 91 and Sandpoint on Lake Washington, crime here would be a great deal easier to control.

When Thad went days, I changed my shift at the hospital to days also. We get to spend more time together that way. Working in the emergency room is always an eye opener. Some of the stuff we see could almost scare a body to death. It seems as the city continues to grow, the worse it gets and now there is all that talk about war in Europe. Who knows where all that will go.

I should close now and get some things done. Oh yes, Amos sent his thanks for the birthday present. He received it last week two days before his birthday. It was lovely and I'm sure that he will get a lot of use out it. Thanks again for everything mom. You are always in our thoughts and we miss you terribly. I hope that we will soon be able to get out to see you. It sounds like Bar Harbor is a wonderful wild place.

Love Cindy, Thad and Amos

Becky set letter in her lap. *Amos, I was so pleased when they named the baby Amos after Dad. He is the spitting image of him and so gentle. I'm surprised that he became a police officer, but I guess he's like his father that way. They love the action. Oh how I miss the children. If I weren't for my age and aching bones I would move back to be with them. All my business affairs are settled now, but I do enjoy the isolation here on the ocean and I have my volunteer work. Sometimes I even forget the hole left in my life. He would have liked it here too.*

Becky felt a chill and stoked up the fire and put in another log. The rain had gotten more intense and it's drumming on the roof was soothing. She settled back in her chair and drifted off to sleep.

With the rain beating on the roof and the wind picking up, Becky almost didn't hear the tapping at her door. She had melded it into her dream, which now she could not remember. *Was that someone knocking or was it the wind? There it is again who would be knocking at this time of night?* Becky picked up the fireplace poker and started toward the door apprehensively. The tapping started again, not a loud knock but a soft tap. *I wish now that I had put one of those peepholes in the door like the handyman suggested.*

Cautiously Becky opened the door a crack and peeked out, the poker out of sight but raised and ready.

"Who's there?"

The soft voice responded, "Becky?" She opened the door further, the rain blowing across the door spattered into her face and she focused on the shadowy figure standing on the porch. He wore a long rain slicker and a hat with the large brim beaten down and covering most of his face except for the beard and his mouth. He made no attempt to come in or approach further.

"You're as beautiful as ever Becky" the brim of the hat raised slightly and then she saw them, those soft warm eyes that looked into her very soul.

"Chad, oh Chad" the poker fell from her hand.

Is this real? Is this just another dream like all the others? Becky reached out to touch him, totally oblivious of the rain blowing against her face.

As her fingers touched his face, the tears exploded from her eyes as she sobbed uncontrollably.

"I'm sorry Becky, I'm so sorry."

Becky fairly threw herself at him wrapping her arms around his neck.

"Hold me Chad, just hold me"

They clung to each other on the porch, both sobbing not caring that the wind was howling and the rain was soaking them. All was now right with the world.